(. . . shards . . .)

(. . . shards . . .)

Ismet Prcic

Black Cat
New York
a paperback original imprint of Grove/Atlantic, Inc.

Published simultaneously in Canada
Printed in the United States of America

FIRST EDITION

ISBN: 978-0-8021-7081-1

Black Cat
a paperback original imprint of Grove/Atlantic, Inc.
841 Broadway
New York, NY 10003

Distributed by Publishers Group West

www.groveatlantic.com

11 12 13   10 9 8 7 6 5 4 3 2 1

To Henrijeta.
To Melissa.
To Eric.

Be not too tame neither, but let your own discretion
be your tutor: suit the action to the word, the
word to the action; with this special observance,
that you o'erstep not the modesty of nature: for any thing
so o'erdone is from the purpose of playing, whose end,
both at the first and now, was and is, to hold, as 'twere,
the mirror up to nature; to show virtue her feature,
scorn her own image, and the very age and body of
the time his form and pressure.

William Shakespeare

Who broke these mirrors
and tossed them
shard
by shard
among the branches?
. . .
L'Akdhar (the poet) must gather these mirrors
on his palm
and match the pieces together
any way he likes
and preserve
the memory of the branch.

Saadi Youssef,
translated from Arabic by Khaled Mattawa

(. . . an excerpt from
notebook one: the escape
by ismet prcić . . .)

In wartime, when his country needed him the most—his shooting finger for defending, his body for a shield, his sanity and humanity as a sacrifice for future generations, his blood for fertilization of its soil—in these most pressing times, Mustafa's special forces combat training lasted twelve days. He ran the obstacle course exactly twenty-four times, he threw fake hand grenades through a truck tire from various distances exactly six times, he practiced marksmanship with an air rifle so that bullets were not wasted, he got covered with blankets and beaten by his peers for talking in his sleep at least once. He did countless push-ups and sit-ups, chin-ups and squats, lunges and curls, mindless repetitions designed not to make him fit but to break him, so that when he was, the drill sergeant could instruct him in the ways of military hierarchy and make him an effective combatant, one who was too scared not to follow orders and who would fucking die when he was told to fucking die.

At some point he was introduced to the real weapons. "This is an Uzi, this is how it works, we don't have any Uzis,

1

so forget what you just learned. This is an LAW, this is how
it's used, we only have a limited number of them and they are
in the hands of people who already know how to use them,
so you'll never get in contact with them, so forget what you
just learned." And so forth.

The knife guy taught him where to stick the knife for what
effect, and he stabbed hanging sacks of sand with people
drawn on them. The mine guy showed him how to set up
antipersonnel and antivehicle mines and pointed out all their
deadly charms. The army doctor took a swig of plum brandy
and told him that war was a giant piece of shit and that he,
Mustafa, was a chunk of corn in that shit and then warned
him not to come to his office again until he had a gut wound
so big he could canoe right through it. That was, about, it.

In the end he got a Kalashnikov like everybody else, one
clip of ammunition, one hand grenade, and one knife and
was sent to the trenches with the regular army for a week,
just to sample what war had to offer, to read the manual, as it
were, before they decided what special unit he was fit to join.

NOTEBOOK ONE: THE ESCAPE*

(. . . cheese . . .)

As the KLM flight finally touched American soil, the white-knuckled Bosnians in the back—people for whom just a few months ago airplanes were but thin lines of cloud, silently crisscrossing the skies above their godforsaken villages—erupted in spontaneous applause. I joined them, despite the queasy feeling in my stomach brought on by the cheese and fruit we'd received somewhere over England. The cheese had been yellow and maybe rancid, and throughout the flight I'd hurried up and down the aisles in search of an unoccupied lavatory, where—kneeling awkwardly in front of one tiny toilet or another—I'd find myself unable to hurl.

These people, my people, the refugees, they were fleetingly happy and stubbornly perplexed. They smiled but also furrowed their brows at the unfathomable patter coming from the speakers. The plane came to a stop at the gate at JFK, but the little belt buckle next to the crossed-out cigarette over our heads remained lit. We sat there. The man in front of me, a youngish fellow with a wife and a daughter and a mouth of cataclysmic teeth stuck his head over the seat and peered at me through glasses.

"Are we there, or are we just getting gas?" he whispered to me in Bosnian, eyes bulging, half-fearful and half-embarrassed. Despite

5

his attempt at discretion, everyone heard him, and they turned to me, the only Bosnian on board with any English, for information.

"We're here," I mumbled, nodding.

Murmurs of approval spread from seat to seat. The man turned back around.

"I thought so," I heard him say to his wife.

"Don't pretend you knew," she said.

"You always have to turn the harvest combine off before refueling, otherwise it's a fire hazard," he explained pointedly. "Same goes for planes. Machine's a machine."

"Yeah, yeah, you know everything."

"Shut it, woman."

It had begun with politicians fighting on television, talking about their nationalities, their constitutional rights, each claiming that his people were in danger.

"I thought we were all Yugoslavs," I said to my mother, although at fifteen I knew better. You had to live under a rock not to see that the shit was about to hit the fan. I don't know why I said it. Maybe the Communist message of Brotherhood and Unity had been so thoroughly drummed into my head that it surfaced robotically and overrode my actual experience. She told me to shut up and turned up the volume on the television.

Then reports had started coming in: sieges, civilian casualties, concentration camps, refugees. Croats and Muslims being slaughtered left and right by Serbian paramilitaries and by the Yugoslav People's Army, who, as their actions made evident, seemed not to really belong to all of the peoples of Yugoslavia.

"Which ones are we?" I asked my mother, still playing dumb, hoping that my willful denial could erase the images on the screen, erase my fear, make everything normal again. Again she told me to shut up and turned the volume even higher, until the downstairs neighbor started broom-handling our floor and my mother had to turn the TV down.

All at once your nationality became very important. There were reports of Serbian paramilitaries stopping all men trying to flee Bosnia, ordering them to drop their pants and underwear to prove they were Serb. Being circumcised meant your ass.

All the Bosnian cities and towns, if not overrun, were suddenly under siege. This went on for years. Civilians chopped down park trees, got buried in soccer fields, burned books and furniture, kept chickens on balconies, duct-taped their footwear, caught and ate pigeons, made makeshift stoves out of washing machines, grew mushrooms in basements, replaced broken windows with murky plastic, went nuts and jumped off buildings, drank rubbing alcohol diluted in chamomile tea until it was no longer flammable, rolled herbal tea cigarettes in toilet paper, suffered, hoped, waited, fucked. Authorities emptied the jails and mental institutions because they couldn't provide for the inmates and patients. Thieves and murderers went back to their families. Lunatics walked around town doing funny things like comparing people to watermelons and sad things like freezing to death behind churches. Soldiers fought for all of them and for themselves. My father, a chemical engineer, got lucky and came up with a contraption that turned industrial fat into edible fat and got paid ten thousand German marks by a small business entrepreneur and war profiteer, which saved us. My mother ate just enough to survive, because she felt so guilty about not being able to quit smoking. She rationed her cigarettes as much as she could, walking around the apartment like a restless ghost, playing her solitaire, counting seconds before the next one. Sometimes, my brother and I stole a cigarette when the pack was close to full and

hid it somewhere in the apartment just to pull it out, unexpectedly, when she didn't have any left, just to see her eyes light up for
a moment. Later it would break our hearts to see her fingering the
wool of the large tapestry in the corridor, looking for our stash, her
forefinger touching her lips, her eyes on fire.

The airport corridors glowed majestically. The current of passengers moved us along. You could tell who was a refugee and who
wasn't—facial expressions, postures, surety of stride. The natives
and the tourists walked briskly, trying to get it over with, catch their
next flight, and be somewhere else. Their bodies were streamlined.
The refugees, we walked like somnambulists, clutching our carry-
ons, putting them between our bodies and the new world as if for
protection. Hungry-eyed, we took in the wall posters advertising
liquor and Disneyworld, the tiled floors, our stolid shoes, our knobby
knees, our hands against these unfamiliar backgrounds. We drank
it all in, giddily and guardedly at the same time.

But what I thought was going to be a short, silent, incognito burp
turned out to be a mouthful of cheesy vomit. I stopped, dropping my
bag next to the wall, and choked the burning, foul liquid down. It
made my eyes water. I kept swallowing, trying to coat the inside of
my throat with saliva. Then I realized that no one was passing me.
When I turned around, sour-faced and disgusted, I saw that all the
Bosnians were queued up behind me, waiting, all eyes. They had
been following me. Even the few who had been walking ahead had
stopped where they found themselves, looking over their shoulders.

"You all right there, pal?" the harvest combine operator asked,
carrying his blonde-angel daughter in his arms like a sack of grain.
His wife, a loose white headscarf over her head, was lugging two
bags behind her and scowling.

"*Žgaravica*," I managed, and they all made sympathetic faces. Indigestion. I picked up my bag and started walking again, swallowing. There was poison oak in my mouth, my throat, the middle of my chest.

One part of me felt pride to have fifty people stopping when I stopped, going when I went. The other part was embarrassed by them, by their bucolic cluelessness, their needy, confused eyes. I fought the urge to run ahead and merge with the natives and the tourists, to ape their body movements, roll my eyes at the slowness of the line, pretend I cared about what time it was, and become one of them.

The corridors spewed us out into a huge room. A black woman in a uniform stood motioning with her hands, first to the right and then, just as eagerly, to the left. Her lipstick was bright red and you didn't have to be close to notice that some of it was on her teeth.

"Citizens and resident aliens, line up to the right. Everyone else, please keep left," she said, impatiently eyeing a Bosnian family of six, who, painfully baffled, planted their feet and gawked at her, holding up their manila refugee envelopes like signs at a rally and impeding the flow of traffic.

"Go left," I yelled ahead in Bosnian, and the family hesitated, turning to me. When I nodded, they lowered their envelopes and lined up to the left, checking to see if I really would follow suit.

The right-hand line was moving fast. Immigration officers waved the Americans to their stations, opened their passports, shot some shit with them, stamped the stamp, closed the passports, and, smiling, welcomed them back. Pretty soon the right side of the room was completely empty—until another wave of Americans, from some other flight, crowded it again.

The left side was uniformly compact, with foreigners inching down a monotonous maze. At the front, stepping over the yellow line became an issue. Officers kept repeating their admonishments with disgust, and the refugees kept looking around the floor, wondering why the hell these Americans were yelling and pointing at the tiles, checking their pockets to see if they'd dropped anything important, shrugging their shoulders.

When it was my turn at the yellow line I stood as close to it as possible without going over, like I was about to shoot a free throw. My heart rocked my body; I could feel its beat behind my eyes, on the sides of my neck, at the tips of my fingers, in my toes. For a moment I forgot about the rawness of my throat, about the putrid weight in my stomach, the bad taste in my mouth. I stared ahead at the PLEASE WAIT FOR THE NEXT AVAILABLE STATION screen, praying silently, sending good vibes, and visualizing the perfect outcome.

The screen changed to a flashing number eleven. I swallowed and crossed the yellow line toward the station where a young Sikh gazed at me politely but without emotion. I approached with a smile, psychically projecting Koranic verses instead of uttering them, and handed him my everything.

"Welcome to the United States. Good luck."

I wandered out of the immigration maze on a pair of legs that weren't mine.

There was a man with a sign in his hand that read BOSNIA, a chicken of a man in gray woolen pants, an off-gray jacket, and long navy blue coat. He had one of those comprehensive foreheads that, over the years, creeps up to the top of an egg-shaped head and a pair of eighties-style aviator eyeglasses, the top of which were tinted and flush with his eyebrows; the bottoms drooped to the middle of his cheeks. At the end of the corridor behind him was a uniformed cop—the last line of defense—whose forearms seemed rooted to his Batman utility belt. He was a huge redhead with the voice of a gargoyle and hands that could squeeze a confession out of a sculpture.

"What nation is abusing us now?" he boomed at the man with the sign watching me come down the corridor. But seeing me slow down, the man disregarded the question and came toward me.

"Bosnian?" he asked in Bosnian, and I, surprised, said yes in English. The combine operator and his wife attacked the man with a salvo of overlapping questions. As soon as they heard somebody speaking in a language they could understand, my fellow refugees turned their backs on me. I was instantly demoted from general of this ridiculous comedy to grunt, no one paying me any mind, some even pushing past me to get closer to this tiny man. I remembered how six months ago, on the way to Scotland, aboard a ferry from some French town to Dover, my friend Omar and I had separated from the rest of the theater troupe and walked around the boat, crudely insulting everyone we encountered in our native tongue, terrified and giddy that we might stumble upon the one passenger who, realizing he'd been told he was spawned by an ass-eyed, donkey-raping water buffalo, would kick our heads in.

"If you're from Bosnia, let's gather over here," yelled the man with the sign. "I'm Enes, and I'm from the Bosnian consulate. Welcome to New York City. The majority of you are trying to catch a connecting flight, and I'm here to assist you in—"

The Bosnians went fucking crazy, speaking to him all at once, waving their tickets, their yellow immigrant envelopes, pushing to the front. Enes tried to calm them down, shaking his head, shouting that he wouldn't help anyone if they didn't queue up.

I felt a little sad witnessing this, so I pulled away. My flight wasn't until the next day, so I knew I would have to stay in New York overnight. I meandered a little way from the group, trying to look native. My stomach cramped and again I felt like I could burp. Fooled once, I swallowed down some spit instead.

"The rats are a-coming," said the redhead cop to a passing American who had noticed the commotion. I glared at him, right into his green blue eyes. He held my gaze.

"You speak English?" he boomed toward me, overpronouncing.

There's a word in Bosnian, *zaprška,* which is a culinary term for the finishing touch to a lot of Bosnian meals. It's golden butter melted in a pan with red paprika, a violently orange sauce (the exact color of the cop's hair) that is poured into stews and over stuffed peppers.

"*Zaprška,*" I said to him, smiling my best fresh-off-the-boat smile, "*jebem li ja tebi mater hrđavu, jesi'l čuo!*"

A couple of Bosnians heard me and scoffed and chuckled at the insult.

"I know you understand me," yelled the cop, but I took my ticket out of my pocket, pushed myself in between two Bosnian women and waved to attract Enes's gaze.

"*Hej care, kad je avion za Los Anđeles!*" I called.

I sat there people-watching, the shoulder strap of my bag wrapped around my ankle in case somebody tried to steal my wrinkled clothes and smoked beef and the slivovitz I was smuggling as a present to my uncle—stuff he couldn't get his hands on in California. After telling me to wait, Enes had led the rest of the Bosnians away to catch their flights to cities like Nashville, Fargo, St. Louis. I sat there thinking I was cold. My jaw was jumpy. But the more I pressed my arms against my body the more I became aware that it wasn't the cold making my teeth chatter. I looked around. People: shapes, races, demeanors I'd never seen before. They were walking in groups or pairs, or were at ease with their aloneness, purposeful, while I sat there trying not to puke.

Other men with signs displaying the names of other sad countries rolled by with gaggles of confused immigrants, yelling in exotic languages, leaving behind one or two other petrified saps who, like me, tried to occupy as little space as possible. There was a gangly black man in a black suit sitting with four veiled women (resembling babushkas) in a range of sizes, pretending he knew what was up, but clearly scared. Only a young African woman in dark jeans and a white blouse, with closely cropped hair and shiny eyes, behaved with any sort of confidence. She took her seat, took a book and snack out of her carry-on, something noisy and, by the look of it, covered in salt, and proceeded to read and munch like she was on a park bench. I wanted to lay my head in her lap, to be touched and told that everything was fine.

Eventually, an airport shuttle—a smelly, back-loaded van of some kind—drove us through New York to where we were to spend the night. I caught only glimpses of the passing buildings, cityscapes, and cars; the African woman was next to me and our thighs were warmly touching. Feverishly, I imagined her taking my hand in hers, looking deep into my eyes and loving me wordlessly. I could see us hugging, touching, holding each other, walking along the beach, cuddling on a love seat, checking on our sleeping brown babies with their Slavic foreheads and African lips.

"Here we are," the driver said.

The van pulled into the parking lot of a dingy motel and shat us out the back. The driver said to prepare our documents and follow him inside. I could tell he did this all the time, his body familiar

with the asphalt beneath his feet. He knew to pull the front door
instead of push it, though there was no sign. You could see that he
hated but tolerated the manager, a shaggy man of Arab descent,
who asked me: "How many in the room?"

"One, one," I said showing him my index finger. He looked at my
passport and had me sign next to my name on a faxed list. Then he
shoved a key into my hand. The orange plastic rectangle to which it
was attached read 7. He pointed, then turned to the African woman.

"How many in the room?"

I lingered, acting like I was having trouble picking up my bag, hoping to catch the number of her room, but the driver waved me over.

"Indian or Italian?"

"Bosnian," I told him.

He rolled his eyes.

"To eat! Do you want Indian food or Italian food for dinner?"

I wanted to stomp on my own balls.

"Indian," I said, figuring there was less of a chance of ending up
with a plateful of pork.

"We're leaving at six sharp. I will come and knock on your door.
You should be up and ready," he warned, jotting down my choice.

Rooms 1 through 14 were in the basement, and I followed the
arrows through halls lit here and there with chipped sconces that
shot murky light at the ceiling in repetitive, throbbing patterns. My
room was in the corner, down the length of the corridor from a daz-
zling behemoth of a Pepsi machine. I unlocked the door and went in.

Room 7 was surprisingly big: a king-size bed with magenta sheets,
a TV presiding, two nightstands with lamps, and a table with two
chairs and a phone. It smelled of orangey bleach and dust, of cover-
ups and FBI sting operations, sex for money and crimes of passion, alcoholic self-pity and junky visions—all the stuff I'd seen in
American movies.

I tried to lock myself in but couldn't turn the key. I tried in both directions and it wouldn't budge. I opened the door, closed it, and tried again. Nothing.

I looked through the peephole and saw two teenage girls giggling by the Pepsi machine. One of them had a head scarf and looked European; I wondered if she was Bosnian. She covered her mouth when she laughed. The other one looked Arabic but was in a pair of ripped jeans, which exposed her scabby knees. Their faces glowed red and blue, in turn. I'd always been a loner and proud of it—people were something you had to deal with or avoid—but now, standing on a worn patch of beige carpet, on my first night in America, I longed for somebody, anybody.

Then I felt my stomach turn. Somewhere in all of this, the cheese puke I'd kept down had somehow turned to shit. I ran to the bathroom, and it came out of me in stormy gusts and thunderbolts. When I was done I felt rejuvenated, glorious.

Still, I didn't want someone silently slipping in while I was asleep and cutting my throat or, even worse, knocking me out with a chloroform rag, turning me into a hustler rent boy or forcing me to work twenty-four hours a day in an underground meth lab. I didn't want to wake up with missing kidneys, liver, heart, or eyeballs. *I'm in America,* I thought, and that meant I was in a movie; the fact that I couldn't lock the door from the inside was one of those little details upon which terrible plot shifts would depend.

I was paranoid. I looked through the peephole again—nothing but red, white, and blue lights telling me that I was thirsty. The girls were gone. I opened the door and studied the lock in vain. I dragged over the table and jammed it under the knob. To get in, the crackhead nutter would have to push hard, which would make a noise, which would wake me up, which was my best chance of survival. Now I needed a weapon.

Someone knocked on the door and my heart kicked against my ribcage like an angry baby. I looked through the peephole: the driver. I dragged away the table and opened the door.

"Indian?" he said, looking over his paper.

"Indian, yes."

He handed me a couple of Styrofoam containers and put a check next to my name.

"Tomorrow morning at six," he said, and made as if to go.

"Uhh . . . ," I started, and he stopped.

"What?"

"My . . . my . . . my key," I stuttered, "I . . . I can't . . . uh . . . lock the door on the inside."

He looked at me with obvious disdain.

"It's automatic. You don't have to do anything. You close the door and it's locked."

Before I ate, I jammed the table up against the door again, together with the chairs and all my luggage. *Fuck the driver,* I thought, *he might be in on a plan.*

The shower had no faucet, just a knob in the middle of the wall, and I couldn't figure out how to make it get hot, if there was hot water in this place to begin with. The best I could do was not-icy, and I stepped in for a quick soap and rinse. By the time I was done—two minutes tops—my lips were the color of eggplant.

Channel 4 was news—fast, indecipherable English I found comforting in the absence of flesh-and-bone humans. I shivered under the covers. I heard the click, click, clicking of women's shoes outside my window and snuck a peek through the magenta curtains, up through a grate below the street. I saw a woman's legs and a big man in a mink coat holding both of her wrists and yelling at her. *I'm fucking staying up all night,* I told myself, but I woke at five thirty to the sound of the alarm, alive and unmolested, all organs intact.

* * *

The driver drove us to the airport. The African woman sat behind me this time, so I got to see some of the city. It was mostly New York motorists in profile, sipping from thermos bottles, yelling out of windows, smacking their dashboards, smoking, putting on makeup, singing, dozing off and waking up just in time to brake, playing air guitar, looking at me with what-the-fuck-are-you-looking-at on their faces.

Enes met me at LaGuardia, showed me where I was to wait for my flight to Los Angeles, shook my hand limply, and shoved off. I sat on another plastic chair and waited.

I kept thinking, *You made it, man,* not believing it. I looked at my hand, this thing I'd been living with all my life, and it felt like I was seeing it for the first time. It seemed only vaguely familiar, yet I was somehow in control of it; it was my hand to use. I glanced up to make sure that what I saw around me was America, confirmed that the seat next to me was a part of that country, then placed my strange hand on its cool plastic surface, and told myself again: *You made it; you escaped.*

Two other Prcićs made this journey before me. There was my granduncle Bego, who fled the Nazi invasion via Paris, settled in an apartment in Flushing Meadows, and died there, alone. And then there was my uncle Irfan, who fled the Communists in 1969, ended up in California, and twenty-six years later invited me to live with him. We were all from the same town in Bosnia but had fled three completely different countries. Bego escaped the Kingdom of Serbs, Croats, and Slovenes. Irfan, the Socialist Federative Republic of Yugoslavia. And me, the newly formed independent state of Bosnia and Herzegovina. Says something about the Balkans: Regimes are plentiful, they don't last long, and they make people want to run away.

What came to me then was the voice of my paternal grandmother. She had told me once that every time Bego or Irfan returned to

Bosnia to visit, they had seemed to her like different people. Unrecognizable. She had blamed this on America.

I looked at my hand again.

Through the airport window, I could see a homeless man in a filthy camouflage jacket sitting on a curb, his back to me, playing fetch with a dog. He'd fight the plastic bottle of Dr. Pepper out of the Alsatian's mouth, tease her with it, and then throw it down the sidewalk. She'd chase after it, her swollen teats swaying, bring it back to him, and the scene would repeat. I sat there mesmerized, telling myself again that I had made it, wishing I had a dog or something warm to touch, to look in the eye. It was then that the morning sun sliced through the clouds, its light hitting the window in such a way that suddenly I saw my reflection. I saw a young man sitting alone on a plastic chair, white-knuckled and wide-eyed and zit-faced, happy and perplexed, and I knew why my grandmother couldn't recognize her own son, why I was wielding a stranger's hand. I knew that someone new would get off this plastic chair and board a plane for Los Angeles and that all the while an eighteen-year-old Ismet would remain forever in the city under siege, in the midst of a war that would never end.

Just as it came, the sun went away. The homeless man threw the bottle. The bitch ran after it. I looked at my hand, then at everything else. I was new and America seemed too big a place to be alone in.

From the air Los Angeles was vast and gray and pockmarked with light blue pools. Down at LAX, it was hot for a winter afternoon; it was amusing. There were palm trees through the terminal window and people wore sandals in earnest.

Coming out of this one corridor I saw a man and a woman in their fifties, white, dressed in shiny red-white-and-blue frocks and top hats with stars all over them. They walked through the crowd, handing them things. The woman came up to me with an ear-to-ear smile.

"Hello, sir!"

"Hello."

"Could I ask you a couple of questions?"

She was speaking slowly and clearly. I was glad about that.

"Yes."

"Where are you from, sir?"

"Bosnia."

"Are you visiting us for the first time?"

"I am refugee."

"So you're here for the government cheese."

She said this very loudly, looking around and trying to get everyone's attention.

"Well, sir, here you go," she said and gave me a brick of yellow American cheddar. "Welcome to America!"

I noticed that there was a man with a camera taping me. I smiled and waved the cheese at him.

Isn't this something, I thought. *In New York they call you names and in Los Angeles a lady wearing the American flag gives you some cheese.*

I knew then that I was going to like Los Angeles much better than New York.

Excerpts from Ismet Prcić's Diary from September 1998

Mother, oh, *mati*, I'm sorry; everything I write to you is a lie.

I'm *not* okay.

I *don't* have enough money. Thousand Oaks is expensive. I eat once a day. I boil a quarter of a packet of spaghetti and pour Campbell's cream-of-mushroom soup over it and use my roommate Eric's salt and pepper, Eric's dishes, Eric's cutlery. Sometimes, when he's not home, I take a sip of his Mountain Dew in the fridge or sneak a handful of his cereal into my mouth like a monkey. He's a good man, don't get me wrong. He shares stuff with me all the time, but it makes me feel bad when he does, makes me feel like a cliché, a poor Bosnia boy. But I have to accept. But I can't. But I do. I accept every time. Sorry I'm not more like you.

I'm *not* healthy. I'm thinner than I was in Bosnia in wartime. There are twenty-one stairs from the courtyard to our first-floor apartment, and by the time I reach the front door I'm wheezing and flashes of light burst in the periphery of my vision. I fainted the other morning.

I got up from my mattress and made it to the bathroom. I saw myself in the mirror, holding a toothbrush, and then I didn't see myself anymore. I woke up on the floor with my abdomen all scraped up and raw. I'd scraped it on the sink as I fell.

I *never* call or go see Uncle Irfan, even though he lives five minutes away. I'd rather throw myself eyeball first into a cactus. Maybe one day I'll tell you what living with him was like for two years. But I cannot stomach him any longer. He makes me physically ill. *Daleko mu lijepa kuća.*

I'm *not* studying bookkeeping in college, but theater and writing. I'm sorry.

I started to write a memoir about my journey here. You wanted to be an actress and a poet but ended up a nurse and miserable. I'm not gonna do that. I only wish you could read the first chapter about my arrival and tell me how to continue, tell me if it's any good.

I *don't* sleep well. I almost don't sleep at all. I dream of going to my college and mowing people down with a Kalashnikov. I dream of throwing hand grenades out of my car window. I dream of being shot.

I couldn't go to a real doctor, because here you have to be insured or pay up the nose, so I went to this Dr. Cyrus guy who volunteers on campus and he prescribed some sedatives, which I eat like M&M's.

He says I have post-traumatic stress disorder. He says that the pills are only a short-term solution and that in order to really get better I need to put my experience in a larger framework to help me make sense out of the whole thing.

He's the one who gave me the idea to write a memoir. I asked him what I should write for this therapy to work and he said, *Write everything.* I asked where I should start and he said, *Start at the beginning.*

At first it worked; I wrote about my escape, about my childhood, trying to keep to the facts. But as I kept at it, things—little fictions—started to sneak in. I agonized over them, tried to eradicate them from the manuscript, but it made the narrative somehow *less* true. When I put them back in, it became truer but it didn't exactly fit what I remembered, not in every little detail.

When I opened up to Dr. Cyrus he laughed, said that what I was experiencing was normal, that our brains are peculiar computers that constantly augment and even edit true events out of our memory when those events do not fit into the narrative that we tell to ourselves every day, the narrative of our own lives.

We're all heroes of our bullshit is how he put it. *Don't worry about what is true and what is not, you'll drive yourself crazy. Just you write. Write everything.*

(. . . suicide attempt number one. . .)

Mustafa never wanted to be born.

His mother, she wanted him out and he didn't want to go. So he finagled the umbilical cord around his neck and big toe, hoping to choke himself to death. But the space was wanting and he was already ten pounds with a head like half a loaf of bread and he didn't really know what he was doing. He kicked and wiggled, more out of frustration than anything else.

She misdiagnosed his tantrums for eagerness to emerge. His father took her to the hospital, but the doctors and nurses were celebrating the eighth of March, International Women's Day. They were all tipsy and loud, greasy around their mouths from all the syndicate food. They made his mother wait until the next day. Although this was working out to his advantage (more time to really do himself in), he could still detect the errors of their ways, and had he been able to talk he would have characterized the Yugoslav Health System as cruelly negligent.

He kicked and kicked and blacked out and that's when they used his sudden motionlessness to pull him into life. There was much rejoicing, everywhere but in his head.

(. . . some early sorrows . . .)

EARLIEST MEMORY

Hot summer day. My grandmother brought a hatchet from the shed and hung it on the branch of a thin cherry tree in the backyard, smiling. I sat on a sheepskin rug in the shade of a rosebush watching a hen trying to flee, flapping its white wings, one of its yellow talons tied by rope to a stake driven into the middle of the lawn. It would get a meter or so into the air and then, anchored, flap back down. For a second it would stand there balancing on one foot, blinking, cocking its head sideways, and then it would try again.

When grandmother approached, it went crazy, flying around in a whirlpool of airborne feathers. The sound of the wings was deep and muffled like glove-handed applause. Grandmother sniggered as she stepped on the rope closer and closer to the hen, gradually reducing its fly zone. Finally she caught it, untied the rope, and with the wide-eyed hen under her left arm, took the hatchet off the cherry branch, and walked behind the shed.

I got up and waddled after her, but she heard me and yelled at me not to look. I stood around the shed's corner for some time not moving, then peeked out anyway. I saw her kneel down on the bird, trying to subdue its wings, trying to get a good grip on it so she could place its head on a low stump in the clearing full of sawdust and wood chips. Her back was to me, so she couldn't see me.

The first *thwack* of the hatchet missed completely. The second was weak and it hit too close to the thick of the breast and didn't do much. The third connected with the neck but failed to sever the head. The fourth one took the head off all right, but my grandmother lost her grip on the hen and it took off flying for four or five meters, landing in the grass right in front of me. It took a couple of steps and stretched its wings as if thrilled with itself that it got away. Its neck spurted blood that reddened its white plumage something awful, but that seemed not to be an issue. It fluffed its feathers, getting some specks of blood on my bare legs, then scratched the grass with its feet, leaned down, and, obeying a terrible instinct somewhere in its muscles, made as if to feed, as if to peck the ground with its beak that was meters away on a small dune of blood-sprinkled sawdust already stilled by death.

AGE THREE

The moment Marshal Tito died* I shat myself. These incidents were not connected.

It had to have been a weekday because I was at my grandparents' in Gornja Tuzla. My parents mustn't have gotten off work yet—they would come to visit every afternoon after work on workdays and would take me home to Tuzla on weekends and holidays—because I don't remember them being there. I was sick as a dog from gorging myself on something or other and was lying in a fetal position on the L-shaped sofa.

---

*Yugoslav "benevolent" Communist dictator Josip Broz Tito died in Ljubljana's Clinical Center on May 4, 1980, three days before his eighty-eighth birthday.

It was cold. My grandfather sat in his armchair by the window and smoked his cigarettes. He sat on his right foot with his left knee drawn to his chest and stared intently at his ancient black-and-white TV with a pensive expression, mostly in his brow. I felt my stomach cramp and suddenly my drawers were filled with wetness and warmth. It took me a second to realize what had happened and when I did I immediately burst into tears. My grandma was in the adjoining kitchen behind these green curtains and when I called her my grandfather howled at me to shut up.

He had never raised his voice at me before. I fixed my bulging eyes on the TV to see what warranted this kind of explosion. On the screen was a gray town square somewhere with all the people standing frozen wherever they found themselves, dark against the asphalt, crying. The sound of wailing sirens came through the speakers. Then the weepy and grandiose voice of some TV announcer shouted things with emotion.

Scared and shitty I started to cry again and my grandfather called my grandmother to shut me up and turn up the television because Tito had just died. She stormed in and picked me up, automatically praying for the departed soul of the Communist leader in Arabic. Her hands were wet and cold from whatever she was doing in the kitchen and they smelled of apples. She patted my chest and whispered that we had to be quiet because it was an important day, and then she turned the volume knob to an almost unbearable level and carried me through the green curtains into the kitchen.

AGE FOUR

We lived on the eighth floor of an ugly, gray building on Brčanska Malta. All three rooms of our apartment faced south, which meant facing the newest, biggest twin skyscrapers in Tuzla. I was in the kitchen/dining room drawing an orange bulldozer unloading a mass of yellow sand into the back of a red truck. There was a construction site in between our building and one of the skyscrapers that I was using for inspiration.

Looking out the window I noticed a large gray coat swell with wind, disembark from a clothesline on a balcony on one of the skyscraper's highest floors, and fall straight down to the ground. It must have been a very heavy coat—it fell that fast. But then passersby started to gather around it, dozens of them, crowding, walking urgently toward it, pointing, and clasping their hands over their mouths.

I told my mother about it. She came over and hugged me from behind and looked out too. The passersby ran and waved to the cars on the street. A white Cinquecento drove up over the curb onto the sidewalk, and over the sidewalk onto the grass, and sped all the way to the crowd, honking its horn.

Why are the people looking at the coat? I asked.

Mother put her hand over my eyes and asked me if I wanted lemonade. She closed the blinds and turned on the radio.

AGE SIX

I started first grade when I was six, which, because both of my parents worked—and it was my brother's turn to stay with our grandparents—made me a latchkey kid at six. I both loved and hated this. I loved sleeping as long as possible, having the TV on all day, and "reading" all the books in my mother's library—the medical ones with pictures of naked people were staples. But I hated being a child and alone, being vulnerable and scared. I hated being petrified when people rang the doorbell: door-to-door salesmen, beggars, Gypsies asking to fix your umbrellas, older kids collecting old newspapers and bottles, trying to earn some money through recycling. I never opened the door, just like I was told. I hated when they would hear me inside and ring the bell two or three times, just waiting there as I trembled in fright and tried to silently put on the chain. I hated having to walk to school by myself with my huge backpack while all the other kids walked in groups and fucked around. I hated the silence that filled the apartment when I was alone, the silence that made me leave the TV on even during the news and boring history shows and intermezzos. Those TV intermezzos were the worst. They would show a tape of a bird flying and play classical music for hours.

It happened out of the blue. I was watching *The Little Rascals* in the living room and eating a butter and honey sandwich when the phone rang. We had a red rotary phone that had a little light on it that flashed when the phone was ringing. I imagined this light to be a camera through which whoever was calling could look into the apartment and see me even though mother told me it was for deaf people to see that the phone is ringing. I was not supposed to be watching TV that day because I had a lot of homework to finish, nor was I supposed to eat in the living room, which was why I turned off the TV before I answered the phone and why I finished chewing my last bite, too.

Making a good-boy face to the flashing light, I picked up the handle and said hello.

There was silence on the other end but not a dead one. It was the silence of an empty room or a room that someone was keeping quiet in to give the appearance of an empty room. It was the kind of silence that sound people in the movie business have to mic and record because they can't have the absence of sound, because it sounds dead, unnatural, and because they need more nuanced silences to make their movies sound alive. The silence I was hearing on the other end of that line was definitely an *alive* silence.

I repeated my hello at a higher pitch as my heart climbed into my throat. This time I heard something, a noise as though someone were sniffling or trying to subdue a whimper. I swallowed. I thought, hopefully, that it was a bad connection, that the whimperer simply couldn't hear my voice. And just as I was about to go into a third, louder hello, a woman's voice said something that I will never forget. She said:

Little boy, Dr. Stefan Tadić is your daddy. Do you hear? Your daddy is not your daddy. Dr. Stefan Tadić is your daddy.

I hung up, hard. It hurt my knuckles. I heard my heart in the silence of the apartment. I didn't understand what she meant, but I knew it was bad what she said, really bad.

The phone rang again and I covered the light with my hand.

It rang again.

And again.

Again.

Again.

Again.

Again.

Shaking, actually hearing my teeth chatter, I waited it out, and when it was over I dialed my mom at work. The operator told me to hold. I held. My finger was bleeding a little. I held until my mom answered and then I couldn't hold it in anymore.

AGE SEVEN

I was lying in my bed with my right arm stretched uncomfortably over the cold plastic of the night table to hold my baby brother's hand as we listened. She was screaming at him again. She was breaking things.

He was saying, *Don't do it; why would you want to do that?*

She was saying, *Enough. Enough. Enough. I can't take lies anymore.*

There was noise: the banging and sliding of kitchen drawers, the jingling of utensils, the clanging of cutlery. There were hurried footsteps down the hall, and then the door to our room opened and Father barged in. My brother cried first. He cried, *What are you doing?* I followed closely. I cried, *Don't fight, please.* We were up on our feet already and Father ushered us out.

He was saying, *I don't know what's wrong with her* and *maybe you can help her.*

We came into the hallway awkwardly in our pajamas. The linoleum by the front door was cold on my bare feet. The light on the electricity meter on the wall was glowing red. It meant the nightly cheap rate had already commenced.

Mother came out of the kitchen with a knife, and when she saw us she hid it behind her back.

We cried. We wailed. Father was behind us with the front door behind him.

Let me go, she was saying to him.

Calm down, Henrijeta, he was saying to her. *Be reasonable.*

*Step away or I'll—*she started and stopped herself. She thought about it. Her eyes darted around. Then she finished: *I'll do something ugly.*

I remember thinking that it was a weird thing to say. In English you can get away with it, but in Bosnian it sounds weird. It sounds awkward. Nobody says a thing like that. It sounds cheesy. She was not saying what she wanted to say. I remember thinking: What does she mean?

Why? he was asking. *We have an apartment, we have good jobs, we have two children. What's so bad?*

You are, she said. *I am. This is a fiasco.*

She took a step back into the kitchen and looked at Mehmed and me. *Never forget this,* she said, *we're all living a lie.*

AGE EIGHT

My dream was to become that sinewy ice-cream vendor from Kosovo who owned that tiny shop by the autobus station in front of my building. At my age I couldn't imagine a better job in the world, sitting in a matchbox of a room between the bank and the station on Titova Street, selling cheaply made refreshments to a wide range of citizens, from badly dressed businessmen with damp underarms to tough-handed peasants on their way to and from the nearby Little Market. My mouth would water at the mere idea of being in proximity to that giant ice-cream machine, buzzing with the sweet inner workings of its metal womb, a touch away from those three levers and the mad swirls of chocolate and vanilla behind them. Mmm, ice cream.

My mother allowed me one piece of bread a meal, a heart-breaking decision for her that probably saved me from childhood obesity, considering my appetite back then. I was never permitted an allowance either. Every time someone would slip me a coin at a family gathering my mother would bring out my kitty bank and make me put it in there. Tough love and all, though, at the time, I just thought she was mean. She took my weight gain seriously, unlike the rest of my extended family, who joked about it and piled macaroni on my plate whenever my mother was out of the room. They called me *poguzija*—an endearing, domestic way of branding someone a fat-ass.

Stop eating, my paternal grandma would say, *or your ass will climb on the back of your neck.*

My mother encouraged me to go out and play, made me. I would do so begrudgingly, and instead of running after a soccer ball or climbing a tree I would stake out the ice-cream vendor in our building. The sight of people buying ice cream, pulling their tongues around and over it, savoring its frosty succulence, never failed to give me a boner of a sweet tooth. Soon enough my eyes would fire up with ravenous gleam, and I would abandon my stakeout position to circle the shop like a shark around a scuba man in an underwater cage—a trancelike state.

Then one day I was awakened from my daze by the vendor. I don't know how long I had loitered in front of the shop, scaring away the customers with my tongue dragging on the smoldering pavement and my eyes feverish with that outlandish, insatiable need. It was as if the world suddenly came into stark focus and I saw him poke his head out of the door and motion me over, his mustache twitching up and down like Chaplin's. My legs took me there, closer to him, though my mind bellowed for them to stop, to quit, to turn away and run.

I knew he was giving me that free ice cream to get rid of me, out of pity. To him I was a poor child salivating over something I couldn't afford. And it was true; I couldn't afford my ass climbing up my spine to sit on the back of my neck, the cruel teasing and pinches, girls snickering during recess. I knew I shouldn't take anything from strangers, and, of course, there was also the question of dignity. But despite all that my hand rose, and a chocolate-vanilla ice cream exchanged hands, and it was on my tongue and down my throat so fast that I blushed. I stood there staring at this man from Kosovo with his knobby chair-leg arms, muttered guiltily my feeble thanks—more habitually than expressing my real gratitude, which was bittersweet at best—and walked away.

I never went by that place ever again on account of shame. If I had to go past it I walked in step with an adult passerby, keeping my gaze locked ahead of me and fighting off all sorts of discomfort.

That charity ice cream didn't sit well and I ended up spewing under some stairs.

AGE TWELVE

In elementary school I was into math. I liked that there was only one solution per problem, that nothing was vague and that you didn't have to interpret what the author meant by this or that. I had it all figured out for the first four years.

It was later, as the math got more abstract and elusive and you had to remember formulas and draw coordinate systems and such, that I developed animosity toward the subject. Suddenly there was more than one solution to a single problem and I started to lose my footing in reality as I knew it. I remember being obsessed with the notion that a straight line can go on forever and never touch another straight line that was parallel to it, that, seen from the side, a straight line is just a dot, which I thought could not be proven, since the line would go right through your eye and brain, rendering you blind and dead. Tragically, I said this out loud in class and my comrade-teacher thought I was trying to be funny and made me stand in the corner facing the wall for hours. My peers snickered at the size of my ass, and I visualized myself turning into a dust mote and wafting out through the crack under the door.

But mostly my change of heart came when *she* walked into my life, my comrade-teacher Radmila. She was a plump brunette in her forties, with pleasant features and nicely manicured nails but with some kind of growth on her cheek that allowed her to smile only with one side of her mouth, making the effort seem cold and halfhearted. She was capable of such astonishing mercilessness that I pissed myself twenty minutes into a class because she wouldn't let me out, because *that's why we have breaks in between classes*. I sat there in lukewarm dampness, inside an acrid cloud, thinking of comic book heroes.

I stopped doing my homework. I convinced myself I couldn't get it. I faked being sick to cut class. I prayed not to be called on. I copied other students' work.

By the third trimester I had accumulated a plethora of bad grades, got caught cheating on an exam (little pieces of paper with formulas glued to the underside of my fat ruler), and was sent to the principal's office. The principal, whom we called Rooster because he had a piece of loose, leathery skin connecting the tip of his chin to the center of his collarbone, ripped me a new one and then gave me a second chance. If I did well on my final exam he was going to let my *conduct unbecoming a student* slide.

There was no way I could have prepared a school year's worth of math in two and a half weeks. I told myself that I was trying. In reality, most of my energy was directed at conjuring up an elaborate scheme that would excuse me from taking the final. I fantasized about being hit by a car and lingering between life and death. I prayed for a communicable disease.

It just so happened that my mother had to go with her nurses' club to a symposium on how to battle alcoholism somewhere in Macedonia right about the time I was to take my final exam. Knowing this ahead of time and realizing that I was going to be alone with my pushover of a father, I hatched my master plan.

See, a couple of years back my cousin Adi had an inflamed appendix that needed to be taken out. Due to the operation and some complications, he didn't have to take any final exams and still passed into the next year. My plan was to find out from him all the symptoms of an appendix attack and act them out for my father in hopes it would get me under the surgical knife. In the dictionary it said that the appendix is a slender, closed tube attached to the large intestine near the point at which it joins the small intestine. I had no problem sacrificing that.

Not only did my father buy into my performance but so did the doctors in the ER. I went out of my way not to blurt out the list of symptoms like an amateur. I just picked a few good ones and mentioned them offhandedly. There was no empty doubling over or cries of pain. I kept my cool.

It worked. By the time they got me into one of those surgery slip-ons and led me down the tiled floors of pacifying mint green and bleach, I did get cold feet but it was too late. The anesthesi-ologist started telling me a joke and zonked me out just before the punch line. When I tell this story I often exaggerate and say that my last thought as I was going under was *Motherfucker!* Like I said, an exaggeration.

I dreamed that my inflatable raft got ruptured on some craggy rocks just under the surface and that I was about to sink into the depths where some dark shapes were sliding around.

I came to in a corridor with terrible pain and a confusion of squeaky wheels and people talking and bleach and iodine. I was wheeled into a room, moved to a bed, and the boy next to me had some complications, so they left him open with a tube dripping yel-low pus into a plastic container. He looked miserable. The girl on the other side of my bed was bald. She had lice, among other things.

I remember the ravenous sounds my stomach made when they brought in food for everyone but me and the pus boy. I remember his haircut—a little like Hitler's—and the way the liquid glucose dripped down the tube and into my vein for lunch. My mom re-turned from Macedonia early and pulled some nurse strings to come and visit me beyond the visitation hours. She seemed to have bought my performance as well.

She was there when my doctor came into the room looking more like a butcher than a doctor, with oily skin a-sheen, an unshaven neck, and a mustache as solid as a chocolate log. He told us that I was a very lucky boy, that if I hadn't gotten to the hospital when I did I would have died, that the inflammation of the appendix was at such a late stage that it was full of pus and ready to burst. He then produced a jar of yellowish liquid with what looked like a fat piece of decomposing red licorice, twisted and curled.

The biggest one I have ever seen, he said. *That's including the grown-ups.*

Let me get one thing across: I never, not for a single second during my performance, felt any pain. None. So what happened?

Here are some possibilities. Perhaps the doctor found a perfectly normal appendix and realized I was lying and decided to play a little joke on me. Or perhaps I got so far into the role of a boy who's having an appendix attack that I psychosomatically caused my appendix to inflame. Or maybe God found a twisted way to tell me I needed an operation when my body refused to warn me the usual way.

So what happened?

A realization: *There is no one solution. Everything's up for interpretation. It's all about what the author meant by this or that.*

My mom made me go to school after missing only six days. I took the final exam. Got a C.

(. . . germs . . .)

Mustafa was crawling around the apartment pretending to be a scuba diver, like one he saw on *Survival*. He had on a pair of welding goggles and a red thermos bottle taped to the back of his shirt as a makeshift oxygen tank. In his hand he brandished a straightedge, his harpoon gun, which he fired at things around the apartment, emitting slow, guttural sounds of underwater battles with sea monsters.

Chasing a particularly nasty and elusive hammerhead, Mustafa rolled into the hall when he heard them talking about germs in the living room. His mother had a guest and he was told not to disturb them. His mother's friend from work, the doctor who talked weird, was over for a cup of coffee. He had given Mustafa a chocolate earlier, which Mustafa had devoured in three, enormous mouthfuls. He could see him now sitting on the sofa, holding his eyeglasses by their rims and sucking on one of the plastic tips meaningfully.

"Children of physicians often suffer from verminophobia," the doctor said.

"Is that what it's called?" his mother asked. From where he was lying, Mustafa could see only her bare foot lightly bouncing under the coffee table. It bounced sporadically against

37

the doctor's shin until the doctor moved it closer so the foot rested against him and the bouncing stopped altogether.

"Verminophobia is an unwarranted fear of germs, yes."

Mustafa didn't believe in germs. The smallest thing he ever saw was a grain of sand on a napkin, and he didn't see anything on it resembling the multilimbed creatures whose photographs his mother pointed out in one of her books. He thought if they existed, they existed somewhere else, in the dirt or in the muddy water, in pond scum, but not here in the apartment. Otherwise he would have seen one by now, especially crawling around on his belly.

The pressure cooker hissed like a train and his mother jumped and ran to the kitchen, apologizing all the way. The doctor pulled out a kerchief from his pocket and started to clean the lenses on his glasses when he noticed Mustafa lying there in the hall. He smiled and motioned him over.

"Gentlemen do not eavesdrop on other people's conversations," the doctor said.

"I'm not a gentleman, I'm a scuba diver." Mustafa stood up. The man laughed.

"That is quite humorous, Mr. Scuba Diver," he said and put his glasses back on. Mustafa, on the other hand, took off his goggles because they were beginning to fog up, inverted them, and let them rest against his forehead, still attached to his skull by their elastic band. He squinted at the doctor:

"Can I ask you a question?"

"May I ask you a question."

"May I ask you a question?"

"Always, son."

"Is it possible to die from germanophobia?"

"Do you mean verminophobia?"

"When people are scared of germs." Mustafa said *germs* with skepticism and disdain.

"I'll tell you a story if you promise not to tell your mother that I've told you it."

"I promise."

"A certain physician from Tuzla would wear surgical gloves at the dinner table. If he dropped a pen on the floor in his own house, he would put on gloves, pick it up, dispose of it, remove the gloves, wash his hands, and open a new package of pens. Once, in the winter, his car wouldn't start, so he had to take public transportation to work. The bus was full and he had to stand. The driver pressed the gas pedal a little too eagerly, the vehicle jerked forward and the physician from Tuzla lost his balance, fell headfirst into the edge of a seat, cracked his skull badly, and later died in the hospital from head trauma. He refused to hold on to the rail for fear of it being contaminated by who knows what kind of germs. That physician . . . that was my brother."

"Is that a yes, then?"

Excerpts from Ismet Prcić's Diary
from October/November 1998

The other day I was in the cafeteria at school and out of nowhere I thought there was shelling. They were shelling Moorpark College. I dove for nothing.

How is it that some shell that exploded long ago in Tuzla can reassemble itself, fly backward into the mouth of the mortar that shot it, get shot again, and reach me here at the Moorpark College cafeteria? How is it that I can exist in both the past and the present simultaneously, be both body and soul simultaneously, live both reality and fantasy simultaneously? How is it that the smallest units of light can be both waves and particles simultaneously, depending on how you look at them? Where's the logic? Where's the sound mind? How am I to interpret?

Mati, you'd kill me, but I drink. You have no idea how I drink!

I have a gun, *mati*, a lady pistol made of chrome and steel. I stole it from someone's bedroom, from underneath their leopard-patterned pillow covered with dandruff, at a Halloween party last year. I was Pinhead from the Ramones song. I keep the gun hidden in my bookshelf, right behind the complete Mayakovsky, wrapped up in a rag. Eric doesn't know. There are bullets in it, six of them, but only the first one matters, right? I'm sorry I'm so much like you in this respect.

In what way am I like my father? Sense of humor? Ability to turn off the outside world? In what way, *mati*?

I love a girl. Melissa. Her hair oozes like honey. It's orange in the sun. She loves me, *mati*. She's American. She goes to church. She wears a cross right where her freckles disappear into her cleavage. She volunteers. She takes forty minutes to scramble eggs over really low heat, but when they're done they explode in your mouth like fireworks, bursts of fatty yolk and coarse salt and cracked pepper and sharp melted cheddar and something called thyme. She's sharp. She drives like a lunatic. She's capable of both warmth and coldness, and just hanging around her to see what it will be that day is worth it.

I *don't* miss home, *mati*. I'm there all the time. In the past. In fiction.

Excerpts from Ismet Prcić's Diary
from January 1999

More things I can't tell you, *mati*:

I asked Melissa to marry me. Not now, obviously. Sometime in the future. Her friends hate me for it. They think she's too young, that she's supposed to go wild and crazy now, guzzle beer, experiment. That I'm too old and serious, that I drink too much, eat too much mayo. *If they only knew.*

I'm turning American, *mati*. I don't go by Ismet any longer. Eric gave me a new name, a rock 'n' roll name. Izzy. He has been schooling me in the ways of American culture, helping me assimilate. He's a living encyclopedia and he knows what books I need to read, what TV shows I have to see, what albums I need to know by heart. The night I turned twenty-one, at midnight, we jumped the apartment complex wall, trudged through some abandoned compounds all the way down to Thousand Oaks Boulevard to a 7-Eleven there. I put a six-pack of Becks on the counter and the clerk didn't even notice it was my birthday, didn't say anything. He just swiped my driver's license through a machine and told me the total. Eric and I went back home, lit some fat candles, and he played Tom Waits for me, made me follow along with the lyrics on the record's inner sleeve. It was then, *mati,* that love was born in Izzy for America, for its sadness and madness, for its naïveté and wisdom, for its vastness, its innumerable nooks where a person can disappear.

I look at Eric. He loves his girlfriend, his record collection, our giant couch. He hates his work, driving this vet around the Valley so that he can look at X-rays, but he bears it, makes it work. While waiting for his boss in clinic parking lots, he rocks out or writes or reads, smokes like a chimney (alternating between regulars and menthols), and warms up his lunch sandwich on the hood of the van. He loves his projects, making mixed CDs, putting together seemingly clashing artists into a unique and unified whole. He's obsessed with Faulkner and has created a map of Faulkner's imaginary county and a bunch of family trees of his characters, trying to look at all that fiction and make it as real as possible. He loves his TV and records almost everything on VHS tapes of which our storage room above the parking space is full. He loves his family and they talk on the phone every day; he swings by their place all the time. We hang out at night looking for boobs on cable and every time he goes out on the balcony to smoke or to the bathroom to take a whiz I yell, "BRIEF NUDITY!" and he scrambles into our living room to see.

I live this kind of life, this day-to-day, too, but you haunt me, *mati.* I have two minds about everything. Side A(merican) and side B(osnian). I wish I could find a way to drop off the face of the planet and leave my minds behind, get a new one. I dream of disappearing, cutting all ties, becoming a derelict, free to rave. I'd be calmer, happier. Or better, going back to Bosnia and telling no one, not even you. Just live there in the same city, grow a beard, and watch you go to the market from a café across the street through a pair of sunglasses, never letting you know who I am.

(. . . premonitions . . .)

The fall of 1990. My mother said:

"There's going to be a war."

On TV some suited fathead behind a podium yelled into a microphone and shook his sausage finger in the air. The crowd in front of him roared, sporting his framed photographs and holding lit candles. My mother repeated her sentence absentmindedly, staring into the corner of the coffee table on which meze was served. My father, chewing on smoked beef, laughed and said that it was all just talk, that people were not stupid.

He poured himself another slivovitz. The parakeet screeched in its cage and pecked at its cuttlebone. Mother just kept on staring.

To me and my brother, after my mother went to sleep, he said:

"Don't listen to her, she's paranoid. It's from the concussion."

A month before, she had walked into a low stop sign in front of our building on the way to the corner store and knocked herself out. She was in a coma for a day.

Every once in a while from then on she would act . . . weird: say weird things, stare off into space for hours, clean maniacally. Mehmed and I were scared for her. Father told us everything would be fine.

But nothing was fine.

The people *were* stupid.

There *was* a war.

Sometime in the eighties, seeing how most of his friends were doing it, my father was persuaded, after an all-out nag attack from his mother and sister, who themselves were not doing it, to take out an onerous bank loan and buy a piece of land on the outskirts of Tuzla on which to build a weekend house. He was notorious for his indecisiveness, waiting for the last moment, always making the wrong decision anyway and drunkenly lamenting his choices for years to come with I-should-haves, I-shouldn't-haves, if-I'd-been-smart-I-would-haves, if-I-knew-then-what-I-know-nows, and so on and so forth. Bereft of imagination or creativity, he believed himself an adherent of a philosophy of sorts, which could be summarized by the counsel he gave me some years later, shortly before I was to flee Bosnia:

"Ismet," he said, "if you don't know what to do in life, just look around and see what other people are doing and then do the same thing."

After months and months of making up and then changing his mind about the location, he had settled for a verdant parcel in Kovačevo Selo, a predominantly Orthodox Christian village some fifteen kilometers outside our town. He acquired it from Drago Stojković, a rich farmer who lived with his clan in a huddle of buildings on top of the hill overlooking all his land. To get to it you had to suffer through an off-roading experience. First there was a nerve-racking 40 kph roll across a shimmying bridge. If you attempted to cross at a slower speed, it would droop in the middle like a hammock and emit agonizing groans. Then there was a sinuous, hilly, mud road that slalomed between scattered houses and sheds and made the cars wheeze going up and whoosh going down the hill.

Our parcel was the last in a row of five others, which all already contained pretentious attempts at the idyllic: picturesque cottages in various stages of construction, loud beds of flowers, absurd white statues of swans, lions, and armless Greeks. All of them were wrapped and rewrapped in barbed wire and guarded by overly passionate dogs and owners who yelled and brandished their double-barrel shotguns if you dared to pick up a plum that fell from their trees. Our little plot of land was a forty-by-eighty-meter rectangle choked with grasses and weeds battling for dominion. It was bordered by the woods on one side and a calamitous cloud of blackberry bushes—that looked like it was slowly rolling downhill from Drago's house—on the other. In the middle there was a pear tree to end all pear trees, the oldest tree I've ever seen. It looked scarred and gnarly and even its leaves and fruit were wrinkled and acned with age spots.

The first thing my father did was put up barbed wire all around the property to match the neighbors'. Then he got stuck. Too many people were telling him too many things: what to build, what not to build, how to build it if he was building it. Some were advocating not building at all. In his small, gray, calculating head he didn't know what to do, so he shut down. He stopped driving up there on the weekends, opting instead for televised sports of any kind and long afternoon naps.

Then it was up to my mother.

Over the years we got to know the Stojkovićs pretty well. They helped us dig our well. We helped them scythe, rake, and stack up the dry grass for their cows. They would bring us slivovitz and fresh cottage cheese. My dad would bring them gift packages of cleaning products from the factory. If we were around they invited us to their parties, weddings, and get-togethers. We invited them when we had people over to show them the progress on the house. By all accounts we were really good neighbors.

Mehmed and I befriended Marija and Ostojka, Drago's two granddaughters, and spent large chunks of our summers playing in the woods with them. We gathered wild strawberries, observed adders hunting tadpoles in the gaunt creek, pretended we were stranded in the wilderness, climbed trees, fell out of them, those sorts of things. Ostojka and I played show-me-yours-and-I'll-show-you-mine in a cow barn, although neither of us showed anything because we were too busy fighting about who should go first.

I'm not saying there were never any blemishes. There was that whole affair with my father's scythe. He took it up to Drago, who said he was going to take it to a man in the village to have it sharpened. Weeks, then months, passed and Drago hadn't brought back the tool, and my father, being that kind of a guy, hadn't mentioned anything, either. Our property started to grow first a shadow, then a stubble, then a full-on scraggly Socialist beard. When my father finally— after my mother's constant pestering that something might bite us from the grass—macheted his way out to the fence and walked up the hill to inquire about what had happened to his scythe, Drago denied that he was ever given it in the first place and started yelling as if offended by the whole thing. Father then minced the matter to calm him down and even went as far as asking to borrow Drago's scythe for a day, which of course turned out to be his own. After my mother gave the property a once-over—she was the one doing the majority of the physical work because of my father's supposed bad back and actual laziness—my father promptly returned his own scythe to Drago and had to borrow it intermittently from then on.

"Why did you do that?" Mother asked him afterward. "It's our scythe."

"It's just a scythe. Fuck the scythe. Not worth starting a war over it."

But you could see on his face that he was chagrined. His already thin lips disappeared completely and he looked away, not saying anything for a while. Only his crow's feet got deeper as he squinted at his swarming thoughts. Mother smoked pointedly. Mehmed and I went to throw a makeshift ninja star made of tin into the pear tree.

That same night after a couple of shots in him, my father, of course, regretted returning the tool. He said that he shouldn't have done it, that my mother was right, that it was our scythe, and that he would get it from Drago the next weekend.

But the next weekend he again returned it *to* Drago. When he climbed back down the hill he was whistling. He walked by my mother and started locking up the shed, avoiding her blazing eyes.

"You said you wouldn't give it back," Mother hissed.

"What?"

"The scythe."

"When did I say that?"

"Last week."

"I don't remember saying that. Are you sure?"

Mother's hand flew to the scar in her hairline. She turned from him and walked to the barbed wire and stared into the woods until he had the car packed up. On the drive back to Tuzla he said "Fuck the scythe" again, but Mother said nothing. The Fiat's belt squeaked. The air was hard to breathe. In the backseat Mehmed squeezed my hand. I took it away from him. Father whistled through his teeth.

*   *   *

In 1990 the weekend house was done. The final addition was a beautiful outside stairway to the large attic room, which was my favorite place to be. There I had my collection of comic books and magazines, my futon bed, my posters on the wall, a TV, and a secret stash of candy, everything a tubby fourteen-year-old boy needed to avoid boredom indoors. As for the outdoors, it was impossible to be bored there.

One particular morning, a Saturday near the beginning of autumn, while we were waiting for our mother's side of the family to show up and spend the weekend with us—which meant that we would have another boy, cousin Adi, to get in trouble with—Mehmed and I were playing the stealth game. The goal of it was to sneak, with our ninja masks on, from the well on one end of the property, through the garden, behind the rows of raspberry plants, around the house, around the shed, to the car, which at this time of year was never parked under the pear tree because of the falling fruit, and to the gate on the other side, without being noticed by our parents. After we had both accomplished this wondrous feat several times, we decided to up the ante and try to retrieve something from inside the house, the candle in the shape of a cat from the top of the downstairs TV or a Pluto mug from the kitchen, without being seen. That proved to be next to impossible because Father was watching tennis and Mother was kneading dough. We were going to change the rules a little bit, but that's when everyone showed up: Grandma, Uncle Medo, Aunt Suada, Adi, and his two sisters.

My father had the annoying habit, which I have regrettably inherited from him, of carrying on with a joke or a prank for much longer than necessary.

That day Father led our guests to our brand-new stairway and told them that he himself had designed it. That was hilarious to me because I knew he couldn't pick a straight line out of a group of curvy ones. I've always been puzzled as to how he got his engineering degree—probably paid somebody off. I knew for a fact that he could not even imagine a shape in his head without seeing it with his own eyes first, no matter how perfectly you described it to him. That's why he never read books. That's why Mother had to build a model of the weekend house and explain where every piece of furniture would go before my father would green-light any expenditure.

The guests didn't know that Father was pulling their leg, and he kept at it, dropping names of fake schools of architecture and non-existent designers whose work, supposedly, inspired him and coining design-related nomenclature full of crude puns, all with a straight face. My aunt and uncle intuited that something was not right but were too polite, too conditioned by provincial Communism and their own sense of blue-collar unworth to overtly question somebody who went to college. My grandma actually believed him and kept saying "really" and "Mašala" and "good, good." They trusted and respected him because he was an engineer, because his family descended from the *begs* and *agas* of the proud Ottomans, because (as he told me and my brother on a million occasions) his grandfather owned half of Tuzla before the Communists took it all away.

They respected him for all the wrong reasons. Truth be told, my great-grandfather Abdulaziz-aga did own some forty houses in Tuzla, one of the first automobiles in Tuzla, and a lot of land on which Tuzla's new neighborhoods stand today, but he didn't own these things because he was noble or learned. He owned them because he was an unscrupulous businessman who clawed his way to the top by pushing and shoving and signing his dotted lines with a smudge of a fingerprint or a wobbly X.

There was meanness in what my father was doing, condescension. His joke was unsalted, cruel, tasteless. It just wasn't funny anymore, not even to me. But he kept at it, and Grandma kept saying "really" and "Mašala" and my aunt and uncle kept looking down at their bare feet, stoically enduring this treatment without a word.

Then my mother, up to her elbows in flour, came out and told them the truth, that Father was pulling their leg and that the design was hers. My father burst into his evil little laugh and told everyone to lighten up, that he was just kidding, and we all smiled through our teeth, even Grandma, but her face had a glassy, wide-eyed tint of hurt.

I was going through a massive ninja phase at that time and so was everyone around me. They didn't have a choice, really, given how obsessed I was. I rented every B movie that had the word *ninja* in the title. In them, masked stuntmen jumped fifteen feet backward onto tree branches and roofs, had two-minute sword fights in mid-air, and disappeared and reappeared in small explosions of smoke. These grotesquely formulaic stories, all of them shot on the same location or two, starring someone named Richard Harrison in a purple or a magenta ninja suit, were being made in order to cash in on the Ninja Turtle mania that was sweeping across the world at the time. I organized the younger kids from our neighborhood into a ninja school of sorts, made them call me "sensei," gave them secret names, and made them secret ID cards written in a secret alphabet that they had to memorize and then destroy. I cut out step-by-step martial arts demonstrations from *Black Belt* magazine and had them go through the motions ad nauseam. I doodled gruesome ninja battles in my school notebooks. Even my mother, bless her heart, knew the Japanese names of all the wooden replicas of traditional weapons I kept receiving through mail order.

"Ismet, you left your *kusarigama* on the balcony. If I trip over it one more time I'm throwing it out!"

The seed of this obsession was planted much earlier, when I came upon Uncle Medo's stash of trashy, pornographic novels about the only blue-eyed American ever allowed to master the art and magic of *ninjutsu,* who was taking out the world's major players of organized crime and, in the process, fucking their trophy wives, their teary-eyed girlfriends, their redheaded secretaries, their favorite prostitutes, their nymphomaniac daughters, their beach-bunny sisters, their lusty S and M mothers, their accidental passersby—pretty much anything that moved. If a woman was introduced in the novel, you knew she would get fucked at some point. I was such a late bloomer that the ninja action passages excited me as much as these ridiculous sexual excursions.

So after an early lunch of homegrown-squash pie, I stole the dull old butcher knife from the kitchen drawer, and my brother, Adi, and I went into the woods to play. We sat on lichen-garnished stumps and pretended we were meditating, slapping at the bugs on our necks, knees, knuckles with the intent to commit insecticide. We threw the knife, trying to get it to stick into the trees but mostly twanging it off the sides of the trunks and then hunting for it in the ferns. We imagined convoluted plots in which we were a ninja team on a quest to save a kidnapped victim or steal back a priceless artifact or assassinate an evil drug lord and his band of mercenaries. The better these plots became the more we were aware that we were just playing, that it was all just make-believe, and that we wanted something more, a touch of real danger.

Throughout that whole summer Mehmed and I had spent a lot of time clearing out a particular part of the woods with Marija and Ostojka, attempting to make it into our own park/botanical garden. We wanted ponds with goldfish, fountains, and waterfalls. We wanted bridges, benches, and trash cans. We wanted tree houses and rope swings. All of those things were in the works in our heads, but in reality it was just a cleared-out portion of the forest where we had swept away the carpet of leaves, shaped the shaggy bushes to appear round and pleasing, and hung a vibrantly colored wooden sign declaring it our park.

When my ninja team came upon it that day, I had an idea of how to spice up the game. I told Mehmed and Adi that Marija and Ostojka had never met Adi before, that they had no idea he was even there, and that we could use that to set a cool little plot in motion. First we composed a generic ultimatum on a page from my journal, and each one of us penned every third letter in order to disguise our handwriting. It went something like "If you don't pay us [insert trivial amount of money here] we will destroy your precious park." Next, Mehmed and I went to lure Marija and Ostojka to the park to play, leaving behind Adi along with the knife, a smoke bomb we made out of a cut-up Ping-Pong ball wrapped in aluminum foil, and detailed instructions on what to do when we brought the girls to the park. He went along with it because he got to do all the action stuff himself.

We found Marija tending to the pigs. She looked like she had spindled into the beginnings of adolescence a little too early and a little too fast, resulting in a mouthful of teeth that were a little too big for her skull, and a tall, hipless frame with limbs that were a little too long. She wore her hair in two flaccid braids, and they swung as she toppled a bucket of meal over the fence of a pigsty to the sheer ecstasy of its inhabitants, who screamed, bumped each other, and chewed with their mouths open. We invited her down to the park casually, covering up our giddiness, and she said yes. She said we should do some more work on the bushes, perhaps expand the whole park a bit, and fetched Ostojka, who looked like the daughter of a different mother with her moody, brown eyes, so unlike Marija's bland, blue ones, her bronze complexion, so unlike her sister's freckled paleness.

It was something in the way we descended the hill, running and wielding our rakes and shears like battle clubs or banners, that suddenly rang a thousand alarms in my head. I saw flashes of un-specified violence in the future, attacking movements of color and bared teeth, and a part of me was aware that it had something to do with the turmoil in the country. That part of me tried to decelerate, digging my heels deeper into the dirt, but my fat-assed momentum shot me across the creek and into the woods.

Marija and Ostojka looked so happy. They were telling us how they'd seen a wild boar last week and how fast it had run through the leaves. They asked me if Muslims were allowed to eat wild boar. I told them I wasn't sure. I started to sweat. I thought of telling them what to expect but didn't. I couldn't.

We walked to the edge of the park when something flew from the thicket and fell some six paces in front of us. It spun hissing on the damp ground, billowing a cloud of acrid smoke that smelled of burning hair. Through the smoke things started to look slow and unreal. Ostojka screamed. Marija ducked behind a tree. Mehmed looked at me to see what I would do. I just stood there, watched.

Wearing my ninja mask, Adi threw his body parallel to the ground, executed an inept somersault, jumped up to his feet, and stabbed the ultimatum into a tree trunk with the kitchen knife. He then hopped and kicked the wooden sign that swung on its rope, but it got caught on a low branch and stayed up there in the foliage. Seconds later there was only the shushing of dry leaves as he hauled ass into the forest and the shrill screaming of the girls.

When I conjured this plan I expected Marija and Ostojka to buy into it the way kids buy into plays written for them. I never antici-pated the hysteria that would take over their faces and minds, or those shrill and elaborate curses that no child can come up with on their own but have to overhear from adults to remember, curses against Adi's mother (they're always against a mother, aren't they?) speckled with words I didn't quite expect to be uttered there, words like *fundamentalist, Turks,* and *terrorist.* I never anticipated that Adi would have to dodge the flying shears or dive headfirst across a barbwire fence into someone's cornfield. I never anticipated that Ostojka would stomp on the smoke bomb and that Marija would take the knife and the ultimatum out of the tree and that they would salamander up the hill, screaming for their dad and grandpa.

Amid all that panic the woods suddenly felt perilous and dark, and Mehmed and I felt compelled to run for our lives, too. It was like we'd awakened something big, something ancient. The forest came alive. The trees leaned in trying to scoop us up with their talons. Blackberry bushes shot out their sticky tentacles at our ankles, tripping us, tearing at our socks. The ground itself secreted a noxious sludge of putrid, dead leaves and animals, trying to bring us down, trap us, and slowly digest us over time, reducing us to petite skeletons with glass marbles and ninja masks in our decomposing pockets.

We reached our property white with fear and Grandma asked us where Adi was and we said we were in the middle of a hide-and-seek game. She said that the hot pot was not going to be ready for another hour or two and that if we wanted a snack we should ask our mother for a piece of bread with plum jam. Then Adi wandered in, all sweaty and scarlet-faced, out of breath, hair full of cobwebs, knees stained, acting like nothing was out of the ordinary. We said we were going upstairs to read—of all things—and nobody was fooled. My mother and aunt were halfway up the stairs to inquire what had happened when they noticed three generations of Stojkovićs rushing down the hill, blackening the green.

*   *   *

55

To both my family and the Stojkovićs it was quite obvious who did what. The Stojkovićs knew that we were the only boys playing in those woods. That was clear to my family, too. What was peculiar, though, was that both families ignored the obvious and put on an act that was incomprehensible to me.

The Stojkovićs came out yelling, cursing malicious extremist Muslim elements who were sent to burn our forests, threaten our children, set neighbor against neighbor, and destroy our whole country. They cursed their Turkish mothers, their dirty prayer rugs, and their whole lineage all the way back to Muhamed. They kept repeating that it was not us but some extremist Muslims on a mission to obliterate the Yugoslavian way of life. For some reason all the grown-ups in my family agreeably hung down their heads, denied being a part of anything, mumbled pacifying words, and endured this salvo of curses directed at some other Muslims, not us, although we were the only ones there, in the whole village.

I started to buy into the Stojkovićs' version of the events myself, happy that everyone seemed to think I had nothing to do with it, and I was amazed at how well organized this Islamist terrorist cell had to have been to even find out about our shitty little park in the woods around Kovačevo Selo and how important it must have been to them to send an operative to destroy it. But that only lasted about half an hour, until the neighbors dispersed and there was hell to pay.

"How could you do that?" Grandma yelled at us that night as the three of us stood lined up in the middle of the room with our hands on our throbbing asses and tears on our cheeks.

"These are very dangerous times to play those kinds of games," said my uncle. "Don't you know that?"

But we didn't. Not really. We knew the politicians were fighting on TV a lot, that there was a lot of talk about what religion everyone was, about tensions between different nationalities, their constitutional rights—all foreign words to Adi and me, who were on the verge of crossing the border from the world of ninjas, marbles, and comic books into the world of new, curly hairs, cracked voices, and minds crammed with pussy, let alone Mehmed, who was only eleven.

"There'll be a war," my mother said, her lit cigarette as though forgotten in front of her face. Everyone looked over as though she had said that Venusians were about to land. But there were flickers of real fear in everyone's eyes.

"God forbid," yelped Grandma, shaking her head as her calloused fingers tapped against the plastic balls of her *tespih* and she continued to count off *zikr* prayers.

"I don't think it will come to that," said my uncle, though his words rang hollow.

Mother kept silent.

Father sent us upstairs. In bed I tried to imagine war and saw images from the Communist propaganda films in which the good guys, the partisans, machine-gunned Nazi dicks on their motorcycles with sidecars. I saw Rambo. I saw Arnold. As I understood it, war was good and exciting if you were a good guy and just the opposite if you were bad. But was I good or bad? Wasn't it my idea to deliver the ultimatum?

Quickly I thought, *She couldn't have meant war.* I rationalized that by *war* she probably meant something like a feud between the neighbors, the kind that Dad wanted to avoid by swallowing his pride and giving up his scythe. She was messed up from her concussion, I told myself. But I couldn't fall sleep.

Soon enough even my father would realize that people *were* stupid enough to fling a hefty piece of wet Balkan shit right into the blades of a turning fan and expect not to get soiled. The war would come just as prophesied, and for years a part of me would believe that by coming up with that bit of mischief, I had somehow caused it all, and I would feel guilty for all the dead and the dead-to-be, and sitting in the basement with my town groaning from destruction above my head, I would wish for a time machine and another go at that day.

By the next fall, scarred by the experience and about to start high school, I grudgingly put my ninja phase behind me. Solemnly, like an aging warrior with failing eyesight and unsteady hands, I retired my trusty mail-order swords to the cobwebs behind the ironing board and hung my nunchakus on the coat hook. I felt like something was ending, my childhood, perhaps, or the good ol' times or pick your cliché, and something else, something forever foreign and foreboding, was coming to a boil in the country, in my city.

It crawled out of manholes and hissed out of pipes. It fell down with bloating rains. It blew in with stormy weather. It settled on souls, minds, concrete. We trudged upon it on the asphalt and in the grass. We kicked it around on dead leaves and trash. We breathed it in with dust and gulped it down with food. We washed it out of our hair and shed it with dead skin. It Freudian-slipped into our words and belly danced in our dreams. It was everywhere, yet we couldn't recognize it, couldn't see it for what it was. The best we could do was smell its ozone breath and sense its dead calm before the storm, attribute it to the changing seasons and blame it on the fall, then winter, then spring. All of us were fooled by it, by the war, except, of course, my mother.

The night Adi, Mehmed, and I pulled off our little stunt in Kovačevo Selo my mother dreamed of Chetniks, although she'd never seen one in her life. Her subconscious conjured them from grainy black-and-white photographs in books about World War II, pictures showing long black beards, black caps and uniforms, big knives, and X-shaped sashes of bullets across the men's chests. She told us that she saw herself running before them, carrying small, faceless children, presumably my brother and me. She saw headless bodies tumbling down an embankment into a muddy, swollen river, haystacks ablaze, buildings splotched with holes, and storm-pregnant clouds so close to the ground they obscured the tops of heads.

She refused to stay overnight in the weekend house anymore and made every excuse not to bring us, the children, at all. She and Dad would make quick trips up there to do some garden work, harvest the vegetables, clean the leaves out of the drainpipes and such, and would always return before nightfall. My father, the champion of taking the path of least resistance, humored her when she was around and made fun of her when she was not, saying stuff like: "Your mother and her conspiracy theories," and "Your mother had a dream and now we can't sleep in our own house."

One time when we did go with them Mother had just finished making *ajvar* and was in the process of transporting the still-warm jars into the shed when Marija and Ostojka's mother walked by the fence on her way to retrieve a renegade yearling.

"Oh neighbor, what are you making there?" called the woman.

"Just a little bit of *ajvar*. We got tons of eggplants this year and the peppers weren't bad either. So I figured I should make something out of them instead of freezing them whole and overstuffing my freezer."

"Make it, make it, who knows who'll get to eat it," the woman said and then jumped over the creek into the woods.

Mother froze, a jar in each hand, swirling the sentence in her mind, trying to work out a nonthreatening interpretation. She stood there breathing, smelling the resin and the nearby outhouse, hearing the insects buzzing and screaming for someone to mate with them, feeling the breeze. And after a while, scrutinized by this most intense contemplation, all those stimuli began to make a new kind of sense. Her brain deciphered the code laid in the fabric of reality and she became aware that everything was saturated with terrible, mounting wrongness. She looked at our house and for a moment actually saw it roofless, stairless, and empty.

She then walked to our dark blue Fiat, opened the trunk, and placed the jars of *ajvar* inside. She returned to the shed and did the same with another two jars, then another two, then another two, and she didn't stop until the trunk was filled up with jars of *ajvar*, pickles, pickled peppers stuffed with shredded cabbage, pickled beets, pear jam, raspberry jam, bottles of rose petal syrup, bags of potatoes, bunches of carrots, boxes of dried valerian, whole pumpkins, everything. She told Mehmed and me to get in the car, then found my father fussing about the well and told him to drive us home. He did and that was the last time she ever saw our weekend house or the property.

"To me it's as good as torched," she would say when Father would try to change her mind. From then on our weekends were spent around the TV, with my father taking naps and drinking and my mother staring into the void and chain-smoking.

As for the TV, it constantly showed news footage of what had happened in the Croatian town of Vukovar, just a little north of Tuzla, its buildings turned into debris by artillery, its citizens fleeing up snow-covered roads with all their possessions on horse-drawn buggies or in bulky suitcases or mere pockets, its projectile-plowed streets now full of Serbian banners and music, and dancing neo-Chetniks, rocking left and right in the backs of their trucks, smiling at the camera as the truck tires, unseeingly, crunched through the flesh and bone of those who had too many holes in them to evacuate and were lying there, hugging the streets.

At that time we still lived in the old apartment on Brčanska Malta, at the intersection of Titova and Skojevska, the latter of which led all the way to the Husinska Buna military base. I would wake up in the middle of the night to pee and find my mother in the darkness of the kitchen/dining room staring through the closed lace curtains with a pair of opera glasses eight stories down to the street on which convoys of military vehicles moved to and fro nightly. She would take a cigarette break and give me the number of the moment.

"They just moved in forty cannons," she'd whisper from the fuzzy darkness.

"So what?" I'd say. "You should go to sleep."

"You go. I'm not tired."

Sometime in April, in the new apartment, just before my parents sent Mehmed and me away, my mother got to say her first I-told-you-sos.

Prior to that, my father's blind optimism had turned into the worst kind of selfish naïveté; he saw the war with his eyes, but the message had yet to reach his brain, or at least the part of it in charge of self-preservation. He would come home from work and, while kicking off his shoes, peck my mother on the lips for my benefit. This performance of affection was transparent, insulting. It was supposed to make me feel better, like the family unit was intact, like the parents knew what they were doing, like there was no reason for alarm. He would walk into the bedroom to change, and Mother would follow, closing the door. I would sneak closer and listen to the hiss and the mumble of their muted conversations, which would always end abruptly with him emerging in his sweatpants, with a face like a red mask, white only around the lips, which were pressed together hard. He would take the kitchen route and materialize in the living room with a shot glass and a bottle of brandy in his hand. His chair would squeak when he dumped his weight into it. I would get shushed and the TV would pop on and blink at us all night with pain and violence and talk.

Despite recognizing his stubborn denial of facts and beginning more and more to believe my mother, I did my share of blocking out the shit when I was with my friends. We avoided talking about politics and religion. Instead, all horny and in love, we walked the streets hoping to catch glimpses of our "girlfriends," who were clue-less that we even existed. We drank Cokes and coffees in crowded cafés, went to one another's houses, and played cheesy computer games and out-of-tune guitars. We lied to one another about sexual experiences, traded Italian comic books and German porn mags, told gross jokes, and bitched about school.

The number of friends eroded with each wave of impending violence, though. Suddenly Boban had a sick grandpa in Pančevo and had to go visit him for a while. Sead's family decided to move to Germany with his uncle, and we had a good-bye party in his week-end house before they sold it. Jaca left for Slovenia with her dad; Tarik flew to Turkey, and my friend Mile went to Banja Luka for his cousin's wedding. Planes and helicopters flew over the town a lot.

The next thing I knew my brother and I were quickly kissed and hugged, then hurried into the back of a white Opel Kadett belong-ing to our cousin Garo. The interior was solid with that new-car stench, and the pungent, coconut-scented air freshener hanging off the rearview mirror made me want to retch. With Garo driving and his sister Amela yammering nonstop from the shotgun side, Mehmed and I looked at the scenery, vaguely scared and perceptibly giddy because most of our friends were in school that morning and we were going on a trip to stay with some family of ours in Zagreb *until this whole thing simmered down*. For a week or two, my father said.

Zagreb, 1992. The two-house complex on Ilica Street was already teeming with my father's distant relatives, some of whom were natives and most of whom were refugees from other parts of Bosnia. It was like hanging out in a locked-down airport terminal with people sleeping among their luggage, sitting on lined chairs, eating bread and smoked sausages off their hanky-covered laps, with their toddlers running amok and slapping at everything with their sticky little fingers, leaving smudges of grease. Everything had the feel of old Russian movies and third-world misery. I was appalled.

Mehmed and I moved in with Cousin Zvonko and his wife and daughter in the add-on attic apartment of the first house. Zvonko was a massive man, with a light brown comb-over and blue eyes behind rectangular specs, obese to the point of not being able to cut his own toenails. He breathed with a resonant wheeze that started on the third stair up, and by the time he reached the apartment he would cough and have to sit down for half an hour, drenched. His wife, Zana, was the exact opposite of him physically, to the point where you wouldn't be able to fathom the image of the two of them in the act of coitus even if, by some twist of fate, you happened to witness it.

The apartment was almost all one room except for Zvonko and Zana's bedroom and the bathroom. It was broken up by beams and chimneys and smelled of sun-bleached wood and dust. All the way in the corner, on the floor behind the TV cabinet, fenced off with low bookshelves featuring googly-eyed dolls and girlie trinkets, was our mattress. Before we got there this nook served as Zvonko's daughter's secret room, which was probably why she was a total shit to us and hated our guts the whole time. I didn't like being called a refugee, so I spent the money Father gave me for essential foods on Ramones records, Coca-Cola, and sugary cacao powder, and the hosts were, let's say, angry.

"Do you know there's a war going on?" they all kept asking. I cried and ran downstairs, slalomed my way through a gaggle of raggedy refugee toddlers and ended up in an office, the door of which I locked from the inside and whose phone I abused to call home. I told my dad we were ready to be picked up.

Mother did come a week later but not to pick us up. She was in one of the last buses that crossed the bridge into Croatia before it went, first up into the air and then down to the bottom of the Sava. Father stayed behind to keep his job, take care of the apartment, and feed the parakeet. Mother showed up in jeans with a bunch of bags and moved into the attic, as well.

With that commenced our official exodus.

In mid-May we saw our old apartment building on Brčanska Malta on TV. In the middle of the intersection that my mother spent nights monitoring with her tiny binoculars, an olive green ammunitions truck sat ablaze, its tires melting, its cargo crackling like a fireworks display, spraying projectiles indiscriminately. Behind it, stretching up Skojevska Street, were more trucks, some burning, some shot to shit, some stalled, some untouched but driverless. There were holes in the buildings. There were no soldiers except for the ones lying around, dead.

A gray ashworm of about half my mother's cigarette died, unsmoked, against the filter and fell silently onto the carpet. I scooped it up into an ad from a magazine and threw it in the trash. Coming back I saw her bring the filter to her lips, realize it was just a filter, and then look around the floor for a singed spot or a small fire, mildly amused that she could find none.

Father called right before dinner, said he was okay, said that the Yugoslav National Army, mirroring what they had done in Sarajevo, attempted to evacuate the base and move all its artillery to the hills around town, where they would be in a perfect position to systematically shell it, and that the local group calling itself the Patriotic League ambushed them and seized . . . He got disconnected midsentence and didn't call again. My mother served the dinner to everyone except herself and sat smoking by the open window, assuring us all that she just wasn't hungry. I forgot and made the cardinal mistake of audibly slurping up a couple of spoonfuls of my hot hot soup and Zvonko lost it. He turned purple, smacked his napkin against the table, and gave me another lecture on how to eat with my mouth closed like a civilized human being. During the rest of the dinner nobody said anything.

I read late into the night, something inappropriate for my age, something about rich couples lounging in Jacuzzis filled with champagne, rubbing cocaine on their gums and the tips of their pink penises and rubbery, swollen clitorises, and fucking, fucking, fucking all night long. When I finally turned off the lamp I noticed an orange dot of fire across the attic room in the darkness above where my mother's mattress was, silently turning brighter for a moment or two and then dimming down again.

Whispers:

"Mom?"

"Yeah?"

"You still up?"

"Yeah."

"Are you okay?"

Silence. Then:

"Yeah."

I didn't know what else to ask, so I let the silence win. It gloated there in the dark, humming. I closed my eyes and pressed my cheek against the cool side of the pillow.

"What are we gonna do?" she whispered, and my eyes shot open. Her voice was so quiet and out of nowhere that it sounded like thoughts in my own head. "I can't . . . I just . . . I can't stand it here. I'll break down. The way they're treating . . ."

She stopped herself. The orange dot did its lighthouse imitation.

"We have to be thankful to them for letting us stay here."

"What did you say?" I asked, though I heard it well enough.

"Nothing. Go to sleep."

The last straw came the very next day in the form of a field mouse.

For more than a month while we were in Zagreb, Mother felt so bad about burdening Zvonko's family that she took it upon herself to work like a maniac and earn our keep. She provided and made all the food, paying for it with our meager and rapidly dwindling savings. She scrubbed every square inch of tile, polished every wooden surface, every chimney brick and window. She vacuumed all the rugs and did all the laundry. She did all the dishes and then she did some more. She had become, pretty much, a live-in maid, this voiceless creature in yellow rubber gloves, kneeling on the floor and scouring, stopping only to stare and smoke. The problem of course was that Zvonko and Zana, and even their daughter, got used to food just appearing on their plates and dirty clothes vanishing off their floors only to reappear washed, ironed, and folded in their drawers the next day. They started to complain if their socks weren't folded the way they wanted, or if there was no beer in the fridge, or if the vacuum cleaner was fucking up the TV reception. On top of all that, they were my father's cousins and, like his immediate family, thought my mom of inferior birth.

Our last day in Zagreb, Zvonko was watching TV, Zana was in their bedroom with a migraine, and Mother was looking for a pot when a little mouse ran out from the pantry and stopped, shivering, in the corner of two cabinets. Being grossed out by a thing like that, Mother asked Zvonko if he could take care of it. Annoyed, he called for Zana to do it, who in turn called him an idiot and told him that her head was about to split open and what the hell was he thinking. Puffing and swearing, he wrestled his ass out of an armchair, which perked up and grew like dough, thundered into the kitchen, and stomped on the little creature with his heel. Blood spurted on the cabinets, over the tile. He picked up the minuscule remains, threw them in the trash, and walked back to his armchair, leaving bloody heel prints on the tile, on the hardwood floor, and on the carpet. Mother suppressed a gag and asked him if he could please take out the garbage, and he said that it was not Friday yet and turned the TV on really loud.

That was it.

Mother first smoked a cigarette, looking out the window, her back hunched, her elbows on the sill, and then took the garbage out herself. It took her a long time. When she came back she went straight for our stuff and started packing. Zvonko was outraged. My brother cried. I sat there with a book in my lap, dreading the fact that I, judging by the gleam in her eye, probably wouldn't get to finish it. Even Zana walked out of the bedroom in her nighty, her face like a storm on the horizon, hissing her deeply wounded whys.

"Thank you for all the help," Mother said, "but we've been here over a month now and it's time for us to leave. We don't want to be a burden anymore."

"Where are you gonna go?" asked Zvonko, as if calling a bluff. There was nowhere to go.

"To the Red Crescent with the rest of the refugees," she said and gave me a crazy look, signaling. I swallowed, put the book on the coffee table, rose, and picked up one of the big bags.

"Think of your children," boomed Zvonko from the top of the stairs as we made our way to the front door.

We sat on our bags in front of the Zagreb mosque, in the parking lot, in the sun.

The heat made the black asphalt look like crusted-over lava, throbbing and emitting visible waves of the red hell that seemed to boil beneath it. Cars wavered in this radiation, their contours melting, collapsing. Shirtless Bosnian men sat on curbs or squatted in the patches of grass, staring vaguely in the direction of the closed doors of the Red Crescent, their skin baked from field work, their spines, pelvises, ribs evident through it in detail. Their head-scarfed wives, sisters, mothers sat clustered on towels and blankets, fanning one another miserably with newspapers, calling their ill-groomed children to come back.

Mother smoked and rummaged through our bags, zipping open all the compartments and slipping her hand inside them, looking for something or satisfying a compulsive need to touch everything she owned. She offered us sandwiches and consolations and every half hour or so walked over to a phone booth on the corner. Through the glass we saw her go through the same motions of putting a card into the phone, pressing buttons and listening, listening, listening for a while, then hanging up, pulling out the card, putting it in her purse, stepping outside, and lighting a cigarette, every time.

Then at some point Cousin Seka showed up in a van with this blond man in a faded Hawaiian shirt. Zvonko had called her and told her what happened, where we were going. Both Seka and the man worked for the Red Crescent, driving food and medicine over treacherous terrains in monthly humanitarian convoys to besieged Bosnians. Mother told us to watch the bags and they walked off a little way and Mehmed and I watched them talk, trying to discern what they were saying from their gestures and body language. When they finally started walking back there was a different aura around my mother.

"Let's go, guys," she said, picking up a bag.

"Go where?" asked my brother. I lifted our biggest bag, but the blond man patted my head and took it out of my hands.

"Your cousin Pepa's in Đakovo," Seka said. She had a man smoker's voice and cool little eyes. I had never heard of any cousin Pepa.

"But we're not staying in their house," Mother corrected her. "We're gonna have a place of our own."

"Does that mean that we're not refugees anymore?" asked my brother and everyone's heart broke a little. Mother put down her bag and hugged us.

Đakovo is to Zagreb what low shrubbery is to a redwood forest.

The tallest things around were several grain silos and a full-size, redbrick cathedral, the proud symbol of the township. From the steeple, they told me, you could see fields of corn and wheat as far as your eyes could reach.

Cousin Pepa, a jolly gray man, showed us the house where we were to stay. It belonged to his Serbian neighbor, who had left for Belgrade the night before the war and asked Pepa to take care of his plants. The place was dark, unfinished, an architectural vomitus. Humidity had turned the layers of dust into invisible syrup that coated everything. Fingertips stuck to it like to wet envelope glue and you had to peel them off surfaces with a slight force. The second floor had a big room with a TV, an adjoining dining room, and a kitchen, and mother told Pepa that we loved it and thanked him. We left our stuff on the floor and crossed the street to Pepa's backyard gazebo, where we were to have a party.

Mehmed and I met some new cousins and neighborhood boys, sneaked into someone's strawberries, squatted there, and spoiled our dinners. Mother had a few glasses of Riesling and we saw her laugh a couple of times.

A month later Mehmed and I knew all the kids in the neighborhood. We spent our days throwing rocks into this large pond the color of white coffee that the local kids told horror stories about. They said that there were a couple of entire houses under the water and that someone named Vedran Tomašević had drowned there— after taking on a dare to bring something from the very bottom, he had dived right down into a chimney, got stuck, and died. They took us to a German bunker from the Second World War and told stories of gang rapes and bludgeonings, Nazi ghosts and overdoses, and they pointed to beer bottles, syringes, and used prophylactics as pieces of evidence. We believed. We had our doubts. We spun our own wild tales.

At the house Mother would turn into a bitch when the news was on and would apologize, kiss our foreheads, and give us snacks when it was over. I imagined what Father was doing in the apartment all by himself. I envied him in a way.

Mother took on the house and cleaned, scrubbed, scoured, polished, washed, sponged up and down, and threw basins of dirty, dark water into the overgrown yard. She revealed dormant colors of wooden furniture and cooked thrifty but scrumptious meals that Mehmed and I pushed around our plates. She sobbed when she thought we weren't around and sang when she thought we were. She held her fist against her stomach and belched her quiet belches, doubled over by her numerous ulcers. She cut off all her hair in front of the mirror and adopted the look of a mental patient, complete with the eyes of glass, long wall stares, and overly eager song.

Father called sporadically, telling tales of empty stores, deadly shellings, and basement-dwelling dynamics. He said he had to let our parakeet loose because he ran out of birdseed. He said that the hamster was still around.

I read and watched TV and read. I sneaked downstairs and rummaged through the stuff of our unknowing hosts, stealing books, trinkets, tapes they left behind. I jerked off to their magazines, family albums, medical books. I caught flies on their windowpanes and threw them into giant spiderwebs, watching them try to free themselves. Giddily, I observed the spiders tie them up with their butcher's twine and store them off to the side for later. Mostly, though, I read books.

A day came when Mother decided that she didn't have anything to lose and she was going to go out and try to feel like a normal person again, despite everything. She made us breakfast of bread and honey and tea and then put on her best outfit, reddened her lips and blackened her lashes, tied a scarf over her jagged do, and walked into the town. She checked out some shops, ran her fingers over fabrics, asked if they had this blouse in a more neutral color or a better size. She bought a fashion magazine, stopped at the corner café, ordered a cappuccino, and asked the waiter if they had any Bosnian music, anything from across the Sava. He found some bad pop and she sat there in the shade, flipping the colorful pages, her mind in a knot.

In time, she switched to beer, hoping it would loosen her up, which it did, and when she came back to the house the skin around her eyes was mucky with mascara, and she told both of us what had happened, how, while sitting there, she had this amazing vision of standing on top of a mountain, on the edge of a crude road, facing an abyss of crispy pastures and tumultuous foliage in the early, green morning air. She described to us a flock of shivering sheep draped with a gauze of patchy, disappearing fog. She said it was an omen. A good one.

Father telephoned out of nowhere after not being heard from in two weeks. He said he was at the bus station in Đakovo and needed directions to the house. He had arrived there on one of the first buses to successfully sneak out of the siege of Tuzla. I flew recklessly across the street to Pepa's house, screaming my brother's name and jumping over things.

Father was sallow and thin. His clothes caved in on the places where protuberances should have been. There was film in his eyes like he was dead, or old, or just born, or drunk. He ate fast. He was unshaven. When he talked, he talked low. When Pepa would give him wine he talked louder and more often. He shook his head like he still couldn't believe what he had seen, felt. But talking about war he still was optimistic, still claimed it would not last long, that people were not that stupid to drag it into the winter. At night he talked with Mother, and Mehmed and I lay under our covers, eyes wide open, holding hands, and trying to eavesdrop. We caught words like *America* and *Zagreb*, Mother's crying, and Father's consoling mumbles.

Four days later, despite well-meant protests from Pepa and his family, our parents made up their minds and we were on a bus heading back to Bosnia. Before we left Mother threw away armfuls of clothes and packed our bags full of cans of oil, bags of flour, tins of meat and fish, packages of coffee and sugar, yeast and dried milk. Again I had to leave my books behind.

"We're going to be fine," Mother said when we sat in our seats and she saw me crying.

But she hung a plastic bag containing her cigarettes and a bottle of cognac on the side of her window. It was a little weird but I didn't say anything.

Somewhere around Karlovac, still in Croatia, the bus broke down and we lost half a day waiting in the sun by an abandoned gas station for a new part to be delivered from Zagreb. I searched my mother's eyes to see what she was thinking, but she was smoking and I couldn't really see inside her head.

Later we all took a pill and slept. Or at least Mehmed and I did. We were on a ferry for a little while. It was dark. Then we were on a bus again, going slowly, stopping, showing papers, starting again, sleeping.

I awoke at dawn and when I did Mother immediately took my hand, her face stern with fear, and squeezed. People mumbled from the semidarkness like at a funeral. The air smelled of puke and rancid mayo and motor oil and old sweat. A child was crying in the back and a mother was telling her to shut up and act her age. My father was up on his feet, leaning into the aisle, copying what other men were doing, trying to figure out what was going on, looking busy.

We had stopped on an incline and we couldn't move. The drivers debated something, deliberately keeping their voices down and their faces stony until one of them finally descended from the front to the middle of the bus and, looking down, told us that the engine was too weak to climb such a steep incline and that we should all get off, unload all our luggage from the belly of the bus, and try to push it up the hill.

Later on, while the men were pulling out the pudgy bags from the swollen bus—their faces so determined to be useful, to be strong, making the fear in them that much more visible and pungent—I saw my mother walk to the edge of the crude road and saw her shoulders go limp.

I realized then just how high up the mountain we really were and how wet green everything below must have looked from where she was standing, and I didn't have to hear the distant tinkling of bells to know that the sheep were there as well. I went to her and saw it all in awe.

"This is what I saw in my vision," she said, but I knew that already.

Home.

We walked around the apartment, in and out of rooms, looked in every corner, opened drawers and cabinets, dragged our fingers across the walls, slipped our hands under pillows and in between cushions, picked up glasses and trinkets and set them back down. Later, we lit a candle and sat around the table listening to Grandma talk, looking in disbelief around our dining room, which the shivering candle was making unreal.

The grown-ups talked.

Mother said that the cognac was in case some Chetnik stopped the bus at gunpoint and climbed aboard and tried to get near us, her children: that it was to be drunk straight out of the bottle to kill the paralyzing fear, so she could then jump at the fucker's neck and tear his throat out with her bare teeth.

Father said that he saw our property in Kovačevo Selo and that everything was gone, looted—the barbed wire, the raspberry plants, the stairway, the roof, the windows, all the furniture, my comic books—and that the only things he found were a broken spatula in the grass and a framed poster of *American Ninja*'s Michael Dudikoff from the attic room way up in the pear tree.

Grandma said that she had fed the parakeet rice and that it died in its cage.

Excerpts from Ismet Prcić's Diary
from February 1999

I love you, *mati*, but when I come to visit you I won't stay.

Melissa's moving to San Diego with her two best friends, those girls that hate me. You know when on nature shows those ice cliffs in Antarctica break off and crash into the ocean? Well that's me now.

You'll see me this summer. I don't know how to feel about it. One thing I do know, though. I *will not* stay. No matter what you do, no matter how many times you try to kill yourself, I will not stay. Izzy has to follow Melissa to San Diego. That's all there is to be said about that.

Pills and alcohol don't work as well as before, *mati*. I take a sedative before I go to sleep, and I wake up half an hour later, covered in sweat. I get hammered on vodka and pass out and the same thing happens. How do you stave off the thought swarms, the brain chatter?

Dementophobia, it's called. Dr. Cyrus told me. Fear of going insane. *Last thing you need,* he said.

* * *

(...shards...)

This is how it happens: I think I hear a murmur. In my head? From downstairs? I mute the TV, listen. It's still there. I go on the balcony, and through birdsong and car noise, I still hear it. A man whispering urgently, as if through a beard. I go back in, unmute the TV, turn it way loud. The murmur is still there. I chug vodka straight out of the bottle. It's still there. It's still there. And when I begin to panic I see things: you, Father, Mehmed, soldiers, and I'm transported into a random memory, a random occurrence of a life that might or might not be mine.

(. . . the night you return
to bosnia . . .)

You wake up in the middle of the night. It's one of those awakenings that messes with your head. The nightmare is still vivid enough to appear almost real, but the waking state is too hazy to offer any consolation of safety. Your shoulders tense up as if expecting a blow. There is no grounded reason for this yet somehow that doesn't matter. The sense of awful urgency is overwhelming and you wait for reality to kick in. You wait for things to start making sense. Time drags its feet.

The air is hot. Your pajamas stick to you. Your eyes slowly adjust to the dark and your surroundings start to ring a bell: the Donald Duck sheets, your brother sleeping on the other sofa, the funky rug, the constant squeaking of the hamster wheel—you are back home. Back home?

You ransack your brain to discover nothing but leftovers of an already distant nightmare. You can't recall your age. The baseless urgency you feel sitting on your chest borders on panic and you have no idea where it's coming from. The hamster wheel stops squeaking and you tense up even more. The silence is pressing. You wait for something, anything. *What the fuck is going on?* you think.

BOOM!

You don't even move. There is the sound of broken glass, then footsteps and the banging of doors in the apartment above. Your heart vibrates like a caught sparrow. You sit there, still waiting.

Your dad appears in the doorway in his tighty-whities. "Don't be scared guys," he says. "This is their usual night treatment." You look at your brother, but he's still half-asleep. You could fire a cannon right from underneath his blanket and he would hardly stir. Your dad helps him up. He keeps on talking but you can't hear him. The source of your heartbeat seems to be in your inner ear, muffling everything else. In the noise you make out some words like *bomb shelter* and *hurry*. He goes out. You keep on sitting there. The siren starts wailing in the night. Loud.

Then you remember everything. Your body goes on automatic pilot and you put some clothes on in haste. All that time your mind keeps repeating *This is real. This is real. This is* . . . In his cage, Rambo the hamster runs in place like crazy. His wheel goes *squeakety-squeak*. You run out into the corridor after your brother. Your mom is shoving handfuls of plums into a plastic bag, her face pale. The sweatshirt she has on is inside out. The seams are littered with lint. She urges you toward the front door.

Outside the door, the stairway is dark but alive. Some neighbor with a flashlight descends from the floor above with a little girl in his arms. He has only one slipper on. The circles around his eyes make his face look like some kind of a mask. He looks like a scavenger bird.

"They haven't shelled for quite a while, Mirsad," your dad says to him sarcastically.

"Fuck 'em!" the man says.

BOOM!

Everybody rushes downstairs. You plunge into the current, staying behind your parents and your brother. You go down seventeen stairs, then turn. You do this four times again as more people join the current on lower floors. You feel a boost of adrenaline make your head light. The last stairway is longer and it takes you into the bowels of the building.

Soon you are in a huge concrete room with two lines of bunk beds stretching the length of a soccer field. Metal pipes crisscross the ceiling. They are wrapped up with black duct tape. They still leak in places. The bun-shaped lighting fixtures beam unevenly from the walls. Their light is gray. It makes everything look greasy and damp. People go to the beds like skeletons climbing back into their grave slots in a mausoleum. You stand there speechless, your heart in your heels.

Your dad points to two bunk beds in the corner. He looks proud and focused, purposeful. He tells you not to be afraid. You sit down on the bottom mattress of the one on the right. Your mom ends up on the one on the left. She asks your brother if he wants a plum, rummaging through her bag. He declines. She squeezes a plum with her thumb and index finger and brings the two halves of the fruit closer to the light, inspecting for worms. You wonder how come she's so calm. This is her first taste of the war, too. Looking down she notices her sweatshirt is inside out and bursts into tears, letting everything fall to the floor. Your dad gives her a pill. She takes it and lies down, sobs rocking her upper body. She looks straight into your eyes. She says, "You're not a traitor." You have no idea what she's talking about. She smiles for an instant. You cannot hold the terrified gaze any longer, though, and you look away.

You notice a family of four arrive and settle on their two bunk beds across the way. They look average, nondescript, their movements mechanical. The son is kind of weird, though. His light hair is full of cowlicks and his shirt says DON'T FUCK WITH CHUCK in English. The dad pulls a flattened cardboard box from underneath one of the beds and reassembles it. You watch in astonishment as they all produce a number of playing cards from their pockets and resume the hand that's obviously afoot. *They're taking it well*, you think to yourself and look at your own family. Your mom is motionless now, as though made of wax. Her eyes are glass. Your dad is making the rounds around the "neighborhood," shooting the shit with the "neighbors." Perhaps he's

BOOM!

Third one. It strikes you that it has probably been only three or four minutes since you awoke, five tops.

Your brother is asleep. *Wow*, you think.

BOOM!

Close one. They sound more sinister underground. You move to the foot of the bed and look. Some apartment dwellers curse. Others pray. Most of their faces are in midcringe. They look like people who don't want to die. Only the family across the way stands out in their cheerfulness, playing gin rummy. You witness the dad win the round and smile. His wife calls him a lucky bastard. He tells her, "He who's unlucky in cards is lucky in love." She pushes him playfully. He produces a cigarette and licks it all over. It burns slower that way. He lights it, takes one long puff, and extinguishes it promptly on the wall. You realize that they are playing for puffs of smoke instead of money. On the wall behind them somebody has spray-painted a huge phallus in green. The family doesn't seem t

BOOM!

You recall the twenty-four-hour bus ride you took from Croatia yesterday. You recall the checkpoints with guards in at least three different uniforms. And land mines alongside the street. You re- member your dad saying that you don't need any papers when you are coming in. It's only if you want to leave Bosnia that they look for documentation. You recall the unshaven face of a young ma

BOOM!

You wonder if this is what war is all about for a fifteen-year-old: sitting in the nerve-racking safety of a bomb shelter, listening to mortar shells explode on the surface. You cannot imagine anything more terrifying. On TV wars are at least exciting, you recall. In reality, in the safe concrete mausoleum, you stare at the halved plum on the dusty floor. Nothing. Yet your heart still races as if you're running a marathon.

Your mother is asleep now. The pill has kicked in. Your father is still talking to some people five or six beds down. While in Croatia you imagined being thrown across rooms by detonations. You imagined walls crumbling and dodging bullets, all that TV crap. At least you would know why your heart pumps so hard. The halved plum stares at you from the floor like a pair of moist eyes. You lie down and try to sleep.

BOOM!

BOOM!

BOOM!

You sit back up. You stare at the family playing gin rummy. The mom has shitty cards. The DON'T FUCK WITH CHUCK kid is dozing off. His sister looks at his cards when he does. Somewhere a baby wakes up and does what babies do best, very loudly. After a while you pray for another explosion just to shatter the monotony of the screeching.

BOOM!

Thank you, you say to yourself. The dad wins another round and you ogle him as he inhales the smoke and puts out the ever-shrinking cigarette yet again, so happy.

A movement across the room catches your attention. A woman. She's sitting on a wooden plank and rocking back and forth as if in some kind of a trance. She's wearing a skirt but is not concerned that she's flashing everybody. You can't help but stare at the whiteness of her underpants. Her makeup is running down her face in streams. The baby is still crying. You stare at the panties. Your mind wants to sleep but can't.

BOOM!

Your mind plays tricks on you. You visualize the woman getting up and pointing at you. The running mascara makes her face look like an inkblot test. She looks like one of the guys from Kiss. In your mind she screams, *TRAITOR!* Everybody looks at you then. Everybody condemns. They all know you haven't been there since the beginning. Some of them are mourning relatives.

You shut your eyes tight. You shake your head to cast off the pressing thoughts. *TRAITOR!* the woman screams again. This time you don't know if you're imagining it or if it's real. You jump up. People look at you. The woman keeps on rocking and wiping her nose from time to time. Seconds pass and people go back to minding their own business. You don't know if they looked at you because you jumped up or if the woman really screamed.

It's not possible, you think. You deduce that there's no way that you just imagined her voice. It sounded way too real. It's not possib

BOOM!

le. . . . Le? . . . Not possible. . . . What? . . . You forget what you were thinking about. You are not sure. The baby keeps on crying. You feel like you just woke up but you know it's not true. Somebody touches your shoulder. You turn. It's your dad. He asks you a question. You say, "Yeah."

BOOM!

You try to recall the question. "What was the question?" you whisper to yourself. You can't remember. You lean on the wall behind you. Suddenly the prospect of spending your days in this room makes you feel like

BOOM!

You can't remember anything. You push your body against the wall. ... .

BOOM!

. . . the wall is rough . . .

BOOM!

. . . nothing . . .

BOOMS!

(. . . by the code . . .)

Mustafa's grandfather was born in a shed. The shed was right next to a puny, derelict house, where the rest of his family sat in miserable silence. They were awaiting this newest addition to the already swarming Nalić household with dread. The room was pungent with smoke from a malfunctioning chimney, and all of their bellies crackled with need. The first milk from his mother's breast was sparse. When she brought him into the house the family looked at him and saw not a son or a brother but an enemy.

One of their two rooms was larger than the other; it served as a kitchen, a living room, a dining room, a children's room, and, at night, a bedroom. His parents slept in the remaining room unless they had guests over, in which case they would give up their privacy and pile in with the children. There was a single outhouse in the backyard, a little way from the shed. Two other brothers camped in the shed unless it was wintertime, in which case they, too, would pile in with the children. One of the older brothers had recently married and found a small, derelict house of his own.

Their father was a pious mason and a spare-time farmer who demanded quiet at all times. He ran his family according to the unwritten code of seniority he'd grown up on, the code of not speaking unless addressed, of politeness to the point of belly crawling, of always telling the truth even if it meant your death, of never smiling, because others might be miserable, of never crying, because others might be cheerful, of keeping your honor in the community by any means necessary, of saving your best food for guests even when you had to put a piece of glass over a handful of shredded cheese so that the smallest of your children would think they were eating it as they dabbed away at the glass with dry bread. The minutest transgressions would be answered with beatings.

Their mother hardly spoke, would walk ten steps behind her husband and turn away to cry despite her veil.

Unlike his siblings, Mustafa's grandfather was good at school. But the spines of countless books were broken against the walls of their room by his father, who couldn't stand anybody being engrossed in another world while he suffered in brutal reality. Often he tore the yellowy manuscripts from his son's hands and fed them into the mouth of the furnace.

Things were like this until the imam of the local mosque, the most respected elder they had, congratulated him on having such a clever son and said that it would be a shame if the boy didn't go further in his studies. *The ink of a scholar is more valuable than the blood of a martyr,* he told the congregation. This would have had no bearing on Mustafa's great-grandfather's decision to mold his son into a bricklayer like himself had it not been uttered in the company of influential villagers after a Friday prayer. As it was, it became a social obligation. So with great reluctance and minimal allowance,

Mustafa's grandfather, at the age of eighteen, was sent to a *medresa* in Tuzla to become an imam.

Another world war started and some bearded men of Orthodox Christian persuasion, exploiting the lawlessness of the time, ambushed the Muslims of Međaš at dawn one day. They raped and murdered the slow and scattered the quick. The houses were ravaged. Mustafa's grandfather's married brother, seeing ten men with tall black woolen caps and sashes of bullets across their chests advancing up the hill, split his wife's head open with an ax. He couldn't risk her being raped. When they broke down the door, he brought down the ax again, taking off the first pillager's left ear, snapping his collarbone like a pencil and continuing downward through the heaving rib cage. The others shot him in the legs and took their sweet time carving crosses into his flesh. They disemboweled him, then burned him alive next to an ancient wooden ottoman, the only piece of furniture he owned.

His parents and siblings were some of the quick ones. They returned to their property two days later to find it still smoldering in the morning rain, some crows jumping sideways through the damp ashes.

Having no place to live, Mustafa's grandfather married into a farming family from Gornja Tuzla and left his home behind. This would turn out to be a very fortunate decision. In 1945, just as he was finishing up his degree, the same bearded men from four years earlier realized that the Communists were winning the war. They shaved their beards, replaced their nationalistic emblems with red stars, and joined Tito's partisans before pillaging Međaš once more, in somebody else's name now but for pretty much the same reasons. The Nalićs weren't as quick this time around.

After the war a new country was born, bloody all over and enveloped in a new ideological placenta. Its people, divided by faith before, were now forced to unite in godlessness. God was beaten, threatened, blackmailed, tricked, and lured out of the starving populace by the new regime. It was the worst time in the world to be an imam.

Religious institutions were shut down or heavily monitored, and Mustafa's grandfather found himself jobless. He lived with his wife and three quick children in a house that looked like a clammy cardboard box. They survived on the sporadic donations of secretly pious villagers and his wife's awesome ingenuity. At one point he was offered a job as a secretary in an elementary school and accepted wholeheartedly. But when a colleague asked him to partake in some slivovitz to celebrate, he declined, citing his religion. He was fired on the spot for being an enemy of the party. From then on, every once in a while, in the middle of the night, beefy men would show up at his door, take him away in his pajamas to a dark concrete cell where they would drip water on his head for hours, and then let him go in the morning without a word of explanation.

But everyone gets a break at one time or another. Mustafa's grandfather was hired in 1951 as a security guard at a new detergent factory in Tuzla by one of his neighbors, who worked there as a staff supervisor. This man never mentioned to his comrade-bosses that the skinny, ghostly man who was to be the guard was not a proud member of the Yugoslavian proletariat, nor that he was a God-fearing man. It was an act of courage that brought Mustafa's grandfather to tears. The neighbor was named Salko, and that name was uttered in the Nalić household only with deep reverence. It gained the status of a family savior.

The job consisted of sitting in a booth in front of the building and writing down in a notebook the name and ID number of everyone coming in and out of the factory and the time at which they passed him. That was the day shift. At night, every half hour, he patrolled the premises with a handgun to make sure that nobody was stealing the detergent. He took his job seriously and performed his duties with methodical dedication despite their tedium.

And better times came. The factory took off and mushroomed into a chemical industrial complex unmatched in all of Yugoslavia. As the air in the region became more polluted, the workers' wages went up. In ten years' time the county's cancer rate had hit new heights, and Mustafa's grandfather had accumulated enough money to build a house his father would gasp at if he saw it. He filled it up with books and children. When each one was born he swore to make himself unlike his father, to modernize his views and improve upon things for his children's sake, but the old way, the code, was too ingrained in his fibers to be eradicated by sheer conscious effort. It was like trying to repel darkness by boarding up windows with planks.

His offspring turned out to be an intelligent, honest, and well-behaved bunch, yet also meek and voiceless, subservient to anyone older even if he happened to be stupider than dirt. They all, without exception, had rage bubbling in their stomachs, unyieldingly tight lips, and eyes watery with heat.

His wife, tired of waiting for him to bring electricity to their shed, which she used as a summer kitchen, did it herself without any training apart from remembering how the electricians put it in the house. And when her first son went to serve the mandatory year in the army, she taught herself to read and write, so she could send him letters. The letters were crookedly written and grammatically hilarious.

In 1983 cartons of various cleaning products began vanishing from the factory's warehouse. This went on for a few weeks, until it dawned on Mustafa's grandfather that one of his coworkers, someone who knew how religiously he stuck to his half-hour patrolling routine, was probably at fault. Greatly disappointed that someone could be so vile, he forced himself to alter the order in which he checked the buildings and discovered, one night, a laborer by the name of Sead loading a fortune in furniture-polishing liquid into a raggedy white van. When he tried to stop him the young man knocked him down, called him an old fart, and then walked off and started the vehicle, snickering. As he pulled away Mustafa's grandfather unholstered his handgun for the first time in his life. Running alongside the vehicle, he took short, concentrated aim and fired a single round through the van's side window and into Sead's neck. Death was next to instantaneous.

There was a trial. Not guilty.

When he came back to work, his coworkers regarded him with a mixture of respect and fear. Even the bigwigs, who had barely given him a glance as he wrote down their names in the morning, now smiled and said hello. Their handkerchiefs dabbed worriedly at their foreheads. He was congratulated on his industriousness and given a small plaque for protecting the Workers' Property and for helping the Brotherhood and Unity of the nations of Socialist Federative Republic of Yugoslavia. Behind his back people laughed at his rigidity. Behind his back only.

Privately, he stopped using utensils and became obsessed with death. He moved up to the attic and spent whole nights practicing religious calligraphy in Arabic under a single naked bulb. To fall asleep and not wake up screaming was an achievement; his eyes, over time, dropped into the shadowy craters of his skull, where they gleamed with red, magmatic intensity. His veins seemed to run not under his skin but on top of it. His teeth got loose and tipped to the right. His hair thinned. He started addressing persons not present and often failed to answer simple questions without going on and on about the destiny of mankind and about how many times a day one had to remember death in order to go to heaven.

Another war in 1992. Ancient grudges that had lain dormant for some time awakened full-grown and rested, and new pillagers, while waiting for their beards to grow, cast away their red stars and pinned the hateful emblems of their fathers back on their coats and here they came again, with crunchy boots and swearwords.

The factory was shut down and its workers sent to the front. Some of them, too old, were allowed to perform their regular duties for almost no compensation, just to preserve the feeling of everyday lives going on uninterrupted. Thus, Mustafa's grandfather patrolled the empty facilities, checked building after building for nonexistent crooks, and locked and unlocked the rusting fences like it was 1989.

In the winter of 1994, the year of the worst shortages, Mustafa's grandfather spotted a figure in the packaging department dismantling one of the conveyor belts for sellable parts at three in the morning. He sneaked up behind the figure, took out his gun, and yelled for the man to freeze and turn around.

It was Salko.

Mustafa's grandfather's face wilted. He backed out of the building in silence. He wandered over to his booth and sat motionless until his family's savior walked by with a wheelbarrow full of parts. He watched him get smaller and smaller, dark against the snow.

He sat there a while, staring first at the chips of paint flaking off the radiator like dandruff, then at an abandoned, dusty spiderweb between the desk and the wall, and finally at the seam of his son's busted hiking boot on his left foot, still a little wet from the snow. He was looking for what was right.

When he found it he wrote it down under the OUT rubric of his notebook, took off his heavy jacket, folded it into a bundle, and shot himself through it. Since what he wrote didn't make any sense to anyone (it was not a classic suicide note), the police considered his death to be a murder. Their thinking implied that suicides don't shoot themselves in the abdomen to die in prolonged agony.

"By the code," the note read.

*   *   *

Going through elementary school Mustafa heard all about
the code. It was usually shoved down his throat by his mother
to illustrate how good he had it.

Once, he'd lied to her about his grades; when she found
out the truth at a parent-teacher conference, she sat him
down in the kitchen and told him about an ancestor who
happened to be at a market where another farmer had a
gigantic pumpkin on display. The farmer claimed that his
was the biggest one that year, and when Mustafa's forefather
said he had a bigger one in his shed, the farmer accused
him of lying. So he went home, loaded his pumpkin onto a
coach, took it back to the market, and had it measured in
front of witnesses. When it was discovered that his pumpkin
was indeed larger than the farmer's, he stabbed the man to
death for calling him a liar.

The moral of the story ricocheted off of Mustafa's ill
humor, but he said he was sorry and that it would never happen again. She sent him to his room to study, and he sneaked
one of his ninja novels inside his history book. Ninjas were
his favorite because they were well-trained assassins who
could use any means to eliminate their enemies and had no
code. They were not bound by Bushido like samurai. They
didn't have to fight fair.

Excerpts from Ismet Prcić's Diary
from July 1999

I don't recognize my hometown, *mati*. I'm standing right in front of my graffiti-covered high school and I miss Moorpark College. And Moorpark backward is Kraproom.

I look at Father. Who the fuck is this guy?

I look at Mehmed and he has an Adam's apple now, his voice like from the bottom of a barrel. A grown-up, full of rage. That's the only part of him I understand. He blames me for everything, I know.

I look at your face, *mati*, your tired, angry, pious, broken, miserable, warm, beautiful face, and I'm dying for Melissa.

You're still fighting with him, still claiming he's having an affair. He still keeps telling everyone you're insane, and you keep trying to kill yourself instead of him. You should cut his throat when he's sleeping. Mehmed is on his side. You should cut his throat, too. I have no choice but to be on your side, *mati*. Please, cut my throat.

* * *

(...shards...)

I wish I were Izzy, *mati*. I wish I were mad and hungry in his room, where it's possible to suffer in peace.

Greetings from sweltering Tuzla, Izzy.

(. . . the cult of asmir . . .)

In 1993, Mother suspected Asmir of being a pederast, out to take advantage of me under the pretense of being my director and mentor, out to make me "do things" by brainwashing me into submission. There was nothing in reality to support that kind of thinking, but she was the kind of person who needed no proof. She believed herself to be fine-tuned for detecting hazards to her children, mistaking common prejudices for mother's intuition. Mere suspicion was proof enough that something was wrong. Hers was where-there's-smoke-there's-fire reasoning—smoke being the fact that I was doing physical theater, that I hung out with the director even after the rehearsals were over, went to cafés with him, read books he wanted me to read, swore by him no matter what. Granted, there was something cultish about our theater group, about Asmir's status as an artistic leader, about our blind trust and willingness to take extreme chances in the name of art, but nothing like what was ripping her mind asunder.

When I look back I can see her sitting cross-legged behind her cigarette, glassy eyes fixed on the images overtaking her mind, violent head shakes when they got too graphic, waiting for me to come back from a rehearsal. I remember, at times, marveling at the ferocious results of her housework. It's amazing how polished the furniture can get when polishing is not on the polisher's mind. I also think I remember a peculiar tremor, clumsily disguised, behind her inquiries about the rehearsals, who this Asmir character was, and when she would get to meet him. Poor woman.

We held rehearsals in the "Home of the Army."

For this statement to make sense you have to understand the nature of the Yugoslavian brand of Communism. Take architects, for example. Say a public building is to be made. In Communism it's not the best architect who gets to make the building; it's the guy (almost always a man) with seniority in the Party who happens to be an architect that gets to make the building. And to get seniority you have to kiss a lot of ass, sit on committees for stuff you know nothing about, endure years of boring speeches, write and deliver years of boring speeches, and get drunk nightly with the bigwigs to show that you're involved in both the community and its social life. By then you're 98 percent bureaucrat and 2 percent architect. This is the reason why the public buildings in the Balkans all look like filing cabinets and why, in turn, they are almost always called "homes" (Home of Health, Home of the Youth, Home of the Workers, Home of the Army): to evoke that warm feeling inside to compensate for their actual soullessness. It's shit in your mouth, but officially it's called ice cream.

We held rehearsals in the Home of the Army.

Home of the Army used to have an olive-colored cannon in front of it, next to a bed of well-groomed tulips and a perpetually bored guard at arms, sometimes with a rigid German shepherd at his heel and sometimes without. But at the beginning of war, the cannon was hauled to the front lines, the tulips were garroted by weeds, the dog disappeared, and only the guard remained, wearing his face like a gas mask.

Inside this "home," the air was gray, the chairs were on their last legs, the ashtrays were heaping, the ceilings pressed on your head, the corridors were long, the doors were massive and ocher, the young men were uniformed, and the shadows on their faces were sacred. The floor tiles looked soiled despite the kneeling, would-be soldiers with their toothbrushes and elbow grease. The walls were smoky. The art was small but dense. The frames were grand ornaments. Where there was no art, there were impeccable white squares from where the mandatory Marshal Tito portraits used to monitor the army that used to be everyone's army until it became just the Serbian Army, better known as the enemy.

Down the main corridor, third door down, just after the johns, was the auditorium of fixed, foldable wooden chairs, slightly slanting toward the raised proscenium and its musky velvet curtain. The stage was of wobbly parquet, bombarded for decades by politicians' shoes, army bands, and touring folklore dancers. Centered on the cyclorama hung some kind of backdrop, leftover from the last regime, full of factory chimneys and soot-faced miners with rolled up sleeves and bulging biceps, the beams from their helmet lights cutting through the darkness.

I was with "Torso Theater" then, a group of amateur actors doing cheap comedies for food led by a bald man everyone called Brada. We had just wrapped up our completely unrecognizable version of Molière's *Precious Maidens,* in which I played the second henchman and got to wear a ninja mask and twirl around a pair of nunchakus to "Boom Shack-A-Lak," which was popular at the time. That was the first time I ever got paid for doing something. I was fifteen. What I received as payment was a plastic bag with two kilos of low-quality, all-purpose flour, a can of vegetable fat, a couple of packets of powdered milk, and three or four cans of American corned beef. My heart was as big as a mosque.

There were talks about new projects, but the plays Brada was looking at had too few characters and some of us would have ended up jobless and we didn't like that. To appease us he announced that he was splitting Torso Theater into two groups, seniors—he and five or six of his personal friends, all grown men with factory jobs hoping to get some food packages on the side by clowning—and juniors, and that he had found a willing director to do a show with us juniors.

Enter Asmir: this guy wearing red warm-up bottoms and a rag of a wife-beater, carrying books and binders. He started talking right there in the doorway. Suddenly there was energy in the auditorium, like things bursting. The almost-shaved head with chiseled cheekbones and angled eyebrows like the way people draw seagulls in the distance and the insatiable, childlike eyes—that was him.

I would soon find out that food was not a reason to do theater.

For the auditions he made us talk and move, sing and dance, and draw squares in his fat book of art. I talked and moved okay, sang a chantlike rock song disastrously, and danced like a Pithecanthropus. As for the squares, we were supposed to pick a painting we liked, divide it into three parts with pencil lines, and number the parts to tell a story of sorts. I picked a monochromatic print of a haloed baby Jesus in his mother's arms and somebody's sad, upraised fist in the sky.

The callbacks were in a week, yet no one called me. One of the fellow troupe members, Jelena, told me at school that Asmir had left a message with her mother for her to come at 5 PM on Sunday. She was surprised I didn't get the call. To tell you the truth I was surprised that she'd gotten it. Although she was pretty, her stage presence was meandering at best, and she played everything with reserve, not giving herself up. At first I thought Asmir had lost my number, but as Sunday rolled on I realized I hadn't made the cut. And it hurt me. It hurt me so much that I got angry and told him off in my mind, told him that his fucking audition was retarded, that I didn't wanna be in his stupid play anyway. But I did. Especially after I didn't make the cut.

Around 4:30, that lazy calm Sunday feeling washed over me like rage, ironed my brow, and corseted my thoughts. It happened while watching my hamster spin his wheel of misfortune, relentlessly. I realized that the best course of action was to go to the callbacks anyway and play dumb. I put on my Reeboks. My mother was a porcelain sculpture in the living room, entitled "Waiting." She was smoking one of her five daily cigarettes. Her coulisse of smoke was unperturbed. I slipped out with a quick bye, not wanting to stand around and explain where I was going and how long I would stay there.

"What are you doing here?" Asmir asked at 5 PM, the parquet squeaking riot from under his bare feet. Everyone else was mute, pretending to look away or look for phantom items at the bottoms of their backpacks. "Did I call you?"

"Jelena said the next rehearsal was today. I didn't realize . . ." I played dumb. He stopped to look at me, burrowing through me. I held his inspectorial gaze, letting my mouth open and close like a bass in the grass.

"Well, you can stick around and watch," he said and had everybody but me climb the stage. I had to smile. I had to smile as something scrambled up my esophagus and into my throat, yanking at the fraying tissues, sucking away my breath, destroying me.

It so happened that the guy Asmir picked to play the father character in his play had a bit of a speech impediment that he had concealed masterfully during auditions, was too short in comparison with his supposed wife (played by Jelena), and didn't know how to take criticism at all. The guy mouthed off one too many times and Asmir finally told him where to go. That was how I got my second chance.

Asmir was unorthodox and pregnant with a vision. Nuts, really. A lot of people, including Jelena, couldn't get over the nuts part and dropped out. He'd say stuff like:

"Fuck musicals! Fuck the dead, cold, classic masters and their dead, cold, classic words. Fuck the chickenshit modern masters and their need to eat and have a roof over their heads and pay bills. We have to change theater! We should go berserk and improvise. Fuck entertainment! Leave it to the cinema. We should show the truth with all the mistakes of our perceptions. Fuck aesthetics! Pretty is a lie. We shouldn't cut, revise, rewrite. We should rave and ramble. The truth is chaotic and it makes no sense."

He'd say that democracy is not the way of the theater and if theater is to be worthy there is lots to be learned from dictatorships.

He'd do stuff like halt the whole rehearsal for Jelena's replacement to learn how to shriek. This girl was supposed to play a mute mother who at the crucial point in the play unloads a mind-shattering scream, but she just couldn't get there. Asmir made her stand alone in the limelight, with everyone else watching her in silence, until the pressure mushroomed thickly and she shrieked a blinding ray of hate and frustration and it was the realest thing I ever heard. It broke me in half.

It took her an hour to do it. Later, I realized that watching her stand there for an hour was more interesting than any play. The rawness of it. The nude beach of emotions. The piecemeal swelling of truth within a human being, her inability to contain it any longer, and its orgasmic release, all inhibitions stripped away. Now *this* is theater, I thought.

In Asmir's kingdom rehearsals were sacred, every day for four hours, rain or shine, snipe or shell. They would start with the ritualistic removal of footwear, then go into a collective meditation with everyone on their backs, eyes closed, mouths partly opened, palms down. The cassette player usually played Vangelis. After this it was movement exercises, then voice stuff, then character stuff, then the play. Afterward it was out to town for a cup of coffee and to meet up with Asmir's best friend, Bokal, and talk about everything.

Bokal claimed to be a lot of things: an artist, a model, a sign maker, an actor. He claimed to be working on a book called The Way of the Ram that would one day top all the best-seller charts. He claimed he beat up Tuzla's worst hoodlums and soccer hooligans. He claimed he lost a kidney due to a terrible inflammation he acquired in the wet trenches of the Bosnian front lines. He had a scar to prove it.

It was like that for awhile: Asmir ruled and Bokal claimed. I kept my mouth shut and belonged for the first time.

My character, Father Karamazov, demanded quite a transformation on my part. He demanded straight lines, no imagination, direct approach, body fetish, soldierly conduct, rigid discipline, and everything else that wasn't me. He was all about the mindless repetition of a man who dug trenches through life's manure, made a couple of wrong turns, ended up where he started, and from fear of being ridiculed convinced himself that his path was not only legitimate but the only one and kept walking it over and over again.

In the play I had to march the square perimeter of the stage from the beginning until the crucial point where Karamazov has an epiphany, realizes he's going in a circle (a square, actually), and, knowing he has to change something, starts to march in the opposite direction with as much conviction as before.

Years of lugging oversize schoolbooks over one shoulder and hanging out with punks on curbs, gravestones, and staircases gave me the posture of a shirt thrown on a hat rack. So, in rehearsals, Asmir had me carry different things around in order to even out my shoulders—a potted plant, a cassette player, a wooden frame.

I marched on and on. In a square. Every day. I learned to walk straight. I learned not to cut corners. I breathed in through my nose, tight-lipped. I stomped loudly. My voice carried far. I got into shape. Pretty soon Karamazov was marching for me, set in his ways, taut like a bass string, while in his mind's eye the red carpet unfolded over the rotting cadavers of his enemies, and admirers crowded alongside, waving little flags, smiling and chanting, and he knew he was the only one.

The morning of the premiere there was shelling. I woke up to the whistle and boom and wondered if the performance would be canceled. There were footsteps in the hallway and I closed my eyes. Didn't feel like talking. Mother opened the door, counted her children, and then went back to her solitaire, the normal run of things. Sirens blared their warnings more than ten seconds too late. I opened my eyes and watched my brother sleep right through everything with his mouth hanging open.

Later in the morning Asmir called. The show must go on. He said to meet him in front of the Bosnian National Theater and to bring a snack. I was the first one he called. Mother stole worried glances at my giddiness.

* * *

I was there right before the show started. That I remember. I stood in the wings in my costume, waiting for the houselights to go down. I could see my mother in the second row. The boots were squeezing my feet and the march hadn't even begun yet. Air came in and out of me in small increments, spasms like I was freezing. The audience thundered indecipherably, ominously. There were spirits swirling around the old lighting fixtures, kicking up dust, swooshing down my spine, whispering obscenities, encouragements. I repeatedly made fists, clutched at an imaginary rope with all my might, then uncurled the fingers as though giving up. I bit my lower lip. I shook my head. The shit you do to try to kill the butterflies.

The houselights went down and then right back up again and it was all over. There was applause like rain upon a sunroof and boos like birds fighting birds, and I didn't bow but had to find a quiet spot, for the world was suddenly too much for me, standing there drenched and gasping, existing in it. I didn't know that time could be so dense, so true, and that a sliver of it could envelop you like that, overpower you. *Then* was as dense as *now* is fleeting. I was aware of *then* as I wish I were aware of *now* right now instead of writing about then; it's pathetic.

A few days later we watched the recording. On the videotape this . . . person marched around the stage, his feet crunching down on the floor like he had a beef with Mother Earth. He knew all the lines. His smile was maniacal, something I hadn't seen before, couldn't even imagine before. Later I tried to smile like that on my own and failed. My face muscles simply wouldn't stretch and flex in those ways. He had my ponytail. And my wide thumbs. And I knew in my head, intellectually, that it was me; I had blisters on my feet to prove it, too, but . . .

It couldn't have been. It was someone reminiscent of me, for sure. But I don't remember any of it, as if I was put on hold for the duration of the play, as if the archetype that is Father Karamazov rented my body to rave and rage and show me how it's done. The tape rolled and he marched. Asmir kept analyzing, praising, finding faults in others, patting himself on the back.

"This is amazing," he said. "You guys have to be aware of what we accomplished with this play."

I just sat there rubbing my thumb into my wrist, feeling the heat, proving to myself that I was there doing that.

Something happened right after the show, an incident. Brada and the other Torso Theater seniors summoned us all to the green room, walking silently among us like health inspectors around a questionable establishment, with long coats and everything. Shit was a-brew, I could just see it. They sat us down but remained standing themselves, Intimidation 101. They murmured to one another while keeping us in silence, waiting for Asmir, who was still out there talking to people.

"What's happening?" someone asked them. The answer was hissed. Apparently a bunch of people walked out because they didn't know what to make of the play. Didn't understand it. Booed it. Asked for their money back. Add to that the fact that another bunch never showed due to the morning shelling and that we were rather cavalier with our comp tickets, giving them to a considerable bunch of friends and family. Money that was expected to be made was not made. They were furious.

"You'll have to perform this another ten times just to break even," Brada said with malice.

There was silence after that. Brada and his buddies stood by the door, hands crossed at the crotch. They looked like Communist politicians paying last respects to a dead comrade. We, the partly costumed performers, still between the two worlds, still beautifully empty between reality and art, tried to occupy as little space as possible and waited for something concrete to establish itself. Silence played tricks and seconds stretched into hours, but it was already wearing off when Asmir came in with Bokal right behind him.

"This is just for the company members," Brada said, attempting to dismiss Bokal, who lumbered by him as though he weren't even there.

"What's it to you?" Bokal asked without inflection and to no one in particular. He gave me a high five and sat down next to me.

"Well, that was the worst performance of the worst play in the history of the universe," Brada said to Asmir.

I looked at the carpet.

"I trusted you to put up a show that people would want to come and see, not a show that makes people threaten to break the glass and strangle me in the booth if I don't give them their money back."

I went over the patterns on the carpet, memorizing the angles of designs, the subtle shifts in coloring, the locations of stains, anything just not to be there in full. Asmir sounded quiet and confused.

"Who are we trying to appease here, the judicious or the groundlings? 'The censure of the which one must in your allowance o'erweigh a whole theatre of others.'"

"What are you talking about? I'm not gonna debate you. We're taking the Torso Theater logo off the poster and you are going to perform this shit until it pays itself off. Then you can do whatever you want with whomever you want."

"When you don't have quality you have to compensate with quantity," said another one of the seniors.

What happened next branded me.

What happened was that Asmir unreeled. The self-taught know-it-all with confidence and know-how up the wazoo, the king of his theatrical kingdom, this man peeled off and what was left in his stead was a child, an angry, hurt child. And I loved him for it, for this nakedness and innocence and passion. He went from age twenty-five to five in an instant, bawling at the injustice and ignorance, at the malice of people who knew only profit and wouldn't know art if Dalí signed their limp, melting dicks.

"It's the way it is," Brada said—ignoring the uncoiled, sobbing Asmir—his lizard eyes scanning a piece of paper in his hands. "To-morrow you'll go perform in Lukavac, then two more here on Friday and Saturday. Then we'll see where we're standing."

"You have . . . no clue . . . ," Asmir blurted in between spasms.

"It's the way it is," Brada repeated and smiled. Smiled. He actually smiled. "I think we're almost finished here."

Silence filled the green room like gas. Asmir's tear ducts were empty, spent. Only the motions of crying persisted. We sat inside our rigid bodies, containing our screaming minds with the conditioned limpness of will, an instinct, really, when you're young and dealing with long coats reminiscent of the Communism you grew up in. The patch of carpet in front of me was memorized. It lasted forever.

"Can I say something?" Bokal asked, rupturing everything. It was a rhetorical question.

"You're not even part of this group," said one of them, a short middle-aged guy with a mustache. Bokal didn't look at him.

"You people are dicks," he said.

"What?"

"You are dicks! The man is crying here. What's wrong with you?"

"You have no voice here," Brada said, his smile wiped out finally. "I'll have to ask you to leave!"

"*You*'re gonna ask *me* to leave? Do it, by God! Let me hear you ask me to leave!"

Brada was perplexed for only a moment, and he would have come up with something cruel any second had Bokal not stood up in his bubbling fur-lined jacket and taken a step forward. Brada aborted the comeback in his throat.

"Well?"

"Calm down," Brada said, suddenly a peacemaker. "We're all on edge here. I was just stating the facts."

"No, you were treating people like shit. And I'm not gonna *ask* you to leave. I'm gonna tell you to get the fuck out of this room before I spill you like a bag of rice."

The Torso Theater seniors, all of them grown men, tucked their tails and drew back toward the door like in a movie. Brada looked at Asmir:

"Is he making your decisions for you now?"

"Yes he is," Asmir said.

"Fuck off! They don't need you!" Bokal said and took another step forward.

"You'll never work in this town again!" Brada said and followed his buddies out.

"Fuck the town in which the likes of you have that power!"

That was it.

That night, on the way back home, I tore my Torso Theater membership card into four pieces and threw them into a gaping garbage container. The moon was frozen to the night, stuck in its vast blackness, witnessing. Like a perfect bullet hole in the tinted window of a Black Maria.

Mother waited up for me, playing solitaire on the kitchen table next to an empty ashtray, her forefinger lightly touching the partition of her lips. By this point in the war our funds were scarce, and cigarettes were expensive. Her hands would shake, constantly flying up to her face to handle the phantom cigarette, and finding nothing, would flutter around sheepishly like a pair of confused sparrows, only to end up on a deck of cards or on her lap, twitch there in agony for a while and then try again. She said that this character was the best thing I'd ever done artistically—so much so that my transformation terrified her and that the play blew her away, that she forgot about smoking. Coming from her—with her tough-love, no-bullshit approach to everything my brother and I did—the comment made my chest expand with joy and suffering. In my bed, I wept with it.

The next day, during my quasi-continental breakfast of barely baked bread (sporadic electricity), plum jam, vegetable fat, and chamomile tea, there was a telephone call. I was expecting it. Asmir had bounced back with a fuck-the-Torso-Theater attitude, with new ideas swarming in his mind, new confidence and vigor, new drive, his gums flapping nonstop: "New group, new approach, new rehearsal place, new everything." It was like I was getting a double dose of Asmir and it was intense and exciting and terrible. He asked me if I wanted to be a part of it all and I said yes . . .

. . . because he cried the night before when the vultures were tearing apart his baby. Because he was a five-year-old and I wanted to play.

From then on the theater became a playground rather than an office, a lab rather than a classroom, a religion rather than a hobby, a cult rather than a troupe. It became everything.

Bokal wanted to do a painting of the troupe, so Asmir made a hefty wooden frame on which the canvas was to be stretched and lugged it across town to the new rehearsal place. We moved from the Home of the Army to my old neck of the woods, the Home of the Youth. Instead of the stage and auditorium, now we had a large room stuffed with crap: generic, Communist-looking chairs, dismembered drum kits, a selection of snapped mic stands, a behemoth of a filing cabinet made of solid wood, and dirty-beige curtains you'd just love to set fire to. The reason that we even got *this* room was that nobody else wanted it. All its windows faced southeast, making it a very likely target for a mortar.

The carpet was the color of decomposing cigarette filters with a fragrance to match. My God, everything happened on that carpet, from shit to divine intervention, from trivial drudgery to magic. Everything. It was on that carpet, in the moist, sweltering air and pungent dust, barefoot and aching from theater and life, that I was the happiest. My God, I forgot.

We had one of those amazing rehearsals of Asmir's play when everything was awesome and meaningful and you felt like a real artist. Afterward we went out to celebrate, lugging that huge wooden frame. We walked to Café Galerija but, as none of us had any money, ended up in the park, on a bench, leaning the frame on a nearby poplar. We watched people go by, scared people, miserable people, masks of suffering on stick figures. No one was fat. Everybody was aware. Even old people had a bounce in their step, knowing what war could bring at any point. It looked grotesque, unnatural. If it were on TV it would pain you to see it.

It was like we were driven to put that frame in front of us. To make a difference on those people's faces, you know. Something. We let it sit in our laps, held it erect, and ceased all movement. We became a painting, staring out through the frame into the real world. And soon the real people stopped to stare at us, the painting, forgetting for a moment about the war, the oppressive psychosis that permeated everything. People have to look at art no matter what.

A bunch of children swarmed around us trying to catch a facial twitch and laughed giddily, waved their little hands in front of our eyes, and scratched their little heads when we wouldn't blink. Adults mostly stared from a distance, wondering why anybody would do this. Two elderly men with their hands behind their backs looked at us with brutal disgust, shaking their heads like the end of the world was coming and we were somehow responsible. And it would all have been an exercise in craft, a spur-of-the-moment performance-art piece, something nobody would remember for long, had it not started shelling and had we not, in our madness, remained motionless in spite of it, among the mad-dashing citizens.

(. . . anatomy of a flashback . . .)*

In May of 1999, right around the time I was supposed to fly to Bosnia, I found myself in the parking lot of a Ralphs in Moorpark, California. Eric had dropped me off too early because he had to go to work, and I was killing time before my train to San Diego. Melissa had moved down there earlier that year, and my ability to bear things had been decreasing each day without her. I was living from weekend to weekend when I could go visit her or when she would come to me. I would breathe in with sadness on Sunday night and exhale with joy on Friday afternoon, both in her arms. While holding my breath, I fought off my brain by stuffing myself with words people wrote, beverages people distilled, and sleeping pills people manufactured.

The flashback started earlier at the station with the sudden roar of a freight train going by. The sound pierced me. I fell to the ground. For a moment it was happening right there. I didn't go back to Bosnia this time. The war had come to me. An explosion rocked the walled-off neighborhood beyond the station's parking lot.

---

* This piece was written on two napkins bearing the logo of a Café Leonardo in Tuzla and was found stuck in the diary that Ismet Prcić was keeping in 1999 when he was visiting his mother.

I felt an onrush of warm air in my face. Debris sprayed everywhere, clanging into parked cars. A palm tree toppled over onto a green Chrysler. A Mexican kid fell off his bike, smoke devouring the cul-de-sac behind him ... then it was blue sky, and cars wavering in the heat, and the Mexican kid contentedly riding in a loop, and the train disappearing toward Simi Valley, and nothing was happening, absolutely nothing was going on.

I started walking toward the Ralphs shopping plaza a little way down the street. I shook off unwanted thoughts and focused on my sneakers stepping ahead of me, carrying me forward. I enjoyed the flatness of the asphalt against the bottoms of my feet and imagined the inner workings of my ankle during the action of walking. All the pushes and pulls, pressures and releases. The mechanism. But the thoughts started to advance again (I heard them buzzing, then murmuring in my head) and in panic I tried to remember where I'd bought those sneakers, and when I remembered that, how much they'd cost, and when I remembered that, too, which one had I put on first this morning, which was an easy one since I'm a creature of habit, and fuck there was a child's foot, lying sideways against the curb, a trickle of gentle blood behind it, smudgy torn-up sock with the Adidas logo caving inward where the child's ankle used to be, its mechanism no longer intact, and my heart played a drum solo devoid of beat, just endless rolls, from snare drum to timpani, from timpani back to snare drum, an occasional chilling cymbal, and a sinister, frantic bass drum so reminiscent of mortar fire.

Bosnia materialized around me and I hit the ground. Shut my eyes. Covered my head. Prayed. Hard.

A bag lady brought me back.

"Wake up!" she screamed. "I ain't getting off at Solana Beach until I know for sure all my shit is off this motherfucker!"

There was a flesh-colored hearing aid inserted in her ear like a piece of dough. I thought, *Do deaf schizophrenics still hear voices?*

She rolled her shopping cart delicately, avoiding the potholes, aristocratic in her posture.

"You're too much in your head, cracker!"

If you only knew, I thought.

Excerpts from Ismet Prcić's Diary
from August 1999

I saw him, *mati*. I saw Father holding some woman's hand in front of a bank yesterday. Later he denied it. I can't tell you this, though. I don't think you can take it. I told Mehmed and he didn't believe me. *He doesn't look like a Don Juan to me,* was how he put it. I guess reality doesn't matter if we ignore it.

I punched a kid in the face today, *mati*. Behind Albatros restaurant. Sixteen or seventeen years old. Good-looking. Smiling. I punched him and he just sat down. I ran away. It was so good to feel my heart pound like that. BOOM! BOOM! BOOM! BOOM! BOOM! BOOM! BOOM! BOOM! BOOM!

I can't wait to get out of here, *mati*. I can't wait to leave you again.

(. . . love, interrupted . . .)

JANUARY–MARCH 1995

Somewhere, somehow I convinced myself that a pink Levi's jacket was a good decision. By then my hair was long and I had lost all that weight and was ready, really overdue, for everything. I buried my old self and hurled the new, unapologetically, into the city under siege, locking eyes, smiling coyly, positioning myself in front of a light source every time so the girls could see my insides. I cracked gross but witty jokes that disarmed even the holier-than-thous. I flaunted talent until they noticed it, then turned up the modesty. I did all that, my part, and waited for her to emerge out of the crowd and love me forever.

The way love happens in high school, a friend of a friend gets drunk in front of the theater one night, comes up to my buddy Omar and me and admits that Asja has a crush on me, and I do some research to find out who Asja is and almost shit my pants when I meet her eyes in the hall in front of the bathrooms, smitten. The next morning I spy her coming to school and arrange it so I pass her and strut my stuff, but right when I'm about to display a dashing smile, an insect, a bee of all things, flies right into my nostril. I start bucking in my pink jacket, and shrieking, and slapping my face, and blowing my nose, and generally acting like a precious maiden in the presence of outlandish vermin.

Hers was the beauty of petite, fairy-tale shoes with buckles, black turtlenecks, and eyes that can take you in the way the skies can take in a bird jumping out of the nest for the first time—only they were brown eyes. Hers was the beauty of lips so lush they folded onto themselves in everyday speech; what happened to them in the act of kissing I could only imagine. Hers was the beauty of little hands, abashed, buried under arms, or shoved into pockets, or barely poking out of extralong sleeves. Hers was the beauty.

Mine was the agony of knowing that she liked me (or did she?) and not knowing what to do about it. God forbid I should just walk up to her and mumble a hello. For a month I took meticulous care of my appearance while I waited for things to be kicked into motion by the friend of a friend who naturally sobered up and kept acting like she hadn't said anything to me. I bathed every other day, which was an astonishing feat when you consider the amount of work that goes into bathing in wartime: the shelled-to-shit waterworks, the shortages, the restrictions, the fact that even when our part of the town got water, there was not enough pressure to shoot it up to the fourth floor. You had to take buckets and canisters, tubs and basins, pitchers and plastic soda bottles, go to the basement and stand in a line of murky, pissed-off apartment dwellers for your turn to fill up your receptacles, then carry them to the apartment in three or four trips (guess what, no electricity), get wood from the balcony, start a fire, wait until the stove was hot enough, heat a huge pot of water on it, carry it to the bathtub, mix it with cold water until it was bearable, and finally pour it over sections of your body from a coffee mug.

I grew paranoid about having things stuck in my teeth, so I brushed them psychotically every time I happened to be around a toothbrush. At school I dug at the seams of my clothing, trying to rip off a piece of thread long enough to wrap around two fingers so I could floss out a particularly stubborn chunk of lunch wedged in the crevice of my molars. I combed my hair like an excited schoolgirl (at least thirty strokes for each side) and let it hang down around my face in shiny, voluptuous whorls. I refused to wear my glasses to school so I wouldn't appear nerdy, had to move to the front desk, and still I couldn't see shit. I constantly sniffed at my pits. A part of me longed for the earlier times when I was fat and nothing mattered. A small part of me. That fat kid in me.

The friend of a friend had one of those bland Bosnian names you can never remember, like Jenny in California. She was an impish person, pointy in all directions, short and unremarkable-looking, like a female gull. I stalked her for weeks, walking behind her, sending telepathic vibes in ripples at the back of her head and her hippy hairdo. When that didn't work I'd go in front and face her, making feverish eye contact.

Come on! I thought at her.

Her eyebrows would twitch in alarm and she would look down, grab at some friend's elbow, and walk away in a swift stride, whispering, shaking her head, glancing backward like I ought to be institutionalized.

At night, I would sit crumpled in my bed, agonizing over whether I had hallucinated her drunken slip of the tongue that night or whether it had actually occurred. I played this moment over and over in my mind's eye, me standing in front of the theater with Omar, freezing my ass off despite two jackets, her stumbling down the street, catching my eye, and turning to her friend, saying, "Is that him?" then walking up a couple of stairs, unzipping my top jacket, placing her boyish hand on my chest, saying, "Pink jacket, that's him!" then leaning in with harsh spirits on her breath, whispering, "I have a friend that really, really likes you; she's a beautiful, beautiful girl," and my heart growing, growing.

I just realized something. I was wearing two jackets because it was wintertime. January, I believe. February 28 was the first day Asja and I went out. How is it possible, then, that two mornings after I found out that she liked me a bee flew up my nose? Don't bees hibernate in this part of the world? I think they do. But I do remember that happening—the bee incident, I mean. It did happen to me. I'm sure of it. I remember the humiliation. I remember the lesson learned. I remember the distinct knowledge of being put in my place by the universe for trying to appear better-looking than I actually was. It had to have happened some other time, then, in front of some other girl. But why did I bunch the two memories together? Why can't I remember the other girl?

Someone, I think it was Omar, said to me once that memories are like tapes and that it's important to keep as many as you can so you can play them later on and be able to recall who you were at the time. I always considered this to be bullshit. I still do. Memories are nothing like tapes. Tapes record reality. Minds record fiction. My mind was never one for remembering things right. Too much fantasy. Too much muggy past. Too many daydreams. Plus, the present reality, with all its tedious details, is just way too complicated; wherever you look there is something existing in itself: a file cabinet full of words, Mother smoking, an extension cord on the floor, a dirty sock, the shadow of my foot throbbing against the white sheets underneath me, and that's just a sliver of a second from a corner of my eye. Who can keep track of it all when our eyes are open so wide and when seconds are so short and cheap and when we spend them so easily?

Mother is in shambles, broken. My father is away on business. At least that's what he said. She thinks, knows, he has someone. My brother won't come out of his room, thinks she's nuts. The women in the neighborhood knit their gossip sweaters. Mother sees them nudge one another with elbows when she passes them on the way to the store. She stays in bed for days, eats nothing. Just smokes and prays. She's skeletal, sallow, slime-eyed.

When I first got here she was great. The energy of my return popped her out of her routine and we talked and took walks and she told me more stories about her childhood and I wrote them down. Then she started to say the same things over and over again, wallowing as depressed people do, and it became harder and harder for me to be there for her. I'm not the sanest person in the world by a long shot. Who am I gonna help? I can fool myself and deliver convincing everything-will-be-all-rights, but only up to a point. Months into this, I feel drained, depressed.

This morning I decided I would go visit my old stomping grounds to see if the sight of the theater or the high school building or the park would make it easier to write about puppy love, but Mother had an attack. She had warned me about these. Apparently, she's fully conscious during them; she just cannot talk or see well or swallow. She was in bed talking to me and then suddenly stopped and her eyes got really big and she slowly put her cigarette in the ashtray and turned onto her side. I knelt by her and held my hand on her forehead. The veins on her temples swelled and her lower jaw started to shift to the right, disfiguring her mouth. Her tongue oozed out through it and her breathing became strenuous. I tipped her head down more to make it easier. She started to drool and I wiped at it with a handkerchief.

It lasted ten minutes. After it was over her face muscles ached and she felt terrible and took a bunch of pills and went to sleep.

I paced through the house for an hour, tried to read a story by
Nabokov, fought with my father and brother in my mind, pounded
their faces into pulp. I tried crying, but it never comes when you
want it. I wanted to kill myself.

Then I took a bunch of paper, went down to the store, bought
a two-liter Pepsi Light and a fifth of rum, came here to the park,
and drank it all. I went to see where Asja and I carved our names
into a pine tree across the street from the Orthodox church, and
it was still there. I sat at the base of it, tried to write about my
youth, and ended up writing this instead.

I turned out not to be insane after all.

It was a Wednesday and I was hopping, blue-lipped, in the hallway
in front of a classroom, breathing out clouds of steam, but with both
of my jackets undone so everyone could see my trendy Beavis and
Butt-Head T-shirt, which I'd borrowed from Omar. Earlier in the
week a shell exploded off the side of the building right across the
river and two pieces of shrapnel busted the window of the second-
floor hallway. They covered the hole with plastic, but someone
nicknamed Paša had sliced his name in it with a knife and the wind
made curious sounds when it forced itself though the slits, a bit like
silenced gunfire. There were two shrapnel holes on the wall, which
somebody else had encircled with a black marker and made into a
huge smiley face. I was appreciating its grotesqueness when I felt a
light squeeze on my elbow and spun around.

The friend of a friend looked pissed off and somehow different
with eyeglasses on. Her face was curt and scrunched up, not even
trying to conceal its disgust at having to speak to me.

"Remember me? Jaca? Little Mario's party?"

Of course I remembered who she was, but there were no words
in my head, let alone my throat. There was nothing remotely as

organized as words anywhere in my body. My mouth dropped and there was a crack-and-hiss noise in my ears, as though from a soda can being opened. Then I couldn't help but smile. The power of it was bigger than I. It was as if I had two fishhooks in the corners of my mouth that pulled my lips up and up and up, and no matter how much my ego screamed that I probably looked like an idiot, like an eager beaver, I had no willpower to choke this one down. She took a step back.

"Well?" There was a pinch of alarm in her voice.

Unable to talk yet, I overnodded.

"A friend of mine wants to meet you," she squeezed out. It was apparent what she herself thought of the idea.

"Asja," I said, finally managing a word. Her mouth screwed up in surprise. The alarm left her face and she reclaimed the distance between us.

"You know about Asja?"

"Yeah."

"How do you know?"

"You told me. Like a month ago? In front of the theater?"

"You're shittin' me!" she said, punched my arm hard, and then busted out laughing. "Is that why you were acting like a psycho? I thought you were nuts."

"I thought I was nuts."

"Why didn't you fucking come and tell me, you idiot?"

"I thought I made it up in my head."

"You're an idiot. Let's go before the bell rings." She took my sleeve and pulled me along. It suddenly dawned on me what was about to happen. My feet got heavy going down the stairs.

"Right now?"

"Yeah, right now. When would you do it?"

"I'm scared."

"You're an idiot," she said, and without having time to sniff at my pits, or cup my hand in front of my face to check if my breath stank, or tongue my teeth for something in them, I was pulled toward and introduced to Asja, a petite person with straight brown hair, wide eyes, and an even wider smile. Her tiny hand popped out of her sleeve for a quick handshake and popped back in like a turtle's head.

"Asja. Nice to meet you."

I blurted out my name. Jaca stepped aside and a bunch of nosey teens crowded around her, smiling, glancing over. I waved to Asja to follow me and I think she asked why, but came nevertheless. We walked down the hallway, away from her schoolfellows, in a giddy silence, our feelings in almost visible little explosions in the air around us.

"You wanna go out tonight?" I heard my voice say. It sounded like a small-caliber bullet bouncing back and forth inside my skull.

"I can't."

I felt myself waning, drying up. Good thing I had that voice that kept on talking, this other me, while I suffered.

"How about tomorrow?"

She made a hurt face. "I can't."

"Why not?" my voice asked, lightheartedly.

"My parents don't let me go out on school days."

My suffering shifted into a lower gear. Dumbly, I asked the obvious question:

"How about Friday then?"

"Okay," she said, and I stopped suffering.

The Bridge with the Statues was where she said it would be. I knew where it was, too, but when I left the apartment I literally followed the river, in a fit of insane compulsion, just in case. I found myself on the bridge forty-five minutes before the rendezvous, walking back and forth in beastly, agonizing strides and counting my steps.

The bridge was an oppressive, parallelogram-shaped coffin of solid cement and steel, spanning the emaciated, shivering river at an angle. Its stone guardians, these identical quadruplets, stood forever on the corners, facing away from one another, slumped under the weight of light they were designed to deliver. Massive lamps pressed down upon their shoulders like globes, like crude, cement disco balls, and they endured it like Atlas. With one leg, knotted with muscles, erected back against the base, and the other one, barely bent, set forward for balance, they were obeying their meaningless destiny, holding up the dead lights, extinguished for a long time by shrapnel or detonations or lack of electricity. One of the brothers even had his elbow taken out by a metal shard, exposing his wire skeleton, but he was still withstanding his job, his expression unchanged, his eyes forever blind to the absurdity of stone or flesh here in the world.

But then again, the way things looked might have been, just as easily, a result of my proclivity for self-torture, presently lapsing into pensiveness, which in turn was bordering on lunacy. The distance between the two brothers on the same side of the river was twelve steps, between the two brothers on the same side of the bridge thirty, between the first set of brothers on the opposite corners of the bridge twenty-six, and thirty-four between the other. I kept measuring and remeasuring the distances between things to take the edge off waiting, to kill the paralyzing thought that maybe she would never show. But as soon as I was aware I was doing it, it became futile and I started doubting that I was even in the right place and searched my memory for another bridge with statues. After much obsessing it became obvious that there wasn't any, and I looked at each stone brother for reassurance.

The river hummed the freezing blues from within its embankment walls, and the buildings hunched like peasants in a summer hail, dreading the unseasonable showers of propelled destruction that had become oh so frequent as of late. Utterly unhampered by it I stared in the direction from where she was supposed to come and tried to recognize which one of the moving dots in the distance would morph into her figure. Every one of the little smudges of color made me heady as I watched them grow like cells; slowly, one cell of blue would become two cells of blue, then four, then eight, and after a while the blue would become a Windbreaker with bubbly little arms, still headless in the snow, and then the head would bud out with a little black atop the blue, and the little legs would connect the blue blob to the ground and this child's drawing would walk toward me, evolving into an impressionistic painting, then into a realistic one, then become a scene from an Eastern European film with blatant social realism that made me want to shoot myself.

I awaited them, trembling, and despaired when I saw them become someone else, a man with a beard, someone's grandmother, a lunatic. Their faces actually caused me physical pain because their features weren't hers. I gulped down my pain and kept on walking and counting steps, picked another dot on the street's horizon, observed its evolution into a stranger, then did it all over again.

When, finally, she did turn from a blob into herself, right on time, by the way (the Catholic church across the street tolled and tolled), and with my insides a-quiver with the sheer insanity of their inner life, something changed and a miraculous calm came over me. It was like something, a male something, incapacitated my inner critic, slapped me a good one across the mouth to snap me out of the funk, took me by the collar and straightened my posture, whispered a word of male encouragement into my ear and sent me onto the battlefield with a pat on the ass.

Thus improved, I waited as she came over with the pitter-patter of a toddler, wearing a black winter jacket—that billowed around her like her own personal cloud—growing more elaborate and beautiful with each small step.

"Hi," she said, smiling hugely, eyes squinted against the wind and a sole section of hair, ripped out from her ponytail, glued with the wind's force against and across her face, splitting it into two uneven halves. She cocked her head sideways to remedy this, but her effort was fruitless. Asja reached way up into the sky to free her right hand from an oversize sleeve, brought it to her forehead, and gently brushed the renegade section away.

I reciprocated the greeting and reached for her hand, my palm facing outward and my thumb down as though aiming, gangster-style. It was the boldest gesture I had ever attempted at the beginning of a first date and it worked; she took it with a smirk and we started walking.

"Did you wait long?" she asked.

"Two-to-three minutes."

The first step or two were mechanical because we were both manifestly overwhelmed. Her hand felt cold and she immediately curled it into a fist and placed it into mine, as if into a padded envelope. I smiled. She was making herself comfortable. Five steps later she briefly uncurled it and tickled the inside of my palm with the tips of her nails, looking at me for reaction. Stupidly gleeful I did it back to her. We smiled, thus acquiring our first ritual.

"Wanna chewing gum?" I asked, fingering a pack of it in my right pocket. It was a rare commodity in those days, but my father had received an aid package from his ex–business partner in Slovenia and that's where I got it.

"No," she answered, dropping her smile, her body stiffening as though hit with something, something disgusting. She looked at her feet, then away from me.

"Okay."

I produced the pack, freed one of the individual foil-wrapped pieces of gum for myself and removed it with my teeth. She saw me do it and her smile returned.

"Oh—that chewing gum. I do want that."

I looked at her, bewildered. Controlling her laughter, she took the gum from between my lips, unwrapped it, and popped it in her mouth. Her cheeks awoke with redness.

Then I realized what I had asked her and a terrible "Ohh" escaped before I had a chance to swallow it. What I had asked was on a par with: "You wanna suck face?" "Chewing gum" was a crude local colloquialism for "French kissing." The crudest one possible.

"You didn't think—"

But we were already bursting with healthy laughter, as if we had always known each other. Less than fifteen seconds into our first date and we already had a little story to tell.

Moments die as they pass and as they do their cadavers are dunked into specimen jars full of formaldehyde where they float with eyes shut and little fingers perfectly curved, as if they are alive, holding on to something—a pickled fetus I saw in my high school biology class. They become memories, nothing but perished moments marinated in brain chemicals to preserve the fact that they came into being once and were alive just as these present moments are alive, moments that I'm wasting by writing these words, leaning on the wall of my parents' living room on a terribly hot day in September 1999.

Mother said she doesn't want to talk today, that she's sick of talking about my father, about what he did, that talking is useless, and that she has said it all before. Fuck his mother, she said, then apologized to God in Arabic. Her lip was quivering. She said she wanted to pray and that I should close her bedroom door behind me and have some alone time, that she senses my fatigue, that I have writing to do. I know it's all bullshit. I know she's really down but I did close the door.

Am I an asshole? What kind of son am I?

Yesterday I bought a shitload of those little bottles of booze. I unzip my luggage as slowly as I can so she can't hear me next door when I take out a couple of vodkas and a couple of brandies. I knock back one of each and shove the empties in my backpack. The other two I put in my pocket. Asja, Asja, Asja, I think.

Went to first base the night of the first date under a streetlight in Batva after botching the first attempt at it a few minutes earlier at the entrance to the Tušanj football stadium due to inexperience. Walked home in euphoria as though I had single-handedly liberated a country.

Mother sobs in the bedroom. I open the door and go to her. He never stood up for me, *she says.* His own cousins would grab my knees under the table during family gatherings. I would tell him in the kitchen and he wouldn't say a word. He would just stare into the void. Waiting for me to stop talking. *I take her hand and she squeezes it hard. She cries silently for a couple of seconds and then calms herself down.* Don't worry, *she says,* it's like this all the time. I have to get it out of my system. Go back to your work. *I come back and leave the door open, sit on the couch. All I see is her thin wrist when she closes the door. I reach into my pocket. I reach for the backpack where the empties go.*

Went to second base—never, really. One time timidly brushed my hand on the outside of Asja's right breast while making out on a bench in Banja Park. The other time playfully pushed her away and ended up with one of them in my hand. Let go of it immediately like Jackie Chan in one of his films.

I can hear her again, moving about. I get up and open the door and right then the midday prayer sounds from the nearby mosque. I see her praying: standing up, bending forward, standing up again, kneeling down, touching the serdžada with her forehead, and murmuring throughout all of it. I close the door. I reach into my pocket but the muezzin's voice is loud and full of God and I don't dare.

Went to third base—never. One time Asja straddled me next to a fountain and we were uncharacteristically spontaneous and so close to everything, but then an old man with a cane walked by and chastised me like I was a pedophile (Asja was very short), messing up my game. For the rest of the night had silent arguments with the geezer in my head and couldn't be spontaneous anymore.

TV from the bedroom. Dialogue in English. Mother's quiet. I feel a little better about myself. I drink the brandy.

Home run—not a chance. Utterly without any idea how to even talk about it, let alone do it, I put the ball in her court without telling her. Wanted love and romance first (had honorable, PG-rated intentions). Believed that sex would come later (after marriage, perhaps,) unless mentioned by her before then. She was too shy to mention it. I was too proper. We were chronically horny.

The TV gets louder. Songs. I remember how I . . .

Walked from Stupine to Irac through a mythic blizzard and paced for two and a half hours from a curb to a building, counting steps, being molested by wind, freezing my ass off in my two jackets. She didn't show. Later, said it was too cold.

I realize why the TV is so loud. I open the door and her face is buried in the pillow. I go to her and hold her hand, pat her back. Tears come to me. They come and as soon as they do, hers stop and she's dabbing my cheek with her moist handkerchief. I'm mostly mad at myself, she says. I know who he is; I know he has no spine . . . no heart, no balls . . . and I still stay here like a cow . . . Like a . . . Like . . . She stares off for a moment, then lights a cigarette. I think I stay because I knew you guys would grow up and move away and I don't want to be old and alone. She smiles at the irony, looks at me. Go, honey, she says. I'm fine again. I close the door and stand there looking at the couch, the armoire, Grandpa's calligraphy on the wall, the radiator, the lace curtains, my stuff on the floor. I remember being so in love with Asja, so sick, so saturated, blissful, and I feel good that what I'm feeling now will one day become just pictures and words, too, nothing that can really break my heart again.

I drag my luggage right next to the couch so I don't have to get up later. Brandy in my pocket. It's medicine. Pen, too.

It's nighttime. I hear my mother cry, barely audible. It sounds like rhythmic squeaking. She cries into the pillow. It's a private depression, she likes to joke. She does things like pull down her sleeves when she's around me so I won't see the scars on her wrists. So I don't get sad. So I don't worry. Usually when I hear her, I jump up and go tell her that things are going to be okay. Usually I'm warm. Usually I know how to distract her, how to put things, how to smile.

But now I'm exhausted.

Now I just lie here and listen to her cry.

I'm sitting on our park bench, Asja's and mine, drinking Fanta and vodka out of a Fanta bottle. I keep wondering what would happen if I bumped into her one of these days while I'm in town. There's an old man on the bench a little way down the path and he keeps smiling at me and shaking his head. I keep smiling back politely.

I haven't seen Asja since the day I left. Some said she waited for me for a year, asking around if anybody knew when I was coming back. But then she married a distant cousin of mine, had a baby.

"She stood you up, huh?" says the old man, suddenly standing next to my bench.

"I'm sorry?"

"You're lucky. It's better that she leaves you now than later on when you're sick and old like me."

He pats me on the shoulder and shuffles away. I can't breathe.

Excerpts from Ismet Prcić's Diary
from October 1999

Back in the USA, *mati*. Exit Ismet, enter Izzy. You have no idea how good it feels to be another.

. . . taking a break from the fake memoir.

(. . . the spitting bee-girl . . .)

Despite the shame and the embarrassment of the bee fiasco, he said yes.

Mustafa said yes because she was cute and petite and coquettish. Because she wore Doc Martins and ripped jeans and he kind of had a crush on her. Because he believed that they could end up being together for a long time.

Bullshit. He said yes because at that age you never, ever say no to anybody who one day, potentially, might pop your cherry.

When she winked at him and said, *Let's go,* he said yes. She said, *Yes, what?* and he said, *Yes, let's go.* They made out in the dewy grass in front of her building until ten minutes before the curfew when she had to physically push him off her. She gave him a handmade bracelet she always wore and asked him, *Do you know what this is?* He didn't really, but he said yes and she killed him with a kiss. Then he hauled ass home.

The very next night Mustafa made an almost fatal mistake by teasing her and calling her a little girl. She was fifteen then. They were in front of the Bosnian National Theater, the newest hot spot in their fun-filled besieged city. She slapped his face and stormed off just to come back a minute later and throw a bloody tampon at his head, right in front of everybody. He was more confused than a glob of human sperm in the third chamber of a frog's heart.

That same night, as he walked home alone, she jumped out of the bushes by the river's embankment and kicked him in the groin. The gun looked huge in her little hands. She squatted over his convulsing body and aimed at his right eye. She kept spitting into the grass over his head. She squatted there for a long time, spitting, looking.

There was no doubt in his mind that the brain behind those fierce eyes was going to send a motor stimulus to the muscles of her tiny hand, which were going to squeeze that trigger and send him to the land of wooden poles and toilet bowls for good. And he couldn't think of a single thing, to say or otherwise. His life didn't flash in front of his eyes. He didn't think of loved ones. He didn't think of hated ones, either. He just cupped his nuts—a laughable move when faced with the business end of a 9 mm Zastava.

He would later come to believe that she saw something in his eyes that made her decide not to kill him. Perhaps it was the total absence of him from himself. Whatever it was she calmly removed the bracelet from his wrist, walked away, and never looked at him again.

Things changed big-time for him after this incident. He stopped going out and spent most of his time with the base-ment dwellers, which is what everyone called those people who never accepted the war as normalcy and lived in fear underground.

A year later somebody found the body of a guy named Goran, who he heard was her second boyfriend, in the middle of Banja Park. He had been shot and stabbed numerous times. The story was that he pressured her into having sex with him and then, during a quarrel, threatened to tell her dad, a devout Muslim, about it. Apparently she convinced her little brother to help her take care of the problem and they killed him together. Since her mother was a judge, she ended up in Kreka Psychiatric Hospital.

And even though Mustafa was drafted and made to go and fight, and had seen people blown to bits, cadavers rotting in the trenches, children's heads atop wooden sticks, crosses carved into abdomens and foreheads; and even though he had a lot of close calls like that time the shrapnel went through the van and through the folds of his shirt around the midsection when he was bending to tie his boot, still the closest he had ever been to death was the moment before she reclaimed her bracelet. In all those other instances his life did flash before his eyes and he did think about loved ones and about those he didn't like.

(. . . mustafa nalić
goes to war . . .)

His dreams were boring, like life. They were saturated with a few humans he had never really met, doing everyday things inside a home he had never really been in, but that he got to know quite well over time. Their routines were forever alien while he was in them and forever familiar when he woke up. The details were mind-bogglingly boring. He dreamed of watching TV and remembered what he watched in the mornings.

Most times Mustafa suffered these virtual nonadventures the way one would suffer through a tedious, artsy-fartsy film when there was nothing else on. The only difference was that he was in there, conscious of not belonging, like an understudy who hadn't even read the play. Conscious in a dream. Once in a while the B quality of it all would make him lose it and he would drop his character and scream something dramatic like "Who are you people?" or "Where am I?" or "You don't exist!" He threw punches at his costars, and his fists would go through the fabric of the dream, shattering it, bringing forth rude awakenings of unsolicited sensations of fear for no reason.

So when he awoke at seventeen, shaking and flustered, with a pair of glasses on, in a corridor that smelled of disease and harsh cleaning products, among some thirty nervous males of his age, clutching seemingly identical paper files in their hands, looking like they were awaiting execution, it didn't take him long to decide that he had to compensate for the dullness of his dreams and make his life noteworthy. The glasses had to come off. There was nothing wrong with his eyes. He squinted a sinister smile as his new attitude kicked in with a wave of shivers up his spine, sending invisible ripples of energy up and down the corridor, affecting everything.

"Are they gonna take our blood, do you know?" a broad-shouldered giant next to him squeaked and boomed, his voice going in and out like the spin cycle of a busted washer. The incongruity between his pubertal looks of oily, gangly awkwardness, radiating almost observable puffs of sharp fear, and his imposing size, topped with a full beard, made Mustafa cringe.

"Oh yeah," he answered.

The paper file made a tiny crumpling noise as the giant hands that held it started to visibly vibrate. Then they caught themselves and, with feverish, insectile tenacity, smoothed out the file and laid it across the giant lap. Once free of the important papers and no longer responsible for their safety, they shakily drove the giant elbows into the giant knees and opened upward to receive a giant petrified head.

Mustafa found it astonishing, this guy's horror. The kid was obviously from the country, his body in bloom, made gigantic by field work and caloric homemade food, the opposite end of the spectrum from Mustafa's own pale, tubercular body. He'd probably never received a shot in his life, and his dread of all things hospital related was theatrically apparent. It was probably his first time in a town, a place he would never go to unless he had to have an emergency operation or, in this case, get drafted to fight the war.

"Make sure you keep breathing when they do it," Mustafa said to him. Something inside made him say it, some kind of envy. He couldn't stand so much fear inside a body that strong and that much better than his.

"Why?" the giant said, looking up, his eyes popping out.

"You don't wanna have a heart attack. They have a syringe this fat right up in your vein here. If you stop breathing for a second"—he made a dramatic pause, held it, held it, then dropped the bomb—"you die."

The giant's lips quivered in agony. His Adam's apple bobbed up and down like he had an alien entity roaming under his skin there. "Oh, mother," he said and buried his head back in his hands. Mustafa smiled, both keyed up and sickened by his work. The rest of the recruits snickered, trying to hold in their laughter.

The nearest door swung outward and banged against the wall. At the sound, murmurs dropped off a cliff and heads turned. The swinger was a meaty nurse with bejeweled fingers, rings she could never get off without Vaseline or oil.

"Next five," she barked and waited until Mustafa, the giant, and three more lads stood up to form a line. The giant's knees were shaky. He crept ahead, hunched like he had a cannonball around his neck.

"Hey, big man, hurry up! You look like you dropped a load in your pants." She laughed a callous little laugh. There were a few obligatory chuckles around the corridor. Mustafa felt like she was stealing his spotlight as the entertainer of these guys.

"Take your shirts—"

Mustafa farted.

"—off and—" Her instructions got eaten up by billows of laughter from a number of newly matured voice boxes, something that couldn't be said for their owners. Her eyes searched the line for the perpetrator and met Mustafa's cool leer. There he was, the knower of his audience, looking her in the eye, not budging. Laughter started to die.

"How can you be so disgusting?" She tried to sound like a disappointed mother.

"Inspiration."

Without ever dying completely, the laughter ignited with a vengeance, and since there was no point in trying to scream over it, she sternly pointed to the door, her eyebrows flying up. Mustafa gave the giant a gentle push in the back and the line of five stepped into a white room as if into the afterlife. The nurse followed and banged the door shut.

"Documents on the table!"

They obliged, some of them still trying to suppress residual chortles. Mustafa's papers got buried under others, but she fished them out and put them on top of the pile, cocking her head to read his name.

"You first, jester! Take off your shirt and sit up here!"

Mustafa tried hard not to be affected by disrobing in public, and it showed. He lingered as though trying to find the bottom of his sweatshirt, and then hesitated slightly before he pulled it over his head, revealing a tight wife-beater—his brother's. Her face exuded ridicule.

"The undershirt, too."

There was no need for that. He looked at her, then at his exposed veins, unhampered by any clothing, then back at her. She held his gaze. He waited a second and then got rid of the wife-beater, uncovering his accordion rib cage. She looked at him and chuckled.

"No comment," she said and turned to prep the needle. Mustafa's eyes wandered across the room, caught the giant's smile, and instantly blazed with fury coming to a boil somewhere within. The giant, that pitiable hulk of dense meat cowering at just the thought of being pricked by a needle, was laughing at him, at his scrawniness, at his pathetic patch of pubiclike hair halfway between his nipples, at the absence of any discernable musculature, at his fucked-up posture. As the nurse drove a needle into Mustafa's vein, concerned with gentleness not at all, he closed his eyes, uttered a short scream, collapsed backward off the stool, and started to twist and spasm, twitch and shake. She panicked for a second, then ran over to a cabinet, trying to remember what to do when someone has a seizure. From the corner came the thump of a giant body hitting the floor abundantly. The bigger they are . . . The nurse turned around, wide-eyed, with a syringe in her hand and found Mustafa back on the stool like nothing had happened.

"Better give that to the big man over there."

Mustafa was on a roll. He farted again while blowing into the thingamajig that measures lung capacity—and received a standing ovation. He told the ear-checking nurse that he lived with constant voices telling him to burn down cinema "Center."

During the optometric exam he claimed to be seeing gnomes all over town, climbing trees, holding hands, riding Vespas. He got patted on the back and cheered by his audience. The nurses weren't so amused. After what he had done to her, the first one kept following him and warning her colleagues.

"Watch out for this one! He's a real jester! Oh yeah! Funny stuff. It's too bad he doesn't know that jesters shouldn't ridicule the king lest they end up headless."

Mustafa replied with another inspired toot.

But in the basement they made them strip naked in front of the army committee behind prison tables. A gaggle of civilian girls crowded the high windows, looking down through the metal bars, giggling and covering their mouths. They flashed sheets of paper with numbers on them like figure-skating judges. Mustafa got a 4, a 5, two 6s, and a 7. He tried to swallow, but it all came back up, battery acid. It would have made him look down, except he couldn't face his nudity.

An army nurse counted their balls and wrote things in their files. She smiled facing the giant's package. You could paddle yourself to safety with that thing. He stood there, still scared shitless, with a shiner on his cheekbone, and cried.

"Pull 'em up, ladies!" she ordered, discarding the latex gloves with which she had touched all of them. "Move along."

Behind the tables, uniforms were unbuttoned, eyes were bloodshot, hair was prematurely gray, mouths curved downward, and a ballpoint pen was tapped against the edge of the table in a steady rhythm. A hand was extended to receive

Mustafa's file, and eyes were made to read the printed letters and numbers. No longer naked, Mustafa felt again the
twinge of his new attitude. It was like madness in the back of
his mind, devoid of survival instinct. A cheap-laugh whore
he was.

"Where do you go to school?"

"The gymnasium."

"Are you good at math?"

"Oh, I'm brilliant."

Salt-and-pepper eyebrows were raised at the blatant sar-
casm of Mustafa's answer. His face was sternly inspected. A
pause was given.

"What branch of the military forces do you think you're
most suitable for?"

"I'd have to say the navy, since I'm a . . . a brilliant swimmer."

And although Bosnia and Herzegovina does have something like a two-inch-wide access to the Adriatic Sea, the
Bosnian Navy was obviously a joke. All voices died in the
basement room. The ballpoint pen ceased its percussive as-
sault on the table. Behind it, lips tightened and eyes squinted
in anger. His file was stamped like someone squashing a roach.

"I think you'll enjoy the special forces, funny man. For a
short while at least. Next!"

He's lying on his back and staring into the night sky, looking
for the face of God. He's murmuring ancient Arabic phrases
that carry no meaning for him, since he learned them phonetically when he was a kid. He has shit himself. He has
pissed himself. He's cold.

(...shards...)

The sky is getting carved with projectiles. Explosions. Gunfire.

He's praying the only way he knows how and hugging his empty rifle.

He's halfway between the trenches.

Excerpts from Ismet Prcić's Diary
from November 1999

I went insane, *mati*. Again. And I thought I was okay. It's Melissa's coldness that does it every time. We were at her parents' house in Thousand Oaks (they weren't there, thank God) and we were fighting about something inane. She wanted me to wear my good sweatshirt for the dinner with them that night, one without holes and without the half-naked cowgirl on the front, and I went on a sanctimonious diatribe about how I wanted her parents to know the real me, and what the fuck is wrong with a hole under the arm if the person at the table is courteous and loving, and shouldn't we stop judging books by their covers, and she. turned. cold.

I'd seen it before, this transformation, but I didn't expect it then. It was reserved for severe fights. Obviously, this wasn't about the sweatshirt. She sideswiped me with a glance that made me freeze, that made me feel unwanted. I turned on the waterworks, but she sustained the same level of coldness. I begged her to say something warm. She thumbed through a cooking magazine instead. My pain turned into rage.

On the floor at the end of the hallway there was an empty laundry basket and a gallon bottle of laundry detergent, seemingly empty. I punted the first as hard as I could and watched it clatter down the hallway with hilarity. That didn't satisfy me, so I punted the bottle, as well, which turned out to be full. I heard my big toe snap, but heated by adrenalin, I barely noticed it. I put on my sneakers, slammed the front door, and walked away.

When I hobbled back home two days later, Eric barely recognized me. He was sore I hadn't called, but I couldn't. I couldn't call, because I had no idea where I'd been.

Back in therapy, on Melissa's request. Or should I say ultimatum? Dr. Cyrus insists I have to keep going with the "memoir," that my trip to Bosnia put a snag in my recovery. He insists I arrange things in chronological order, write the name of a month, and go into what happened that month. Simple as that.

We'll see.

(. . . scaling the serpent . . .)

Donju Tuzlu, Donju Tuzlu
opasala guja
Lower Tuzla, Lower Tuzla
is surrounded by a serpent
Bosnian sevdalinka song

LATE MARCH

I turned eighteen in 1995 and was supposed to be a man already but didn't like being one yet.

Sure I had an Adam's apple and a penis in a cloud of pubes and could break big chunks of coal with an ax, gather the pieces into huge, heavy sacks, load three of those bastards onto a wheelbarrow at a time, haul them across the war-quieted city, then carry them, one by one, over my shoulder up sixty-eight stairs to our fourth-floor balcony. Sure, I could bang a nail in straight with two or three hits and could put away however much booze you set in front of me and still have the tenacity and audacity to yammer about David Hume. Sure, I could hold my own at man talk, too, sitting around with the boys and talking about weapons and pussy, even though I had yet to see either one up close and personal. Sure, I could do those things, but only because I'd been an actor since I was six, because I knew how to play parts and keep the illusion going, how to get into different characters. I knew that people always believed you if your performance was good, and I *was* good. I didn't mind acting in real life as long as I could go into my head after the performance and, up there, resume being a kid.

I had developed many roles to pacify the people around me. At home I acted like a dick, an angry teenager to whom the world was owed, which of course warranted whining, and door slamming, and locking myself in various rooms, and playing my music at earsplitting decibel levels, and tormenting my brother. At school I acted cool, flaunted my sense of humor and my trendy long hair, was popular, everyone's best friend. In rehearsals I was quiet and hardworking, a tenacious artist with balls of steel, a man who lived for his art. With my best friend, Omar, and the rest of the town's punks I was a mysterious and tormented creature, dark and willing to do any drug first, a monster in a mosh pit.

With my girlfriend I had tried my best at first to act like a man but had a tough time giving a good performance. It was easier fooling multitudes than a single person. On the highly intimate stage of a one-on-one relationship, broad strokes that were a hit at bigger venues didn't hold water. I was a theater actor having trouble transitioning to silver-screen close-ups, and it showed. I kept messing up, but fortunately Asja found my attempts at being a man for her amusing and she stayed with me nonetheless. Over time I realized that she liked me best when I inadvertently slipped into my kid self, and the longer we were together the more comfortable I was being that in front of her. Thus our relationship was innocent but deep, our trysts in Banja Park filled with kisses and caresses, with love so dreamy it could make you comatose, so syrupy it could make you puke.

But a month earlier I had been drafted into the army, and it was everything you would expect: intimidation, humiliation, obedience.

Some camouflaged asshole actually rubbed his hands together and told me he couldn't wait to get my mane under his clippers and my ass into the trenches. During my psych evaluation I played tough but lied and told them that I was good at math, hoping to be trained as an artillery man so as to put the greatest distance between me and the enemy when they sent me into the eye of the war, but the prematurely gray colonel said that we didn't have much artillery and what we had was already being handled by people who knew how to handle it and how about a bright future in the meat grinder, instead: infantry? It was a rhetorical question. He said to report at the base on September 15 to serve my term, and he stamped my file red. FIT, it said. I acted nonchalant. Acted.

I started feeling like I had an expiration date, like my life would end on September 15, 1995, and I had to milk joy out of every moment I had left. I focused on spending as much time as I could with Asja or by myself, in my own head. I stopped sniffing paint thinner with Omar because I wanted "to be there for my life." At one point I freaked out that I would die without knowing all the stuff there was to know, so I stayed up at night with flashlights or candles, reading through my mother's library of classics. I crammed myself full of Pushkin and Pasternak, of Dostoyevsky. Every four or five days when our ward would get three hours of electricity in the middle of the night, I would play Bergman and Tarkovsky films I borrowed from Asmir, while my mother baked loaf after loaf of bread in our electric stove. I did sentimental things like go through my old diaries and cry over who I'd been.

One day in late March, after tossing all night, staring at my brother sleeping with his mouth open, and suffering millions of thoughts having orgies in my skull, I came up with a plan that involved and depended on Asja. Life was short; we had so little time. I got up at first light, forced down some cornbread and beef fat, washed it down with cold chamomile tea from the night before, and left the apartment before anyone else got up. Not that I cared if I woke them: I had clanged around the kitchen like it was the middle of the day and slammed the doors with gusto. I didn't bring my backpack with schoolbooks but hid it behind my bed.

Outside, Tuzla was stolid and chilly and you had to push your way through the wet haze. There was barely anyone around, just silent shadow people slipping into murky vestibules, stirring up nothing, making no mark upon the world. The parking lots were full of dead cars, juiceless for years, their sides peppered with corroded shrapnel holes. Their windows, if they were there at all, were fogged up and blind. There was no wind, and the greening trees were quiet like everything else. It felt good to be alone in this way.

I crossed the street by Hotel Tuzla, in front of which a blond man with a red face was drinking his coffee and reading a newspaper like he was in Paris or something. Foreigners were like that. They didn't feel part of the surroundings, because this was not their war and somehow this made them feel immune to its hazards. They'd jog, whereas Bosnians would run, as though Chetnik shrapnel could tell American flesh from Bosnian. Granted, the mortars were eerily quiet for a couple of months, but before that, the mornings were their prime time, as Chetniks tried to discourage the populace from going to work or tried to kill them en route.

The Jala was swollen from snowmelt, its clayey waters barely a meter below the lips of the tall concrete embankments, rushing away from here. It hummed with odd power, and instead of proceeding alongside to my high school, I walked onto the bridge, somehow drawn to it. Approaching the guardrail I felt that power in my gut, in the immediate weakening of my muscles, as if the river were somehow robbing me of my life force, dispersing me. I made sure my hands were tight around the rail before looking down. One moment there was a chair leg in the current below, bobbing in and out of the brown and brandishing all its gnarly woodwork in detail; the very next, it was a black stick way down the stream, then nothing at all. Gone.

I imagined it getting away from here, from this city under siege, all the way to the Spreča, which would smuggle it through the enemy-occupied territory east toward the Drina. The Drina would then hook it north between Bosnia and Serbia, hiding it in the blood of the people from both jagged borders, and give it off to the Sava. The Sava, as big as it is, would have no problem getting it to the Danube, and the Danube, that behemoth, would provide a safe passage for it through the middle of Belgrade and then take it away from this godforsaken peninsula all the way to the Black Sea. But once in its inky waters, what would the chair leg do, beautifully carved as it was but broken off, without the rest of the chair? Without anyone to sit in it? Without anyone to climb upon it to screw in a lightbulb? Would it wash up on a beach somewhere and become driftwood, end up in a glorious bonfire as young people celebrated their youth beside it and jumped over it drunkenly? Would some tortured Bulgarian soul scoop it up at the docks of Varna, fashion it into a small sculpture of a mother holding a child and make it immortal? Or would a common villain pick it up and bash his victim's skull in with it on the backstreets of Istanbul?

Looking straight down at all that turbulent water rushing away from me, it felt like I was on the back of a boat that was taking me away, away from September 15, but then a UN jeep screamed across the bridge behind me, its engine roaring, its driver sporting a red pair of sunglasses even though the sun was hidden, and I bucked with fear and ran to the shore, and when I realized I wasn't really being run down, I snatched a stone from the ground and hurled it after him. It ricocheted off the asphalt three or four times and came to rest in the bushes in front of the hotel. I saw his brake lights turn red as he slowed to take the corner and then disappeared around the hotel toward my neighborhood. The man with the red face glanced at this occurrence and then returned to his newspaper. Everything but the river returned to silence. I put down my middle fingers and made my way to the high school building.

Asja was an early riser and I knew that she would be one of the first students to show up at school. She did anything to be away from her parents, who were strict, old-fashioned, and overprotective, suffocating, really. We could hang out only on Friday and Saturday nights and during our brief encounters at school. Lately I started walking her home, too, and that was an extra hour of hand-holding and kissing before I had to disengage from her (by the entrance to the soccer stadium close to her building) and let her get smaller and, with a little wave, disappear behind the newspaper kiosk every time.

I also knew that she liked to use the shortcut by the river to get to school instead of taking the long way down Južna Magistrala, so I planted myself halfway down the gravel path and found a plank to sit on and wait. The plank had a knurl in it and it kept digging into me, so I had to stand up every once in a while to rest my ass. When I saw her coming in her black sweater I hid in the shrub above the embankment, and when she passed by me I jumped out producing inarticulate sounds, trying to scare her, but she just turned around and punched me in the chest.

"You goober," she said. "I saw your head from Shoe People's bridge."

"You're saying I have a big head?"

"I'm saying you're a goober."

I braced for a long kiss (I needed it), but she just touched my lips with hers and then withdrew, took my hand, and started walking. Usually we didn't stop sucking on each other's faces until we ran out of breath, like barnacles. Clearly this was bad news, but I so didn't want it to be that I ignored it and staked everything on my little plan.

"What classes do you have today?"

She squinted. There was coldness in it. "What are you up to now?"

"I was thinking maybe we could skip the whole day of school, go up to the park, make out."

She grunted. Playfully, I poked her rib. She squirmed and hid her hands in her sleeves. I tried again but she slapped my hand away.

"Don't!"

"What?" I went to embrace her from behind, but she wangled her way out of my arms.

"Stop it!" she said and started walking away. I walked behind her.

"What's going on?"

"Nothing."

"Nothing, my dick."

She threw up her arms. Her feet crunched down the wet gravel path. The river hummed. My feet crunched, too, but off beat to hers, so the noise of the three of us in the world was continuous and sounded like grinding.

"Why are you doing this?"

We kept on grinding.

"Talk to me, please."

Grinding. And suddenly I couldn't handle the percussive monotony anymore and stopped. It felt like the only thing to do, like the last thing I could do: stop. The river hummed and sounded like a river now. Without mine, Asja's footsteps sounded like the footsteps of someone walking away.

She came to a bend in the path and halted as if paused by a remote control. My heart hopped. She couldn't walk away. I thought she was gonna turn around and come back but she just stood there. It looked unnatural, her rigidity, her stillness. It went on for a long time, too, so long that I thought briefly that I was hallucinating, that she was already gone but that my brain, unable to deal with her departure, had taken a snapshot and buried me forever in this moment of heartbreak. Then her right hand moved back a little. She bent her whole arm at the elbow until her hand slowly traveled to the middle of her lower back and started to frantically rotate there.

What the hell?

Puzzled but recharged, I went to her. She took one excruciatingly slow step back toward me, her hand still doing somersaults and cartwheels against the black wool of her sweater, then halted again. I came up to her and kissed her neck from behind. She smelled of mothy clothes and soap. I took her possessed hand in my right and hugged her against me with my left when I felt her squeeze my fingers like she never had before. I thought it was out of obdurate love, but then I saw the dog.

Five meters in front of us, cocked and crouching, its jaw open and slobbering bile, was a huge Great Dane and my knees buckled under me. Its eyes were feral and livid. Its ribs glared through the mangy coat. It growled once and I felt my body ossify and my mind rush back in time, away from the two teenagers who were huddling petrified on the river path. Age six, my cousin Garo's German shepherd clamps me on the thigh when I try to pet it. Some man yells and beats him with an open palm but it doesn't let go. The man starts to use his fists. The thuds sound hollow and meaty at the same time. Age eleven and I'm riding my bike under the line of willows by the river and a little shit of a black terrier named Johnny takes after me, and in horror I grab the first branch I can reach and clamber like a fat monkey all the way into the treetop as my beloved green "Pony" rolls itself down the embankment and into the water.

For a moment I see the two teenagers take a shaky step back and the animal in front of them jerk up, reclaim the distance, and then crouch down again. For the moment when it's upright, it truly looks mastodonic. But I see it (remember it?) when it's still a puppy in a litter of six. I remember it being picked up by a thin woman with dark circles around her eyes. She's a poet and employed by Tuzla's National Theater to do dramaturgical work. She can't have children, and her husband agrees to get the puppy so their house on the hill won't be so silent all the time. He's a professor of music and a concert violinist (he has once played for Tito) and silence is not his cup of tea. He genuinely likes dogs, grew up with them. I see the puppy grow fast, see the woman sneak pieces of calf liver and chateaubriand to it, and see the man repeatedly throw a fat piece of rope with a knot at each end way down their property from the terrace and the dog fetch it every time. I see it take over his side of the bed and the man drag it by the collar over the polished parquetry with much difficulty to put it outside. Later, when the man is asleep I see the woman let it back in but keep the bedroom door closed. I see it jump over the fence one day, going after a cat, and get nicked a little by a blue Renault. I see the war come, and it's getting harder and harder to find dog food, so the woman has to buy butcher scraps and offal and cook these pungent soups, crumble bread into them, and feed that to the rapidly diminishing dog. Dark circles return to her eyes. Shelling makes the dog whine and hide. It makes the woman despair and she hugs the whining animal in the basement and sleeps next to it on a cot. The man sleeps in a rocking chair. The first winter and it becomes obvious that the dog is suffering and that they cannot do anything about it. Their own clothes hang off of them like ponchos now and the man has to punch new holes in their belts. They try to give the dog away to a shelter but the employee laughs at them. They try to give it away to anybody who will take it, even walk all the way to the UN base in Šićki Brod and try to give it away there. Nobody wants it. He says they have to let it go or put it to sleep. She says no, no, over and over. What else can we do? he asks. No, no, she says. With the last of his gasoline the man drives it to the edge of the town, feeds it a meal of cooked cow lungs and bread, throws a fat piece of rope as hard as he can toward the woods, and when the dog bolts after it, climbs into his car (without bothering to pick up the dog bowl), and drives away. He tilts his rearview mirror up and keeps his eyes on the white line in front of him. I don't see the dog anymore, but I see the couple still. No, no, she screams at him when he comes back and melts through his arms and his fingers to the floor. No, no, she locks herself in the basement and refuses food. He breaks in after two days and the next-door neighbor drives them to the hospital. The hospital is full of crazed doctors and legless soldiers. They sedate her and send her home. The man cooks for her, spoons soup into his wife's mouth every day. He changes her clothes, washes them by hand in the tub. She refuses to move or talk. The war keeps on. Their food stash is dwindling and so is their money. There are no concerts or plays in the town under siege, not the ones that people would pay for, and they have no income. What he's getting from the music school, monthly packages of flour and oil, is not enough. He has to sell things from the house. They used to live well, so they have a lot of nice things that he goes to the market and sells for dirt cheap: a mink coat for a small bag of potatoes, an antique grandfather clock for a sack of cornmeal. He comes home one day and finds her dead, suicide maybe, but nobody has time to autopsy. Every morning he goes to her grave and picks up dead leaves or brushes away the snow or pulls up the spindling weeds. He gets thinner, starts playing violin publicly, making it cry for a cigarette here, a worthless coin there. He refuses to sell it. Going through his wife's stuff, he finds a can of German dog food that got overlooked, sleeps with it for a couple of days, and then, after selling the collected works of William Faulkner for two boxes of pasta, heats it up and mixes it with half a squishy, rancid onion and some ketchup from the bottom of a plastic bottle—he cuts the top of the bottle with a serrated knife pours hot water into it and makes sure to get every last smidgen of red out of it—adds it to the heaping plate of rigatoni, and devours it. And before I see him sell his violin to a bus driver, I am aware that the dog's name is Archibald.

I see myself get my right hand out of Asja's and give her the left one instead and step in between her and the dog. I hear myself

"Archibald!" I yelled to the dog, and his ears suddenly perked up and his tail went down between his legs. He closed his cavernous jaws with a whiny yelp, jumped sideways toward the river, realized he couldn't go that way, made a tight half circle around himself, took off like he was spring-loaded over the fence that separated the path and somebody's war garden, and vanished.

For a moment I actually felt heroic. I turned around and saw Asja trying to comprehend what had just occurred, her hand still breaking my fingers, when a mortar shrieked over us and rocked somewhere nearby, sending everything running, everything except us.

We had no legs to run, no lungs to breathe. We just dropped to the ground and lay there holding hands as one, two, three sirens started to shrill at different pitches and filled the vast skies above us with their morbid symphony.

No other shells fell. We looked for them against the gray and white sky but the gravel became uncomfortable and we scooted closer to the river into the dewy grass. When I tried to let go of her hand she crumpled her fingers in mine.

"Don't you dare," she whispered.

"I won't."

She was silent for a while. I felt so close to her, never closer.

"I heard," she said, still whispering.

"Heard what?"

"You guys are going to Scotland."

Asmir had met this British woman aid worker and brought her to see some of our shows. She loved them and asked if we wanted her to put out a good word for us in the UK, that she knew some theater people. Asmir said yes but then completely forgot about it. Then, a couple of weeks ago, we got this invitation from Edinburgh to participate in some kind of festival. It was supposed to be in August, but there was no way the authorities would let us go. Bokal was in the army, Asmir was evading them although he was twenty-five, and Omar and I had both just gotten drafted. They didn't let anyone out, let alone potential soldiers.

"Nobody is going anywhere. We just got invited, that's all."

"You didn't tell me."

"It was nothing. We got a letter. When is the last time you heard of anybody getting a passport? It's impossible."

"You didn't tell me."

I sat up and tried to let go of her hand but she wouldn't let me.

"Don't you let go."

I leaned away a little but she pulled me on top of her and into a feverish kiss. It was insane and outlandish, as though my consciousness went into every cell of my body and I was there in the curve of my lips, at the tip of my tongue, on my dewy back, where her hands were coldly pressing, and down there where my erection was pressing at her. It was wonderful.

It wasn't until the sun poked through the clouds and some children rode by on ancient BMX bikes and made fun of us that we got up and decided we might as well go along with my plan for the day. We crossed the Shoe People bridge and saw the smoke from behind the Shoe People building. *Shoe People* is this horrid cartoon for small kids—all colors and no heart. Right before the war started, this monstrosity of a building had burgeoned in the middle of the town, and some genius had painted it in a combination of pastel yellow, pastel blue, hot pink, and brown, which is why Tuzlaks started calling it the Shoe People building.

The earlier shell had hit the parking lot in front of it, lifted this VW bug, flipped it, and brought it down atop a little Citroën. By the time we got close, you couldn't see what colors they were, as they were burned extracrispy and still burning. The bug looked a little bit like a turtle on its back. Some pissed-off storeowners were sweeping their broken windows off the pavement. There were shrapnel holes everywhere. We overheard that two women were killed, but we walked past the jail and up to Banja Park to make out.

Sitting on our favorite bench overlooking the town we could have been photographed for one of those cheesy love calendars that eleven-year-old girls across the world keep on their walls, all breathtaking nature and saccharine love. At one point something ran through the bushes behind us and we startled, but it was some old man in too small of a suit jacket, crazy we guessed.

"I thought it was Archibald," she said and I couldn't stop laughing. "Where in the world did you get Archibald?"

All I could do was point to my head. She punched my arm and kissed me.

"You goober, don't you ever leave me."

APRIL

Asmir, Bokal, and I decided to go out after rehearsal. The Galerija was a toilet of a café, two low-ceilinged rooms crammed with bulky wicker chairs and smelling of rotten drywall.

The guy behind the bar ignored us. Bokal had to go down to him and order our long coffees as Asmir and I settled into our chattering chairs.

"Do the waiters here have to go to a school to learn to look this disaffected?" I said.

"The less he comes this way the better," Asmir replied.

Last night he had mooched forty marks off a Dutch humanitarian worker he was fucking and lifted a bottle of Johnnie Walker from her pantry when she went to the bathroom to clean herself up. He wanted to do something that would end their arrangement, because he was getting sick of her. He said she gave good blow jobs. In the dark. That was his joke. She was fifteen years older than him, or more, and he said he could only do her in the dark. Asmir was a bit of a bastard when it came to women.

Bokal came back smoking a cigarette we knew he didn't have when we came in.

"Where did you get that?" Asmir asked him.

"Look who you're asking."

Bokal called himself the king of lying, scrounging, borrowing, and freeloading and was proud of it. Once I witnessed him leech a mark from a Gypsy beggar kid, honest to God. We were sitting in some other café and this little kid came over to beg from us and Bokal told him that he was in trouble, that he had ordered a coffee he didn't have money for, and that the owner of the café would kick his ass when he found out. The little guy felt bad for him, took a wad of small bills out of his sock, and gave him a mark to pay for the coffee.

The waiter/barman, with a gap in his teeth you could push a beer cap through, brought over three long coffees and put the receipt under the ashtray. I couldn't stand the taste of coffee and so put in three packets of sugar.

"What do you think, Asmir, God doesn't see you fornicating with all these foreigners?" Bokal asked out of nowhere. "They come over here from who knows where to help Bosnians and you treat them like shit."

"Hey, I'm Bosnian. They're helping *me*. Get off."

Asmir laughed through his nose at his own joke and we did the same. There was something disarmingly childish about him that you just couldn't hate no matter what he said or did. He had a knack for downplaying his faults, a particular kind of charisma that made you let him get away with murder as though it were mischief.

"Pass me your cups and keep pretending like you're talking," Asmir said.

Bokal and I carried on a mock conversation while Asmir, hidden by the tablecloth, poured some Johnnie Walker from his shoulder bag into all our coffee cups.

"Let's drink to us making it to Edinburgh," Asmir said, and I saw all the good humor go out of Bokal. His face went sour. We clinked our cups and drank the stuff. It was terrible but it burned in a good way. Bokal leaned back and the wicker under him woke up and groaned under his bulk. He glanced at the remains of the cigarette in the ashtray.

"Fuckin' walls," he said.

"What's up Bokal, you don't wanna go to Edinburgh?" I asked him, trying a jovial tone. He looked at me like *you lucky kid*, and I remembered that he was in the army, that even if the rest of us, by some Miracle, got our passports, he probably wouldn't.

"Look at that painting," he said, nodding to the wall next to me. It was kind of a caricature of downtown Tuzla, with its signature buildings all being squeezed at the bottom by a huge white snake. "What does it mean?"

"It's from that song, right?" I prided myself on being a badass punk rocker, and admitting that I knew all about *sevdalinke* would betray my bad rep. I took a huge gulp from my cup to reinforce my badassedness.

"Do you know what the snake represents?"

"The wall?"

"Wrong."

"What are you talking about?" Asmir butted in. "There used to be an actual wall around the whole downtown. There are still pieces of it left up on Banja Park, that old armory up there."

"Yes, but do you think that somebody would write a song about a fucking wall? No. The snake is the invading army of Omar Paša Latas, who was dispatched from Istanbul to quash a rebellion in these parts. When he was done he surrounded the whole town with his troops and just hung out there for a while to show off the might of the Ottoman army and make sure nobody else had any funny ideas."

This was startling coming from Bokal, who was known to us more for his street smarts.

"So what's your point?" I asked.

"My point is that us thinking that we can escape the serpent's grip is just a very funny idea."

He downed his cup and slid it in front of Asmir.

"Branka said it's possible," Asmir said and, keeping an eye on the waiter, poured him another Johnnie, this time unmixed. I quickly finished my drink, too, and presented Asmir with my own empty cup.

"Possible, my shlong. If they let anyone go it'll be all the young'uns in the troupe. Me, you, him, whoever can carry a gun, we're just dreaming."

"If anyone can do it, Branka can. She'll fight for Omar to go and he's Ismet's age."

Branka was the woman in charge of the Home of the Youth, where we rehearsed; she was an ass-kicker taker-care-of-things and Omar's mother. Omar was part of the troupe, too, because he wrote and performed the music for one of the plays in our repertoire, a re-imagining of Saint-Exupéry's *Little Prince*. I played the Little Prince. Omar's little brother Boro played the Little Prince as a child.

"What is she gonna do, sign the passports instead of General Lendo?"

"Richard Bach says that when you wish something strongly enough, the universe shifts to make it happen." It was like Asmir to pull infuriating New Age quotes out of his ass like this. Bokal stood up, tightened his fists, and shut his eyes.

"Here, I'm strongly wishing for my kidney back," he said, opened his eyes and fists and pulled his polo shirt out of his jeans. He turned and revealed his operation scar to us. "Oops, tough titty. It's still gone."

He pulled himself together and walked down to the bar.

Outside, the day was dying and the thin, exhausted, fun-starved people were slowly starting to fill the garden seating area for the evening.

"That's Bokal for you," Asmir said, "no faith." He grabbed my forearm to make me look at him. "We're going to Edinburgh, you mark my words."

And somehow a part of me knew we would. That was Asmir's power. Despite his hypocrisy, you didn't doubt that he believed.

"From your mouth to God's ears," I said.

"What are you going to do with Dunda?" he then asked. Dunda was what everyone called Asja. The question blindsided me. A sort of panic rang through my skull and rattled down my limbs. There I was wishing and praying to be away from this town, plotting to do so, believing I was out already, and not for one moment did she ever enter my thoughts.

"Nothing," I heard myself say. "I'll go to Edinburgh and I'll come back."

"Don't be stupid," Asmir said. "She's your first. I know it feels strong, but she's your first. You can't throw away your life just because you think you know what love is at seventeen."

"Eighteen."

"Even worse." He took a sip. "Nothing's gonna come out of that."

Bokal lumbered over to us and brandished another cigarette he had scored.

"Ismet says he would come back if we made it to Edinburgh."

"Come back here? Why?" Bokal looked flabbergasted.

"He loves his girlfriend."

"Listen to me. If you get out of here and then come back, you better hide from me. If I see you on the street I will cripple you."

"Why do you care?" I laughed, though I knew he was serious.

Bokal ignored me. He and Asmir talked about art and about the girls going in and out of the restrooms. I said not a word. A part of me wanted to run all the way to Batva, ring Asja's doorbell, have a man-to-man with her father and win him over, marry her, go to war, liberate villages, and come home from the front lines every week to my love. The other part saw myself on a boat, alone, escaping September. I imagined myself in Scotland, what it would look like. I imagined green pastures and jolly red-bearded Scotts, long-haired yaks and ancient castles, wet cobblestones and mythic monsters hiding in lakes, things I read about.

At some point we heard two gunshots ring outside and all the people in the café leaped and charged into the night to the edge of the park where something exciting was taking place. Tipsy, we followed the dark crowd, and there was this mountain of a man out there, standing in the moonlight, a foot taller than anyone else, slinging what appeared to be an antique two-shell shotgun over his shoulder and pointing to the ground where everyone was looking. Some smokers flicked on their lighters to better see whomever he had shot, and I saw that the big man had a top part of a ranger or security guard uniform on. For a moment I saw him squat out of sight and had to blindly follow Bokal, who cut through the crowd with ease. When the big man reemerged I saw his face and remembered him.

He was in my batch of draftees for the physical and psych evaluations, which made him my age, but unlike me, he looked like a soldier that day. With his shirt off he looked chiseled out of a boulder, had the full beard and body odor of a man. They wanted him for an MP but he kept begging to be in the special forces. They said no, but he kept ridiculing them, pushing their buttons, farting, and finally he pissed off one of the brass, who assigned him to the unit with an average life expectancy of about a week.

The crowd parted a little and what I saw lying there was lean and furry.

It was Archibald.

I kneeled next to him and touched his hind end. I felt like crying. His rib cage was devastated with a hole. There were bones protruding and they were white in the moonlight.

"Was it yours?" asked the mountain man.

"That's Archibald," I said and walked back toward the café. Asmir snickered, thinking I was messing with the guy. There was an omen here, and I was drunk and ready to go home.

MAY

On May 25, after rehearsal, I went over to Omar's without calling ahead. It was in the late afternoon. I yelled his name from in front of his house and his head popped out of the second-story window.

I wanted to go out, but he felt like staying home, asked me in. I caved, as usual, and he sent his ten-year-old brother down to unlock the door. I teased Boro that he had a girlfriend and he told me to "screw off," so I chased him up the stairs, a routine.

Omar was sitting by the window, smoking, trying to blow the smoke outside.

"Shut the door," he said and sprayed jasmine-scented air freshener around in hisses.

I perched myself in the usual spot on the sofa, with my back against the stereo, and picked up a guitar that had seen better days some ten to fifteen years ago. It sounded like it was on hallucinogens.

I don't remember what we talked about or did. I don't even remember if it was still light outside. I just remember freezing in midsentence when I heard the muffled discharge of a faraway cannon—by this point everybody could distinguish between the sound of a cannon and that of a mortar. There hadn't been any shelling since that morning in March.

Time imploded. My internal clock, trained to turn on as soon as a discharge was heard, started counting seconds before the projectile would reach the town, three seconds in all—everybody knew that, too. Three seconds to find cover, or run, or pray, or hold a thought, or remember. Three seconds.

One, one thousand.

Two, one thousand.

Three, one thousand.

Movies don't do it justice—that's all I'm going to say about the thought-collapsing, breath-stealing sound a spinning shell makes as it pierces the air on the way down toward the center of your town, in between three of the busiest cafés and a little bit to the right of the popcorn vendor in the midst of hundreds of citizens who are pretending that everything is okay, that the war is winding down. But I didn't know that yet.

Three seconds passed in silence, then BOOM! A close one. Sirens blared. We rushed to the living room because it overlooked the center, Branka already at the open window.

"Stay away from the windows," she said.

"Come on, Mom," Omar replied and looked outside.

"You guys wanna go to the basement?"

"It's not like it's our first time."

We listened for more discharges. Everything was quiet.

"You smell like smoke," Omar's mother said to him and he grunted in feeble protest. We kept on looking out.

A car sped down Južna Magistrala, a red Fiat Zastava 101, back-firing and leaving clouds of gray fumes behind it. Then came other cars. Then bicycles. Then people running. Everybody was hurrying toward the center.

I decided to walk home, as I knew the police would shorten the curfew tonight. I said my good-byes and left. The night was quiet and I took the path by the river. Walking past the gymnasium, I saw somebody graffitiing one of the walls and I hung out in the grass until I figured out what it said. It said: HALLOWED BE THY NAME, and judging by the face of a zombie cyborg by the name of Eddie next to it, I suspected it wasn't a religious message.

When I got home my parents were beside themselves. Mother was angry, unable to utter a word. Father wanted to know where I was, why I didn't call. I went past him into the kitchen and poured a glass of water.

"Open your mouth so I can tell you," I told them. It doesn't translate well into English but means something like *It's none of your business.*

"What's wrong with you? Don't you know what happened?"

"Yeah. A shell fell downtown. Very exciting."

He just stood there, so I went to my room where my pallid brother was watching TV.

I saw it all on TV: a severed child's foot by the curb, survivors piling the wounded into the backs of cars and banging on the roofs when they couldn't fit any more in, to signal the drivers to step on it, blood trickling into a manhole with popcorn sprinkled in it, dozens of humans on the cobbled ground, not many of them moving at all, and a decapitated body in a green sweatshirt sitting upright inside the Gate Café, a cigarette still burning in an ashtray in front of him.

That was the last shell that fell on my town.

Body count: 71.

Average age of the victims: 23.

Wounded: around 124.

Cousin Garo died in this shelling and so did a bunch of guys I hung out with at one point or another.

My brother and I weren't allowed to go to the funeral. The town was petrified of another deliberate attack on the mass gathering of civilians, so the time and place of the funeral weren't announced on any media.

They ended up being buried at dawn a few days later on a clearing in Banja Park. Both my parents were in attendance. Mom later told me that, as it was happening, swarms of birds took off from the forest, circled the area above the gathering, then flew off. She said she had never seen so many birds in one spot.

When I went to that special graveyard for the first time to pay my respects to Garo, every grave sported a photograph of its occupant.

I walked around the mounds of still-wet dirt, peering into unfamiliar eyes, recognizing a few faces here and there, looking for my cousin. His grave was perfect. It smelled like a plowed field. "1964–1995," it read.

I walked away from the place, then stopped and returned. There was a little bug of a thought that made me do it, made me feel like I'd missed something. I retraced my steps, looked at the photographs again, and when I saw it it killed me. Garo was my cousin, and seeing his grave didn't affect me as this stranger's did. The picture was murky, not the best likeness, but I recognized those eyes, that full beard, those broad shoulders, and something squeezed in my chest. I got a head rush. I had to sit down in the wet dirt.

"Mustafa Nalić," read this grave, "1977–1995."

The man who shot Archibald.

From then on I had trouble falling asleep. The dark of my room would seep off the ceiling and cover me with its morose particles. I would pull up my childhood covers, with their succession of sleep-walking Donald Ducks, over my head, but I couldn't keep my eyes closed. The dark would find its way through the wetness of my eyes, through my pores and the roots of my hair all the way into my thoughts, and the shadows of my room would spring like screaming dogs or ominous storks, beaks dripping with dead, vile flesh.

I dreamed of him. I agonized over my two memories of him, tried to remember them perfectly. I imagined his life before death. Who was he? What was he like? He never left my mind.

I started to see him. I saw him everywhere. I saw him first from my balcony. He was standing in front of the arcade downstairs, watching kids play Double Dragon. Then I saw him at school, on the staircase. He was an extra in the movies I watched when there was electricity. He was a guest in my house, sitting on my parents' bed, silently nodding approval. I found his toes in the residue of gunk in our bathtub.

Why?

He was just this guy, this stranger. A random fucking guy who begged to be in the special forces.

But now he was Mustafa Nalić. Now he was dead and pieced together like a puzzle in a shallow coffin, parts probably missing, swept into the gutters, and washed away by the cisterns of industrial water from the chemical plant. Maybe bits of his skull were gone, never to reunite with the rest of him. Or perhaps some of his fingertips still wiggled somewhere under the asphalt, never to rest in peace.

I staked out the graveyard trying to meet somebody he knew. Nobody prayed at his grave.

I asked around about him, about his family, his friends. Nobody knew them but people told me things anyway:

"That kid's name is Mustafa, Muće they called him. He used to work at the lodge renting hunting equipment. Ooh, is that kid messed up."

"He lost his father, too."

"I don't know where he's from, some place in the valley of the Drina, I bet, but people say all kinds of stuff about him, that he's not all together. They say, and you can believe it or not, that he wasn't right to begin with but that the war really pushed him over."

"He loved his father."

"Nalić? Nalićs are crazy! There are stories about a Nalić who killed a man over a pumpkin. Stabbed him in the gut with a knife, and then went insane and starved himself to death in his attic."

"He killed his own father. Everyone knows that."

"He lost his whole family, the poor bastard."

"My neighbor lived next door to them, pure truth, this. Refugees. When the Chetniks came into their village, he saw his father hide in the septic tank. When they came to their house, they took away his mother and sister to rape them—who knows?—and cut off a bunch of his older brother's fingers, his nose, his ears, gouged his eyes and sliced open his scrotum, and made him, Mustafa, chew on the stuff—eat it—horrible things. Then they said that if he wanted to live he had to cut his brother's throat and that he did it. Can you imagine that? I can't vouch for that last thing, but the other stuff is pure truth."

JUNE

Branka's office at the Home of the Youth smelled of bureaucratic dust and conservative perfume and oniony sweat. It wasn't much of a dressing room. There was furniture everywhere: boxy desks, orphaned chairs, yellow, top-to-floor cabinets filled with tomes that made you feel bored and exhausted just looking at them. The girls' stuff was strewn everywhere. Prop and costume boxes cluttered the floor and looked like their innards had exploded. It was our turn to get into costume now—the girls had dibs on the office first and had taken their sweet-ass time—and now we had only fifteen minutes before the show.

It was kind of like a dress rehearsal marathon, all three of our plays in a row with fifteen minutes between each, starting at three o'clock. Branka was trying to make the Edinburgh thing happen and had invited all the bigwigs and all the military brass to watch it. In Bosnia, the bureaucratic machine in charge of issuing papers to the citizenry was vast in peacetime, but now it also included the military, who had the final say. No matter how you sliced it, any citizen leaving the country in wartime was a matter of national security, especially with

the population numbers dropping precipitously on a daily basis and
the end of the war nowhere in sight. Branka in her diligence nagged
all levels of officials until she got the promise that General Lendo,
the guy whose signature on your passport made it valid, announced
that he would attend this afternoon.

"What if I did the show like this?"

The three of us guys turned and looked at Bokal, who was standing by the door in black socks, baby blue briefs, a laboriously ruffled
white shirt, and with a crown upon his head. He played the King in
the *Dream About the Little Prince,* the first play on our list tonight.
We all laughed.

"I'm not kidding. It's fucking hot, man."

He wasn't kidding. It was forty degrees Celsius all day and the air
was hotter on the way in than on the way out of your lungs. Every
place where one part of your body touched another was moist. Even
eyelids stuck together when you blinked and it took some force to
pry them open. You just wanted to be naked and spread-eagled and
suspended in the air.

"Don't you say a word," Asmir said, already drenched in sweat
in his soiled winter coat and a beanie. He played the Drunk. Little
Boro and I giggled. Our costumes were identical and pretty light
compared to theirs.

There was a light knock on the door and then Branka's blonde
head was in the room with us.

"He's here," she said.

"Mom!" Boro protested.

"It doesn't matter who's here," Asmir said. Branka beamed at
him with hatred.

They had this dynamic of disgust toward each other. Asmir
thought her a heartless, talentless, self-promoting bureaucrat, and
Branka thought him a selfish, pretentious, uneducated asshole;

neither hid their feelings from each other or anyone else. They were both control freaks who needed each other and hated their predicament.

"Yes it does, Asmir. We have to show him that we are serious about this if we want to get the papers."

"*We,*" Asmir said, indicating us and brazenly excluding Branka, "are serious about this. We always have been. We don't have to do anything extra to show anything to anybody, especially not some career soldier who never read a book in his life."

Branka's eyes turned into slits. I looked over at Boro and we both grimaced and rolled our eyes. Bokal on the other hand was very loyal to Asmir, and as soon as he saw the struggle ensue between them, he hurried to tip the scale to Asmir's advantage. Nonchalantly, he took off his briefs. Asmir sniggered like a teenager.

"Asmir, can I talk to you outside?" Branka asked.

"There's no time. I need to get ready. Can it wait?"

Bokal made a show of leaning bare-assed into one of the prop boxes and rummaging through it.

"It's about what we talked about."

Asmir had told us earlier that Branka wanted him to cut some things out of the play to appease the brass, stuff that was making fun of the military. In Saint-Exupéry's *Little Prince,* the main character leaves his tiny planet to see the world of the grown-ups and finds out that it is absurd, that everyone is alone in their own fictional world, which they perpetuate ad infinitum. In his adaptation Asmir added a character of an archetypal soldier because it was relevant to our daily experience.

The second and bigger problem that Branka had with this portion of the play was that there would be a real weapon on the stage. Ramona, the girl who played the role of the Soldier, brought her grandfather's WWII Schmeiser from home for every rehearsal. The weapon was an antique and was obviously empty, but the military had ordered all citizens to turn in any and all weapons in 1992 when the war started because there was a serious shortage. If General Lendo saw it used in an artsy-fartsy play instead of being in the hands of one of his men on the front lines, he might not be as sympathetic to our cause. I agreed with Branka on this one. The gun was not crucial. It was not like we could have taken it to Scotland with us anyway. Asmir just wanted to exercise his ego, to piss Branka off.

"I'm not changing a thing," Asmir said simply. Branka's chin trembled.

"Do you understand what you're doing?"

"I'm doing my job and maintaining the play's artistic integrity."

"You're sabotaging everybody, including yourself. Not to mention possibly ruining all the work I put into making this happen."

"What work? And what did you make happen? We got invited to the Fringe. The troupe. Doing the play the way we do the play. Not you, not the Home of the Youth."

"You can only leave the country as an institution."

"We can be an institution."

"But you're not. As far as the government is concerned you're a bunch of individuals trying to leave the country in the time of war. You're not an official company, you have no credentials, no business cards, no bank account, no permanent or mailing address, no telephone, no fax, and you don't pay taxes on anything. To the state, you're virtually nonexistent."

There was a knock on the door and Branka opened it without looking. Ramona stood there in a stylized black uniform with a cap that was reminiscent of Parisian gendarmes. The submachine gun hung horizontally across her midsection. At the sight of her, Bokal turned away from the door and scrambled into his royal breeches. Ramona tore her eyes from his ass.

"I'm sorry but we're starting," she said.

Branka turned to Ramona.

"I really think it's not smart showing that to the military."

Ramona looked up at Asmir.

"The gun stays. The costume doesn't work without it." Asmir pushed past Branka, almost knocking her into the door frame. "Thanks to you, now we don't have time for our meditation."

Somewhere, Omar played the first notes of his original score on the piano. I took Boro's hand and we ran like mad through two corridors to the open doors of our rehearsal room, in front of which all the girls in their costumes gestured for us to hurry with almost synchronized arm movements.

"What took you so long?" they whispered and straightened out Boro's costume. On the third measure of the piano melody, right on cue, Boro turned on his flashlight and walked into the room.

"Which one is him?" I asked the girls, scanning the clammy and uncomfortable faces of the audience members sitting along the wall with their arms crossed or balled up in their laps. Seven or eight of them were in uniforms. The girls pointed to a massive man with white hair and a bald spot, his black beret shoved through his shoulder strap, his camouflage shirt damp under the arms. I watched him. His brow was downcast but something in his eyes almost showed fear. He listened to Boro's opening speech as though ashamed of something. You could see he'd rather be anywhere else but here where this long-haired child with big eyes was putting simple but crushing words into his skull. You could see he preferred the front lines, where the world was divided into us and them and you lived in your muscles instead of your head because matters were crystal clear and nothing was up for interpretation and there was no need to use the head at all apart from planning maneuvers, dreaming, and remembering.

I could say that the reason he let us go to Scotland was that we knocked him on his ass, that our art, the truth of it, got to him, and that he realized we really deserved to show the world that there was beauty in Bosnia, and heart, and love, and that we weren't just victims of madmen, experts at suffering, beggars crying for help, vegetating in our towns and waiting to be picked off while the world watched it on CNN. I could say that, but it wouldn't be the truth.

The truth was that he only stayed for the first play to make sure we weren't a bunch of scammers, and in that sense I guess we did our job well. In fact, the only time during that hour and a half when we did something that actually reached him had nothing to do with our art. Quite the opposite. The only thing that reached him was a mistake, a momentary absence of art in one scene when Bokal broke character and let reality become part of the make-believe world.

In the play, the character of the King rules a planet of which he's the only inhabitant, and when the Little Prince shows up the King tries to convince him to stay so he can finally have a real subject. The Little Prince quickly figures out that the guy's orders are meaningless and starts to leave. It was at that moment in the scene—right as I turned to the audience and was to deliver my "the grown-ups are certainly very odd" line that finished off each scene—when Bokal cleared his throat and boomed the following words:

"All right. You can go. You can go if Lendo lets you go."

There was a gasp in the audience.

Some people scoffed, tried to pass it off as coughing, and then quieted down. For a few moments I felt disembodied, surprised by where I was, who I was, what I wanted, why I was so sweaty. I looked through my long wet hair and saw the general's clenched jaw, his adjutants looking at him, waiting to see what he would do. He held his mouth clenched for a second longer and then his face opened and he started to laugh. He laughed with abandon, like he was alone or with friends. The rest of the audience soon safely followed suit. I remembered, then delivered, my line and began walking to another planet as Omar played the melodious theme.

The next day we were told to gather proper papers and get photographed.

Luckily and disturbingly, nobody even noticed that Ramona's Schmeiser was the real thing.

LATE JULY

Right after I had given up looking for anybody who knew Mustafa, a piece of information landed in my lap—his family's supposed address somewhere in Mejdan. I went to Omar's to get him to go with me, because Mejdan was a tough neighborhood, but he had found a bottle of paint thinner in his basement and he wanted to huff it.

"I can't go by myself, man."

"I know what can give you some courage," he said, dangling a plastic bag with a soaked rag in it in front of my face.

I saw myself: I'm crying and kissing Asja on a bridge and she turns and walks away and I try to go after her but as I run around the corner it's nighttime in a foreign city and the tumultuous skies are pouring water on me and wet I dart under the bridge and slip in the grass and fall down the embankment into the river which is frozen and I think I'm a fat child until I look down and see my camouflage pants and the cold shaft of the Kalashnikov in my hands and the walls of the roofless house I'm in are eroding with projectiles until they disappear altogether revealing a gut-dropping view of a thin distant bridge stretching from a palmy shore across the ocean into the red of the setting sun.

When the high subsided some I marched up the hill to Mejdan and found the address as though in a daze. Once there I didn't know what to do. It was hot and my mouth was dry and everything looked meaningful, so I sat on a makeshift bench across the dirt road from the property, looking at the little house, the yard.

This is where he lived.

In place of flower beds, every available piece of the yard except for the path to the front door was planted with vegetables in no discernable order. It was like a blind man had done it. There were heads of cabbage strewn among the flattened scallions, tufts of carrot hair popping out of the lettuce, bean vines overtaking the fence and squeezing the tomato plants. Three stalks of corn leaned against one another like drunken buddies. A sunflower was propped on its toes, looking for the master.

Somewhere behind me a radio murmured about no-fly zones, cease-fire agreements, and what Richard Holbrooke had said at the press conference about the Srebrenica massacre. And like that it is a week earlier and my mother wakes me up and tells me to get dressed. What are we doing? I ask, but she just says, Come with me. We go outside and she's carrying this ocher plastic bag. What's in that? I ask. Food, she says. Look, she says. I look and see a UN truck pass down Južna Magistrala and, for a second, cannot fathom what's in it. We walk closer as we watch. It disappears but another one appears—it's a convoy—and I look closer and still can't see. I see movement. Things are moving on these trucks. Here and there. We get closer, closer. Up close and we see the people, all women, so packed in the back of the open trucks that they look like solid, uniform blocks of human meat. The ones on the outside are pressed against the railing, immobile, their backs crooked, their arms jammed against their neighbors', faces made of misery, eyes made of empty. We can hear wailing. Here and there. But mostly they don't wail. They are so compressed that there isn't enough air for breathing and wailing. Just breathing. Barely. What is this? I ask. Refugees from Srebrenica, my mother says. We walk and walk, alongside. Even when the whole convoy passes us and the street is empty, we walk. We walk where they are going. To the sports arena, where I saw my share of basketball games and handball tournaments, boxing matches and humanitarian concerts. Now I can't see the parquet floors beneath the thousands of wailing women moving around like insects or sitting on yoga mats and blankets, their faces in their hands. We climb from the nose-bleed section down to the court, and the place is deafening: wailing, sobbing, sniffing, screaming, shrieking, crackling of plastic bottles of water, calling of the names of the living, calling of the names of the dead, calling of the names of God, yelping, whining, sighing, banging of fists against the floor, singing of sad songs, singing of happy songs, cursing of mothers, swearing to Gods, blowing of noses, shuffling of clothes, crying of children, crooning of lullabies, and the sounds of my heart booming in my skull. Mother kneels on a blanket. The woman she's trying to help is red. Veins bulge out of her forehead and neck. I can't watch. I turn around. I smell shit. An old invalid flops on a mat. Only arms flop. Paraplegic. Incontinent. She calls a guy's name. No one comes. I look up. The ceiling of lighting fixtures, the arena's baskets on elaborate blue, metal arms folded against it. Nobody's gonna score here for a long time.

* * *

Across the road some old-timer came out of his house, slowly, as though his shoes were too small and made of wood. He wore the black French beret that generations of Muslims traditionally wear in these parts. It was too small for his big, white head and looked clownish. He went around the house, reappeared with an ax in his hand, and painstakingly made his way to a dried-out plum tree in the corner of the yard.

Is this his grandfather?

He looked up at the tree, shook his head with sadness, put his hand against the sun-bleached trunk, and pushed at it. The treetop rustled and some brown leaves parachuted down into the yard.

His father?

Chop went the ax. The old-timer's swings were measured and slow but he knew what he was doing. Splinters of wood flew from his ax like sparks.

"*Merhaba*, grandpa," I heard myself say, and felt myself walk across the road toward him. The man turned to look who it was, then put down the ax and leaned on it like on a cane.

"*Merhaba*, son, *merhaba*."

"Time for doing some work, huh?"

"Yeah . . . we got hit this spring. One of their . . . shells. It hit right there at the base of the house, you see, and all the bullets made all kinds of mess in the yard."

"Not bullets, grandpa. They are called shrapnel."

"They're metal and they go fast and they kill and break things. They're bullets."

"Makes sense," I said.

"Of course they're bullets . . . I didn't mind the broken windows or the goat but they hit this here plum tree. Thirty years ago I put a stick no thicker than my little finger into the ground and look at it. Every winter I wrapped it in plastic. I picked bugs and worms off of it with my fingers, one by one. I scraped pigeon shit off the roof, mixed it with water, and used that to feed it. It was the best plum tree in Mejdan. But these animals . . . these mountain people . . . and look at it now."

He reached up and bent one of the small branches, which snapped off in his hand.

"Look," he said and broke it effortlessly in three places and showed me the lamentable twigs. "Nothing."

"It's not nothing," I said. "It's good firewood."

"I guess," said the old man. "My sons said the same thing but I didn't let *them* cut it. I told them, I said, I don't wanna see you near it. I thought it might pull through, you know, rejuvenate itself. God can do that. But I can't look at it anymore. Every time I see it something cracks in my chest. What a pity. Thirty-some years. Burn it up in a stove."

I shook my sympathetic head. We both stood there for some time looking up at the tree. The old-timer's eyes were wet slits, trifurcating into crow's feet.

"You don't happen to be a Nalić?" I asked him, to my own surprise.

He came closer to his side of the fence—holding down his beret as if afraid that a gust of wind might nab it off his head—and looked at me.

"Nope."

"Do you know any Nalićs?"

"I had a couple of refugees living with me, brothers."

"Mustafa?"

"Yeah, he's in the army now."

"I'm sorry, what?"

"Commando, I hear."

"Big guy, with a beard?"

"You know him?"

"I was drafted on the same day as him."

"What unit are you with?"

"I don't know. I go in September."

"Mustafa's been in the army for a year now, son."

I looked at a wristwatch I didn't have, rubbed the place where it would have been if I had one.

"When's the last time you heard from him?"

"Yesterday. He brought me some cornbread."

"I think I have the wrong Mustafa, then," I said, backing away. "I was looking for the family of the guy who died in the last shelling, at the Gate."

"You mean Bakir?"

"Who's Bakir?"

"Mustafa's brother. He died at the Gate."

"Why does the grave say Mustafa?"

"The grave says Mustafa?"

"There's a picture of Mustafa on it, too."

"Are you kidding me, son?"

"No, I swear to God, grandpa."

"I have no idea," he said. "I'll have to ask Mustafa."

My neighborhood lit up just as I was walking across a children's soccer game in the parking lot in front of my building. As soon as they saw the lights they all started to cheer and ran home to their TV sets and Atari pedals in full gallop. Three or four seconds and they were all gone. Only the boy with whose ball they were playing lingered for a moment longer to retrieve his property from under a shell-mangled Cinquecento; then he, too, disappeared into one of the vestibules.

For the first time in who knew how long I used the elevator.

When I opened the front door I could hear the pressure cooker hissing in the background already, some terrible turbo-folk music from one wing of the apartment and the demented ramblings of World Wrestling Federation's Macho Man Randy Savage from another. I knew exactly where every member of my family was and what they were doing. I also knew that there was no way of avoiding them. The only unoccupied room was my parents' bedroom and I had no desire to go in there.

I stood in the corridor by the coat hooks, trying to decide where to go. I took two steps toward the living room—where I knew my father, dressed in his sweatpants, was sitting in the rocker and hoarding the remote—then halted, and went the other way. The door to my room was ajar and I saw my brother jump, elbow first, off of a chair onto a sofa cushion on the floor. The crowd cheered loudly through the speakers, as though for him. I took a deep breath and started to go in but then just stopped and stared at a sticker on the door, a yellow and red triangle with a silhouette of a guy being struck by a serrated spear of electricity. HIGH VOLTAGE, it read. I exhaled.

The parquet floor squeaked under my right foot and I lifted it off. I stood there on one foot, staring at the sticker. I stood and I stood there. I stood breathing deeply until the door to the kitchen opened behind me and I heard my mother freeze in the doorway.

"You're home."

I put my right foot down. The parquet squeaked imperceptibly.

"What are you doing?"

I faced her. Mother was up to her elbows in flour. Her graying hair was in a ponytail, her arms chalky white.

I went up to her and kissed her cheek, said hello. She looked at me sideways.

"What's gotten into you?"

"What?"

"Listen, I think you guys will make it to Scotland."

One of the parquetry squares had a dark node and I made it appear and disappear under my white sock. A tear worked itself out of my eye and dropped two centimeters north of the node. I pressed my big toe on it. When I lifted my foot, it was gone.

"I just don't know what to do." My voice was whiny, stupid.

Mother stepped in and half hugged me, keeping her floury forearms away from my useless T-shirt.

"Let's talk about it."

"Listen," my father said from across the coffee table, "I talked to Branka today and she thinks you guys are going for sure."

On the TV was a blonde woman opening and closing her mouth into a microphone and swaying idiotically. The sound was muted.

"She didn't tell *us*," I said.

"I know," he said, condescendingly nodding his head. He couldn't help himself wanting to be important, acting like he was. I hated that. "We would like to know what your plan is."

I looked at my mother smoking in the armchair. She held my gaze but said nothing.

"What plan? If Lendo signs the passport I'll go to Scotland with everyone else."

"And then?"

"What do you mean 'and then'?"

"He talked to Ramona's father," my mother said through her personal haze.

"Ramona will stay in London after your tour," my father said.

This was no news to me. Ramona had an older sister in London and the whole troupe knew she was planning on staying in the UK. We also swore not to tell anyone about it.

"I hope you didn't tell Branka that," I said. The singer on TV finished swaying and bowed to us.

"I didn't. Her father did."

I looked at him.

"Yes, he talked to Branka and arranged everything. Branka's gonna let her stay. That's better than having to run."

"Did he have to pay for this?"

"Don't worry about that."

"What does this have to do with me?"

"I could arrange the same thing for you."

"If you want him to," my mother added.

"To stay with Ramona in London?"

"To stay in Zagreb on the way back."

"What for?"

"To get papers to go to America."

Heat came out of nowhere and I thought I was spontaneously combusting. It spread from inside out, all over me, saturating my flesh.

"Your uncle Irfan phoned earlier today," Father said. "He says you should come stay with him in California, go to college."

I thought nothing.

"So what do you think? Ismet!"

I looked at Mother, her worried eyes. "What are you thinking?"

"I don't know."

A gray-haired man was strumming a silent guitar on the screen now and the back vocalists behind him clapped their hands in unison.

"I think I want to come back," I said.

Father leaned back in his rocker and turned to the screen, his hand distractedly rubbing his face, rasping against his weak stubble. Mother took deep tokes of her cigarette. I could hear the smoke whir through the filter and into her lungs. When it came out it was silent like the TV, climbing slowly to the ceiling.

"I don't know what's smart," my father said. "Who knows how long the war will last. It can go on for years or end tomorrow."

"It will not end tomorrow," Mother said with venom.

"Why don't you want me to come back?"

"We do—" my father started.

"Because if you die on the front lines, I'll kill myself." It was Mother.

The room swung, the gray-haired man strummed his guitar, the three women behind him clapped, and the smoke billowed toward the ceiling. All things were in motion, not making a sound.

AUGUST 2

"When are you gonna call me tomorrow, goober?" Asja asked and I felt angry. It was 8 AM and we were on our favorite bench in the city park and I had just told her that there was a big chance Lendo had signed our papers—we were to find out later that morning.

Her brow was mountainous. A light breeze picked up portions of her hair and let them go, picked them up and let them go.

"Did you hear what I just said?" I asked.

"My dad'll be home all day but he usually goes to work on our car around ten o'clock," she said.

"Look at me," I said, but she wouldn't.

Instead, she put a kiss on my lips, unexpectedly, and sensing it was going to be a brief, devastating one, I leaned into it more and felt my pursed lips fight for purchase against hers, trying to protract the mellifluent contact, and then it was all over. She stood up, told me to call her tomorrow morning, and walked away forever. I watched her devolve from the flesh-to-flesh contact, to a specter down the street, her peach-colored backpack bobbing slightly, noiselessly, her hand flying up for a wave, then—foliage.

* * *

I was waiting for the County Office of Personal Documents to open. I guess I looked like a down-in-the-mouth late-blooming virgin with heartache, because the first thing Asmir said when he walked up with Bokal was:

"Why are you sad; you haven't even given it to her? By the time I was eighteen I had more pussy than salad."

He ruffled my hair like I was his fucking nephew or something and I punched his hand away.

"Get the fuck off me!"

"Whoa," he cried out, trying to shake off the pain as though it were a crab clamped to his finger.

It took me all that time to notice that Asmir had on new clothes. He sported a pair of Levi's—fake and probably made in Turkey, but crisp and jet-black and nice-looking. On top he had a striped polo shirt and in his hand was a plastic bag with more stuff. Both of them had on brand-new Converse All Stars, also fake.

"How did you get the gear?"

"Oh, our troupe was sponsored by an undisclosed German humanitarian organization today," Asmir said.

"Well, some members of it anyway," added Bokal and the two of them cackled like children.

"You got a sponsorship for the troupe and you went shopping for clothes?"

"Do you know what I had to do to secure this sponsorship?"

"What?"

"Six, no, five and a half times I had to sexually please a forty-seven-year old aid worker with pussy flaps the size of elephant's ears. I think I deserve a pair of sneakers out of it."

"Not a word about this to Branka, though," Bokal said.

"Or her sons."

To the left of the County Office was a rectangular hole that used to contain a pane of bulletproof glass but now was boarded up with a sheet of plywood. We heard some scraping coming from the inside, and the top of the sheet tipped back. Four fingers wedged themselves between the plaster and the wood on each side and the whole sheet disappeared inward, revealing the disgruntled face of a county employee, a youngish fellow with dark hair and a week's worth of stubble.

"Are you open?" Bokal asked.

"What do you think?"

As I was closest, I went to him first and gave him my ID card.

"Here to pick up my passport and the license to travel out of the country."

He snatched the ID out of my hands and disappeared inside. When he came back he held the navy blue document and a sheet of paper.

"Ten marks," he said.

I took the note out of my pocket, straightened it out, and handed it to him. He folded the piece of paper twice, stacked the ID card on top of it, put the whole thing inside the passport, and gave it to me.

Asmir stepped up next. I opened up the passport and stared at my picture. It was a little crooked, but the signature to the right of it looked official.

"Wow," I said. "I can't believe we really are going."

"I can't believe they are charging us," Bokal said. "You have ten marks to lend me?"

"Sorry, man. My old man talked to Branka and she said bring ten marks."

"Didn't I tell you we're going to Scotland?" Asmir said, holding up his passport, then spread his arms and mimed flying like a bird.

"Fuck," Bokal said. He walked up to the window and put his ID in front of the man, who just looked at it without picking it up.

"It costs ten marks to pick up the passport."

"I'll go get it; I just want to see if they approved mine."

Grimacing, the man took the ID and once more vanished into the back. Bokal turned to us.

"To tell you the truth, I don't have ten marks at home, either."

"Fuck, Bokal, why didn't you tell me? We just spent a hundred and fifty on the black market."

"I didn't know they were gonna charge us."

The man coughed to get Bokal's attention.

"Your passport is here, but your license to travel was denied on account of your being a member of the military."

"What does that mean?"

"It means that you can take this passport and wipe your ass with it, is what it means."

"What's the point of giving somebody a travel document and forbidding them to leave the country?"

"What's the point of trying to make sense of the bureaucratic lapses of an infant state in the fourth year of a devastating war?"

"So what am I gonna do now?"

"You can go home and bring me ten marks and I'll give you a worthless document. Or you can go home, take those ten marks, buy a bottle of moonshine, and drink it until the colors of the world melt off."

"I can't drink," Bokal said, changing tack. "I lost a kidney in the trenches."

The man sighed.

"Listen, if the passport is void anyway, why can't you give it to me for free?"

"Because it cost the county ten marks to print it."

"But if I don't pick it up you're gonna lose the money anyway."

"What can I say?"

"You don't have to say anything. Just close your eyes and hand me the passport and you'll never see me again."

The man shook his head and placed Bokal's ID on the sill but kept the passport. Bokal scooped it up and turned to us. For the first time ever I saw Bokal scared. He bit the nail off his thumb and spit it into the grass.

"You'll have to sneak out illegally. The passport will work outside of Bosnia."

"You think?"

"What do you think, that some embassy worker is going to call Lendo on the phone and ask him if one Bećo Bokal got permission to leave the country?"

"You're right."

"I know I'm right. Let's go to my place and get the money."

"I don't want to go all the way to Ši Selo."

"What do you want from me, Bokal? You want me to go and get it for you?"

"Hold on a sec," Bokal said and went up to the window again.

"Hey, it's me again."

"What's up?"

"You don't happen to need a pair of red Converse All Stars?"

"No, I don't."

Bokal folded his right leg and took off the sneaker without having to bend down. He presented it to the man like an expert shoe salesman.

"I just bought them at the market for twenty marks and am willing to part with them for my passport."

"I can't do that."

"Come on. These are good sneakers. And trendy."

"They're too big for me."

"They are not big. Just wear two or three pairs of socks. Winter is coming. They'll be perfect and warm."

The man started to laugh.

"What's funny?"

"You are. You're relentless."

"I need that passport."

He laughed again, shaking his head.

"All right. Put 'em up here."

Bokal took off the other sneaker and reunited it with her friend. The man gave him the passport and Bokal casually stuffed it in his back pocket.

Minutes later Asmir and I watched Bokal shuffle down the street in his black dress socks. Asmir stayed behind to wait for the rest of the troupe to show up and help out the younger ones. He reminded me that the bus was leaving at ten p.m. from the front of the National Theater building. I went home to pack.

Walking homeward I felt that I was there, putting one foot in front of the other and advancing through the familiar locality the last time in this direction for who knew how long. I felt the hardness of the sidewalk, on my heel, then on my toes, on my heel, then on my toes, and I saw my feet come down upon it, left one then right one then left one, swallowing distance, and what I felt and what I saw matched perfectly. That was how it was at first, anyway, because as soon as I started thinking, as soon as I said to myself *It's happening, you're leaving tonight*, things started to shift and not make sense. It felt like there was a charge in my chest and in my brain, and looking down I saw my feet move in their Reeboks, but all I could feel was the crushing weight of Asja's *goober*, of Mother's *I'll kill myself*, of Father's *I don't know what's smart,* of Bokal's black socks and Asmir's outstretched wings. And suddenly I walked into something. There wasn't anything in front of me that I could see—the tree-lined October Revolution Street looked the same as always—but I walked into something. I could feel the impact. For a second I felt dead and empty and couldn't help but stop moving. When I looked I saw myself from the back, walking away, carrying on. I stood there, close to the sandbagged entrance to the main bank and saw myself walking away with a purpose. It sure looked like me. It sure looked like I knew what I was getting myself into.

Then I was moving again, my sneakers swallowing meters of gray sidewalk, but something was off. Something was missing. I slowed down and turned around, and there I saw myself standing in front of the bank, unable to move, unable to catch up to me, as though there were an invisible barrier separating two possible futures that only a certain percentage of me could pass through. I wanted to stop and go back, but my own feet kept on moving.

At home Mother packed my bag, made sandwiches for the road, tightened the caps on bottles of water. Father gave me a thousand deutsche marks, and I put them in a tobacco pouch and hid them in my underwear. Mehmed kept touching me, patting my back, my forearm, his eyes different than usual, fearful with love. We all sat around in the low glow of a small neon tube and pretended nothing was changing. Father made the same ancient jokes, Mother smoked, shaking her head, Mehmed and I smiled. At nine we all walked out and through the town to the National Theater. There were a lot of people there, children and parents. They swarmed around the bus, loading it. Some families were louder than others, mothers wailing, fathers yelling last-minute instructions, jumping up and banging on the bus windows.

Once my bag was in the bowels of the bus, we, my family, quickly and quietly hugged and kissed and I climbed aboard. Quickly and quietly was the only way to say good-bye.

The back of the bus was all adult actors from the National Theater; the front of the bus was all us, Asmir's troupe. But Asmir wasn't there. And Bokal wasn't there. Branka said she didn't care. Asmir showed up a minute before the bus left and found me in my seat. He said he was staying behind to help Bokal sneak out illegally, that a friend can't leave a friend behind.

He took my hand like my mother did and said that if somehow he didn't make it to Edinburgh, he trusted me to lead the group in his stead. He said I was an artist, like himself. He then gave a short speech to the front half of the bus, said *see you in Edinburgh,* and stepped off onto the street. Doors hissed closed behind him. The bus crept ahead and a jolt went through the crowd of parents, whose hands flew up to wave and whose eyebrows went up together with their lips to cover up with smiles the fact that their hearts were descending into their stomachs.

Soon enough there was nothing but the hum of the engine and the war darkness outside the windows, and a creeping feeling that I had left something important behind.

Excerpts from Ismet Prcić's Diary
from February 2000

I'm a lizard, *mati*. Eric got married in January and I had to move out of our place. I pay a hundred dollars now for a room in my theater teacher's attic. There's no place in it where I can stand up. I crawl around like a fucking lizard. I'm a lizard.

I hate going downstairs. My teacher's kids hate me. I live on bread and peanut butter, which I keep in the room. I piss into a two-liter Mountain Dew bottle and pour it out the window when everyone's asleep. I only get out to go to classes and buy booze. I shit and shower on campus.

On weekends I take a train to San Diego. To see Melissa. Her roommates still hate me. I met one of their mothers. When I told her where I was from she said, *Oh, I didn't know there were any white people in Bosnia.* I wanted to take my gun and shoot her in the face.

Mustafa is back, *mati*. I can't get him out of my head. I spend hours daydreaming his life as I wait for mine to make sense.

I'm waiting to hear from UCSD, whether they will take me. Everything depends on that. If they let me transfer in I'll be with Melissa.

My gun tastes of ancient cutlery, *mati*, but its mouth smells of Bosnia.

(. . . the man called meat . . .)

1.

In wartime, when his country needed him the most—his shooting finger for defending, his body for a shield, his sanity and humanity as a sacrifice for future generations, his blood for fertilization of its soil—in those most pressing times, Mustafa's special forces combat training lasted twelve days. He ran the obstacle course exactly twenty-four times, he threw fake hand grenades through a truck tire from various distances exactly six times, he practiced marksmanship with an air rifle so that bullets were not wasted, he got covered with blankets and beaten by his peers for talking in his sleep at least once. He did countless push-ups and sit-ups, chin-ups and squats, lunges and curls, mindless repetitions designed not to make him fit but to break him, so that when he was, the drill sergeant could instruct him in the ways of military hierarchy and make him an effective combatant, one who was too scared not to follow orders and who would fucking die when he was told to fucking die.

At some point he was introduced to the real weapons. "This is an Uzi, this is how it works, we don't have any Uzis so just forget what you just learned. This is an LAW, this is how it's used, we only have a limited number of them and they are in the hands of people who already know how to use them, so you'll never get in contact with them, so just forget what you just learned." And so forth.

The knife guy taught him where to stick the knife for what effect and he stabbed hanging sacks of sand with people drawn on them. The mine guy showed him how to set up antipersonnel and antivehicle mines and pointed out all their deadly charms. The army doctor took a swig of plum brandy and told him that war was a giant piece of shit and that he, Mustafa, was a chunk of corn in that shit and then warned him not to come to his office again until he had a gut wound so big he could canoe right through it. That was, about, it.

In the end he got a Kalashnikov like everybody else, one clip of ammunition, one hand grenade, and one knife and was sent to the trenches with the regular army for a week, just to sample what war had to offer, to read the manual, as it were, before they decided what special unit he was fit to join.

2.

The morning was shitty and opaque, pregnant with grayness and cold moisture. A slothful, hungover rain tapped them on the shoulders as they waited for the trucks to take them to the front line. Those who were issued caps now put them on. The others just hunched, made their necks smaller, and continued to suffer the water torture.

To Mustafa it all felt, a little bit, like the first day of school or a funeral. Everybody was dressed the same, standing around, stupidly, looking at everyone else, not knowing what was appropriate. Faces were knotted with wretchedness, working too hard not to collapse, melting away from the skull bones.

Around them, the base was just waking up to the sounds of drill sergeants rampaging through the barracks. Steam was billowing out from the side of the kitchen. The guards at the gate were fucking around in their guardhouse, tossing a paper cup, laughing, as if nobody could see them through the glass. Some pigeons landed on the soccer field and strutted up and down and around, mocking military discipline.

Mustafa curled and uncurled his toes, already freezing in his oversize boots. Actually, his whole uniform was oversize and the camouflage patterns on the pants and the jacket didn't match. He had asked for a medium and they had given him an extralarge. When he complained, they made him scour the kitchen storage room with his toothbrush. Now the side pockets of his pants, which were supposed to be at his thighs, were tickling the tops of the boots. Looking down he noticed the laces were untied again. The fucking things were rigid and slippery and no knot could survive for long. He bent down, his jacket ballooning in front of him as if he had a prop belly on, and laced up.

"Your ration," somebody said behind him and Mustafa turned. This scarecrow of a soldier was handing him two packs of Ronhill, staring off somewhere with his eyes like wounds. There was something about him, a veneer of divorced guys in cheap motels on rainy afternoons, staring into swirls of wallpaper and throttled dreams.

"I don't smoke."

"Yes you do. You just don't know it yet," said the scarecrow, tossing the cigarettes on the pavement, sick of holding them in the air. He walked to an older soldier with a hood on.

Mustafa finished tying another provisional knot and picked up what was given to him.

"I swear to God, the only reason I'm fighting in this war are these shit sticks," said the man with the hood on, grinning. He dug through his pack fanatically, holding it in front of his face like a hamster. Behind him, the gate opened for four dirty trucks and a van, causing a stir.

"Well, fuck it! Now they come." He spat, putting the pack away, his fingers shaking, his eyes dying. He stood in line next to Mustafa, sighing and pouting like a toddler.

A thick man in a pristine uniform and with a fancy sidearm, the captain, stepped down from the back of the van and everybody saluted. He touched the rim of his cap casually, as if checking to see whether he had put it on at all this morning, and ordered one of the lower officers to read the list, to do his job. He lit a cigarette instead, leaned on the van, and smoked. In comparison to everybody else he looked like a soldier of some other, superior army.

A corporal with misaligned, yellow teeth shouted the last names into the morning, and corresponding soldiers climbed into the trucks. When he was done Mustafa was still standing at attention.

"What's the problem, Private?" asked the captain, walking up to him, letting the smoke come out of his nose like an angry dragon.

"I did not hear my name called, sir."

"Did you listen for it?"

"Yes, sir."

"Bring me that list!" He motioned to the corporal like he was going to kick his ass. "And you give me your ID."

Mustafa handed him his military card. The captain started

scanning the clipboard and in no time found a match. He flogged him with a stare, then chucked the document right into Mustafa's face.

"Get your ass on that truck! I didn't hear my name called, sir! Next time open your fucking ears!"

Mustafa ran to the closest truck but found it full.

"And don't you think I'll forget about this! I'm like a fucking elephant!"

There was no room on any of the trucks. Mustafa turned around in confusion.

"What is it now?"

"There's no room, sir."

"Well, I guess you'll have to ride with me."

3.

The back of the van had no side windows, just the little one up front that looked into the back of the driver's rotund head, and two on the back doors. It was hot in there and dark and humid and noisy. The captain slept, sprawled over two seats like Caesar, his heaving belly testing the limits of his shirt's buttons. The corporal sat like a robot, suffering through his life with conditioned mindlessness and fatalism that was intolerable. There was barely anything behind his gaze, anything alive anyway. Mustafa held his shit together in the midst of this.

The radio was garbled, its voices extraterrestrial, aloof, ill. The tires made out with the asphalt, making that constant slurping sound. Raindrops banged covetously on the thin metal roof. The captain woke himself up, looked around, licked his seemingly salty lips, and then closed his eyes again. It was then that Mustafa noticed that his boot was untied again. It was only the left one this time. At first he was going to let it be, since he didn't have to walk for a while and he was fed up with tying them all the time, but the little insects of compulsion gnawed at his thoughts, reminding him that untied laces were in an unnatural state, that the universe ached because of it, that he had to do something about that.

As he bowed down, all he realized was that it got lighter in the van, and that there was a tug on the front of his jacket and shirt, a lover's tug when she feels horny and wants you closer to her. His fingertips reached the laces as the sound arrived, a sound so big it changed the density of things, and the air became solid like Plexiglas, trapping him, freezing him. It was like God decided to show Itself, and the fabric of reality wasn't made to bear it, so it gave way, accommodating. Only Mustafa's thoughts, the little monkeys of free will, still darted all over the place, and he remembered having crippling abdominal pain when he was a kid and how he was scared to tell anyone because he thought he would die if he did, and how his mother would sing to him his favorite lullaby, the one about Grandpa's house, and how that one time when his dad took him to a soccer match, he couldn't see anything because everybody would stand up in anticipation whenever a team had a chance to score, and the terrible paralysis he fell victim to when a girl asked him out in a dark passageway through a building that smelled of human waste and burning matches, and just how much he hated this kid Vlado, and his thin, freaky, witchy fingers . . .

4.

No, Mustafa didn't die.

5.

It was a 120 mm mortar shell, discharged at random in the direction of the town in order to keep the populace up-to-date and in fear. It hit by the side of the road just as the van was passing. The denser the surface a shell hits the bigger the devastation, since the shell gets to explode aboveground, giving its shrapnel wider range. It so happened that the rain had been falling for days, turning soil to muck. It missed the cement kilometer marker by a foot, submerged itself in the mud, and did its thing. Most pieces of it were channeled upward, giving the nearby treetop a frontal lobotomy, but a few found their way to the van. One ripped apart the front right tire, one smashed the passenger side window, wedging itself in the lining of the cabin roof above the driver's head, one took out the muffler for good, and one made a pencil-size slit in the side of the van, went through Mustafa's jacket, ripped up the front of his shirt without touching him, went through the jacket again, and exited through a hole the size of a coin.

When he saw the holes for what they were, Mustafa couldn't think anymore. Heady elation was in the air, as if he were frozen in the middle of a sneeze. He touched the hot skin of his abdomen and began to laugh.

6.

"And this is your first day?"

"Yes, sir," Mustafa said with a smile that was strained, a little too wide. His hands did a drumroll in the air, culminating in the noiseless crescendo of an imaginary cymbal. He put his hands on his knees for a split second, and then flung them up again, somewhere above him, like he was trying to catch something.

"I don't know if you're lucky or doomed," said the captain, mixing up a deck of playing cards with naked women on them, trying to hypnotize him, calm him down with his voice and the slow, repetitive shuffling. They were sitting at a wooden table under a ribbed, plastic roof in someone's front yard, waiting for the driver and the corporal to change the tire. Mustafa's knees jumped up and down with adrenaline. His face got pulled this way and that, unconsciously. Every once in a while he chuckled like a lunatic.

"Do I look like a doomed man?" asked Mustafa in a voice that pushed the limits of a private-officer relationship. The captain let it slide, though obviously miffed.

"You're in shock," the captain said. "We'll play poker and get your mind focused."

"There's nothing wrong with me," Mustafa said. He laughed, uncontrollably opening and closing his fists.

"Put a gun in those hands and you're a liability."

Mustafa tried to stop fidgeting and found it impossible. He chuckled, looking at his hands, sprightly entities with minds of their own.

"I'll deal first," the captain said in a deliberate monotone.

"What are we playing for? You can't play poker just for shits and giggles." It was apparent that Mustafa couldn't help talking that way. There was so much energy just being wasted off him. The captain swallowed.

"We can play for smokes."

"Yeah! I don't even smoke, man, but you won't either by the time I'm done with you! You won't have any cigarettes." He laughed a little too hysterically and a little too long. The captain did his best to hold in his annoyance, but what came out still sounded harsh.

"Pay attention here!"

He slammed his palm on the wooden surface, attracting Mustafa's gaze to it, and dealt.

7.

An hour later the tire was replaced, they were on the road again, and the captain had lost all his cigarettes and his deck of cards. There was nothing to be done about the muffler, and sitting in the back of the van was like being inside a jackhammer. The captain's forehead was ridged with irritation as Mustafa kept looking at him and shrugging as though apologizing for his good luck. The captain turned his head away and reached for a nonexistent pack in his pocket.

"I need a smoke, Private," he said.

"Too bad you lost them all," Mustafa replied, dismissing the captain's outstretched hand, which presently started to tremble.

"What did you say?"

"I said too bad you lost."

The captain's eyes shrank, squeezed down by his overactive brow, suggesting waves of pain issuing from somewhere within his skull. For a long moment he was speechless. His military demeanor left him and he suddenly looked like a salesman or a high school teacher. Mustafa was cool and detached, acting like his superior.

"But you don't even smoke," was what he said, "and look at my hands."

Mustafa rolled up his sleeve and showed him his arm.

"Look. I got all goose-bumpy from how much I care," he said and watched the dumbfounded captain soundlessly open and close his mouth.

8.

When the racket of the van with the busted muffler got replaced by the far more dangerous clamor of the front line and thunder, when the giddy energy became plain horror as the shock caught up with him, when he marched in a line into a cluster of faceless houses with their eyes gouged out and their brains spilled, the debris of their caved-in skulls all over the grass, Mustafa knew that he really did smoke but just didn't know it yet. The rain fell in self-perpetuating ropes that looked like you could climb them all the way up to God's leaky basement; the soldiers' faces drooped, as well as their mismatched uniforms. The captain had his power back, barking over the explosions, not flinching as the wandering bullets zinged into drainpipes and thudded into brick. He designated which house was the preliminary command post and started calling the names of the first shift of soldiers to replace the ones in the trenches. Mustafa expected his name to be found on that list, after everything that had happened, but it turned out he was wrong.

The captain had a different plan. He ordered the second and third shifts to take cover in the houses until it was their time to man the trenches, pointing specific groups to specific houses. When it came down to Mustafa, he personally led him to a roofless, shelled-to-shit summer kitchen right between the rest of the houses and the trenches up the hill, its walls eroding from rain and projectiles.

"You're in here!" the captain yelled over the explosions. "Alone!"

Mustafa looked through the empty socket of a window and saw a knee-deep pond of water covering the entire floor. It was deafening in there from the sound of water hitting water. He turned to the captain.

"I wasn't issued a tarp, sir."

The captain smirked, rolled up his sleeve to reveal his non-existent goose bumps; he showed him how much he cared.

9.

By nighttime, leaning against a wet wall in his heavy, wet uniform, Mustafa was coughing a heavy, wet cough. There was something wrong with his mind, too, and he kept mumbling songs that wouldn't leave his head and dozing into hallucinatory dreams. He kept seeing scenes from someone else's life intermixed with his own, confusing him: two mothers, two fathers, a sibling, a watercolor of an overcast day above a swollen Russian river on the dining room wall, the corner of its frame chipped. His lips were chapped from fever and he kept licking them. In the midst of all that water, and being chiefly made of water himself, Mustafa was feeling dry.

"Third shift!" someone yelled into the night. He came to and peeled himself from the wall, shivering.

10.

He slept in the trench, sitting on a birch log, his rifle across his knees, dreaming of a play he was in, how something was wrong with the rigging and how the lighting fixtures kept crashing down. He woke up every once in a while when the other three soldiers in the trench with him fired an occasional burst up the hill and swore at the enemy. They mostly left him alone, seeing the state he was in, and kept playing cards under a tarp. Refa, the guy in charge, gave him an aspirin and a swig of a deadly alcoholic beverage out of a flask, something homemade and terrible.

Around three in the morning Mustafa hallucinated a man with a beard jumping into the trench. Only when he closed his eyes and opened them again, the man was still standing there, pale like a limestone slab, trembling. His eyes were raw and he was holding his rifle by the barrel, sniffling in the cold air. Mustafa didn't know what to make of him, so he just looked on, flabbergasted.

"I came to give myself up," the man said. The sentence lingered. Slowly, Mustafa's brain kicked into gear.

"Are you a Chetnik?" he asked without moving.

"Yeah," said the man.

Mustafa jumped to his feet, fumbling to flip off the safety. A huge head rush made him blind for a second and he almost lost consciousness. When the world faded back in, the man was holding him up, helping him.

"I came to give myself up."

Mustafa brushed away his hands and regained balance on his own. He turned the rifle on the man and just stood there, not knowing what to do. His heart drummed fast, pounding in every part of his body, it seemed.

"Where do you want me?" the man asked, still trembling.

Mustafa didn't know, so he ushered him at gunpoint to Refa and the other two. Refa was hammered. The other two were almost there. They didn't even notice their approach.

"Refa," Mustafa called and swallowed. He barely found any voice.

"What's up, rookie?"

"Look here."

Refa turned around and noticed the man. There was a dumb silence all around.

"Who's that?" he asked, holding his hand against his chest, hiding his cards.

"A Chetnik," Mustafa said.

"Where did you get him?"

"He just jumped in."

"I came to give myself up," the man said. Refa looked at him like he was insane.

"What's your name?"

"Nebojša."

"Nebojša what?"

"Nebojša Banjac."

"How did you get here, Nebojša?"

"I crawled."

"Through the minefield?"

Nebojša's eyes grew wide and glassy. He had no idea. Refa started to laugh and turned back to the other two soldiers and their game. They laughed, shaking their heads, and continued playing as if nothing had happened, as if there were no enemy combatant in their trench, holding his gun by its barrel and trembling. Mustafa stood there fighting an urge to vomit. His heart pounded circles around itself.

"What now?" he managed.

"Take him down to the command post," Refa said without

turning. At the prospect of really doing this, Mustafa couldn't hold it in anymore and started to spew a pale, acidy liquid.

"That man is sick," Nebojša said. "He's in no state to do anything."

"What are you, a doctor?" asked one of the gamblers with a sneer.

"Yes I am, as a matter of fact."

Refa put his cards facedown on the trunk in front of him and stood up. He swayed over to Mustafa, looking like a man who was told that he had to take out the garbage right in the middle of his game on TV.

"Hey rookie, you want another aspirin?"

Mustafa dumped another load of vomit into the mud. Refa sighed, pinched the fabric of Nebojša's uniform at the shoulder, led him to the trench leading downhill, and pointed into the night.

"Okay, Dr. Banjac. This is what you're gonna do. See that big house that looks a little bit like a skull? The white one? That's the command post. You're gonna go down there, you're gonna find the officer in charge, and you're gonna tell him that Refa sent you and that you're giving yourself up. Okay?"

Nebojša swallowed hard. Even the little color he still had in his face was now gone.

"By . . . myself?"

"Don't be afraid. It's gonna be fine."

"I'll get shot."

"You're not gonna get shot. Just tell them that Refa sent you."

He gave him a little push in the back. Nebojša made a timid step and halted again.

"What should I do with my gun?"

"Just bring it with you. What am I gonna do with it?"

"But they'll kill me if they see me with a gun."

There were tears streaming down Nebojša's face now. He tried to hold them in but couldn't. A glob of snot oozed out of his right nostril and he sniffled it back in.

"They won't kill you. Trust me. Just tell them that Refa sent you."

This time he had to push him a little harder to get him going. Nebojša headed down, focusing on the skull and sobbing. He held his rifle with two fingers only, as far away from himself as possible, and kept on sobbing.

Refa returned to the game and Mustafa puked again.

11.

The next day Refa, Nebojša and Mustafa were reunited. The truck that brought the food to the trenches also brought two military policemen, who proceeded to arrest Refa for being drunk on duty and needlessly endangering fellow soldiers' lives by sending an armed enemy into the command post without prior notification.

"I told him to tell them that I sent him," Refa said, defending himself in a raspy voice while being led, handcuffed, onto the truck. "He could have killed us all in the trench if he wanted to. But he didn't. He wanted to give himself up, man. Tell them!"

But by then, Nebojša, who was already on the truck in his own pair of handcuffs, sitting like a God-fearing man before an altar, with his hands interlocked, crushed by the vise of his knees, didn't feel like talking much. He moved his pale face a little to the left, as if considering whether or not to look at Refa and respond, then sniffled, and went on staring down at his boots. He looked like he was dead already and waiting for the afterlife.

The MPs brought the unconscious Mustafa on board on a stretcher, his rifle between his legs, his face ablaze with fever; you could light a cigarette on his cheek. They set him down like a repossessed dresser and gave the driver the green light to go. Refa kept demanding justice, demanding to be heard out, explaining himself. His face was bloated with hangover, his wrinkles fat and deep, his sense of self-preservation relentless. The MPs told him to save it for the judge, that if it had been up to them he would have already been wearing his wooden kimono.

They went back and forth like that, the decibel level increasing: who would do what to whom if they weren't handcuffed, who would do whose mother, how and in what location. It would have probably ended in blood had Nebojša not screamed for them to shut up. They turned to him with their faces suddenly vacant and agape.

"This man is dying!" Nebojša said. "If we don't bring down his fever he'll suffer brain damage."

It took the MPs several seconds to regain their attitude.

"What do you know, cunt face?" snarled one of them.

"No, no," Refa interrupted. "He knows. He's a doctor."

They all looked down at Mustafa's burning face and his cracked, gibbering lips, telling them, in their own hallucinatory ways, perplexing accounts of what was new in the borderlands.

12.

What was to be his introduction-to-combat week turned out to be just a week, one spent in a squeaky, collapsible bed, one spent without electricity, with nothing to read, and with insipid lentil soup. He slept there among the amputees, whose phantom limbs itched, and among crazies, who screamed and screamed and screamed. It was there, in the swarming military hospital, that Mustafa started to smoke, and no nurse or doctor discouraged him or stopped him from doing it; nobody gave a shit about that.

13.

On a Saturday afternoon, a letter in an official army envelope came by a courier and Mustafa didn't realize it was for him, even though he found it lying on his pillow. Nobody wrote to him ever and he naturally assumed it was some kind of a mistake. He tossed it onto the mangled crate serving as his bedside table, meaning to tell the nurse to take it to its rightful owner. Then he went out into the corridor for a smoke. He didn't have to do that—everybody smoked in the room—but the guy next to the window had started screaming again, yelling for someone named Steamboat not to leave him behind, for God's sake not to leave him behind. Mustafa felt much better with a width of the door between him and that sound.

When he came back the soldier on the bed next to him with a shrapnel hole in his cheek and no left hand shook his head slowly, fearfully, and said:

"You're fucked, man. I'm sorry."

This came out somehow wet and muffled, as most of his teeth had been shattered by shrapnel. The lines of his face were deep, pointing downward, disfiguring him. He made a movement, like a shrug, and it looked so grotesquely saturated with pity that it froze Mustafa at the door. The man's

211

elbow and what was left of his forearm were bandaged so heavily it looked like he had a hand puppet on, one with a turban atop which a blood-colored fez was showing through.

"Apaches are sent to the worst fronts. Their life expectancy is like two weeks. Look at our screamer. He was an Apache," the amputee went on, his stump bobbing through the air, trying to help out the words.

"What are you talking about?" Mustafa asked, still at the door. The guy next to the window abruptly stopped screaming and somebody thanked God.

"The letter. You're transferred to the Apache unit."

"That's not my letter."

14.

Apaches were young and crazy. They wore bandanas and rock 'n' roll T-shirts and their faces were like warrior masks, painted in swirls of green and black and brown. Their eyes were blank from the things they saw, from experience, and there was dirt under their fingernails, and blood, and war. Some of them were nothing but bone and gristle; others still had baby fat in their cheeks and on the back of their necks. One they called Ninja carried a samurai sword across his back and never said a word. Another one called the Claw had a small crossbow and couldn't shut up. Sooty always had his hand inside his pants. Steamboat was like an old American gas hog packed inside a European two-door sedan. They were all like something.

Apaches didn't salute and the captain couldn't make them. They didn't have to stand at attention or be neat or shave or button up—none of that mindless discipline bullshit. All they had to do was complete insane missions or die trying.

"What's this?" the Claw asked the captain, standing in front of Mustafa, looking right at him. His irises fluttered upward, and he blinked several times in order to bring them down again; it was a tic. Mustafa's gaze fell to the barn floor littered with sheep bonbons. The Claw's breath was rancid.

"That's my present to you," the captain said without even a slight nod of the head toward Mustafa, like he wasn't worth even that much. He was hunched over what seemed to be an old refrigerator encased in a shoddy wooden box and tipped on its side. There was a map on top of it.

The Claw shook his head disgustedly and his tic took control of his face again. He looked like an android taking a second to process new information. Mustafa felt obliged to say something since the Claw was in his space, standing too close, breathing out clouds of rottenness.

"I'm Mustafa," he said, trying to sync his breath with the Claw's, so he didn't have to smell him.

"No you're not," the Claw whispered into his ear so matter-of-factly that Mustafa seriously reconsidered whether he really was who he claimed to be. He wanted to back up, but the space behind him was occupied with something solid, a barn wall. The Claw came so close that at one point his lip touched the shell of Mustafa's ear, sending a peculiar shiver down his leg.

"Mustafa is the name of somebody who's either dead or alive. My grandfather's name was Mustafa. He's dead. Right now you're neither. Your name is Meat. All the rookies are called Meat until further notice. My name was Meat. If and when you survive your first two weeks you'll get your proper

Apache name. We don't want to get, you know, attached to a cadaver-to-be. If you're wondering, why me, how did I end up with these lunatics, what did I do to deserve this, those are all legitimate questions which you have to ask the command or God or yourself. All I can tell you is I'm sorry, that's how your beans fell."

In Bosnian this last sentence rhymed: *Meni je žao, al' tako ti je grah pao,* sort of a fatalistic little rhyme illustrating one's lack of power in the ways of the universe. The Claw smiled, but not with his eyes, and gathered around the map with the rest of the unit. The captain talked about the mission, where he thought their positions were, how many of them, where the minefields were, and what the best tactic was to retake the village on the plateau up the hill. He wasn't briefing them. He was discussing. The Apaches stood around him like equals, although they were technically just privates. Sooty played pocket pool right smack in the middle of it and Mustafa just stood there stuck to the wall, his mind elsewhere, trying to cope, as the Claw's last sentence kept playing in his head to a jolly but creepy little tune:

Meni je žao, al' tako ti je grah pao!
Meni je žao, al' tako ti je grah pao!
Meni je žao, al' tako ti je grah pao!
Meni je žao, al' tako ti je grah pao!
Meni je žao, al' tako ti je grah pao!

15.

Mustafa spent the rest of the day and the night that followed in a state of catatonia, forgetting even to smoke. He walked around, sporadically communicating with the members of his new unit, but it all felt both distant and familiar, like he was dreaming about something that had already happened, like he was watching himself do things on tape. When the feeling dissipated and the world sharpened up, it was dawn already and the turbulent sky was about to take a giant wet shit and the Apaches were about to advance up the hill with an enormous yellow bulldozer, and that meant Mustafa had to do it with them.

The army had no tanks, and this particular situation demanded a relatively unstoppable vehicle that could take a few hits and behind which the infantry could move forward and take cover. Somebody thought of a bulldozer. The Claw, who was to drive the monster, had raised its scoop or blade or whatever it's called in front of the cabin as a shield. Sooty lay on its roof, where he had previously mounted a heavy machine gun. The rest started crowding up behind it, checking their weapons in silence.

For a second Mustafa thought it was all just a joke, an elaborate one to scare the rookie named Meat and make him shit his pants. He kept expecting everyone to start laughing and tell him it was all just an initiation joke, an Apache ritual every member had to go through. Instead, the old yellow behemoth awoke with a diesel roar, coughed up black smoke, and started around the barn and up the hill. Mustafa didn't move. There was no power inside of him, as though someone had taken out his batteries. He would have just stayed there behind the barn if Steamboat hadn't noticed him, run up, grabbed the back of his neck, and pushed him into the group. Mustafa stumbled forward, ricocheted between the Apaches until he slammed against the back of a slow-moving vehicle, and was told to stay there and keep up.

Sooty opened cover fire and so did the regular army from the trenches. The enemy woke up from their early-morning slumber and started to respond. The Claw stepped on the gas. Apaches cried their eerie battle cries. The bulldozer went over the first antipersonnel mines, which burst under its undercarriage, causing no damage. Bullets hit its metal bulk, sounding like a fast rhythm machine possessed by the ghost of a virtuoso jazz drummer. The skies opened up, pouring rain over all these silly creatures, and Mustafa just kept up behind the hulk, doing nothing but running and having not a single thought in his mind.

16.

He was not there.

His legs did run behind the bulldozer, and his hand did throw a grenade into the enemy trench, and his right index finger did squeeze off a few bursts to cover Ninja's advance, and when everything got quiet, his eyes did see dead Chetniks with holes in them, and his lungs did push air up through his windpipe, and his voice box did shape itself to turn his breath into a battle cry to match the cries his ears did hear coming from his fellow soldiers all around. Fellow Apaches.

And up in the village his heart did sink when his pupils witnessed children's heads atop picket fences, crosses carved into the heads of women with missing ring fingers, their bodies rotting in a pile by the community well. His stomach did turn at the sight of a hog burying its snout into a pond nearby, red with human blood and chalky with filth. His tears did flow, and his tongue did swear, and his brain did realize that the Claw was right, that what was standing there in hell, seeing this, looking around in disbelief, crying, dying, wasn't anything but meat.

But he was not there in the meat. No way.

17.

He snapped back into the meat only after the side of Steamboat's head exploded with a high-caliber sniper slug, and the Claw yelled, "Ambush! Retreat!" and then called him by his real name, to help him carry Steamboat's meat down to the trenches, since no man was ever to be left behind.

He called him Mustafa and that was who he was.

(. . . on the road
to edinburgh . . .)

PATHETICA

In the moonlight, from the moving bus, Tuzla seemed monochromatic and unoccupied. Dark windows gaped and gawked out of
gray facades. Forsaken sedans with tarps thrown over them looked
like full body bags. It all looked like stock footage from a late-night
History Channel documentary about some sad thing that happened
elsewhere a long time ago.

The interior of the bus was silent and ghostly, like a fever dream
of being on a bus. Familiar faces were off just enough that you
weren't quite sure if you knew them or not, if the people to whom
they belonged, your friends, were really sitting around you or if you
were imagining them, badly, to make yourself feel better.

We drove past the soccer stadium and came upon Asja's street.
With my forehead pressed against the vibrating glass, I imagined I
could see through two buildings and into her room, where her moon-
washed body lay awake touching itself and thinking of me. A part
of me then rebelled against this fantasy, cringed at the cheesiness,
at my own *pathetica. Wake up, you're leaving her, you asshole.* But
quickly I imagined my heroic homecoming sometime from now: me
walking up her street in daytime and in color, entering her building,

ringing her doorbell, her opening the door, and me catching her in my arms just before she faints from happiness. *You're doing the right thing. . . . No, you're a loser,* I said to myself, *a pussy.*

We passed the alien skyline of Tuzla's industrial zone, looped around the Šićki Brod loop, and hooked toward Kladanj. Five minutes out of town and we were farther from home than we had been since the war started.

CHECKPOINT

I dreamed of a man stomping on baby raccoons in a crate, and when I woke up the bus was stopped and a soldier of some variety was checking papers up front. Omar was next to me, listening to what sounded like drizzle in his Walkman. I nudged him.

"Checkpoint," he said too loudly over the noise in his ears. The soldier glanced in our direction, then approached the next row of seats.

I heard the crinkling of a plastic bottle in the seat behind me, a quick slosh of liquid, and then the sound of someone twisting the cap back on. Omar and I were in the middle of the bus on the line of separation between Asmir's troupe and the Bosnian National Theater troupe, twenty or so adult professionals occupying the back half of the bus. A faint smell of plum brandy drifted to me. Omar smelled it, too, pointed back and tipped an imaginary bottle to his mouth. We smiled.

The soldier neared. The rifle hanging from his shoulder was old but real. I reached for my passport but it wasn't in my pocket. A surge went through me and I panicked and started to dig through my backpack. Omar tapped my shoulder and showed me that he had both his and mine.

"You scared the shit out of me," I said.

He pulled off his headphones and the drizzle became the familiar three-chord progression of a Ramones song.

"We passed three checkpoints while you slept," he said.

"Oh."

It was our turn and Omar handed the soldier our passports. He glanced at the pictures, then stared into our faces. His eyes were like puncture holes in a mask.

"Where are we?" I heard myself cheerfully ask.

"In your mother's cunt," the soldier said and threw the passports into Omar's lap.

STUPIDITY ON SHRAPNEL HIGHWAY

The bus was winding its way up a mountain road. Outside, the only visible thing was a jagged line of demarcation between the solid blackness of the dense conifers and the watery dark of the void above it, pockmarked somewhat with faint, throbbing stars. Omar was slumped in his seat as if shot, sleeping. Someone was snoring all the way in the back. I was thinking about my mother, pushing my head against the window, trying to get its vibration to shake my thoughts loose.

The road began to level out when the bus slowed down. A squeal of feedback came from all the speakers. The driver announced that for the next couple of kilometers he had to turn off the headlights. He said that we were coming upon a plateau that was clearly visible to the Chetniks and that among the bus drivers this stretch of the road was known as Shrapnel Highway.

The bus crept ahead blindly in the moonlight. The guy behind me, a man in his fifties with a Super Mario mustache, sloshed another swallow of slivovitz. He cleared his throat and it sounded like somebody choking on vomit. After that, things grew quiet, eerie.

I looked across our row of seats, saw Omar, Boro, and Ramona all awake, overwrought, all awaiting the future.

Then Super Mario lit a cigarette.

A collective gasp rippled through the bus and abruptly died. Everyone stopped breathing.

"Put that shit out!" hissed the driver through the speakers.

Omar stood up, reached over his back support, and snatched the cigarette out of the man's mouth. He took a quick toke from it and then squashed it into a built-in ashtray in front of him. We looked at each other for one, two, three, four seconds when something hit the side of the bus, a tinny crisp crack like a small rock hitting a windshield. One of the girls in front of us screamed. The driver swore and the engine roared like this was a jet and we were clear for takeoff. Velocity pushed my head into the back support.

The kids screamed and screamed and the bus careened insanely through the blackness of the world.

WRONGFULLY ACCUSED

In Kladanj we parked near a mosque whose minaret was missing its tip, an imitation of a snapped pencil. Nobody in the bus was hurt. The driver, his partner, Branka, and the president of the National Theater all went out with flashlights to check out the damage. Their beams found a single bullet hole high in the window above me.

My fear turned liquid in my stomach and I suddenly needed to piss it away. I went to the front and stuck my head out of the bus.

"I need to go to the toilet," I said. The driver shined his beam on me.

"*Hajvanu*, you almost got us all killed," he said flailing his arms, his flashlight unveiling random details in the night, a hole in a wire fence of the house next to the mosque, an overturned traffic pylon leaning on a curb, a black galosh.

"You're lucky they didn't use mortars, you fucking idiot."

I stepped into the street. The night was solid. A river gurgled somewhere. I walked past the four of them toward a shed flanked by some shrubbery.

"It was Super Mario who lit that cigarette," I said.

The shrubbery turned out to be nettles. I pissed in the nettles.

THE PRESIDENT V. THE CONVOY

Creeping down a narrow, precarious dirt road chiseled into the side of a mountain, with the right side of the bus scraping the vegetation growing out of the toothed wall and the left side shaving the edge of an imponderable abyss, I realized I'd been here before. The only difference was that now I was going in the opposite direction. It was Tuzla's only artery, the road my family took to sneak back into the city at the beginning of the war, the road where my mother had her déjà vu, where she hung that bottle of cognac within reach in case we got stopped by the wrong kind of soldiers, where all the passengers had to get out of the bus and help push it up the hill. Here it was three years later and the wear and tear from traffic had made the road even more dangerous, though this time around we at least had a better bus.

The headlights illuminated a clump of makeshift road signs somebody nailed into the trunk of a tree, one on top of the other. All of them were pointing in the direction we were going except one plank that said TUZLA. The others said LONDON, PARIS, NEW YORK, NEW DELHI, TOKYO, ROME, MUNICH, ZURICH, SYDNEY. It was a joke. This was the only way out of the siege.

The brakes squeaked. The engine rumbled. Branches chafed the glass from outside.

Turning a corner we came face-to-face with another pair of head-lights and stopped. The driver got off the bus. He had to hug the side of it so he wouldn't tumble down the mountain. He yelled things in Bosnian and somebody else yelled things in another language. When the two men stepped into the headlights, I saw that the other one was a UN soldier. There was a baby blue beret on his head. They talked and gesticulated and you could see that nothing was being communicated really.

The president of the National Theater, a tall, bombastic man with a shock of upstanding black hair, stood up and made his way to the front.

"I'm gonna goout and takecare of this," he said, but then stumbled and fell to one knee, barely keeping his head from hitting one of the seats. "Fucking fuck!"

Like Super Mario, he was hammered.

"We need someone who speaks English," Branka said, pretending to help him up.

"Are you saying I can't say . . . I can't talk English? To the gentle-man in the blue hat."

"I'm saying you'll fall off this cliff," she said.

"I'm in charge here!" His thumb thumped against his barrel chest.

As this was going on, Ramona slipped past him and went out. She interpreted for the driver and soon they were both back aboard. The president was leaning over Branka's seat and boasting about his engineering degree.

"What is this?" the driver asked. The president flipped around.

"I demand to know whatsgoingon."

"Go and sit down, man. We have to go back."

"*I* decide wherewego. And *I* say we go straight through those fuckingBrits. Make *them* turnaround."

"First of all, that is a humanitarian convoy and there is no way *they* can back up on this road. We have to. Second of all, if you don't go and sit down in your seat I will kick you off this bus."

The driver was two feet shorter than the drunken man and fifteen years older, but I had no doubt he was capable of walking the walk.

"D'you know who you're talking to?" the president asked, pointing at the driver's face. But before he could continue, a drained blonde, his secretary, materialized next to him, hugged his neck, and took him away. He swore and mumbled his outrage.

Branka chortled deliciously.

The driver put the bus in reverse and it labored up the hill like a shit bug. I gripped the arm on the side of my seat and prayed. Omar had his eyes closed and his music on, but I was pretty sure he was praying, too. Some four to five hundred meters back we found a wide spot in the road to tuck the bus in. We parked close to the wall and watched trucks and armored vehicles go by for a long time. They were so close to us we could see inside their cabins, into their lives.

The penultimate truck clipped our side mirror with its own. Ours gave way at the base but the glass itself didn't break. The whole thing dangled on some wires.

The president laughed hysterically from the back.

BOSNIA, HERZEGOVINA, CROATIA

Out of the night, we rolled down into the limestone crags of Herzegovina. As soon as it cleared the horizon, the sun broke out whitely over everything and everyone started to sweat. Outside, the rivers turned fluorescently emerald. Tall, smooth trees hunched down and grew smaller and gnarly. Limestone houses became indistinguishable from the surroundings, and the sky descended upon the world in a serious way.

From a distance half of the city of Mostar looked as if a berserk giant had stomped it into rubble. It shut us all up. Tuzla looked untouched in comparison. I saw half of a skyscraper standing upright and the other, broken-off half upside down next to it. If you saw it in a movie you'd find it unconvincing, cartoonish.

There were more and more checkpoints and we had to wait longer and longer to pass through. At the border crossing, the Croatian soldiers gave us dirty looks, made us take all our stuff out of our bags and onto the asphalt, made us stand in the sun for hours, and then sit in the bus with the windows closed. But we all had valid transit visas stapled to our passports and they had to let us through.

When they did, you could feel the change of pressure, as though the air in Bosnia were really a liquid. We went across an invisible line and I felt giddiness and élan in my legs, felt like I could have dunked. The younger of our troupe members broke into a song, the staple song of elementary school field trips, urging the driver to overtake everyone in front of him. What was it we were feeling? Freedom?

THE BEACH INVASION

The first sighting of the Adriatic was cheered like a victory. There were enthusiasts even in the back of the bus, hooting and singing along with the children. One of these professionals yelled, "Cheers!" and the driver threatened to stop and made an official announcement about no drinking on his bus.

We snaked across the arid hills, in between crumbling rocks, through sun-bleached conifer groves and orchards until the hills parted and we fell upon the blue. We stopped in the first town, at the first beach next to a long dock that cut a block of white into the blue, and when the doors opened we ran out screaming—the younger half of the bus, anyway. The air smelled of pines and seaweed and fish guts, and we ran through the pine needles of a small park and crunched onto the pebble beach, leaned on twisted trunks of olive trees long enough to get rid of our sneakers and shoes, then hobbled like geriatrics over the hot pebbles, causing quite a ruckus among the natives there. They all perked up their heads from their beach towels and gathered their children and stared at these screaming lunatics who ran past them, shedding clothes, exposing cheese-white bellies and backs, and clambering like large insects onto the cement dock.

I was the first one up there in my tighty-whities, screaming giddily, staring one moment at the blue sky, the next at my white feet slapping the hard surface of the white cement, until the whiteness ended abruptly in a horizontal line and I found myself airborne above the blue, beneath the blue, in the blue and going up, up, up. I swear to God I would have been the first human to really fly had I not remembered, going up into the blue like that, that all my money was rolled up in a tobacco pouch hanging next to a pouch of another kind in my underwear.

CRIMES AGAINST SUPER MARIO

On the way north to Zagreb—another night was already upon us —Omar and I decided that, in theory, Super Mario wouldn't be opposed to sharing some booze with us. In practice, though, Omar made sure that both he and his seatmate were asleep. He asked them questions and threw little wads of newspaper at their faces. When they seemed to be dead to the world I lay on the floor, reached under my seat, and retrieved Super Mario's bag. In it were three two-liter plastic bottles of brandy (one almost empty and the other two full), an eroded loaf of bread, two cans of humanitarian corned beef, and a handful of bruised tomatoes in a sack.

At first we were going to just take huge gulps and put the booze back, but when I saw that one of the full bottles was identical to one of the bottles of water my mother prepared for me before I left, I just switched them out making sure to put the water on the bottom of his bag so he wouldn't find out for a while. I returned the whole thing between the man's feet where I found it and Omar and I got ourselves drunk, cracked some ridiculous jokes, and were the only ones laughing. Periodically, I took my English dictionary out of the backpack and checked on the status of my money. The notes kept being almost dry.

JOINT ENDEAVORS

We spent that night at the Zagreb University dorms and in the morning, some of us hungover and groggy, went to the British embassy on Vlaška Street to apply for visas. Branka and the president were snippy with each other, each acting like they were in charge. The president was bombastic about it, talked loudly, flailed his arms, walked with his chest out. He had one of those large peasant bodies on which any kind of suit and tie just looks wrong. His big belly, a shameful thing on a man coming out of a siege, made the front of his shirt come out of his pants and he constantly tried to tuck it in as he marched in between us, telling us how to complete the forms that the embassy personnel had already told us how to fill out. Branka was sneakier, using Ramona's knowledge of English to go behind his back and talk directly to the Brits instead of to the interpreters. After a while it became apparent that Branka was winning this round, because the president's people kept having to come to us for help with English, which made the president seethe.

"I'm the reason everyone is even going to Scotland," he said to Super Mario, but loudly, so Branka could hear. She made a show of ignoring him but not without scoffing a little first. For a second I thought he would charge at her.

"None of you would have taken a single step out of Bosnia if it weren't for me, and you need to remember that!" he yelled, pointing his finger indiscriminately.

"You're behaving outrageously," Branka said, smiling. "This is a joint endeavor. There's no need for yelling."

"Joint endeavor, my dick. You're here courtesy of me. You're traveling under the wing of the National Theater and I'm the president of it, goddamn it, and I demand to know what these Brits are talking about."

"It might look like that on paper, sir, but I have to remind you that the reason you are here is because it was the Youth Center theater that got invited to Scotland, not the National Theater. I'm the president of the Youth Center, so you are here because of me."

"I'm in charge!"

"You're a drunk!"

"What did you say to me, you fuckin' cow?"

"You're a bully and a child, sir. You should be ashamed of yourself."

The blonde secretary came to the rescue again and pulled the president away from everyone as he spewed profanities. Branka beamed satisfaction, victory.

"Neither of them would even know where Edinburgh is if it weren't for Asmir," I told Boro, and he laughed. "It's weird not having him around."

"I know."

In the embassy waiting room, we waited and waited and waited some more, then had our one-on-one interviews with the consuls, who asked us if we would seek political asylum in the UK, if we would seek employment or government aid in the UK, and if we intended to return to Bosnia after the festival was over. Like well-coached parrots we all said no, no, no, yes. We gave them our passports, then meandered around the city until 4 PM, when we came back and were told that our visas were approved.

I called my parents from the post office and told them the good news. They were happy I was alive. Father asked if I still had the money. Mother told me not to have the window open when the bus was moving, that sweat and a draft in combination could lead to an inflamed nerve or even Bell's palsy. Then I called Asja, but it was her crazy father who answered and I panicked and hung up. I stood there in the booth feeling ridiculous. What could he do to me now? I picked up the phone again, hovered over the dial buttons for a moment, then cradled it.

Outside, Ramona was waiting for her turn, and I had an idea. I asked her if she would call and pretend to be Asja's friend so we could circumvent the Nazi dad. She said yes and in seconds I was talking to Asja. Well, barely. I told her where I was, that I really got out. She sounded mad and curt. She couldn't really talk. I told her I loved her. She said she had to go now.

HOW BIG ARE THE PRESIDENT'S BALLS?— SPEAKING BOSNIAN IN FRANCE—THE ORIGINS OF SUPER MARIO'S MUSTACHE

Sitting in the same seats for days and cutting diagonally across Europe on a bus made us feel just how boring freedom was. We drove the tedious highways, saw cities only from a distance, stopped at rest stops and gas stations, public restrooms and supermarkets. Having gone through what we brought with us, we gorged ourselves on prepackaged sandwiches and corn puffs and chocolate, drank sodas and juice boxes and mineral water, and smoked famous brands of cigarettes. Our stomachs were not used to all that, and we barfed into black plastic bags and diarrheaed everywhere.

We went through a long tunnel through the Alps at one point.

At another point the president made a huge scene in the middle of the night and demanded to be let off the bus. He screamed that he was sick of being treated like a child. He pressed the emergency button on the door and stood there in the draft, threatening to jump out into the night, his red tie flipping and beating him about the face. When the driver pulled into a gas station, the president got off, staggered drunkenly some two hundred meters down the road, and plopped on the curb with his head in his hands. The members of his company kept going over and trying to change his mind, and he kept yelling that he had to do this to show some people (Branka) who was in charge, to illustrate that nobody could go anywhere without him. Even his secretary couldn't reach him this time. I fell asleep and woke up twice during the ordeal. In the end Branka told him we were going on without him.

"You don't have the balls for that!" he yelled and vomited on the pavement.

Branka got on the bus and told the driver to go.

"He's a douche bag but we can't just leave him," the driver said.

"Just you go. Let's just see how big *his* balls are."

We rolled on by him but he kept on sitting there, flipping us off. The driver shifted into higher gears and we accelerated away. Around the first curve, where we couldn't see him anymore, we stopped and waited. It wasn't a minute before we saw him hauling ass on the shoulder, falling down, and getting up again. I thought I would laugh, but it was a sad thing to see. When he caught up and got on there was a huge raspberry on his forehead. A drop of blood trickled and got soaked up by his eyebrow. He walked to his seat in silence and nobody said a word to him for a long time after that.

Somewhere around Paris a gendarme pulled us over because of the broken side mirror and escorted us to a mechanic shop, where we had to wait two hours for a woman mechanic to find and install a new one. Nobody spoke a word of French. Omar, Ramona, and I separated from the group and walked into a small neighborhood. We drank Ramona's brandy out of that jar of hers and sat on a patch of grass in the shade of a bakery and loudly described every French passerby in the most flowery negative terms we could come up with, amused that they didn't understand a word we were saying. Sitting there like peasants, we felt like we had the right.

Back on the bus somebody told us a story about Super Mario. Apparently he had had that mustache since he was sixteen years old and had vowed never to shave it. Then, sometime before the war, a famous guest director arrived from Zagreb to do a show at the National Theater and gave Super Mario a part in his production of one of García Lorca's tragedies. At the first rehearsal he asked Super Mario to shave so he could get a visual idea of what he looked like without the mustache so he could make a decision about the look of the character. When Super Mario told him about his vow and how much his facial hair meant to him, the director pressed the matter even harder. What was the big deal? He was an actor, was he not? Did he want the part or what? After some soul-searching Super Mario chose to be a professional and capitulated. He showed up at the next rehearsal smooth as a baby's bottom. The director took one look at him and told him he looked awful and then made him wear a fake mustache—a replica of the one he had just shaven—throughout the rest of the rehearsals.

FRESH ON THE BOAT

The night we crossed the Channel on a ferry it was freezing. Most passengers dozed off in their cars or clustered around the boat's coffee shop, pacing to keep warm, sipping out of steaming Styro-foam cups. They all looked double-knit and miserable, watching and hating us young Bosnians because we ran up and down the stairs with a spring in our steps, screaming at one another, laughing with abandon. They envied our dynamism, the thrill of freedom that returned to our hearts and legs as we got closer and closer to Scotland. Mostly it was the fact that we didn't have to be seated anymore that prevented the freedom from being boring again. On top of that there was the novelty of traveling by boat and the sea wind that stung the nose, infiltrated us, and burned our lungs with chill.

Out on the upper deck the wind bore down on us, nabbed at our cigarettes, smoked them for us. It lifted us off our feet, made us hold onto that guardrail in earnest, made us squint and cry and feel the world in a different way, somehow more corporeally. I went to the back of the boat with Ramona and we stared down at the churn-ing waters and at the lights of France diminishing in the distance. I remembered standing on the bridge by my high school looking at the swollen river below. I remembered kissing Asja and felt again like there was a small hole in my chest that was hissing and letting out my essence. My hand naively went up to plug it.

"Do you miss her?" Ramona asked into the salty darkness.

The wind screamed in my ear, messed with my clothes, pushed me around.

"Yeah," I said.

She pushed me, then hugged me, sideways, with one arm. She handed me a jar and we drank. The slivovitz tasted strange at sea level; plums are grown in the hills.

"How much booze do you have?" she asked.

"Let's just say I've been tapping into somebody's supply."

Omar found us then and we ran around the ferry calling peo-ple names and laughing in their faces and found things to throw

overboard, trash and pieces of rope and paint chips. The lights of
Dover were getting bigger when Ramona went back to the bus to
get another jacket. She returned laughing, told us to keep quiet,
and then led us to where the driver was standing on the hood of a
Peugeot and peeping into his own bus. Ramona went right up to
him, and when he saw us he waved us over and showed us where
to look in silence. When it was my turn on the hood, I saw the
president mounting his secretary in their seat, the slab of his naked
flank flashing in the dull light.

SCOTLAND

The last leg of the trip, northward through England, was the worst.
I was exhausted but couldn't sleep; I was wired but couldn't stay
fully conscious.

We got lost in the maze of London highways and passed the same
graffiti-covered wall three times until someone mentioned it to the
driver. He then pulled up behind a road-assistance vehicle in a half
circle of orange pylons, and the nice man in overalls told Ramona
where we were supposed to make our turn. After a while the driver
got used to driving on the other side of the road.

The weather was cloudy, the hills were a-green, and the haystacks
weren't piled around a pole like in Bosnia but were in uniform yellow
cylinders or cubes that looked like giant boxy toys thrown around
the sides of the highways.

In Scotland it was cloudier and greener, but despite our exhaustion and hangovers it made our hearts grow. We had made it.

On the outskirts of Edinburgh I saw a fat seagull on a chimney
of a house made of stone and thought of Asmir and Bokal.

It was then that Super Mario decided to crack open another
bottle of slivovitz to celebrate. He took a sip, and when he realized

it was water in his mouth, he screamed "Robbery!" and accused his seatmate of stealing his booze, then Omar and me, and then everyone on the bus. The president yelled at him to quiet down, said that we would get to the bottom of this later, but in about ten minutes we were parked in front of the venue and people were taking pictures of us and shaking our hands and welcoming us to the festival and the crime that Omar and I had committed was altogether forgotten.

Excerpts from Ismet Prcić's Diary
from April 2000

I miss her, *mati*. I miss her so damn much. Can't wait to hear from UCSD. They have to take me. They have to.

I hang out with Eric when she's in San Diego, watch *Twin Peaks* with him. He's married and our old home looks different now. Stuff that we had is in storage somewhere. They have new stuff, new blue couches, new entertainment center, new, healthier cereal. I can't wait to have that with Melissa.

I keep finding things in my pockets, things I don't remember getting. I shouldn't be drinking this much, that's for damn sure. I go to parties in the Valley and wake up in people's homes, look at the photographs on the walls, and freak out because I don't recognize any faces. I sneak out and run like hell. In my attic I go through the clothes I wore the night before and find pills, notes written by strangers, keys that open no door I know.

Mustafa is becoming a problem for me.

(. . . allison . . .)

Our venue, Venue 25, was on Albany Street, this old gray building with all of the plumbing on the outside of it, black pipes dividing the facade into random straight-sided geometrical shapes. Off the pipes hung vivid banners advertising the festival, the individual plays. The wallpaper around the threshold was a collage of posters and newspaper clippings. Coming inside, the air smelt vaguely of basements and old glue. There was a downstairs and an upstairs, a narrow stairway leading from one to the other. A stout, pimply lass in an oversize festival T-shirt ushered us up toward the cafeteria. Her name tag read LUCY. She sawed the air with her arms and rolled her r's the way Bosnians do it and it felt a little bit like home. With that bosom, with that smile, I just wanted to hug her.

"We've go' a surpraize for ya," she said.

The doorway into the cafeteria was narrow and we had to go in one by one, maneuvering our luggage so we didn't get stuck. I walked in behind Omar, and there was Asmir in black jeans and a black blazer he had bought on the black market in Tuzla. He was standing on a chair, grinning, his arms spread out like seagull wings, his patented stance. The younger members of the troupe ran to him, screaming. He climbed down and hugged them and ruffled their hair, and there was something eerily staged about it, like documentary footage of Communist dictators meeting schoolkids on national holidays.

"How did you get here before us?" I asked as we hugged.

"What do seagulls do?"

"Fly?"

"There you go."

"Where's Bokal?" Boro asked, and I felt so stupid that a ten-year-old could see through to the essence of things before I. Asmir's smile faltered and his eyebrows went up in unison with his shoulders.

"He took a bus to Split the morning after you left. I told him to come with me, but he said that something in his dream told him to take the bus to Split. I trust he's on the way, unless . . . you know."

Asmir and Branka agreed on the lodging. Asmir suggested that the eighteen-and-over crowd stay in one of the provided houses and that the little ones stay with Branka in the other. He was right and you could see that Branka hated that he was. She made a spectacle of shuffling through some papers, then dropped the bomb that to-morrow morning "we" were all supposed to meet with a drama club from a local high school and rehearse a student-written play to be performed during the last week of the festival. Asmir laughed, ar-gued that we were here not to perform other people's plays but our own, that he didn't know anything about it, that he wouldn't do it. Branka said that it had been a condition of all of us getting visas. Asmir asked why he hadn't known about it then, and said that he wouldn't do it. She said that "we" could do it without him, that, in fact, she didn't care what he did at all. Who's gonna direct it, you? he said, and laughed. It'll be a joint endeavor, she said. It'll be a piece of shit, he said. What do you care? she said. What do I care what *my* troupe is performing? Are you out of your mind? he said. We'll leave it up to them, then, make it voluntary, she said. Asmir then turned to us and announced that we were not required to show up for this meeting *or* do the play with the Scottish kids. Branka said we should do it because we promised we would. *You* promised for us without asking any of us, he said. I did what I needed to do to get us up here, she said. So did I, he said.

Lucy volunteered to take Branka and the young ones to their lodgings and Boro made a fuss. He said he didn't want to lodge with his mother and the kids, and Branka, being an enlightened, modern kind of mother, soon gave up and put him in the care of his brother, Omar, and allowed him to stay with the older crowd.

Asmir led us "old birds" and the musicians away.

"Down this way," he said.

The night fell on Edinburgh like a blanket over a birdcage and a haze crept into the air and made the lights crisp at the source but blurry on the periphery. The chill put bumps on your skin. Ghosts swirled around streetlights and tangled in your hair. Buildings breathed heavily. The streets groaned underfoot. You could feel how old everything was despite the neon, the cars, and the techno music bumping from basement bars.

There were crowds everywhere, walking and laughing, making me dizzy. We passed a group of tourists and I was sure I saw Asja. I thought I recognized her cheek across the street but it wasn't her. The experience made me anxious, panicky. I forced myself to look down at my feet, gave myself the silly task of trying to step on every patch of dirty, ancient bubble gum on the sidewalk. After a while the monotony of it calmed me down. When I looked up I saw I was way behind the group.

I yelled for Asmir to wait, and they all stopped by some street performers until I caught up to them. There was a guy with a red mustache in a leotard juggling chainsaws. I leaned on the

BOOM!

"Incoming!" screamed Omar.

Suddenly I was under a parked bus, hands over head, my mind flashing to the discharge of the shell that scared Archibald, counting to three because three is the number of seconds it takes a shell to arrive.

One:

My mind flashing to a severed foot on the pavement, to popcorn in the

Two:

street, to blood drops on my Reeboks, a car atop another car like turtles, smoldering

Three:

heat, mind bracing for the whistle or the **BOOM**, heart like a pager set to vibrate.

Three:

Waiting for it to come.

Three:

Bracing for the **BOOM**.

But nothing came. Just another distant explosion. Then another. *These shells are defective.* Then the crackle of a series of smaller, tinnier explosions, but not like Kalashnikov fire, more musical, cascading in pitch. *What kind of guns are these? Singing guns?*

I opened my eyes and realized I was face-to-face with a perfectly round bubble-gum stain on the curb in front of me. *Oh, we're in Edinburgh.* I looked up. Red mustache was twirling small chainsaws in the air like nothing ever happened. Some of his audience were looking at me, though, looking at Ramona curled up on the sidewalk, at Omar and Boro crouching next to a building. The audience's thoughts were legible on their faces: Were we insane, or were they witnessing impromptu street performance art?

Then I saw Asmir and our musicians laughing at us.

"What is it, peasants? Never seen fireworks?"

I climbed from under the bus. A hugging couple avoided me in a wide semicircle. I dusted off and looked for my bag.

No, I had never before that day seen fireworks. Neither had Ramona, nor Omar, nor Boro. Asmir and the musicians were older. They remembered with fully formed adult bodies and minds life before the war. Before chaos, they'd known order, before senselessness, sense. They were really out of Bosnia because leaving chaos to them felt like returning to normalcy. But, if you were forged in the chaos, then there *was* no return. There *was* no escape. To you chaos *was* normalcy. And normalcy was proving to be an unnatural, brittle state.

Asmir came over and hugged me.

"Don't shit yourself," he teased but the hug felt good, genuine.

I avoided his eyes because mine were bursting. I turned uphill toward the explosions over Edinburgh Castle, blurting festive fire into downcast skies.

We didn't sleep all night, despite fatigue. We just dropped our bags at the house and then ran around the town in the mizzle, filling our eyes with the fresh and the unfamiliar. Asmir led and we followed him into every store, every pub, just to see what they looked like from the inside. We jumped over tall fences into fancy forbidden parks and kicked the trees to get each other wetter. We drank a mug of beer apiece in this loud place called the Basement where all the employees wore fluorescent T-shirts that said IT'S COOL TO BE DOWN. We buzzed. We vibrated. We were high.

In the morning, through the thicket of a hangover headache, in a small, unfamiliar room that smelled of paint, I heard a doorbell ring.

A door opened somewhere in the house and a moment later someone shrieked—in pain? Horror? Joy? I had slept in my clothes, so I just jumped out of bed, ran and opened the door, and saw little Boro careening toward me down the hallway at full sprint.

"Bokal is here! Bokal is here!" he screamed as his feet fought for purchase on the hardwood. He braked in the fashion of somebody on a motorcycle, swinging his rear end to the front, was still just for a split second, and was already running back the other way before I even left my room.

Bokal looked like a shepherd in his fur-lined jacket, with his face unshaven and his hair oily and matted and sticking out indiscriminately. It was Lucy who had picked him up at the train station and called him a taxi, which dropped him off in front of the house. He stood in the living room with his bag on the floor but with his backpack still over his shoulder as he received hugs and pats on the arms. You could see he was happy and tired.

"Sit down," said Ramona, ushering him toward an armchair. He took two steps, then changed his mind.

"If I never sit again it will be too soon," he said.

Ramona and I decided that we would go to the meeting with the Scottish kids. Asmir made fun of us but we told him that if his troupe was going to be represented in any form—and we knew Branka was going to make all the youngsters show up, because she had their passports and parent slips and pretty much owned their asses outside of Bosnia—we should at least have a couple of senior members present to protect the integrity of the group. He made fun of us again but we were steadfast. Halfway to the venue he caught up with us on foot, with Boro in tow. He went on and on about Branka putting the troupe in this situation and kept apologizing to Boro that he had to talk shit about his mother in his presence. There was no need for that. Boro understood. Boro was smarter than any of us.

In the rehearsal room there were two cliques, with a language barrier between them. The Scottish kids had some kind of scripts in their hands; the Bosnians didn't.

Avoiding everybody's eyes, we immediately took off our shoes and sat on the floor, a routine practice before any Asmir-led rehearsal. The younger members of our troupe responded to the familiarity of it and did what we did, which left the Scottish kids to look from face to face trying to figure out if they should follow suit. Their poor leader, a wide-eyed high school drama teacher, told them to go ahead.

Soon enough there was a circle of barefoot kids sitting Indian-style on the parquet and still nobody knew what to do. Branka asked Ramona to help her talk to the Scottish teacher. Ramona got up and the two of them crossed the language barrier. Just as they did someone else left the circle and walked over to Boro and me, kneeled down, and said hello. There was nothing else I could do but look up and meet Allison.

Allison had the hands of a grown woman, and something passed between us through the handshake. Allison's skin was cold and smooth to the touch. Allison wore a watch. Allison's trousers were black and I can't recall her blouse. I couldn't keep my gaze away from her eyes, a little brown and a little green and a little sad, despite the smile. A little troubled.

"I'm sorre, bu' could you say yer name again, please?" she asked.

"Ismet."

"Izz-matt," she said.

Boro scoffed.

"Ssss," I said. "Izmet with the zed means, uh . . . shit of cow in my country."

All the Scots laughed.

"Why would yer parents do that to ya?" she asked.

Two other Scots crawled over and introduced themselves, too, and I shook their hands but almost never broke eye contact with Allison. They snickered at our connection and *oooooooohed* a little bit and kept mentioning someone named William.

Then Asmir took over everybody's life for the next two hours. The poor Scottish drama teacher had no chance. Asmir just gathered all her scripts and tossed them on some chair in the corner. Then he took off his shirt and lay down in the center of the circle. He might as well have pulled out a gun; everyone was frozen, waiting.

"Ve do relax number one," he said, "number two ve do game of theater, THEN ve do theater."

Branka and the teacher simply backed into a corner each, sat down, and watched with their lips pressed tight. Asmir led us all through a meditation exercise. I was amazed by how seamlessly Allison and her friends merged with our troupe under Asmir's leadership. At first they sniggered at his Tarzan English commands to *close eyes and tink of inside of mother stomach* and *imagine energy of life come out of your eyes like balls*, but soon got comfortable.

We did some warm-ups, some voice and trust exercises. We did that one where one person stands rigidly still with their arms crossed on their chest and has to let two others push them back and forth like a metronome. This blond boy in the Riddler T-shirt and I pushed Allison. Every time her shoulders fell into my hands she smiled. Her eyes were closed and I looked at her chest. I could feel the bra straps through her blouse on my thumbs and I never wanted to stop doing this.

After the rehearsal Asmir went up to the drama teacher to explain his vision of our troupe's involvement with her show:

"Scot actors do text. Ve do dance. Yes? Ve vill pretend ve are the vor. Ve vill come and be very together like a bomb and then ve vill sing like a bomb and start from one end of stage to the other, dancing like bomb, and ven the bomb fall around you, people, ve vill become . . . *geler, kako se kaže geler, jebem mu mater* . . . vill become piece, small piece of bomb, all of us, and dance like different small piece of bomb, killing. Yes?"

The drama teacher stood there, baffled.

Allison winked at me twice during the warm-ups the next day. After the rehearsal she said her father was letting her have a party for all of us that night and that I had to come. She gave me directions and kissed my cheek. It felt like a sunburn on my skin. In my head, it felt like a gulp of brandy. She walked away, and when she finally disappeared from the doorway, I realized that everyone was watching me standing there stupidly.

"Nice going, Ismet!" Bokal said and clapped me on the back. "No wasted time, huh?"

"She has a boyfriend, ya know?" the Riddler kid told me, interpreting the clap.

"I have the girlfriend," I told him.

"Right," he said.

All day the rest of the day, her friends (the "morality police,"

Allison later called them,) kept reminding me that she had a boyfriend, although we hadn't done anything but blush around each other and smile a lot. And hug that one time. And that peck on the cheek, which I didn't reciprocate. Even Ramona and Asmir started bringing up Asja for no reason, trying to make me feel bad.

I kept forcing myself to do the right thing and think about Asja. I would start to remember her, love her, and for a while I would succeed and feel righteous, but halfway into a daydream my mind would insert Allison's face into my memories of Asja. It would be Allison holding my hand in Banja Park, Allison kissing me on "our" bench. I felt scared, deranged, not in charge of my mind. So instead of going to Allison's party like everybody else, I spent the night writing a love letter to Asja, wallowing in self-pity, coming up with pretty words for how shitty I felt.

The next day I woke up with a pounding headache—there was a bump on my head I couldn't explain—and sore all over. Everybody regarded me with admonishment. Allison looked wary of me and I suffered through the rehearsal. She left right after, without a good-bye. I felt marbled with love and anger. So, come matinee time, I performed my ass off out of spite, taking over the performance, upstaging everyone, exorcising my frustrations. The show went well. My feet ached from stomping.

The troupe dispersed and left me in the cafeteria and I was glad. I stood in line and got a croissant sandwich and a paper bowl of fruit, sat down, opened the sandwich, picked out the pork, pressed the halves back together, and bit into it. It tasted like it was made by robots, but I got it down with the steady munch of somebody who knew hunger well enough. Grapes tasted like grapes. Melon like melon.

Then Allison showed up and sat at my table. She just sat there, looking at me for a while, and like that, I fell in love. Or realized that I had. She was wet from the rain and there were clusters of gossamer white foam on her hair where whatever product she was using came in contact with water. Rain slid from her scalp and down her cheeks. She wiped it off slowly, like a movie star. She was beautiful.

I started to cry a little and she took my hand. She said that she saw the show and that I was great and that she was bringing her mother to see it tomorrow and that she wanted me to meet her afterward. She said that I was her friend, that there would be a repeat of the party, and that she hoped there would be no more incidents. *What incidents?* I thought, but said nothing. Just wanted her to keep touching my hand, keep talking to me. She asked me if I wanted to go to a museum with her. I hated museums, but I said yes. Once there, she did cartwheels when the guards weren't watching and we giggled and the stern people in the paintings stirred not.

A week later, a few hours before Allison's second party, I came back to the house and found Ramona, Asmir, Bokal, and the musicians congregated around the fireplace. A green bottle of something was circulating from hand to hand.

"There he is," Asmir said as I was taking off my shoes, "Bosnian Casanova."

Bokal came over with a grin, grabbed my hand, and sniffed my fingers.

"Still ruled by conscience, I see. What kind of Bosnian are you? You'll ruin all our reputations."

The musicians laughed. I saw Ramona's brow bunch up and tugged my hand away.

Bokal said, "You have two more days. It's like the Olympics, man. You're not scoring just for yourself but for your country, too."

More laughter.

"Yeah, yeah, you guys are hilarious," Ramona said and then backed me up into a corner away from the rest of them. She whispered something and I had to bend down to her to hear. There was booze on her breath. "Tell me you didn't do anything."

"I didn't do anything." It was the truth.

"Can the soap opera wait?" spat Asmir. "I didn't send Branka's boys on an errand for nothing. We gotta plan this right, and they're probably on their way back already. So, this is what's going on: We have two more days before we're supposed to go back and matinee performances on both days."

"And the play with the Scottish kids at five, Asmir," added Ramona.

"Fuck the Scottish kids."

"Well, Ismet is letting us down in that department," Bokal said.

"Come on!" Asmir practically screamed. "Do you want to stay here or go back to war?"

The laughter died. Somebody handed someone a bottle. Liquid sloshed. Someone else took a nip.

"We're in a foreign fucking country, and if we don't do this right, if they find some of us before the bus crosses the border, that's it. I know that Ismet and Ramona have arrangements with Branka, but the rest of us don't. This is my *life*, man."

"All right, what are we doing?"

"Tonight at the party, make sure to spread some rumors about where you're going. I want each of those kids to have a different story about where each of us is headed. Tell them I have a cousin in Glasgow, or Ireland. Or a friend. I don't care what you tell them, just make it sound hush-hush, like it's special information just for them."

The musicians nodded in approval, looking surprised that they hadn't thought of this first. I glanced at Ramona and her face was flat.

"But wait a second," she said. "Are we going to finish all our performances, or are you guys bailing on the shit we're doing with the Scots?"

Asmir looked at her almost in confusion, and I saw his mind jump from thought to unknowable thought.

"Well?"

"Tomorrow, we're doing both," he said. "The last day, I'm gone right after our matinee. I don't know about you."

"Me, too," Bokal chimed in. "We need a head start to get away from Branka."

Right then, the front door opened and Omar and Boro walked in with plastic bags of beer. A gust of wind whooshed in with them and it felt like the room imploded a little. Everyone looked otherworldly and stiff. Nobody said anything. Ramona grabbed the green bottle out of the drummer's hands, stomped across the living room to the bathroom, and slammed the door.

The party went into the night. Minors drank tall cans of lager, spilling all over the place. Asmir, Bokal, and the musicians cornered them individually and told them where in the UK their fictitious relatives lived. Allison played the piano in a blue T-shirt and her father kept maneuvering people off his expensive Chinese carpet. The young troupe members were sad because our Scottish excursion was coming to an end, and so were their Scottish counterparts. Everyone took pictures of everyone else, crying, exchanging addresses.

I wanted to spend some time with Allison alone, but suddenly it felt like she was embarrassed that I was there, scared almost. She wasn't the same Allison from earlier in the week, the one doing cartwheels among statues, goofing off, using every chance to be touching me. Maybe it was because her dad was there and she was trying to be someone he would approve of. Maybe she thought about it and realized she really loved her boyfriend and dreaded getting close to me. Maybe she was only toying with me behind his back, the bitch. After all, where was he tonight? In the end I figured I shouldn't have been hoping for anything in the first place. Bad karma. In the end I blamed myself.

At some point Asmir took me out on the balcony and closed the door. The night was cold but without rain. The street below us was empty.

"Don't break your heart over her," he said. "You don't know what she's like."

"I'm fine," I said leaning over the rail. I wondered what it would feel like to be airborne above this street.

"Real seagulls fly alone."

He spun me around and hugged me. His general aura was redolent of beer.

"Tomorrow, after our play, Bokal and I will evaporate."

"You mean the day after tomorrow?"

He let go of me so I could see his shaking head.

"Tomorrow."

There was genuine sorrow in his eyes.

"What about our last performance?" I managed.

"Ismet, it's not the show that must go on, but life." I could see he was very proud of that one.

We both leaned on the railing, looking out. My eyes stung. I looked at my white breath against the gray building across the street and thought about mankind, about how hot we had to be on the inside to survive in such cold environs.

"Where do you think you'll go?"

He didn't say anything. I looked at his profile against the city lights and the city darknesses. His shoulders were hunched. He looked smaller and toothless. He looked like a child, or a father who had lost one.

"Let's go inside," he said.

We found Bokal, and Asmir immediately turned from vulnerable to voluble. We had another round of tall ones and watched a frail fifteen-year-old Scottish girl puke amber into a potted plant. Allison's father had had enough. There was a gong. He gonged it and we started to look for our coats.

As the last of us were leaving in a group, Allison put on a jacket and said she'd walk with us part of the way, to say proper good-byes.

"Don't do it," Asmir whispered in my ear. "You have no idea what these Western girls are like."

"We like each other."

"They like dick, that's what they like. You'll see. I'll prove it to you."

He and Bokal lagged behind as the rest of us took over the street like an invading army. The cold oxygen had awakened us. Scottish high school girls hung off the musicians' arms, cackling. Allison became her flirty self again and tried to tickle me, ruffled my hair, tried to push me off the sidewalk with her hip.

And just as my heart grew big again to accommodate my regained feelings toward her, Asmir came out of the blue, swooped in like a fat seagull to prove his point, took a confused Allison by the arm, and they walked ahead of everybody, like lovers. My heart shriveled up on itself like a raisin. All the love in there escaped in a cloud of steam, exchanging electrons with the misty air, merging with it, and giving it importance. Some other Scottish girl (too many hair clips) slipped her hand between my elbow and me, snuggled in closer, and kept saying words in English while I tried to breathe so I wouldn't die.

I don't know how long I walked, but out of nowhere I saw Allison standing on the sidewalk ahead, disoriented, her body rigid. I saw Asmir cross the street and vanish around the first corner. The hair-clip girl on my arm kept talking until we came alongside Allison, frozen to her spot, and I found myself slowing down as though she had some kind of gravitational pull only on me. I came to a stop and wiggled my arm up and out of the other girl's grip, saying sorry, my face all gushy.

"Please hug me," Allison whispered and we locked in an embrace. Our pupils overtook our irises, opening holes in our eyes so big the world just got sucked right through them and into us. We stood still, clutching each other.

"What's wrong?" I asked.

After what she said I could have killed Asmir.

Later we walked, hand in hand, up the hill from St. Stephen's Church all the way to Princes Street, trying not to step on any lines or cracks in the sidewalk—a game. On the hill in front of us Edinburgh Castle stood well lit and unobtainable, like paradise. Black taxies passed us, somberly gliding up and down, like hearses. The creatures of the night gorged themselves on fish and chips out of oily paper wrappers. Tourists acted like they owned the place, yelling in exotic languages and laughing hysterically for no apparent reason. There were posters everywhere that read: "Amazing, tour de force performance . . ." and "You're stupid if you don't see this one . . ." Some just showed a picture of Salvador Dalí, his mustache like dollar signs.

A group of teenagers passed us on the other side of the street. There was some kind of commotion and someone yelled something with a thick Scottish accent. Allison dropped my hand like a slug and said:

"Shite!"

"What?"

"That's William."

I looked over. This tall, blond guy separated from his group of friends and ran across the street toward us. I saw myself getting bludgeoned, stabbed. I planted my feet and prayed.

But he smiled at me and said, "Sorry to bother bu' I'd like a word with Allison?" or something like that. In Bosnia I would already have been picking my spleen up off the sidewalk.

"No problem," I said all too eagerly.

"I'm sorry," she said to me and followed him a little way down.

William's posse stood around, eyeing me with hatred. I swallowed a lot and counted steps from a bus stop to the building, making it look like I wasn't compulsive, like I was just pacing. My mind kept telling me to run away, but I couldn't. I didn't want to leave without Allison; that gravitational pull again. She and William were standing in front of a jewelry store, two shadows arguing against bright light and burnished gold.

"Hey, fucker," someone called from behind me, and I almost buckled like a piece of lawn furniture. Then I realized that it had been said in Bosnian. I turned and saw Bokal coming my way, holding a painting under his arm.

"What are you doing here?" he asked.

"Shitting myself." I moved my chin slightly, as though pointing toward the jewelry store. He looked over there, recognized Allison and laughed.

"Tonight's the night, huh? All right, I'm gonna leave you to it."

He tried to walk by me but I grabbed his jacket.

"Where are you *going?*" I said through my teeth. "That's her boyfriend and those are his friends. He saw us holding hands."

Bokal glanced at them and scratched his beard, evaluating their potency if it came to a brawl.

"They're not gonna do shit," he said.

"You stick around anyway."

"Hey, check this out." He held the painting up for me. "What do you think?"

It was a nude in blues and yellows, part of a window and a full moon outside it.

"I picked her up in a pub. Said I *needed* to paint her. She took me to a store, bought me a canvas and some paints, and then took me home. When I was done, I fucked her."

"And you didn't give her the painting?"

"It's my painting. I painted it."

I glanced toward the jewelry store and saw Allison and William hug. It was a quickie, like spouses parting in the morning, before going to work.

"I guess that makes sense," I told Bokal.

Allison walked over. She and Bokal exchanged some niceties; then Bokal left. Allison and I turned on one of the streets leading to Queen's Park and I put my hand in my pocket, but she reached into it and took my hand again.

For the second time someone yelled her name from behind us, William. For the second time that night she said *shite.* For the second time I counted steps as they argued, this time in front of a pawnshop with electric guitars on display. For the second time I couldn't just leave without her, despite my ambiguous status, despite the fear, despite myself.

They took longer this time, though, and when she finally came back she said:

"William and I are history."

We walked by a pond and in between the wall-like hedges of some park, the mist meandering in their corners like spiderwebs in the wind. A playground was there, and a soccer field. She swung in the swing and I tried to go down the slide but only got my jeans wet.

"Doesnae that streetlight look like a halo?"

"What's a halo?" I asked.

"Ye know, the sign of the enlightenment, like."

"What's enlightenment?"

"Like God's grace."

"Oh."

I was going to ask what grace was, but I had a vague idea of its meaning and I didn't want her to think I was stupid.

"In religious art, halos are those circles around Jesus's heed."

I suddenly got an urge to run into the middle of the field. She jumped into my arms and we stood there for a long time, just hugging. I became aware of the hot skin on her neck, our cold ears touching.

"Kiss me, I'm Scottish," she said—a T-shirt we'd seen in town.

We breathed each other in. She touched my butt and I got an erection. She checked the grass but it was too dewy to roll around in. We kissed and rubbed against each other and time slipped away and a white police cruiser glided by, almost noiselessly, across the grass, shining its reflector on us, then politely, *Britishly*, carried on. We kissed some more until a little fox came up to us from behind the hedges, regarded us with a pragmatic leer, then trotted away, shaking its head, its tongue out, mocking us.

* * *

I woke up late the next day, found no one in the house. It was ten minutes before the show already and none of the troupe members had bothered to wake me. I rushed into my jacket and caught a whiff of Allison on it and remembered what Asmir had done, that motherfucker. I was gonna kill him. I checked and there was still luggage in all the rooms and miscellaneous clothes, debris from a hasty breakfast all over the kitchen, bread crumbs and cornflakes and smears of orange marmalade. There was Asmir's boom box in the living room. If he was still in Edinburgh, he was mine. I dashed out without locking the front door behind me.

The day was soggy and I ran up the hill like a maniac, rage fueling my muscles. There were a lot of people out and I slalomed in between them, catching a shoulder here and there.

As I turned onto Albany my right shoe started to clap against the sidewalk. Unwilling to slow down, I hopped on my left foot and kicked my right foot sideways to see what had happened. The cheap sole had unglued itself and my heel was a-flap.

"Fuck!" I said and, off balance like that, crashed into a beefy man in front of me, bounced off his bulk, and bailed hard. In the nanosecond blur of being face-to-face, I recognized him.

Mustafa! Could it be?

"Sorry," I said, trying to get up on all fours, but he just kept walking. By the time I was up and cupping the funny bone in my elbow, he was already around the corner.

"Mustafa!" I called after him, but he didn't come back.

I hobbled into Venue 25 and went through the courtyard to the green room behind stage B, where I assumed the troupe was stalling the show until I got there. But as soon as I walked in I knew there wouldn't be a show.

The young troupe members, sitting on sofas in their costumes, looked at me with petrified faces. A gasp went through the room and caught Branka's attention. She was standing with her back to me near the entrance to the stage with Ramona and two men I'd never seen before. When she spun around her face made me tremble. She ran to me.

"Where were you?" she hissed and I thought she was going to hit me.

"At the house," I said and looked at Ramona. "Nobody bothered to wake me up."

Ramona turned away from me.

"Where are Bokal and Asmir? Where are the musicians?"

That's when I realized that Asmir was long gone. They were all long gone.

I wanted to bash his head in for groping Allison when he knew I liked her, for saying he did this to help me understand how the world works, for lying to my face. I remembered how vulnerable he'd looked the previous night on that balcony and it made me even madder. Something inside me came to a boil, and without being able to release the pressure of it in front of this anguished woman, it all came out of my eyes.

"I don't know where they are," I choked out.

"My dick! You're as thick as thieves."

I wiped my eyes, my guts knotting.

"I. Don't. Know."

Her lips curled into a snarl. She grabbed my left sleeve and pointed me toward the sofas.

"Nobody knows anything," she said. "Go sit down. We'll get to the bottom of this."

My friends scooched over and made some room for me in the corner, next to Omar.

"Fucking craziness," he whispered, like it was all his fault.

"What happened?" I whispered back.

He looked toward his mother, who was now pacing from the stage entrance to where Ramona was talking to the two men, waiting for something, it seemed. One of them, a chinless blond, was writing something in a pocket notebook.

"Boro and I woke up this morning and everybody was gone except for Ramona. We thought you were with that chick and didn't even check in your room," Omar said.

"But they left their stuff behind."

"I think to give themselves more time."

"Fucking asshole."

"Who?"

"Who do you think?"

"My mother doesn't give a shit about him or Bokal. They didn't come on *her* bus. It's the musicians she vouched for, that she's responsible for bringing back."

Something in the way he phrased the sentence switched on the silent alarm inside of me.

"What about me and Ramona?"

"What about you and Ramona?"

"Well, she's letting *us* go, right?"

"I know about Ramona. Her father made a deal or something."

The rage in me turned into panic. All alarms blared.

"My father made a deal for *me*," I said, almost crying again.

"I don't know, man. Not with Branka, or I would know."

My hands started to shake and I hid them under my knees, feigning cold.

"Where were you gonna go? To your uncle in America?"

I managed to nod.

"Man, you better do something quick. Those guys over there are from immigration. Mother called them and told them that some people ran away from the troupe to seek asylum."

I couldn't move, not even my eyes. They just stared ahead across the room and locked onto a blue sandbag next to the stage door, a doorstop. Every so often Branka's blurry shape passed in front of it, pacing.

The stage door swung open then and a conservatively clad woman entered. Branka told Ramona to tell her that they found me. Ramona translated, pointing in my direction, and the woman looked at me. She had large, photosensitive glasses and bangs and looked a little like Joey Ramone. I tried to move but my legs felt wooden, my feet bolted to the floor.

Joey Ramone said something to the blond man and I heard the word *passport*. Omar heard it, too. I felt him lean slightly into me.

"If you let go of your passport now you're as good as in Bosnia," he whispered without moving his mouth.

"They recommend you take his passport if you want him to go back with the troupe," Ramona said to Branka, and without a moment's hesitation Branka started toward me.

That's it.

My passport was in the front left pocket of my Levi's jacket. My money was in a tobacco pouch in the right inside pocket. My name was Ismet. The sandbag was blue. Branka was coming. My hands were under my knees. My heart was beating in the tips of my fingers. My brain was churning. My legs were wooden. The room was silent. My throat was closed. Branka was coming. My armpits were damp. The room was silent. Branka was there. Her hand extended. Her mouth was moving. My throat was closed. My brain was churning. And I was flying. Flying above. My name was Ismet. My heart was not beating. I was looking down. At another Ismet. Whose heart was beating. Whose feet were not wooden. Whose throat was not closed. My passport was in the front left pocket of his Levi's jacket. My money was in a tobacco pouch in the right inside pocket. He knew this fact. Branka was there. Asking for my passport. With her moving mouth. My name was Ismet. He reached inside. Pulled out the money. His face screwed up. He dug deeper. Looking for the passport. In the wrong place. He stood up in panic. He looked around. *Where is your passport?* Branka was saying. *I left it in the room,* he was saying. *We'll go with you to get it,* Branka was saying. The sandbag was blue. My name was Ismet. My passport was in the front left pocket of his Levi's jacket and he didn't give it up.

We were on Dundas Street. I was walking downhill, flanked by two open umbrellas and their owners. The purple and white one belonged to Branka. The simple black one belonged to the man with no chin.

My heel flapped as I walked and my shoe took on water. The rain was cold and my shoulders were hunched, no neck. Three times Branka offered to share her umbrella with me and three times I refused. "I like the rain," I said. "My shoe broke," I said in English. The man with no chin was stern.

"I can't believe you don't have your passport on you," Branka said.

In front of the house. A flight of stairs down to the front door. I took it in one leap, removed my shoes, and left them there on the welcome mat. The two with umbrellas were still at street level.

"If you want you can wait here," I said. "I'll go bring it." But Branka started her descent, her face suspicious.

The front door was unlocked and I ran in. I sprinted down the hallway and almost lost my balance because my right sock was soaked and it slid more dangerously on the polished hardwood. But there were walls for balancing and I made it to my room, scrambled in, and shut the door. I locked it from the inside.

For a moment there was panic. I picked up my bag, put it down. I ran to the window, looked out, spun around, ran to the door. I grabbed at my hair, let it go. I heard footsteps. For a moment there was calm.

A knock on the door.

I put my Windbreaker on over my Levi's jacket and climbed on the sill.

"I'm gonna change!" I yelled. "I'm all wet!"

I jumped into the courtyard in my socks.

I muddied my hands and knees, got on my own two feet, ducked under some pillowcases now sopping on the clothesline, and ran to the door leading to the vestibule. I clutched the doorknob and pulled and pulled and there was panic again because it wouldn't budge. I pulled and pulled and looked around, gauging the height of the walls, but then I pushed and the door clicked open and I ran the width of the building to the front, stuck out my head and saw that no one was at the front door, picked up my shoes from the welcome mat in one sweeping move, and ascended the stairs to the street.

I ran on.

And on.

And there was a spring in my step and elation on my face despite the downpour, despite the equally wet socks now, despite what Asmir had done, what my father hadn't, despite who all were left behind in hell, despite uncertainty about the future, the pull of the past, the disjointedness of the present. Despite fear. Despite love.

I ran on across the street with a shoe in each hand. A double-decker straight from a British postcard decelerated and came to a stop. I got on board and handed the driver a bunch of crumpled notes. I climbed the stairs to the top deck, which was empty, went all the way to the back, and threw myself face-first on the floor.

The bus started to move. I lay there for a while, then flipped onto my back. I dropped the shoes over my head. My chest was heaving. My face was smiling. My right hand clutched the left front pocket of my jacket, felt the document inside. My left hand reached into my inside right pocket and squeezed the money pouch. With that I lost consciousness.

I awakened to the sound of foliage scraping the roof of the bus, and as soon as I realized where I was, my heart was a-thump.

WhatareyoudoingWhatareyoudoingWhatareyoudoingWhatareyoudoingWhatareyou

I raised my head, looked down the aisle, and immediately felt a swoon coming. I closed my eyes and leaned into the side of the seat to my right, folded my legs under me, and managed to push myself up and into it.

doingWhatareyoudoingWhat

Slowly, my personal darkness retreated ahead of reality and I was able to look around. Slivers of Edinburgh, made opaque by rain, turned in the frame of the window, one after the other. I couldn't recognize anything. It was the price of freedom.

areyoudoingWhatareyoudoing

I hallucinated I was someone else, someone older to whom the inside of this bus wasn't foreign, someone who knew where they were, where they were going, and how many stops it would take to get them there. It felt both good and unnerving, good because it had a calming effect on the body, unnerving because inside it I knew I wasn't really me. I panicked and fumbled to get out my passport.

I opened it and looked at my photograph. Who was this pale kid? Why was his T-shirt neckband so stretched?

I read the name. Ismet Prcić. I read the name, then looked at the picture, looked at the picture, then read the name until I recognized them both, the features of my face and the slopes and curls of my signature. I held the passport in both hands, closed it and put it back in the pocket, checked three times that the button was secure, pressed my palm on top of it, and felt my heart beat through it.

Whatareyoudoing

My feet were cold. Their once-white socks were now brown and translucent. I peeled them off and dropped them. They looked like two slush-and-shit snowballs melting on the bus floor. The skin of my feet was alien and wrinkled. I looked for my shoes. The back of the right one yawned at me, but they were relatively dry and I put them on my bare feet.

I saw some buildings. I saw some cars, their windshield wipers standing up and lying down. I had no idea what I was doing.

Outside a bigger bus station I got off. The wind blowing there made me aware of every bone in my body.

The inside of the station was warmer, but I couldn't stop shivering. I meandered, looking for a nook, for some cubicle of privacy, to hide in, collect myself, and think about what to do. I found refuge in a stall of a public toilet.

I sat on the closed lid with my head in my hands while men around me pissed and shat, farted and groaned, washed and didn't wash their hands. I checked my passport again, counted all my money (both German and British), then pulled out my address book and read the names and phone numbers of all my friends and family in Tuzla who couldn't help me. I read my parents' number, and even though I knew it by heart, it looked unfamiliar because I knew it wasn't mine anymore. My uncle's number in America seemed too long and obscure, like a line of computer code. Asja's number was sad, like an unread love note found thirty years later.

Part of me wondered if I should just go back to the venue, find the rest of the troupe, and go home. *This is not for you. You can't do this alone.*

Part of me was euphoric, alive, thinking of nothing but Allison. At the museum she'd said that she didn't want me to go back to Bosnia, and I told her not to worry and informed her of my plans. She'd said that if the America thing fell through I could always come and stay with her. At the time I thought it simply romantic and rather unlikely, but now it was the only thing I could think about. Over and over I read her addresses and phone numbers (one at her dad's, the other at her mom's) and tried to commit them to memory.

I bought a triangular cheese-and-tomato sandwich wrapped in plastic, my first meal of the day, and devoured it in four bites. It tasted so good. I went and bought another one for later.

Having gathered a bit of courage and warmth, I called Allison's dad from a pay phone, but he said she was at her mum's. I called her mum and, with my heartbeat thumping in the booth, asked if Allison was home.

"Who's this?"

"Ismet. From Bosnia. We met at the play."

"Of course, how lovely. Allison is still at squl, I'm afraid."

"I'm sorry?"

"She's still at squl."

"Oh, school," I said through a sudden knot in my throat.

"I don' expect her back until sex or seven."

"Oh," was all I could manage as tears fell hotly from my eyes.

"Ismet, are you o'right? What's the matter?"

"I'm okay," I said in a voice an octave deeper.

"Are you sure, luv?"

"I'll call later."

"O' right then. I'll tell Allison you phoned."

"Thank you. Bye bye."

"Cheerio."

I couldn't call again. I stood in the booth with the phone in my right hand, with the number in my mind, with a left hand perfectly capable of pressing the buttons in the right order, with a mouth capable of strongly accented speech, with enough breath in my lungs to turn it into *Good evening, is Allison home,* but I couldn't call again.

Instead I bought a bus ticket to South Queensferry, where Allison's mother lived—or, rather, I saw myself buy it. I saw myself buy it and then it was in my hand, so I must have bought it.

I don't know how long the ride took.

Queensferry.

Somehow I found the street, the apartment building. It's not clear to me how. It took a long time. I remember the bite of the wind, the similarity of cobblestones to the ones in the center of Tuzla, the supernatural emptiness of the streets making me flash to curfews. I walked and walked, looking. I ate the second sandwich. I kept looking. I went into a pub. The statues on swivel stools cracked their necks trying to look me up and down, then turned back to their pints. I ordered milk. I told them where I was from, asked for directions. They heard me wrong. One of them said: "I didn't know there was a war in Boston."

After a while I found the apartment complex. I checked the numbers of the address three times. They were right. I went to the vestibule door and tried to go in, but it was one of those deals where you had to buzz someone to open the door for you. The apartment numbers on the intercom box were worn off. I couldn't get myself to press any button. I didn't know what time it was and I didn't want to wake anybody up. I resolved to spend the night outside and try in the morning.

If you knew which one was the right button, would you press it?

The question just appeared in my mind as though someone had actually uttered it. Would I? I recalled not being able to place the call earlier, either. Why?

The light in the vestibule came on and a young man and a woman exited together. They paid me no attention and I caught the door before it latched itself. I went inside where it was warm and climbed the stairs and found Allison's mother's door. I stood in front of it, listening. Then I knocked.

The answer came to me then. *It's harder for someone not to help you if you're at their door than if you're at their gate, or in another city calling them on their phone.* The cold cunning of this thought surprised me.

Allison's mother opened the door wearing a bathrobe over her pajamas.

"Ismet, luv!" she said as Allison popped her head from behind her.

"Ismet," Allison squealed, "what's the matter?"

Things sloshed in my head.

"I escaped," I said and they took me in.

They drew a bath for me. They gave me some of Allison's brother's old clothes. They made me spaghetti for dinner and sat me down at the dining room table and asked me millions of questions. I told them everything: about why I had to run away, about my uncle in America, about my family, my town, my country, the war, my hobbies, my favorite books, my favorite movies, my favorite color. I told them I had never done anything like this before, that I had no idea what I was doing but that I had to.

"We'll think of something tomorrow," Allison's mother said. "Don't worry."

She looked like my mother in the old days, a blonde and a non-smoking version of her, and I trusted her that things would turn out all right. She went to bed, and Allison and I held hands in Allison's room and talked all night and I felt unreal again, like I was watching footage of myself.

Come morning, during cereal, Allison's mother had it all figured out.

"Yer plane ticket to Zagreb is waiting for you at the Croatia Airlines office at Heathrow. Window seat. On the eleventh."

Allison clapped hands, jumped up, and embraced her.

Inside me: kazoo music, confetti, fists pumping, childish voice screaming *Yes!*

The phone rang and Allison's mother turned to answer.

"Excuse me?" I heard her mother say, then, "Come again?"

Allison's mother motioned to me with the phone, eyes popping out of her skull.

"It might be for yee. It's no' in English."

Mother?

She put the phone in my hand, this thing connected to the wall with a spirally wire, and I felt the weight of it and the weight of whoever was on the other end. My biceps strained to get it to my ear.

"Hello," I said in Bosnian.

"What's up, man. It's Omar."

"Omar?"

Where did he get this number?

"Listen man, we haven't left yet."

He paused and then continued as if I had asked him a question.

"Well, a bunch of people ran away from the group and Branka is trying to round them up. They just figured out where Ismet is."

He paused again. I couldn't even manage a grunt. He continued with his one-sided conversation.

"One of the girls in the troupe spilled to Branka that he fell for this one girl. Branka and immigration called the school and talked to her drama teacher, who released her addresses. They just went by the girl's father's house and didn't find him there. So they are on their way to her mother's right now."

He was warning me. We had been friends for a long time and I knew him well, which is why I didn't expect this degree of devotion, especially considering how close he was with his mother.

"Are you sure?" I asked.

"Yeah. They're gonna pick him up and bring him back and then we'll leave. They know the other guys are in London."

"Thanks, man."

"Okay then. So I'll call you again when I get to London."

The line clicked. I walked to the dining room wall and cradled the phone. I wiped my tears and turned around. Allison and her mother looked immobilized by my body language. I swallowed.

"They know where I am."

Allison's mother put her hands on my shoulders and said, "Nobody is taking you away. No' if I can help it." She called her lawyer friend and asked him what the best course of action would be, and he said that, because I was Muslim, she should take me to a mosque in

Glasgow because there was a very strong and well-organized Muslim community there and they could advise me in legal matters better than he could over the phone. She called in sick, packed me a bag of her son's clothing, and rushed us out of the flat.

I felt pleasantly paralyzed in the car on the way to Glasgow. Someone else was in charge. The heater was working. Droplets of rain traveled sideways across the side windows and couldn't get me wet. Allison was pumping love through my hand. Up front, her mother was reassuring me that everything would be fine, that it was my destiny to make it to America, that I should not let the dream die.

Well, is it destiny or is it a dream?

We pulled up into the parking lot of a pretty big Islamic center and the posterior mosque. The building was made of brick and there was a squat pillar with a speaker on top of it, posing as a minaret. Allison's mother went up to the information booth by herself, and Allison and I held each other feverishly in the backseat and kissed until we couldn't breathe. It felt like the end of things with the rain drumming on the roof.

A man named Tariq, some kind of liaison for the center, received us in his small, simple office. He had one of those white flowing thobes and a Rasputin beard you could hide a cat in. He served us black tea with milk and listened to my predicament with genuine interest and understanding.

Apparently, the center's legal representative had the day off and Tariq said that the best thing for me to do was to stay there until the next day. They had accommodations for refugees and asylum seekers in the back and he would provide food. Allison's mother kept stressing safety and he assured us that I would be taken care of. Allison wanted to stay with me but he said that would not be possible.

Allison and her mother left, said they'd be back tomorrow. Tariq saw me cry and then asked me if Allison was Muslim. I told him no. He shook his head at me and put his hand on my shoulder, said:

"Perhaps it is good that they are gone, yes?"

He showed me around the complex. When it was time for noon prayer he took me to the mosque. During prayer I murmured *suras* that I knew, that my grandfather taught me. I didn't know when to kneel and when to stand up, when to touch the *serdžada* with my forehead, so those aerobic parts of the prayer I copied from the man in front of me. Tariq then took me to his house and fed me some kind of spicy egg dish, which we ate with our fingers, dabbing pita into the mush. *The Death of Yugoslavia* was on BBC and I watched it die, again.

In the evening he drove me back to the center, showed me where I was to spend the night, a small room in the back of the mosque with gym mats stacked in one corner and a cabinet full of gray blankets.

"Tomorrow Dr. Habib will make everything all right, God willing," he said.

Dr. Habib was a skinny Egyptian man in a well-fitting suit, and he did make everything all right. He looked over my papers and said that there were no legal grounds for Branka to make me go back to Bosnia if I didn't want to go. He called immigration and informed them where I was, that I didn't wish to return with the troupe, and they wished me a pleasant rest of my stay in Great Britain. While Allison and her mother were parking, Tariq asked me if I wanted to stay at the center instead and I said no. He smiled sadly and shook my hand. As I left his office I caught a glance of his expression in the glass on the door. The joy with which I was leaving appeared to cause him pain.

Excerpts from Ismet Prcić's Diary from June 2000

On the surface, *mati*, everything is fine. I got accepted to UC San Diego. Melissa and I live together in sin. We found this little house in North Park, a neighborhood in San Diego. We're sharing it with another couple. Ben and Jen are their names. Jen is Samoan. Ben has a cat and Melissa is a sucker for those. None of them has any idea what's going on in my head, where my gun is.

My memoir is a sham. Who am I kidding?

I *might* come to Bosnia to see you again, *mati*. Maybe in a year. If I find the money. I'm looking into this one place that does medical testing, sleep deprivation studies, experimental drugs and such. Maybe I'll sell them a kidney. Or my brain. I don't want it anymore.

I realized tonight that I may have lost my virginity in Scotland. And not with Allison. I remember it . . . I think I do. I had forgotten. Is that even possible?

Allison. Asja. It's terrifying how these people come into your life, do what they do, and get the fuck out. Gone.

(. . . going through the motions . . .)

It was the late summer of 1995 and Bosnia was still bleeding somewhere on the other end of Europe. Mustafa was getting drunk with Allison's father at his party in the posh part of Edinburgh.

Allison's father was a chatterbox and Mustafa pretended he understood more then 20 percent of the words that were coming his way. The Scotsman went on and on about the process of aging whiskey and Mustafa humored him, the whole time trying to strategically maneuver his host so he could steal glances at his daughter. He was in love with Allison. He had met her the first day in Scotland because she did promotions for the venue. She had a boyfriend and was way out of his league physically. He read once that some poets would allow themselves to fall deeply in love and then break up on purpose just to have inspiration for their tragic love poems. He was like that. For him there was nothing better then being young, skinny, and sad about girls.

At first the Bosnians and the Scots did not mix at all, but as alcohol blurred the cultural border, things got better. Mustafa played Green Day songs on his host's Gibson and everybody sang along. Allison's father kept saying that the new generations had no idea what music was and that three chords over and over again did not constitute a song. Allison said to disregard his comments and sat in front of him, bobbing her head. Some of her girlfriends followed. So it wasn't exactly the blackest day of his year.

But by 2 AM the following things had happened: He had had too much to drink, had broken two strings on the priceless guitar and had it torn out of his hands, some fragile fifteen-year-old girl had projectile-vomited into a fern plant and was later carried home in a blanket, and Allison's boyfriend, William, had showed up unexpectedly and she was really happy and almost sucked his face off. Painfully, Mustafa watched William's left hand squeeze her ass in slow motion over and over again.

So he waited until Allison was out of the room to try and head-butt William. The next thing he knew he was outside with a bump on his head, walking arm in arm with somebody in the cold wet night.

Her name was Leslie. She was a busty eighteen-year-old with curly rust-blonde hair kept away from her face with an armada of hair clips. Her eyes were too close together and she wore denim overalls. She looked like a girl one would meet at a county fair.

"Fun-see a reed?" came out of her mouth and he thought she had sneezed. He couldn't remember the phrase to say after someone sneezes, so he went for the literal translation of a Bosnian equivalent. "On health," he said. At that point she thought he had sneezed and her facial features pulled into a grimace of utter confusion. He smiled like the drunken idiot that he was.

"Fancy a ride?" she repeated more slowly and with a touch of annoyance. This time he figured she was offering to drive him home. "Yes. It surely beats walking drunk," was what he said.

Then they walked. He kept waiting for her to stop by a car somewhere but she just kept on walking. He figured she had just parked far away. But then she led him down some stairs and into the basement of an apartment building. She leaned him against a green wall and unlocked her front door. She didn't even bother to answer his questions anymore, probably because he was asking them in Bosnian. She sat him on a queen-size bed and disappeared into the hall.

Her room was a meticulous composition of straight lines and sharp corners that had him feeling like he was in the middle of an abstract painting. The fringeless carpet looked like a flattened sheet of aluminum foil, the desk was a hollow cube, and the lamp a pyramid. It took him a minute to realize there were no round shapes anywhere. Even the screw heads in the furniture were angular.

On the wall was an eight-by-eight-foot metallic frame without a picture. He didn't know if this was a statement or if she hadn't had time to put one in just yet. No stuffed animals. No pillows. He imagined having to vomit into a cube-shaped toilet bowl and freaked himself out.

When she returned she was naked and her face and nipples were painted in metallic makeup. Her pubic hair was trimmed into a perfect triangle. She walked over to the stereo and the sound of a vacuum cleaner came from the speakers mounted over the bed. After turning on the pyramid lamp, she killed the general lighting. He just sat there like a frozen drumstick. She said something in a robot voice and started to unbutton his jeans.

He guessed they fucked, but his brain still remembers it as him being vacuumed. She did it to him mechanically, her on top and him on whiskey. The only thing he remembers doing before he passed out was imagining Allison's bedroom and visualizing it with a heart-shaped bed and fuzzy red pillows, with round windows, and William-less.

Excerpts from Ismet Prcić's Diary
from July 2000

San Diego. Beach, beach, beach. Beach bunnies and beach bums. Meat-market bars. Bush stickers on the backs of ginormous vehicles. Baseball caps, everywhere.

I feel like a pig in Tehran.

I'm afraid to write about Melissa. It seems that as soon as I write about someone I love, they are gone and forgotten. Like Asja. Like Allison. I guess I'm just that kind of guy who has to have someone to love even when he knows the love is doomed. Girls like stepping-stones. *Is it love?* a techno band would ask.

Melissa's hard to wake up for school or work, but when I finally succeed, after at least forty-five minutes of warnings and begging, she graces the living room with her presence (in her underwear), lasers through me with her eyes, and says, "You're fired," then turns to the cat, the ottoman, the love seat, Ben's poster of *Endless Summer,* each time repeating the phrase, after which she stomps off into the shower. She kisses with abandon and to her love is sharing a guava and cheese pastry from a Cuban place down the street, and walking together while holding hands, bitching about the sun, and, if it happens to be raining, stopping whatever we're doing—and I mean *whatever we are doing*—to go outside barefoot and walk in the wet grass, beaming at this magic falling from the sky.

. . . she is slipping away from me.

(. . . zagreb diaries . . .)

My first time on a plane (London–Zagreb) and all I had was this little black leather tobacco pouch hanging in my underpants like a second nut sack, containing all my money. It was digging into to the skin down there like a critter, like it was trying to merge with me and give me more balls. I appreciated the constant reminder that the money was still there—that at least I had that—but all the sweat was starting to give me a rash that I couldn't quite go after the way I would have had I been alone.

The pouch was old-fashioned, with a drawstring, and featured a gold drawing of a mosque, on account of which I was convinced that, any moment now, God would smite me with mechanical failure or pilot error, yet nothing happened. The jet engines kept on humming, and an exhausted, wrung-out businessman next to me, with his tie undone and hanging around his neck like a dead adder, unbuckled and walked drunkenly to the lavatory. I used the opportunity to rearrange the two sacks for minimum sweatage, scratched my balls viciously, and looked out the window.

Down there, somewhere, I had left Allison and her mother in tears against the backdrop of craftily displayed cartons of cigarettes in a duty-free shop and walked through the metal detector without a peep. Allison and I hadn't slept at all on the overnight bus ride from Edinburgh to London, but held hands and watched the almost full moon follow us, peeking through the window like a veteran chaperone, making sure we weren't doing anything naughty while her mom was dozing in the seat behind us. Allison was a mess. She had broken out in zits from all the nervous tension around my departure, and her lips were chapped and sore, so our last kiss was painful and short and full of woe. I had never cried so hard. We promised to write every day and went through our assortment of private, teen, puppy-love jokes and rituals, and then I was gone.

The businessman came back, zipping up, and noticed a postcard in my hand that Allison had signed with a row of *x*'s and a row of hearts. He gave me a spineless, despondent smile, an everything-must-go-today-because-I-owe-some-bad-people-some-money-and-they'll-be-coming-after-my-kneecaps-with-a-lead-pipe kind of smile. With a face like that he couldn't do any better.

He said something in my mother tongue, something sexist and Balkanicly crude, and I screwed up my face like I didn't understand, pretending to be an Englishman. I just couldn't handle talking to a brother Slav all the way to Zagreb. I wanted to be left alone for the sake of both of us. He looked at the *Guardian* in my lap, smiled as if to say, *Okay, I believe you,* then uncapped a knobby bottle of Tanqueray and pushed it through the air in my direction. His hand was clammy, glistening. I declined politely but cuntishly, at which point he blurted out in his loud, creaky English:

"To sveetharts!" and took a seemingly painful swig, shook his head once and put the bottle back into his briefcase. In there I also caught a glimpse of a package of crisps, an overcircumcised summer sausage, and a wedge of sagging Brie, its rind untouched. He gave me another shit-eating grin, simultaneously calling me a faggot in Bosnian and looking me in the eye, probing, searching for a glint that would break my character. But I looked at him as if through a monocle, the way the Duke of Edinburgh in the nineteenth century might have regarded an infectious ape that monkeyed out of its quarantine. I smiled sourly from those heights and turned my gaze over to the clouds and to heartbreak.

From the air the city of Zagreb looked slimy, covered with a gauzy, egg-whitey layer of watered-down clouds. The flaps on the wing started to sporadically deploy, their inner workings churning like intestines, slowing us down. The safety belt sign pinged on and the captain started his garbled prepare-for-landing patter. In his slumber the businessman's face went from slack to a painful frown, which held until the announcement was over, at which point he relaxed it again.

Something began to stampede back and forth in my stomach. It wasn't the landing. Well, it was, a little bit, but mostly I sweated what would happen once I was down on the ground.

"Passport," said the young officer in English, noting the *Guardian* under my arm. He began to smile but when I failed to produce a maroon British travel document and instead flashed my blue Bosnian one, he aborted it and hid it behind a compulsory twitch of the lips. It fell like crumbs off his face.

"Are you aware that Bosnian citizens now need a visa to enter Croatia?" he barked, his voice suddenly an octave lower. His pink, shaky, nail-biter hands fussed over the covers, overtouching them, turning the thing this way and that, flipping it open and closed as if he'd never seen a passport before.

I pointed to the visa.

It trembled there in his hands, stapled crookedly to a page in my passport, its edges sticking out, dog-eared and yellowy from finger grease. He looked at it, touched it, rubbed it with his thumb as if to check its authenticity, looked at it against the light. The only thing he didn't do to it was lick it.

"Is there a problem?" I asked in a language he could understand.

"Wait right here," he said and dialed a number.

The problem, of course, was my Muslim name in the wake of recent clashes between Bosnian Muslims and the Croats in Middle Bosnia, despite the fact that there was a coalition of their respective infant republics standing against the common enemy to the east. Some villages got torched. There were reports and videotapes of children being tossed out of windows onto bayonets.

Anchored with my elbows against the booth I stood there, leaning, fighting off the fear and the rapid light-headedness deflating my skull. My reflection in the glass was ashen. Only the eyes now looked alive. Everything around me, ashtrays, tiles, people—they all flickered and then came into focus, bursting with reality, with the essence of what they were. *This must be the end,* I thought, my eyes grabbing at every image as though I were about to go under. Why else would the tubercular grayness of the tile mean so much to me, unless it were a parting image of this world I was surely about to leave?

But someone screamed behind me, a woman. Then something fell to the floor, and by the time I turned around I saw two men at each other's throats. The woman next to them had one hand pressed against her breasts and the other rigidly fanning the dip where her neck met her breastplate. On top of that her burgundy face, presently shot full of blood, was outraged the way only an Englishwoman's can be.

The two men fought like four-eyed librarians, with their heads craned backward as far away from the fight as possible and both hands blindly flapping in front of them. All the blows were thrown from the elbow with the eyes shut, hitting each other's shoulder or forearm or, mostly, nothing. When airport security finally stepped in and pulled them apart, the Englishwoman's knight, a cotton top in a tweed jacket with an unlit pipe still protruding from his mouth, had the other man's atrocious tie in his fist.

Lo and behold, the other man was the businessman.

"Let me go, motherfuckers, I'll break all your legs!" he screamed in Bosnian, as they dragged him away, his comb-over sticking up thinly as though running away from his wild eyes.

"Pervert!" screamed the cotton top in English and looked at the woman, who in the meantime had changed colors. Now without a drop of blood in her face, she was swooning and he shepherded her into a row of fixed blue chairs against the wall, struggling to communicate with an airport sec—

"Mister!"

A muffled voice from behind me. I turned toward the booth and saw it filled with a meaty shape, loosely humanoid, seemingly made of fodder of the kind that God probably used to sculpt and chisel humans from back in the day. He was fitted into a huge uniform that was still too tight on his bulk. Behind him, the young officer's head looked like a grape in comparison. I froze at the sight.

"Are you aware that your transit visa is expiring tonight at midnight?"

He struggled to move down closer to the rectangular opening in the glass between us to hear me.

If you don't stay with me until the last possible moment I will hold it against ya, Allison had said. But this *was* cutting it close.

"Yes," I managed.

"What is your plan then?"

I had learned this part by heart.

"I'm going straight from here to catch a bus for Tuzla."

"When does it leave?"

"Four thirty."

"How are you getting there?"

"I have family here. They'll take me."

He looked at me with his dull, whale eyes. I tried a smile. Saliva started to accumulate in the back of my throat as he held my gaze, x-raying me. If I had swallowed right then he would have seen through my bullshit. But I didn't and his gaze dropped down to my passport again.

"Do you know that failure to leave Croatia tonight at midnight will result in your incarceration and deportation?"

"Yes."

He licked his lower lip and gingerly, pedantically stamped my passport.

This time around I didn't want to have anything to do with Zvonko or Zana, the cousins my mother, Mehmed, and I stayed with at the beginning of the war, so instead I had Vedad and Neda pick me up in their little car. Its interior was stuffy, almost gooey from a recent fight that was put on hold for my benefit. It was obvious. There was a hateful residue of curses in the air, pushing at me from all sides like a liquid. In the backseat with my hands on my knees I immediately felt like an encumbrance, like dead weight. She snapped at him because he pulled out too suddenly and then made a point of cutting herself off and looking away, out the window. I caught his eye in the rearview mirror and Vedad grimaced something that was meant to be a smile. His role was unmistakable: a husband in the doghouse.

I always called them my aunt and uncle, although they weren't. Neda was some kind of a cousin on my father's side but they were more like friends of the family. She was a droopy woman with eyes like Ping-Pong balls that threatened to pop out of their sockets when she got too surprised. She looked famished and old, and you'd think it was because of the war and its wear and tear, but no. She always looked like that. Her husband was short and portly with thinning hair and the smile of a leprechaun. He had on a spanking new uniform with the Croatian Army insignia.

"I didn't know you were with the army?" I said just to say something.

"He's not," Neda said almost in anger then looked away again. That was the only thing she said for the rest of the ride.

Outside, it was like any place in the world, streets and buildings, big fat heads of politicians smiling constipated smiles from tasteless campaign posters, people walking and carrying things, people stopping to pick gum off their soles, trams sparking, pigeons shitting off wires.

Vedad talked to fill the silence, going over the plan of action once again, what to say to the INS officer, how to dress, how to avoid raids in this recent backlash against Bosnians, how to be thankful to my uncle in America for what he was doing for me. He talked about where I'd be staying and my landlady-to-be (a Bosnian-born spinster), what she's like and how to make the money last. He tried to make it sound like fatherly advice but his voice was devoid of feeling and inflection; he was just going through the motions.

Somewhere close to their apartment a traffic cop stopped us for something. I freaked out silently in the backseat but Vedad turned on a perfect Croatian dialect and started talking about the front lines and at the end of their conversation the cop just shook his hand and simply let us go without even a warning.

It became clear, the purpose of Vedad's uniform. After all, they were illegal, too.

* * *

It felt like being sold, like I was this Cuban cigar or illicit drug, and they had to finish the transaction quickly and get the fuck out. Neda just closed the apartment's door and stood there on a patch of linoleum, not even thinking of taking off her shoes, holding the doorknob in her hand for a quick getaway. Vedad introduced me to this woman, buttoned up to her ears in conservative garb, standing harshly in the corridor like a bouncer, her face austere, almost disgusted, her nose pointing down to her chin and her chin commendably reciprocating. Her gaze penetrated my head and I felt it rampaging in there, turning over tables, ripping up sofa cushions, looking for evidence of my unworthiness of being her tenant.

"Mina. Pleased to meet you," she said, although she appeared to be everything but. "It's best we take care of the business part immediately so everybody knows the rules."

I knew she was talking about money and I asked if I could use the bathroom really quick. I couldn't very well just drop trou and dig my sweaty, musky money pouch out of my underwear in front of everybody.

It was cold and white in there, as though I had stepped through a portal into, like, Narnia. A grid of sterile tiles took me in, leading my eyes around, giving me a modest tour: a small alien sink, a mirror speckled with toothpaste, a curvy tub like a giant bedpan in a corner, a pebble-glassed window overlooking a parking lot, a toilet bowl, a washing machine, and some shadows. I untied the pouch, took out the money, checked myself for a rash, and found nothing but a patch of ordinary, explicable redness. I put the pouch in the front pocket, the money in the back, washed my hands dutifully, inhaled, and stepped back into reality.

"Step this way," Mina said. "This is nobody's business but our own."

She showed me into a tiny blue room with baby blue walls, pool-blue curtains, and two single beds, their comforters a messy composition of blue and turquoise flowers, and closed the door. The wooden furniture was painted white, a dresser and a nightstand. She said her price and waited for my answer, as if I had any choice, as if I could say, *Thanks, but I'll try to find a better deal somewhere else in this foreign city where I'm practically illegal, undocumented, unwanted.* I took a thin roll of German currency out of my back pocket and gave her what she asked. Her eyes lit up and for the first time I thought she was actually a person, someone with thoughts and inner life. But don't get me wrong; the price was fair.

"Welcome," she said and went out.

Beaming with joy that I had a home base for at least a month, I walked out into the corridor where Neda was still clutching the doorknob and tapping her shoe. She looked up at Mina, who asked her to come in for a coffee now that the business was settled.

"We couldn't really," Neda said and leaned over the border of linoleum and carpet to give me a quick hug. "I'll call you later," she said to me. Vedad shook my and Mina's hand and they were out of there in no time, disappearing down the stairs, dying to continue the earlier fight, to curse and vent in their little car, exaggerate, blow things out of proportion, feel righteous and angry, demand to be heard out, cut each other off, and fall asleep facing opposite walls. The front door closed behind them.

I sat on the couch in the living room, stared into the muted TV, and endured a salvo of Mina's questions and comments that left me naked and bruised. It wasn't so much a conversation as it was an interrogation. Everything she uttered had a blunt inflection as though I were disagreeing and she needed to change my mind. I couldn't help but spill the truth; I was afraid that she'd tie me up with a telephone cable and drive shards of glass under my nails to get it out of me. In the end she knew everything, even about Allison.

"That's not gonna last. You're here, she's there, and you're going even farther away. Just suck it up and admit that it's not gonna last."

You don't know us, I thought, not really hurt but pitying her for being old and living alone in a three-bedroom apartment, not knowing what it's like to love and have someone love you. Already a little used to her brash ways, I just gave her a smug smile and let her decipher it on her own.

"Don't be a bombastic fool," she said and turned up the TV, on which a greenish helicopter passed a ridge of dry mountains and landed in the midst of scurrying soldiers and doctors, carrying gurneys, waiting to unload some injured comrades. The letters M, A, S, and H appeared in white with stars between them.

"This is my favorite show," she said curtly and actually rubbed her hands.

She laughed at everything Alan Alda said as I politely and painfully sat there, tracing the swirls of design on the couch with my thumb and thinking of Allison.

At some point someone walked out of one of the bedrooms and went into the bathroom. I saw her through the murky pebble glass on the door, a dark fraying shape gliding by, leaving short-lived, shadowy residue behind. Intrigued, I waited for the toilet flush but it never came. Instead, this shorthaired, salt-and-pepper woman, probably around forty years old, walked in slowly, hunched over as though we were sleeping and she didn't want to wake us up. I stood up like my momma taught me.

"Did I miss it?" she asked, her face drooping with disappointment.

I noticed that her whole right arm was heavily bandaged and tied up, bulging indefinably, oddly, around the biceps.

"Maybe half," Mina said, not taking her eyes off the screen. "Ana, this is Ismet. Ismet this is Ana. He's the new tenant."

She leaned over and extended her left hand to me. I shook it gracelessly and we exchanged our wide-eyed glad-to-meet-yous. Mina shushed us both and turned up the TV. Thus persuaded I sat down and watched the rest of the show with them. I didn't know what was happening but a man with a hawkish face strutted around in a bonnet and a polka-dot dress, saluting his superiors, which was funny.

In the blue-tinted darkness of my room, not being able to fall asleep as I kept remembering more and more about Allison, I stared at the broken red numbers of the alarm clock, wondering how a simple thing like 11:59 turning into 12:00 could make a person illegal.

FROM ISMET PRCIĆ'S DIARY:

September 11, 1995:

I had that werewolf feeling again, all day today, like I wasn't the only one in my body or my mind.

I can't sleep despite exhaustion. My heartbeat shakes the whole bed.

My landlady's name is Mina. Mina is SCARY.

September 12, 1995:

Bad day. Mina just had a conniption because I broke her stereo. She let me have it, her eyes lasers; I'm actually shivering. For a moment there I thought she was gonna kick me out but she just slammed the door to the living room and turned the TV on real loud. My door is closed but I can still hear every word. I need to calm down.

Spent the day meandering around the apartment because she forgot to leave me a key. Ana wasn't there either. Didn't eat anything, just a Scottish Mars bar I had in my bag. Mina made it clear that her food is off-limits.

In an attempt to snap myself out of the funk, I decided to play one of the tapes Allison sent with me. The EJECT button opened the stereo's tape deck, the tape went in, the PLAY button played it. Offspring. I jumped up and down around the living room, played some air guitar, got into it. But when I went to turn the tape, the EJECT button didn't open the deck. I tried every imaginable button fruitlessly. In the end I figured it must be one of those decks that opens when you pull it. I pulled it and it gave. A tiny rectangle of black plastic flew up, clinked against the side of the TV, and fell noiselessly onto the carpet. I knew I was fucked.

September 14, 1995:

Yesterday, Neda took me to some humanitarian organization to apply to immigrate to America. She was in a bad mood, rushing through everything as though trying to shake me off. I kept imagining myself as green slime sticking to her coat. She introduced me to the workers there and disappeared. I'm getting a feeling that I won't hear from her again.

The agency people were nice enough, helping me with the forms and feeding me peanuts. I gave them all the papers to complete my file. They said that from this point on it's a waiting game. An INS officer comes every month to conduct interviews and it all depends on him or her. They said the last one was there just two days ago and that I'd have to wait about a month or more for an interview.

At the main post office I talked to Allison for the first time and we cried. I spelled out Mina's address for her, although I had already sent her one of my letters. Then I called Uncle Irfan in America to give him Mina's phone number so he could call me. He said, "Good luck; we are waiting for you." I bought some food and hurried back to my blue room. Finished Hesse's *Rosshalde* and picked up *Peter Camenzind*.

Mina came home from work in better humor. She kept going on and on about her stereo, how it was her father's, how he left it to her with the apartment when he died, how much these little things mean to her, but she said it with less malice and more sadness. I apologized for the nth time.

After *M*A*S*H* we pooled our food and all had dinner together. Ana said that I could hang out in her room when she's not around and watch TV. The deal with her arm is that she has cancer. She thought she had got it beat but it came back and started swelling in her arm. She's in Zagreb for therapy. I'm a little spooked. I don't know what to say to her.

Today: alone in the apartment all day. The TV programs here are dreadful, just like in Bosnia: badly made puppets opening their mouths to generic children's songs, all of it amateurishly unsynchronized; history show upon history show showing black-and-white soldiers advancing amid explosions, carriers sinking with little planes orbiting them like electrons, Stukas clouding the skies, shitting out cylindrical turds of death and destruction; a fatso with a cigar, a cripple, and a man with an enormous mustache sitting around on a stage somewhere, laughing. In between they show nauseatingly dubbed, racist Bugs Bunny cartoons from the forties and fifties with black people nothing more than giant lips on tiny heads tap-dancing in the background, or domestic music videos of bad rap (Say "yo" for Croatia / say "no" for the war) and even worse pop rock (starfucker, star-starfucker / starfucker, star-starfucker / starfucker, starfucker / starfucker, starfucker, staa-ar).

I left the TV on mute and just read. Finished *Peter Camenzind* and started *Gertrud*. I like Hesse. I like that in books the world is solid and the characters' lives move from chapter 1 to chapter 2 and so on until the end. I like that.

Mina just can't let it go.

September 15, 1995:

I've moved from the blue room into Mina's bedroom. Mina moved into the living room where her TV is. Ana stayed put. My new room is big and cold and nothing like the blue room. I feel smaller, exposed, caught. Every time a car passes, its headlights press the pattern of the lace curtains over the wall above me like a net. I feel like the furniture is monitoring me. I can't sleep in here.

Then I realized what date it is. Today, this very morning, I was supposed to report at the garrison in Tuzla and become a soldier. The dreaded fifteenth of September. Tomorrow, two MPs will show up at my parents' door, looking for me. They will not find me. Not me, brother. Not me.

First I was in a bomb shelter with Mustafa's dark, stormy face screaming at me among the pipes, then I woke up in this strange bed and discovered that all my teeth were loose, and when I touched them they fell out of my mouth with awful ease, like rotten fruit off the branches, and then I really woke up in a strange bed.

I lay there in a dense clump, staring over the blurry precipice of the pillow into the void of a room, afraid to move my tongue against my teeth lest I find a salty, metallic gap. On the ceiling was a light fixture that looked like a starfish. I shut my eyes and checked for my teeth. They were still there.

It took me a while to remember who I was, until I saw my clothes deflated and laid out on the carpet in such a way that it looked like someone had gotten beamed up onto an alien ship in the middle of doing sit-ups. I shut my eyes again.

I visualized my body already in California, wearing shorts and a yellow basketball jersey, driving a beat-up convertible gas hog with a Bosnian flag hanging on the rearview mirror, my biceps bigger, meatier, my long hair in a sun-bleached ponytail, my head bobbing to the radio and to the blasting Ramones. But then Mina's phone rang in the hallway and erased all my ephemeral fantasies and my old life came back to me and I succumbed to it like a junky, like I needed it, like I couldn't live without it.

Beyond the door there were mumbles of a phone conversation, a couple of guttural sounds I recognized as groggy good-mornings between Mina and Ana on the way to and from the only bathroom, and then everything mercifully died down. I burrowed into the pillow like a fetus, trying to enjoy my blanket, stretching it tight across my back to get the sensation of being squeezed or spooned or something and stared into the photograph Allison had sent in her last letter.

There was a single troubling sentence toward the end of her last letter. It read: "Just in case you're wondering, William and I are history." It made me crazy. I kept watching them make out in my mind, his hand hungrily going under her shirt, her gasping for air, almost cross-eyed with ecstasy. I tossed and turned, shut my eyes tightly and opened them again, shook my head, trying to shatter these images, when Mina knocked on the door, a highly irregular occurrence.

"Hey, Hawkeye," she ordered. "Wake up!"

I jumped up like I was spring-loaded.

Ever since I had given her some money (to finally shut her the hell up about the fucking stereo) and subsequently made her laugh a few times, she persisted in calling me Hawkeye, her most beloved character from M*A*S*H.

"Just a sec," I yelped, hustling my way out of pajama bottoms that clung to my ankles, tripping me. My voice was too creaky, too surprised, and I just knew she thought she had caught me abusing myself. I cringed at the image I imagined her imagining. When I came out, the dining room table was set for three and Mina came out of the kitchen and dropped a wooden coaster in the middle of the table.

"Hurry up and brush your teeth," she said. "I made breakfast for all of us.

"It's *uljevak*," she added before returning to the kitchen.

"What has gotten into her?" I whispered to Ana when she got out of the bathroom. She shrugged and giggled. I went to brush my teeth.

My double looked me up and down with disgust, running his palm over his patchy stubble, then suddenly pulled down on his eyelid, exposing the beastly redness of the underbelly of his eyeball. His mouth open wide, he cocked his head sideways and leaned in as though for a kiss, only it felt more like he was about to bite down and tear off a chunk of my cheek. He stopped centimeters away from my own mouth, smiled and breathed toward me like a silver-screen villain exhaling smoke into our hero's face while the latter is gagged and tied to a chair. His something-died-in-his-mouth fumes made the partition between us visible for a few extended moments and I felt a little safer. In the two-dimensional, fleeting cloud that hung between our faces, I drew him a fist with an extended middle finger, reached for my dying toothbrush, and watched him robustly brush his teeth.

"Sit down," ordered Mina from the kitchen as soon as she heard me closing the bathroom door. Ana was already sitting at the dining room table, fork in hand. I heard the scraping sound of Mina's knife against the bottom of the pan as she cut the *uljevak* into squares. Ana sneaked a slice of cucumber out of the salad bowl and put it in her mouth with a face like she was getting away with something.

The doorbell rang.

I looked at Ana in terror. *Police!* something screamed in my head. I wondered if I could survive a jump out of the window, six stories down from here.

"Well, will someone go and get that?" Mina yelled from the kitchen entrance, holding a blackened pan with two mismatched mittens. "My hands are busy!"

The smell of *kajmak* melting over the golden squares of baked dough pounded my head with images of my childhood's summer mornings: sheepskins covering the patch of sun in the backyard, bees humming in yellow blossoms, trees hissing with gusts of wind, Grandpa sitting on his foot, folded over his stomach ulcer, his knee under his chin, smoking. The saltiness of Grandma's creamy salad dressing, infused pink with bleeding tomatoes. Blue heavens above it all, as though open for business, and the time dripping or flying capriciously . . .

I opened the front door and was hypnotized by the sight of two men in civilian clothes. I stared at them as though they were a pair of naked, toothless Bedouin.

"Günter?" said one of them. I shook my head no.

"Günter?" tried the other one.

"There's no Günter here," I managed.

The men looked at each other, apparently devastated.

"*Nein?*" said the first one.

"*Nein?*" repeated his friend.

"No," I said, pointing behind me, "*Nein* Günter."

They craned their necks trying to see beyond me, then slowly backed away, gesturing that they understood and that they were sorry. I closed the door, locked it.

"Who was that?" Ana asked.

"Some Germans . . . I think."

"Who was that?" Mina yelled from the kitchen.

"Some Germans," Ana yelled back.

We ended up having the most marvelous conversation about food, about differences and similarities between Croatian and Bosnian cuisine, about Osijek, where Ana was from, and Tuzla, where Mina and I were from. Mina brought out some old photographs and talked about every single one of them. I watched in wonder at her newly apparent tenderness and heartbreaking pride as she pointed out various members of her extended family, illuminating their black-and-white images with stories of eccentricities, hard work, and triumph. It was as if her furrowed brow and blunt ways, this mask and shield, suddenly became transparent and revealed an extraordinarily good, truth-loving, down-to-earth person. I could have hugged her right then.

Later on in the afternoon, although frightened and unsure, I decided to go out. Part of me felt like a caged animal and all of a sudden I couldn't tolerate it any longer. Usually I gave my letters home to Mina, who had this reliable channel to get them into Bosnia via UN convoys, but this time I figured I would take my letter to the bus station myself and stretch my legs.

Parts of Croatia and most of Bosnia were occupied territories and there was no conventional postal service of any kind between them. If you wanted anything to go back home you had to give it to a trustworthy someone who was going there by bus or bribe the daredevil drivers and hope they were honest enough to deliver it. Trips that in more peaceful times took three to four hours tops now took whole days, because the buses had to go around all the troubled zones and pass through innumerable checkpoints where any military or paramilitary formation could pull you off the bus on a whim and put a bullet in your sad, hapless head.

I was sealing a letter to my mother, thinking about where it would really end up, when Ana came out of the bathroom, hugging her bundled arm like a baby, her face lopsided from pain. She walked by me like I was an abhorrent lamp and locked herself in her room, where she started to moan, a miserable lioness in a zoo. There was something both fuming and desperate about her moaning. "Fuck this arm," I heard her say. "Fuck this arm." Mina closed the door to the living room, which meant don't come in. A man and a woman started to yell at each other in some language from her television. "Fuck this arm," cried Ana.

It was as if the magical breakfast we shared earlier had never occurred.

I went out. It was not my custom to tempt fate and venture outside unless I really had to. I didn't feel like I belonged out there. My month-and-a-half-long quasi incarceration had shrunk my universe and made the outside world seem immaterial. I hallucinated stepping outside the building and sinking ankle-deep into a doughy street and having to keep moving lest I get devoured whole.

Despite all my efforts, this state of not belonging in the world (not just this city) persisted until I saw the cop. I was at the station early, meandering outside the bus parking lot, counting steps, walking back and forth between a bench and a wire fence through which I could see three parked buses with Bosnian stickers and Tuzla license plates. My plan was to call on the driver when he showed up to get the vehicle ready for departure and give him my letter home and ten or twenty deutsche marks, depending on his mood. I was checking the time on the big clock on top of the station tower when I noticed a uniformed cop, his eyes fixed on me, leisurely coming my way.

The street pushed at the bottoms of my feet, hard. There was no way of sinking into it and getting away.

Shit. What now?

While thinking this, something took over my body. I saw myself start to walk toward the cop, smiling. The cop broke his stride a little, shilly-shallied in his step, surprised by this behavior.

"Good afternoon, Officer," I heard myself yell ahead as I pulled out my passport before he even had time to speak.

"Good afternoon," he murmured, visibly miffed that he didn't have the element of surprise as he had hoped. His cap was pulled so far down over his head that it covered most of his eyebrows, making the flat part on the top bulge out comically. "May I see your personal identification, please?"

As he was pronouncing the word *identification* my passport was already in his hand. Seeing the Bosnian emblem etched on the cover he smirked.

"Do you have a visa?" he asked, flipping through the book, which opened to what he was looking for. His lips tightened as he read it and then the smirk returned.

"This expired a long time ago," the cop said, closing the passport with a motion that had an aura of finality.

"I'm just in transit," I said. "I'm waiting to get my papers to go to America, for college."

"Do you have any documents that prove this?"

"No, not on me, no."

"I'm sorry, sir, but you have no papers that allow you to stay in Croatia or to corroborate your story. You'll have to come with me."

He lightly touched my elbow to get me going. For a second I was thinking of driving my palm upward into his nose, shattering its brittle divider, pushing shards of it into his sinuses. I felt a tingling in my right hand. But I kept it at my side and walked toward the station building like I was told.

We walked in and climbed several flights of stairs, past staring citizens, who all seemed to know I was up shit creek, and ended up in a big office on the top floor. It had huge tinted windows on three walls, overlooking most of the station and the parking lot in particular. I realized the cop had probably clocked me wandering around the Bosnian buses from his desk. I might as well have worn a sweatshirt with ILLEGAL ALIEN printed on the front.

"Sit down," said the cop and took his cap off, revealing the reason for wearing it so far down over his head. The top of his head was bald in the way a cue ball is bald while the rest of it was infested with patchy tufts of brownish hair. Hanging his cap on a coat rack he reached for the door.

"Wait here," he said and stepped outside just to return in a couple of seconds with another cop, a younger, pleasanter fellow who took a seat behind the desk in front of me, fed a paper into his electric typewriter, and looked up at his boss, awaiting orders.

"We're starting a report," said the bald cop. "Answer all the questions truthfully, cooperate, and we'll make this as pleasant as possible."

"Of course," I said as if offended by the implication that I wouldn't have told the truth anyway.

"Today is October 29, 1995, 16:05. Police outpost: city bus station. Suspect . . . Name?"

"Ismet Prcić."

The electric typewriter buzzed and crackled under the junior's blurry fingers, recording everything.

"Father's name?"

"Osman."

The bald cop checked the genuineness of every answer against the first page of my passport.

"Date of birth?"

"March 9, 1977."

"Place of birth?"

"Tuzla."

"Your address in Croatia?"

"Ilica 702, 41000, Zagreb."

I had no idea where this believable answer came from. Then I remembered: It was Cousin Zvonko's address with a made-up street number. The junior cop rained it onto the keyboard like it was the truth.

"What are you doing in Zagreb?"

"I'm in transit. I'm waiting for my papers to emigrate."

"You told me you're going to America to go to college."

"Well, yeah. The reason I'm emigrating is to go to college. My uncle lives there and he's gonna be my sponsor."

The cop made a face. He walked over to the window, shaking his head. He stared out in silence for a good two minutes, grooving on his power. I looked at Junior but his face was neutral. He was just there to type.

"Tuzla is the largest free zone in Bosnia," the cop said, not turning around. "Why do you wanna emigrate so bad?"

"Better education."

"Oh, come on! Millions of others have it worse than you do. Shit, the youth of Croatia is over there, risking *their* lives and dying, defending *your* country, *your* town, and you're hiding here like a pussy."

My hands knotted into fists.

"I'm not hiding here because I'm a pussy, I'm hiding here because you're not allowing any Bosnians to stay here legally," I said before I could stop myself. "The reason I would want to enter legally, which I did, by the way, is because Croatia is the closest spot from which I can emigrate. In order to emigrate you need papers. Papers take time and I went a little bit over. Would you pass on an opportunity like this for your son or daughter? Free education in America?"

I wiped the tears from my eyes.

The cop slowly sat down on the edge of Junior's desk and let his left leg dangle back and forth. Dispassionately, he picked up my passport again. His smirk returned but this time with undergarments of malice.

"You're giving me stories without any proof. All you have is this passport and this expired visa. That's all I really know about you."

"But I have all the other papers at home. You cannot expect I carry all that on me all the time."

"Yes I can."

I broke into sobs. He just dangled his foot and played with my passport. Next to him Junior avoided my eyes as though embarrassed by something and pretended to look for things in the drawer.

"I'm sorry about that, Officer," I said, collecting myself.

The cop shrugged.

"I'm afraid that sorry is not going to make this visa valid. We're going to finish this report and then take you to the main station. You can argue your case to them, although, I'm gonna tell you right now, having an expired visa is looked upon as inexcusable. All right, where were we? When did you enter Croatia and how?"

"I came by plane on . . . I believe it was September 11. There's a stamp in there somewhere."

The cop flipped through the rest of my passport for the first time. "If you were really going to America you would have a plane ticket and a visa allowing you to—"

He came upon something in my passport and abandoned the sentence. His brow furrowed as he pulled the passport closer to his face. Finally he looked at me with disgust.

"What is this?"

He flipped the passport open toward my face.

"Oh, that's my visa for Great Britain."

"But you said you're going to America."

"Well, yeah. That's my final destination. But first I have to obtain my refugee status here, then fly back to England, for which I have a visa, and from there emigrate to the United States. My uncle bought my ticket from London to Los Angeles; that's why."

"Wait a second. Back to England?" The cop was dumbfounded.

"Yes. I was there before I came here."

"Why did you come here when you were already there?"

"To obtain my refugee status, so I can emigrate."

"To America?"

"Yes."

The cop rubbed his eyes as the Danube of veins swelled in his temple, empurpling all its curvy tributaries up the shiny dome of his befuddled head. Then he reexamined my visa against the light, which revealed to him a hidden profile of Queen Elizabeth vouching for the document's authenticity.

"When does this expire?" he asked, handing my passport to Junior.

"February, it says right on it," I said a little too eagerly.

"I wasn't asking you," the cop hissed.

Junior looked over the visa himself.

"He's right," he said. His voice was high and screechy like a parrot's. "I'm just wondering about this stamp. This visa has already been stamped."

"They stamp it every time you enter or leave," I offered.

"That's true," said Junior.

"What does this mean?" the cop asked, pointing to something in my passport.

"I've no idea. I had Russian in school," Junior said.

"I know English," I said.

The cop walked up to me and pointed to a phrase stamped in black in the corner of the visa.

"Single entry," I said reading the words in English. "That means something like free access or free to come in. It's a pretty common phrase."

The cop's lie-detector eyes scanned up and down my face, searching for telltale signs of deceit. But I made it look honest, made it look human.

"Why didn't you tell us you had a visa for England?" The cop broke the silence suddenly, aghast at my stupidity and lack of concern for his time. From malevolent judge, jury, and executioner in one he became a high school principal scrutinizing a usually decent student's bad choice.

He gave a sign to Junior, who pulled the paper out of his type-writer, crumpled it into a loose ball, and dropped it behind his desk and out of my sight, presumably into a trash bucket.

"I don't know," I whimpered. The cop tossed me the passport.

"I'll let you go this time but if I see you again . . ."

"You won't."

On the way back the world was all hard concrete and harsh edges, nothing malleable about it. Everything was definitely matter. You couldn't leave a mark if you wanted to, let alone sink into the street.

I walked, pretending to be okay, just a normal, unafraid citizen of the world putting one foot in front of the other, until the bus station tower was out of my line of sight and I knew the cop couldn't see me anymore. At that moment I started running and I ran all the way back to Mina's building, stopping only to exchange a bunch of money, buy a shitload of canned food, and stock up on airmail envelopes. I was never leaving that apartment again unless to go to the INS interview or take a final ride to the airport on the way to sunny California, its iridescent pools, its fake-breasted women— dreams in a jar, labeled and barcoded and all.

FROM ISMET PRCIĆ'S DIARY:

October 27, 1995:

No go.

America, college, kiss all that shit good-bye.

The INS officer was a fucking robot encased in a blob of doughy human flesh. His eyes were devoid of humor. His brain had the motherboard of a Commodore 64 and his thoughts were written in BASIC (IF 1, 2 AND 4 / GOTO 10, 10 being NO ENTRANCE). He was programmed not to see me as a person.

For him it all came down to a simple question: "Do you have a place to go back to?" I didn't want to lie. I said yes. (IF "YES" GOTO 10.) The interview was over.

I thought of just going back home but Mina told me not to. Neda told me there was another agency, the International Rescue Committee, through which I could attempt to immigrate to the United States, so I went and dropped off all my papers there. They said to wait a month or so until the next INS officer showed up.

November 9, 1995:

Officially read every book in the place, including the complete works of Erich Fromm. Around 3 PM thought I was having a heart attack but the palpitation subsided after about ten minutes. Ana said it was an anxiety attack and gave me half a pill of Valium. I tried reading the newspaper but it was atrocious. Kingdom for a book. Don't know what to do with myself.

November 15, 1995:

Mina went to bed early. Ana busted out a bottle of red wine and offered me some, but for some reason I told her I didn't drink. She ended up getting quite sauced and happy and we talked movies into the night. She asked me if I had seen *Pulp Fiction,* "the best film in the world," and I said no. First she screeched and then she proceeded to tell me the whole convoluted plot of it, quoting huge chunks of dialogue by heart in English, reenacting gestures and grimaces and voices. After about three sentences I realized I had in fact seen the film before, just hadn't caught the title, but by then it was too late. She went on and on and I couldn't bring myself to disappoint her. Truth be told, I don't think I would have sat through the whole thing had she not had cancer. Is that bad?

Around eleven her medication started its slow dance with the wine, and in half an hour's time her eyes, little by little, turned into slits and she thanked me for my company and retired.

November 20, 1995:

Felt good and positive, like this America thing will happen after all. Made myself get out for the first time in a long-ass time and walked around Zagreb, had a cup of coffee on Ban Jelačić Square, went to the U.S. embassy to use their library, got out two books on avant-garde theater, and read some on the bench in the park, watching the leaves glide to the ground and dog owners chaperone their pets' bowel movements.

Decided to go to a movie. *Braveheart.* Started crying from the opening image. Camera flying over the highlands and then those bagpipes kick in. Killed me. The Scottish accents made me giddy. The love story made me cry for Allison. All the freedom fighting pumped me up to the point of invincibility. Had a bunch of cops tried to deport me when I left the theater, I would have gone through them like Mel Gibson through a carload of wet cardboard cutouts—no contest. I walked back to the apartment like an invading general, chest out, eyes on fire, letting everyone know I wasn't to be fucked with.

Now I can't sleep.

November 25, 1995:
No call from IRC yet.
Ana is crying in her room. I can hear her all the way in here.

December 7, 1995:
IRC just called! *D-day tomorrow, noon.*

It rained or snowed all morning. My broken shoe was no match for the briny slush that stuck to the city streets like a dirt ganache. I had my wet right foot parked against a lukewarm radiator that stretched the length of the wall right below the window in the waiting room of the IRC in Zagreb.

Outside, on the sill, an old pigeon suffered his life with sagelike fatalism, standing on his one and only leg, unaware of the tragic state of his plumage, and blinking his eye against the wind. Still farther outside, on the sidewalks, citizens in histrionic winter head wear hobbled under the weight of their ex-Communist coats, looked at their shoes to hide their helpless necks from the chill. Something swooshed up diagonally into the window frame, a page from a newspaper bullied by a particularly ardent gust, and the pigeon hopped once to the left, cocked his head back as if contemplating this uncouth agitprop theatrical occurrence, then settled back, unimpressed, into his one-legged meditation.

In the big waiting room people waited in lines they were told to wait in, holding papers they were told to bring, looking at watches and clocks, their faces scared and ready for anything. Employees smiled tirelessly and spoke in subdued, library voices. Every new-comer through the doors mechanically stomped their feet against the welcome mat to get the slush off and collapsed their umbrellas in the same déjà vu manner.

Nobody inside or outside (not even the employees) knew that the INS officer had approved my application to immigrate to the United States. I was sitting sideways on the edge of a bench blending into a group of fellow applicants who crushed their hands, popped their knuckles, bit their cheeks, paced the room, and awaited the official results of the morning and afternoon interviews. I, too, tapped my cold foot nervously against the radiator and examined my nails over and over again, all of it out of solidarity. Like I said, I knew for a fact that I was in. I had shaken on it. The INS officer had said, "Welcome to America," stood up from behind her desk, and initiated a handshake. Unlike her fat automaton predecessor she had gentle, gray human eyes and a soft hand. Her final and most important question had been: "Why do you want to come to live in the United States?" I said I wanted to go to college, which was true. She scrutinized me for a long while, rubbing the edge of the desk with her index finger, saying nothing. Her tongue explored the cavity of her mouth as if it had never been there. A range of feelings and thoughts about those feelings walked to the proscenium of her face, posed for a moment, and then walked off the runway to be replaced by the next one. Next, she wrote something down in my file and said:

"Be good at school."

The weird thing was that I had been really calm all morning. I suppose it had something to do with the pill Ana gave me the night before. I had trouble falling asleep and when I sneaked out to the bathroom I heard her in the kitchen. She was grunting, thinking she was the only one awake, yielding to her pain in private. As soon as she noticed me her left hand dropped off her bandaged arm and she smiled that big, toothy grin of hers, a little embarrassed and a little violated, like I had caught her touching herself. She wanted to know what I was doing, dressed, in the middle of the night. I told her and she gave me a pill to zonk me out, and zonk me out it did. I woke up at nine this morning, completely refreshed and calm as a cucumber.

A healthily plump woman came out of the door marked IRC and read a Bosnian last name off a list and searched for its bearer among us, crushing her clipboard against her bosom and smiling a generally reassuring yet undecipherable smile. Looking at her you couldn't tell if you were the winner of a contest or next in front of the firing squad. A graying man on the other end of my bench shot up desperately, dropping his documents, his face made up in hope and dread. His peasanty hands were knotty and thick and unacquainted with handling papers and it took him some time to pick them up off the carpet. Through the canvas of his face I could see exactly where his sockets were situated as his ogival cheekbones protruded, making twin pointy ledges. The woman waited for him and once he was next to her she led him calmly through a big white door. The rest of us succumbed to murmuring.

When, after some time, he came out, hunched over, slow and watchful as though he were walking through a marked minefield, and came over to our bench to retrieve his coat, he wore his face like a disguise. We all looked at him trying to read into his expression, his mannerisms, and his overall vibe, but he avoided our gazes by stubbornly staring at the floor. He mumbled a quick *good luck* and exited into the street, still in his shirt and pullover. There, he put on his coat, buttoned it up, took out a pair of blue woolen gloves, probed his way into them, raised his collar all the way to his ears, looked to the right, looked to the left, and walked out into the slush.

"You think they let him in?" someone asked no one in particular.

"No way," offered someone else.

From where I was sitting I saw him stop a little way down the sidewalk and stare at the sky and the twirling descent of snow for more than a minute, his legs apart, his arms opening as if to receive a blessing or a punishment. I couldn't tell if he was thanking the heavens for a miraculous break or cursing them for their cold and egregious injustice. Eventually he started walking again and became indistinguishable in the current of people. The pigeon was oblivious and just kept on blinking against the wind.

"Prchich," mispronounced the woman with the clipboard and I rose and followed her through the white doorway, scratching off the stares from the back of my head. As soon as the door swung shut, she asked me to please keep my emotions in check when

I went out no matter the outcome of my particular case, just to be considerate of the other applicants' feelings. I asked her if she could tell me if the man before me was accepted or denied and she said she couldn't disclose that kind of information. I entered the processing office with a smile, realizing I didn't have to act for the time being.

Father was relieved when I told him the news from the carved-to-shit booth in the main post office. He didn't understand why I was still mad at him for not arranging the deal with Branka like he had promised and why I wanted him to give the receiver to Mother. Mother said happy words when I told her. The happier her words the harsher was the unspoken feeling of doom and regret escaping from her voice. Her baby was moving across the globe and the knot in her throat suddenly snapped when this dawned on her, and she started sobbing, apologized for it, said not to mind, that she was just overly emotional, and quickly wrapped up the conversation.

Allison shrieked my ear off, then said happy words that sounded genuine but distant, and the automated voice said we had only another minute and we spent it saying I *love you* in all the languages we knew: *Ich liebe dich, volim te, mahal kita, te amo* . . .

Outside, the street was a-clink with Hare Krishna. The procession of about twenty people, mostly in orange and white, stopped at the entrance to some kind of a superstore and danced and chanted to the accompaniment of a percussion squad. Passersby lingered to check out the festivities. It felt like everyone was suddenly celebrating my personal good news. The *machinal* of reality that I had observed earlier in the day was thus gloriously interrupted and I couldn't stop myself from smiling. I danced and sang and even followed the group when they started marching again. One of the leading percussionists, an American, complimented my huge grin, saying I should do commercials.

By the time I got back to the apartment they had already picked up broken Ana from the sidewalk, gathered all the scattered pieces of her, shoved them in a bag with the rest of her, and taken her away in an ambulance without sirens. They had already come with a cistern and melted away the bloody slush and washed away all the mess. They had already dispersed the gawking crowds and silenced the futile rumors. They'd done all that before I got there and entered the lobby.

I checked the mail and found an envelope with Ana's sister's name on it without any address or postal code and, puzzled, climbed six stories' worth of staircase to Mina's door, in front of which a bald police officer was talking to the teary woman from the apartment next door and writing things down in a little notebook.

Still, both eyes and mouth agape, I had no idea what kind of note I was carrying in my hand.

. . . a story is not compulsory, just a life, that's the mistake I made, one of the mistakes, to have wanted a story for myself, whereas life alone is enough.

Samuel Beckett

NOTEBOOK TWO: SHARDS*

(. . . porcus omnivorus . . .)

You know you're dreaming, because you've seen this sneaker moving like this before. The movement you're seeing is not voluntary. There's an outside force. Something else is moving the foot and with it the sneaker. A hog.

The sneaker is a Reebok, white and baby blue, reasonably clean, its laces tied neatly. It bobs up and down several times, then comes to a gradual, bouncy stop for a few moments of pregnant immobility, then goes through a few sideways moves that make one of the lace loops sway like a noose, after which there's another wicked stretch of time in which the sneaker is not moving because the hog is chewing. You can't see the hog but you know it's chewing, because you've seen the sneaker move and then not move like this before. You've seen it so many times it's boring, like the back of your own hand, like your own dick. Bosnian Muslims don't eat pigs but pigs have no problem eating Bosnian Muslims. Or anybody else. They have no problem eating dead meat. It's all very boring. And before the close-up of the moving sneaker widens enough to show a whole human leg and the hog munching on its thigh, stopping to chew, then digging in again, making the lace loop sway, you come to on a sofa in someone's house in the Valley.

Yesterday, after work, your coworkers said there was a party, that you should come. You took a ride with them because you didn't want to drive, because Jason gave you speed and pot and you felt keyed up and groggy at the same time. They promised to drive you back to your car but here you are still in the Valley on a Saturday, sweating all over someone's couch.

The sofa sags like clammy old tits. The ceiling has a cellulite problem and from a poster on the wall a white man and a black man are pointing their guns at you, about to blow you away. On the coffee table there's an array of remote controls, some smut magazines, mounds of pistachio shells, and a soldier's helmet half-full of peanut M&M's. You swing your feet to the carpet and sit up. The air around you is yeasty with half-drunk, abandoned beers. You try to remember whose place this is but can't picture any faces. It scares you, this inability. What if they don't remember you, either? What if, after coming across you lying on their sofa, glistening, they decide to call the cops on you? You stand up, trying to make no noise.

On top of the paranoia you feel like shit. You feel like someone went through your intestinal tubing with a blowtorch. You're buzzing with this unreachable, untreatable pain. You're vibrating with it. You pick up a long-dead beer from underneath the table and pound it.

There's a short, plosive sound somewhere, a door closing or a collision of two things, then a screech of metal against metal as a shower curtain is pulled open, and a gush of water against bathtub enamel. You set the bottle silently on the table and locate the front door. The next moment you're outside, running across the grass, past parked SUVs and mailboxes and driveway hoops, everywhere underneath the scorching California sun that sits smack in the middle of the merciless blue void.

The Valley is a hellhole with palm trees, a perpetual quasi suburbia. You walk briskly for about fifteen minutes and wouldn't be able to find your way back even if you wanted to. Neighborhood-watch signs make you queasy. You think you see curtains move in the windows. There's a brawny bald fellow tinkering inside the gaping crocodile mouth of an El Camino in a driveway, and you dash across the street to avoid him.

You need a ride. You need a ride or a way to call for a ride, probably a phone. It's a long way back to Thousand Oaks from here.

You check your pockets and find a guitar pick, some bitten-off nails, a rolled-up Sav-on Pharmacy receipt, and no coins. Your wallet has your driver's license, an ATM card, your Bosnian ID card, some business cards with chicken scratches on the backs of them, names and numbers, idiotic ideas, makeshift maps, book titles, band names, bullshit. There's no money, which means you'll have to find an ATM, get out a twenty, take it to a store somewhere to break it, then find a pay phone. You think if you just follow a major street you'll eventually hit a minimall.

Mostly there aren't any sidewalks. Walking is discouraged in the Valley. Motorists at red lights gawk at you or avoid your eyes and lock their doors.

You've seen pigs eat dead villagers: big, pink, fleshy hogs feeding on gray, wet, dead people. You've seen other things, too: chopped-off heads near makeshift goalposts, human-ear necklaces, dickless, toothless, breastless, scrotumless, noseless, eyeless, fingerless, armless, headless, legless, pissed-on, shat-on, came-on, carved-up, stabbed-through, burned-up, bludgeoned, fucked-with bodies of men and women you knew. You've seen all this and yet the images that come back to you now, night after night, nap after nap, are from the TV footage you saw toward the beginning of the war: a close-up of a sneaker, moving, then stopping, then moving again until a slow pan reveals the hog.

Memory is bullshit.

Stop it.

You make yourself look around. Corner of Somewhere and Someplace. The crosswalk signal is red. Cars are zooming by: an Asian lady in white, a fat redhead smoking a cigarette, a man with a thin mustache, a hippie stereotype in a tie-dyed VW van, a police cruiser. You can't stand standing there.

There's a song in your head, something accordiony from back home. You think about firing bullets into unsuspecting bodies, rib cages ripping open, heads caving, oozing stuff. The music in your head gets louder and you realize that it's not exclusively in your head.

A man wearing black slacks and a wife-beater stumbles out of a beige house and opens a tall door to the backyard, where apparently someone is playing a song you know on an accordion. He's yelling into his cell phone and it takes a surreal moment for you to realize that he's speaking Bosnian.

". . . park it on the grass, then, I guess—fuck it!" he says, then waves to someone behind you.

You turn around and find a burgundy minivan there, its driver with one hand on the wheel and the other holding a cell phone to his ear, waiting for you to get out of the way. As soon as you hop aside he has the minivan slanted up the gentle slope of the lawn, its fender kissing a rosebush. You look up and down the street. There isn't a parking spot in sight for miles. It's another party. With Bosnians this time.

Out of the van comes a gaggle of boys and girls, all of them screeching in English. The wife-beater man makes them all high-five him before he lets them squeeze by and fuck off into the backyard.

"Domaćine," says the driver, locking the van with one of those key remotes. *Be-beep!* Both men raise their arms like they haven't seen each other for years, step into a hearty hug, then smack kisses on each other's cheeks, three apiece.

"Come on in, come in!"

"Did you start without me?"

"Shit yeah, we started last night."

"I heard, I heard!"

The driver walks toward the door, then realizes that the man in the wife-beater hasn't moved.

"Are you coming?"

"Yeah, I just want to smoke a cigarette in peace. Go get yourself a beer."

"Hurry up."

You watch all this like it's a play; it isn't until the man in the wife-beater gives you a look that you realize you're just standing there, staring at him lighting up. He's thick and meaty, older than you, with thinning black hair held up and against his skull with what must be bucketfuls of gel, all of it painstakingly combed to give the whole head a ribbed texture, like in Mafia pictures.

"You want one?" he says to you in English.

You don't usually like talking to Bosnians in America. You feel like they stand in the way of your complete assimilation. You don't like the doubling of words in your head, things coming out in Bonglish. But then you remember you still need to make a phone call.

"All right, give me one," you say to the man in Bosnian, watching his eyes pop open, bloodshot and blue, almost teary.

"Are you here for the thing?" he asks, lighting your cigarette, a menthol, nodding back toward the house. You get a whiff of his breath and for a second you're back with your dad and his slivovitz-drinking friends, yelling at the soccer game on TV, clapping yourself on the forehead when they just miss it by an inch, watching them swear and say stuff like "My aunt Devleta would put that in" or "Fuck his mother, he's got two left legs."

"No, man—I was just walking by and heard the music."

"Where are you from?"

"Tuzla. You?"

"The whole of Tuzla a single goat did milk, and then keeps on bragging that it feeds on cheese." It's an old song about your town, and he's smiling like he's proud he remembers it after all these years. "I've been there a million times. My ex-girlfriend studied there. Jasna Babić. You knew her?"

"I don't think."

"Kind of shortish, blonde hair?"

"I don't think so."

"Tits up to here?"

"I don't think so, man."

"Man, she fucked like a pike."

He takes a drag, a sad toke of nicotine fumes and nostalgia, looking glassily away. You try to emulate him.

"She got blown up by our own shell," he says, and smokes. You don't know what to tell him, so you just ape his mannerisms. You read in *How to Make Friends* that it puts strangers at ease.

"I told her a million times to fuckin' get out," he continues, but then stops himself. Something like anger blows across his face. His eyes change. "Oh, fuck her. Her fuckin' choice." He smokes some more and then says, in English, "There's plenty of pussy in the sea," and laughs, smacking you on the back so hard it uproots you. His cigarette is almost to the filter now, and you still have to ask about the phone.

"Listen—" you start.

"When did you get here? To the States."

"Uh . . . end of ninety-five."

"How'd you get out?"

"Got wounded in battle. They let me go."

"Wait a minute, you were a soldier?"

He's suddenly very close to you, looking into your eyes like a lover or a nemesis. You nod, leaning backward. You swear to God he starts to cry a little, embraces you like he did the driver earlier, and kisses you on both cheeks.

"You have to come in and party," he manages through his genuinely shrinking throat, then hugs you some more. Clamping your neck, he maneuvers you toward his house. "I won't take no for an answer. Not even in theory."

"I should—"

"My pops would love to meet you," he says, ushering you past a line of color-coded garbage bins. "He still can't forgive himself for not going back to fight when you guys needed it the most."

Most of the backyard, you see, is taken over by a long, white tent. Underneath it forty or fifty people are packed around a long table, fanning themselves with paper plates, gulping down beers, yelling, laughing, standing up to make announcements. Little kids run in and out of the house with sticks in their hands, marshmallows stuck on their tips. Their mothers run after them, screaming for them not to run. They scream in Bosnian and the kids answer in whiny English, complaining that so-and-so's mother is letting so-and-so do what he likes, look. In the yard's far corner there's a kidney-shaped hole in the grass, the beginnings of a pool, in which a hairy man with a T-shirt tied around his head is using the shallow end to spit-roast a pig. Something is a little off.

"Here," says the wife-beater man, handing you a Beck's. "Let's find you a spot at the table."

As you follow him you figure it out. Next to the tent there's a three-colored flag with a yellow symbol in the middle, an Orthodox Christian cross and a Cyrillic S in each of its quadrants, four S's you've seen before. They stand for *Samo sloga Srbina spašava,* your enemy's creed from the war you fought in and survived: Only Unity Saves a Serb.

You look for the easiest way to get the fuck out of there. Through the house, maybe? Or across the pool, onto that bench, and over the wall into someone else's yard? Definitely not the way you came. Too many bodies to go through. You're mad at yourself. You should have realized something earlier: three kisses for the Holy Trinity, not to mention the pig in the pool. Shit. You sidestep timidly toward the house.

The wife-beater man has made it to the head of the table now, and he leans in and speaks directly to someone sitting there whose face you cannot see because there's an enormous blond hairdo in your line of vision, like a clown's Afro. You don't see him until he stands up, wobbly on his feet, this perfervid patriarch dressed in Chetnik war paraphernalia, *šajkača, kokarda*, greasy gray beard down to his bellybutton, a pistol grip protruding from his pants.

"Where is this soldier man?" he yells, looking around while his son tries to keep him standing. He speaks in a patchy Serbian dialect with a rural Bosnian lilt, only a Bosnian Serb, a wannabe. You're six feet from the back door when his hammered eyes finally find your own. The man smiles and waves you over.

Running right now would not be a good thing. A calm voice from within tells you to do what you're told. You raise your bottle to the man and take a royal swig to buy yourself some time, then saunter over. Some of the people around the table pat your back. Those that can't reach you raise their glasses in your honor, then go back to their conversations.

"Make some room for the war hero," snarls the patriarch at the clown-fro lady, who has a face full of deviled egg.

"I'm done anyway," she blurts, spraying egg bits out of her mouth as she stands. The wife-beater man and his pops shepherd you into her seat. Up close you can see that the old man has an elaborate tattoo on his shriveling forearm, a black shield with a red and blue border. In its center floats a two-headed eagle with two yellow swords held crossed beneath a human skull. Cyrillic letters are inked above and below it: FOR KING AND FATHERLAND. FREEDOM OR DEATH.

In 1993, your unit crawled through a sticky minefield to take out a machine-gun nest as prep work for the early-morning offensive. The Claw, the leader of the unit and a truly insane individual, crept into the nest without his boots on and stabbed the last Chetnik in the back. He came out with a souvenir, a banner with an identical skull-and-swords design. A pirate flag, he called it.

The patriarch claps your back and squeezes your arm, telling you how his dad was a Chetnik in the Second World War under the direct command of General Dragoljub "Draža" Mihailović and so were both of his brothers, and how he, the youngest, was too young to fight back then and how his father liked him the least because of that, and sent him to "Čemerika" without a dinar to carve a place for himself in the world. As he talks you start thinking of a different way to get out of here. Plum brandy.

"We should have a toast for staying alive despite everything," you say, and swig your beer again.

"Wait for us," the son says, looking around for his beverage.

"You're gonna toast with beer?" You turn to the old man. "We need something stronger for this, right?"

"He's right," the father says. "Miloš, go get the *rakija*."

An effete, shuddering fan trained on the back of the old man's head putters to a stop. He swears, leans down to the grass, and fumbles with its cord until, resuscitated, it starts to twirl again, halfheartedly.

"Connection," the old man explains.

You clink your beer against his and you both drink. He starts to talk again.

"See, both of my brothers were savagely killed. Dragiša, God save his soul, was caught and executed by the partisans in 1942 or 1943, we are not sure exactly when. His body was never found. Zdravko, God save his soul, was axed to death by the Zeleni Kadar in northeastern Bosnia. Fucking Turks. They chopped him up into pieces like a birch log. He came back to us in four burlap sacks."

He slams his fist on the table like he's in a bad play. Deviled eggs jiggle on his plate. His eyes well up. You hold his gaze while tightening your lips and shake your head in your best approximation of commiseration.

"After that my father hated me, said that if I'd been with my brothers to watch their backs they wouldn't be dead now. But I was only twelve years old."

Miloš comes back with a plastic Fanta bottle full of yellowy liquid and a tray of clashing shot glasses. As he passes by her a woman in black stands up from the table.

"What do you want that for?" she booms at him. She has a mouthful of gleaming golden teeth.

"To drink."

"You want to kill your father?"

"He told me to get it for a toast."

"It's the middle of the day and he's drunk already. You'll give him a heart attack in this heat."

"Raki thins the blood, Mother," he says, and puts a shot glass in front of his father and another in front of you. He fills them all the way to the lip and then pours himself one as well.

"To survival, despite the enemy's best efforts at achieving otherwise," you say, and raise your glass. Miloš and his father follow.

"Whiny Turkish cunts!"

"Fuck their mothers on their shitty prayer rugs!"

You hold up yours until everyone at the table who wants to join in has a beverage in their hand, then slam it to the back of your throat, feeling like someone napalmed your stomach ulcer. It takes a conscious effort to suppress your urge to vomit. It's not the brandy making you sick.

Your mother's body flashes in your mind's eye, a skeletal figure too brittle and head-shy to hug after her stint at the camp. You shake your head to get it off your mind. In her stead emerge fallen trench-mates, their faces rigid and pale like papier-mâché masks. And before the floodgates are open all the way you slap yourself, hard.

More toasts are shouted from all around the table: toasts to dead relatives, to dead relatives' saints, to the personal saints of the host's family members (his name is Jovan Cvetković, you hear), to slogans like Serbia-to-Tokyo, to President Milošević, etc. Every time a shot goes down Jovan's gullet he tries to stand up, pull out his weapon, and fire into the air, but Miloš and some younger cousins step in and dissuade him. They remind him that he's in the Valley, in America. In response Jovan drops back into his chair and moans. You're livid, but the sight of that Zastava sticking out of the old man's pants keeps you from doing anything stupid.

Meanwhile the food's been served, and now everyone's plowing through it: soups, stuffed squash, stuffed peppers, savory pastry coils. There's an accordion player, a fat person in a green felt hat with a crow's feather stuck in the band and a mustache of the sort that vandals draw on posters. He plays and sings with varying degrees of success. Every once in a while he gets a clutch of people to get up and dance kolo. They wave you over every time, and eventually you tell them the shrapnel in your leg cuts off your circulation when you sit for too long and Jovan yells at them not to bother you. Really there's no shrapnel, just nausea and cloying memories, confusion.

At some point they unload the pig, head and all, placing it on the table so it faces you with one eye closed and the other agape and forlorn. They pull the spit out of its ass and put half a lemon in its mouth. They pour beer over it and laugh and smack their lips and ask for cutlery. They're all really happy.

You're ripping apart. You see your mother climbing through an open window in Tuzla and your arms grab for her in the Valley. Your muscles remember how they had to hold on to her when she bucked and shrieked that day, trying to end it. *Let me go,* you hear her say, and the people around you dig into the pig. Your arms are rigid, holding on to nothing. Your stomach climbs into your chest. The sneaker moves in your mind, then doesn't. You want to run away or cry or start swinging.

In your heart you don't know what you want.

When some woman serves you a big, glistening piece of flesh, you throw up all over it, all over the plate, the side of the table, your lap. Somebody tilts your chair and you hit the grass, still vomiting.

"Lightweight," you hear Miloš say. You kneel there.

The woman, the clown head, helps you up. She walks you through the back door and into the house, shielding your head with her hand when you pass below a chandelier, and puts you in front of the bathroom door. She knocks.

"Hold your horses," says a female voice from inside.

She raises your head.

"Are you all right?"

You grunt.

"Are you sure?"

You nod.

"Okay. Wait until she's done and use the bathroom."

"Thank you," you manage, covering your mouth for her benefit.

"Don't puke on my carpet now," she says, smiling. Then she's gone.

You look around the hallway. Pictures everywhere, collages: Jovan in a Chetnik uniform, Jovan in a suit, younger Jovan with seventies lamb chops and a mustache, his wife in a floral-patterned dress, hugging a baby to her chest. A family portrait with a head count of more than a hundred. Miloš as a child on a donkey at a beach somewhere, Miloš on prom night with a blonde date, Miloš at the wheel of a red Camaro. A huge portrait of General "Draža" Mihailović with his round little glasses and the puff around his eyes and a beard to match Jovan's, only blacker. Next to it, framed in thin wood, is a photograph of a purplish medal. You get closer to see the caption. It reads:

General Dragoljub Mihailović distinguished himself in an outstanding manner as commander in chief of the Yugoslavian Armed Forces and later as minister of war by organizing and leading important resistance forces against the enemy, which occupied Yugoslavia from December 1941 to December 1944. Through the undaunted efforts of his troops, many United States airmen were rescued and returned safely to friendly control. General Mihailović and his forces, although lacking adequate supplies and fighting under extreme hardship, contributed materially to the Allied cause and were materially instrumental in obtaining a final Allied Victory.

—*Legion of Merit award citation given by Harry S. Truman, President, The White House, March 29, 1948*

Underneath, in Cyrillic longhand, someone has written:

The highest award the U.S. government can bestow upon a foreign national.

Your whole life, since you were six years old, your teachers have told you that "Draža" Mihailović was a bad man, a quisling, someone who fought with the Nazis against the Yugoslav Army and ordered the slaughter of thousands of Yugoslavs who were not of his faith. But here he is, an ordained American hero. You stagger away in rage. In fear.

No one's come out of the bathroom yet. You go farther down the corridor, into a bedroom, and find a phone. You dial your apartment and after two rings your roommate picks up.

"Hello."

"Eric, I need a ride from you, dude. I'm in a pickle."

"Where are you?"

"In the Valley."

"Still at that party?"

"No, I'm in the house of a psycho and need to get the fuck outta here, pronto."

"Can it wait? I'm making ramen."

"You should be in the car right now, dude."

As you say "dude" there are four pistol shots in rapid succession: *BANGBANGBANGBANG!* You look around and notice an envelope on the bed stand addressed to some other Cvetković. The mother.

"Are those gunshots?"

Ignoring the question, you read the address into the phone twice. You're pleading now. "Come get me, man."

You hear some commotion out in the corridor, and turn around in time to catch a glimpse of Miloš and his mother hurrying down the hall, arguing about where to hide the pistol, fussing.

You remember a cataclysmic night on the front line, when the snow was the color of bone in the close-to-full moonlight and the branches were spread above you like blood vessels on the anemic belly of the night sky and the bullets dove from nowhere, crashing into soft things and bouncing off hard things, and the enemy mortars smashed everything into powder. You remember the story the Claw told you that night, the one about how, some time ago, he was given orders to crawl up a hill and rendezvous with another squad of guys who were crawling up from the other side. He was supposed to wear a white band around his left arm to distinguish himself from the enemy, since otherwise their uniforms were virtually identical. He told you about how he reached the top and lizarded his way into a trench full of guys with white armbands on their left arms, squatting there, shooting the shit, until finally he realized that they were actually Chetniks, that by some strange twist of fate they'd decided on the same white armband to set themselves apart. You see the Claw keeping his cool, creeping backward, silently cocking his Kalashnikov, and killing them all from behind.

The bathroom's open now and you lock yourself in, determined to wait it out. The little room is decorated in belabored beige: beige tiles, beige shower curtain, red and beige towels, your own beige face in the mirror. You splash water on yourself, take some into your mouth, spit it out, take it in, and spit it out. Through the small, pebbled window you can see the accordion player typing an intricate Balkanesque melody on two keyboards simultaneously, acting like no shots were fired at all. You sit on the beige toilet lid, put your head into your beige hands, and stare at the tile grid on the floor, at a wastebasket, at the grid again. You think of death and Mother. You try to figure out what's right.

The wastebasket is small, wicker, and lined with plastic. You push at the base of it with the edge of your foot and the wads of tissue tumble and rearrange themselves, exposing a dull glint beneath. You reach in and retrieve Jovan's gun.

Your hand knows what to do with it; your index finger turns inward. The grip feels good. You sniff the barrel and it smells of youth, of Bosnia. You switch the safety off and stand up. You cock. In the mirror you look like the Claw, standing there against the beige. You lean closer. Your eyes are all pain.

Police sirens start off low and grow higher until they shut up the accordion player and silence the clamoring Serbs. There are conversations you can't really hear. Questions are asked. Things are blamed on the kids, fireworks. Apologies are given and warnings issued. You realize you're standing there with a gun in your hand. Where is Eric? How long does it take to get here from Thousand Oaks in an Oldsmobile?

You pace the bathroom. You hide the gun. You pick it up again. Hide it. Pick it up. You lift the tank lid, toss the gun in. You close the tank.

Half an hour later a car horn sounds and you know it's your ride. There's a party going on in the backyard again. You focus on what you need to do, take a deep breath, and get out of the bathroom and down the hallway. There are kids sitting around the table in the kitchen, laughing. You make your way across the living room. The white front door is the only thing you see. You can feel it, this elation in your chest, this glee in the muscles of your face. Your lips curl. You reach for the doorknob and wrap your fist around it.

"Soldier!" Jovan yells from behind you. "Where are you going?"

He stumbles toward you, pushing himself off the walls, almost falls but doesn't. He makes it to the back of the giant armchair and, with fifteen or so feet ahead of him without anything to balance himself on, stops there and leans on it with both hands.

"Stay a while longer."

"I have to go, sir. I didn't mean to stay this long. I have some things I have to do."

He grunts. "Eh, okay. Okay, but come over here before you go so I can thank you for what you've done for us."

He raises his arms, stumbles forward, and catches himself just before he hits the back of the chair with his face. The car horn sounds again. You can see the brown Delta 88 right in front of the house.

"That's my ride," you tell him, and start to step out the door.

"Tell me one thing."

You wait. You turn to him.

"How many of them did you—," he stops, dragging his left forefinger across his neck, "—with your own hand?"

You look at him, this son of a bitch. His eyes smirk. You want to say, *I'm Mustafa Nalić,* but you can't. You want to forgive him. In your heart you want to hug him but you're afraid you'd break his spine. You want to shake his hand but you're afraid you'd pull his whole arm out of its socket. You want to kiss his cheek and spit upon it.

"One night I infiltrated an enemy trench and killed six with one clip. They thought I was one of them. They were joking around. I just mowed them all down."

He smiles and nods his head.

"Good for you," he says.

Excerpts from Ismet Prcić's Diary
from June 2003

Melissa is gone, *mati*. Gone.

We kept fighting. For months she kept . . . she said she found motel receipts and drugs in my dirty jeans while doing laundry. WHAT?

She became so . . . cold, like she does, and I felt like I was gonna shoot her, so I stormed out of the place before I did. Drove all night. Camped in the woods. When I came back she was gone.

She's still gone. Ben and Jen (roommates) are gone, too, but they will be back in San Diego tomorrow. From outrigger racing in Hawaii. Melissa won't be. She left for good. I'm alone with Ben's cat, drinking.

I called Dr. Cyrus at midnight. Like a broken record. *Take a Xanax and write,* he said. *Write everything*. He wants everything? Here's everything:

(. . . a full minute of everything, for cyrus . . .)

. . . home sweet home and on a love seat reclined groggy with alcohol and a five-day camping trip with ticks and bears and giant trees you sit in the low glow of a 40-watt bulb with a journal and the TV on and Johnny cat is psychotically chewing his fur off and the insides of his hind legs are even more bare than when you left and his eyes are huge and loveless and the aquarium sits half-full or half-empty the fish have been moved elsewhere since it started leaking and shorted out the answering machine and there's a week's worth of *Los Angeles Times Orange County Editions* still in their plastic auras unread and splotched with desert dreamscapes broken wire fences camouflage uniforms and mushroom clouds and everything is a mess and clustered against the cyclorama of colorful junk mail offering junk food and junk dreams for prices a junky could afford are white envelopes reminding you of approaching due dates and a lady longlegs pokes her appendages at the old wine stain under the strict surveillance of the cat too lazy to get off his fat ass and hunt his own food and a car drives into a desert sunset on-screen and the metallic letters spell out *NISSAN* and then the angry young white man comes back on his baby face wrinkled with tough attitude his whiny voice gets bleeped a lot and he swears by artistic expression and spits on censorship and laughs all the way to the bank and his song bounces in the background and your hand slips to the floor and investigates around until it finds the "Kai Elua Outrigger Canoe Club" mug half-full or half-empty of diet orange soda and Albertsons vodka out of a plastic bottle purchased with your Discover card since your bank account said $18.69 last time you checked some months ago and the liquid goes down with painful ease and your eyes get a bit watery from all the mess around so you press a button to change the things you can change at the moment and the angry young white man vanishes into a representation of a faraway land on-screen with tongue-breaking names for towns split sometimes with a dash and the south is scribbled on with red and black arrows pointing north and the drawings of tanks and planes are harmless and look like something from the Cartoon Network and a white-haired white-collared white dude with a foot and a half in the grave points a pointer with his sagging hand and explains in a loveless voice "what we are doing" using sports rhetoric like "we hit the target" and "our team is easily maneuverable" and "we have the best team in the world" and fairy-tale rhetoric of bad guys and good guys victims and bullies right and wrong and somewhere across the globe civilians are being "liberated" liberated of their lives personal property culture pursuit of happiness and you press the button again as your eyes water a little bit more and the cat licks his ass and more liquid goes down and you find a bump on your back and it better not be another tick that Lyme disease shit is nothing to laugh about and some other white-haired white-collared white dude talks to a handful of white-haired white-collared white dudes about his newest book on multicultural diversity and you mute the sucker silent and imagine him running a marathon in sweltering heat and drinking Gatorade that turns his sweat green and for a moment everything is silent—then the phone screams too loud and the cat sprints into the corridor and your mind flashes to Bosnia and to a mortar shell hitting your high school gym and its detonation tossing you over three meters of tiled floor into a pinup board and your head buzzing like a hysterical motherboard and you barely hearing the sirens you know are shrill and your thoughts are comatose with the overwhelming flashback forcing itself into your awareness reminding you that things might not be so peachy after all and your heart pumps hard but off beat and the way the air escapes out of you without your control over it foreshadows the impending panic attack that freezes you in your tracks and you should go and answer that phone before it rings again screams again but you cannot move and everything is suspended as if paused by a remote control so that the being watching you dreaming you inventing you on the spot can go and take a leak squeeze a zit out and marvel at its chiseled facial features while you wait for the crushing collapse of your inner system and the ascent of baseless fear paranoia will destroy ya but it doesn't come a false alarm and you are relieved and sweaty and only if your heart would start again and then it does and you start for the phone which screams again but this time you're ready and prepared and you put aside the remote control get off the love seat step over a bunch of crap and pick up the telephone.

It isn't Melissa.

Excerpts from Ismet Prcić's Diary
from May 2004

I give up, *mati*. I gave up.

This book about my life cannot be written. Not by me, anyway. I still write but it's not a book anymore. Now I write everything.

I write "*mati*" and I have no idea who I mean by that. It's been so long since I told you the truth. Everything that was meant for you I gave to these pages. You have no clue who I really am.

I read everything I wrote. Why do I write about Mustafa? Why does Mustafa have my memories? Why did I kill off Ana? Why did I make Asmir into such a dick? Why did Mustafa put his own picture on his brother's grave? I think I wanted him to be alive. The picture was Mustafa's scam to not have to fight anymore, to run away, pull off a disappearing act, start anew, live some of my life.

I would like that very much myself. A new beginning. Old body, old mind, old stuff forgotten and done for. New body, new mind, new stuff. What a dream.

* * *

Ben and Jen, they are worried about me. Ever since Melissa moved out of the house they feel obliged to try and get me through it. They knock on my door and tell me jokes. They have people over for barbecues. They invite me to play cards or Trivial Pursuit or disc golf in the park. But there's fear in Jen's eyes nowadays. It's probably the gun. I made a mistake of showing it to her. When she comes home before her boyfriend, she stays in their part of the house—"just picking up," she would have me believe—and doesn't come out until he returns.

I stopped going to school, *mati*. I haven't paid my part of the rent. I think they're gonna kick me out.

I'm sorry you had to give birth to me, love me.
You felt no contractions. They had to induce. When they pulled me out of you I was blue and dead. They unwrapped the umbilical cord from around my neck and depressed my tiny chest inward and blew icy air down my throat. I came alive. They *made* me live.

You tell cute stories. About everybody congratulating you on the size of me. You're a small woman. I was more than ten pounds. Big head. Full of hair. Late, too. I sucked up all the calcium out of your body. They had to pull out a bunch of your teeth. Now, at fifty-four, you've got osteoporosis to deal with. Crumbling bones. And that head on me. You never peed right again. Wore pads all your life, didn't you? Plus your stretch marks. Rivulets. Like the surface of Mars.
I'm sorry about all that.

But you would laugh this off and say that two nurses came in to match the newborns with the new mothers in your hospital room and that the first one carried in six babies, three on each arm, all bound in white and wrapped like minimummies and that the second nurse followed with this one colossal infant all by itself with this big dark head that flopped around—me. I had no muscles to support a thing like that. You would say that it was the best day of your life. But that's just your story. Stories aren't real.

I thought of carrying on with the book, writing about what happened when I got to California, how I met Melissa, the love we had. But one thing about forcing a life into a story is that you become a character and when the story ends you do, too. I finished my story of escape and it finished me. There is no more narrative to conjure up and make it make sense and hide behind. Now there's just the mess of life.

Mehmed tells me to shut the fuck up when I tell him that I'm not doing well. He thinks that getting out of Bosnia is the only hard part, that I'm a wuss, that if it were him here in San Diego he would be happy and thankful. Maybe he would. Maybe if I stayed in Bosnia I would have been happier, too. I have dreams of Mustafa. I think I saw him in the grocery store the other day trying to break a twenty. I'm afraid of what I might do.

Sometime ago before Melissa broke it off for good and moved to Los Angeles with this guy, to this green apartment building on Micheltorena Street (yes, I checked it out and parked across the street in front of the elementary school one Friday and stayed up all night but they never came out and in the morning there was this squirrel that used the telephone wire to cross the street above me and I watched its perfectly balanced tail retain the shape of an inverted question mark the whole time and thought that I understood something about loss and love but already the next day, back here in San Diego, it was just a squirrel running cautiously over a telephone wire and I understood nothing), we were talking about us and she said I was stretched too thin, that I lived too many lives.

Parallel universes, maybe? String theory?

I will never write to you again, *mati,* truth or lies. Forgive me. Forget me.

(. . . shards of i . . .)

"Being a mother is the worst occupation in the world," she said in a letter.

She said she had tried to kill herself again. She said she had a mental crisis and that my dad and my brother didn't believe her and thought she was doing it out of spite and that she couldn't handle it and ran into my brother's room, locked herself in, opened the window, and sat on the sill, dangling her feet from the fourth floor. She said she muttered a final prayer and went to jump off when something stopped her, made her head swoon, and that she noticed four girls waving to her in slow motion from the parking lot below and that the sun made her sleepy and when she snapped out of it there were firemen down there and a swarm of people looking up and that my dad somehow got the door unlocked and pulled her into the room. She said that things in the family had turned to shit ever since I left, that everything changed that night when my theater troupe boarded that bus to Scotland. She said that she misses me dearly, like you would miss a limb. She said she believes in God now. She said that she doesn't know how long she'll be around but that I make her happy.

* * *

Driving home from school at dusk I do this thing. What I do is I get it up to seventy in the right lane, exit Pershing, step off the gas pedal, and coast my way first up, then down, the arc of the overpass with my arms crossed at chest level. My alignment is all fucked up, and every time, the car veers to the left and follows the curvature of the pavement perfectly on its own—no pilot. At the peak of the overpass I usually look to the right and catch a glimpse of the blade that is the Coronado Bridge at this distance, and in this light, and I imagine what would happen if I just simply closed my eyes and never opened them again.

A familiar, recurring thought.

My mind is tainted with the B movies I stay up watching every night because I can't sleep, and often at the top of the Pershing overpass I'll visualize jalopies from the 1970s flying off bridges and exploding before they touch the ground, the arms of the dummies in the driver's seats flopping bonelessly. I laugh at these and take great pleasure in this end-of-the-day-almost-home ritual.

But every once in a while I really do close my eyes. Not as often as in the beginning when Melissa first left, but I still do it from time to time, when she sends me an e-mail out of the blue or when I see a redhead. As I close them, instead of tensing up I grow limp, and instead of grooving on adrenaline I grow sleepy and think of times past. In that darkness I wish I am elsewhere, or elseone, and I let go. For a moment I'm gone like that and it's always a terrible thing that my mind does to snap me out of it, remind me where I am and I open my eyes and grasp the steering wheel. It's a conditioned response, this choosing life; I do it out of habit. Mustafa was forced at gunpoint to eat his brother's testicles, to slit his throat. That's choosing life.

At the first red light I focus on a man in his seventies in short bicycle shorts, his legs tan but shriveled, encumbered with vein knots, jogging painfully across the street in front of me. His face is miserable, the hole of his mouth kidney-shaped, drooping down, letting the air come in and out in short gusts. I'm both delighted and disgusted at this display of human determination to cling to life, to have another good year, another good minute.

When I pull up on Mississippi there's my roommate Ben unloading a boat from the top of his truck. He's in his ratty tank top showing off his outrigger canoeist triceps.

"Are you ready to party?" he asks.

"Again? Where's Jen?"

"Making a shopping list. Listen, maybe you could pick up your room a little bit? We're having some Scripps people over, too."

"I'll close the door."

"C'mon, man, I'll hook you up with a science chick."

"Yeah, yeah," I say and go into the house.

My room is a dungeon, a little cave littered with shit. I shove and kick my backpack and everything else under the bed frame, then lift my mattress up from the floor. There's an off-white rectangle on an otherwise beige carpet where my mattress was. A cockroach scurries behind Melissa's old desk in panic.

Looking at the discrepancy in the color of the carpet I start to cry.

"Liquor out of a beer mug?" Ben says, catching me in the act in the kitchen. "What is that? Gatorade and Popov?"

"I call it Piss Galore."

"You should call it a Bosnian Travesty."

I make another one right in front of him, then go to my room and close the door. I sit in the middle of the bed. It sags, almost collapses. I scoot toward my pillow. It feels sturdier. I bounce a bit.

I look around. My posters. My books. Her old desk. Her old bookshelf. In the mirror on the closet door this destroyed loser in a polyester shirt and a red face. He takes a swig but his mug is already empty. He lets it fall to the carpet.

On my answering machine a light is blinking. When I press the button the message is a single word.

"*Mati*," my mother says, or better, cries out, and hangs up. The sound of it is like a cat meowing or like a recent adolescent with a cracked voice warning his mother not to embarrass him in public.

In the summer of 2003, when I last went home to visit, my parents were at each other's throats, on the verge of splitting up. Father had become the president of the detergent company and had made a lot of money, which changed him for the worse. He bought this new weekend house on Mount Konjuh and my mother often stayed there by herself while he and Mehmed remained in Tuzla. She couldn't handle the constant fighting and the calls from unknown women telling her her husband was cheating on her. Father kept on denying any wrongdoing, expressing concern for her mental health in cold and civil terms. Mehmed was mostly in his room on the computer, washing his hands of us all.

One night that summer, in the new weekend house, I had a dream. In it a black cat grew human-size on our couch, morphed slightly into human form, and started to meow, staring at me. That was it. The cat/person just kept meowing. I woke up but the meowing continued into my waking state. It took me a groggy minute to distinguish between the residual meows from the dream and the meowlike calls that were coming from outside of the house. Barely, I heard someone calling my name.

I got up and walked out into the brisk morning. Father was gone again; the car wasn't there.

"Ismet," called my mother, and by the weird hollow echo of it I realized that she was calling from inside the well, halfway down the slope of our property. I ran to her.

Sure enough, there she was, fully clothed in the cold water up to her neck, pale and terrified, holding on to the unscalable, circular cement walls. I lowered a creaky ladder that I found in the shed and she climbed out, shivering. After a hot shower, and from a bundle of blankets, my mother laughed, said that after surviving the war, all those medical problems, and suicide attempts, it would have been pretty funny if she had died in a stupid accident like that.

But I wonder why I'm recalling this particular memory at this moment. Is it because her voice on the answering machine reminded me of a cat's meow or is it some kind of warning that something is wrong? She has her ways of communicating bad news.

I replay the message.

"*Mati.*"

After some back-and-forth I come to the conclusion that she only wanted to let me know she had called. A routine.

Someone knocks on the door and I become aware of loud music, the din of conversations. *How long has the party been going on?*

"Come in."

It's Ben with a plastic cup of wine.

"I knew I was gonna find you in here, wallowing."

"I was checking my messages."

"Pull your shit together and come out."

Ben and Jen throw laid-back but sophisticated parties for the people from their work, an oceanography lab up in La Jolla. Jen works in administration; Ben dives and cuts kelp entangled around the oceanography instruments with a knife. The result tonight is a houseful of smart, sporty, and sciency people in flip-flops with sand in between their toes, drinking fancy zinfandels and Rieslings out of coffee mugs, swaying to Ethiopian jazz, eloquently discussing anything under the sun, scratching their shapely, tan extremities, and being in every goddamned way better than me.

I drink another Travesty, pretending to be okay with my otherness, my foreignness, and stumble around gawking at female partyers. They catch a glimpse of my face and immediately abort eye contact and feverishly try to rub a stain out of their tank tops, start a conversation with somebody else, the cat, anybody, or leave the room to refill their full drinks or empty their empty bladders.

"Hello." I answer the phone on the last ring before it goes to the machine, heeling my door shut against the din.

It's my dad, solemn, somehow annoyed. He asks how I'm doing, am I healthy. The moment I hear him speak I know something's not right. I ask what is going on.

"Your mother's in the hospital."

"What?"

"They had to pump her stomach."

He can never just come out and say what's going on.

"Pills?"

"Yeah. And this time she cut her veins, too."

A girl cackles in the living room. She hoots.

He keeps talking. I can't stand him. The way he talks about it, like he's the victim.

I wanna stab, burn.

"She says she did it in the bath the night before, but Mehmed found her around noon the next day, in her bed, dressed."

"So she's out of it now?" I manage through my teeth.

"They are keeping her sedated."

I don't say anything. I can't.

"Listen, she's not well at all—" he starts, and I hang up the phone.

I walk to the mirror. I want to see what I look like right now. Right outside my room a chorus of women is screaming how they just want to have fun. My face is pulled. I look like an animal.

The phone rings. I sit on the edge of the bed.

Melissa's old desk. A picture of my parents. Father's sour smile. Mother's crazy eyes.

The phone rings.

My alarm clock. Past one o'clock.

The phone rings.

Melissa's old bookshelf. The complete Mayakovsky.

The phone rings and rings and I wait it out.

I wander out of my room, past some shapes and people.

It makes no sense. If she drew herself a hot bath, took a bunch of pills, and sliced her veins, this was no cry for help. This was a triple-insured plan.

I go into the office and stare at the picture of a jaguar on the Greenpeace calendar for a while. Someone comes in and starts to talk and I move away from them into the darkness of Ben and Jen's room. Through their window I see someone, probably a neighbor, look around to see if she's being observed, then lean over our gate, pick up one of Ben's potted flowers, an orchid, and she's gone.

I see the horrible scenario play out in my mind: my mother naked in the bathroom grinding sleeping pills with the back of a spoon against the top surface of the washer, her thumb digging in hard, crushing them into powder one by one. Or would she be prepared enough to bring a cutting board with her? Probably would. I see her sweep the baking soda–like powder from the cutting board into a glass of water with the blade of her palm and swirl a spoon in there. The liquid is white now, milky. She murmurs a prayer, drinks it, and steps shakily into the steaming bathtub. I see her reach for a knife that she had brought with the cutting board, a thin blade, smaller than a finger. She knows which one is the sharpest. Now I see her face, her faraway, fed-up eyes. I see her mean it and I shudder.

"*Mati,*" her message screams in my ear.

I'm stupid.

So fucking stupid.

Somebody's face is in front of mine, round and bearded. Its mouth is moving, baring American teeth. There is something in each of my hands now, too.

I don't know what to do.

There are pills in my hand. And a beer.

The blade slices my mother's veins; blood squirts out and clouds up the bathwater. Her head bangs backward into the bathtub enamel. Her mouth fills up with water now the consistency of a bland rosé, and only her nose, her eyes, and her forehead stick out of it.

Is she breathing?

My eyes feel like they are frying in oil.

"You all right?" someone says behind me.

"Yeah," I say, without looking to see who it is. I look at my hands instead. One empty bottle of beer now.

"We're all going night swimming."

"I don't know what to do."

"Okay. Suit yourself."

Silence. Past two o'clock.

I aim the pistol at my reflection in the mirror and wonder what would happen if I fired. I wonder if the mirror would shatter or if the slug would only make a hole or if the person in the mirror would suddenly spring a bullet hole in his forehead and slump down dead.

* * *

Past three o'clock.

There's a bottle of vodka in my hand, and a pistol in my hand, and a phone. I go out the back door, lose my balance, and fall into Ben's dewy ice plants. I try to get up and then give up on it, pour some vodka on the lower part of my face, and look around. Through the flimsy hedges I can see the glowing blue surface of the next-door neighbor's pool and nobody in sight.

For a moment it's like I hear gunfire. For a moment it's like I'm in the middle of a war.

Something moves underneath the house.

"Mustafa, is that you?" I call into the shadows.

I remember meeting this Bosnian guy in 1997 who was in Thousand Oaks for some famous doctor to fix his foot after it was blown apart in battle. He was staying with his uncle, and my uncle knew his uncle. He was crazy and scary (kept calling himself Apache) but I hung out with him anyway and milked him for war stories. The things he told me made me hollow. What he had survived made me feel unworthy of calling myself a Bosnian.

I was never forced to eat human testicles or shoot at another human being or watch pigs eat my fellow citizens. No. I ran away instead. That's what I did. That's *my* story. I left my mother behind, my father, my brother, my first love. That's it. The end.

That's why Mustafa is here, the shadow under the house.

"Here I am," he says in Bosnian, confident, smiling.

Mustafa knows the sobering horror of getting a mouth-to-mouth from a gun. He knows the reason why this man in the ice plants grasps for the steering wheel at the last moment, why he can't pull the trigger now. He steps up and takes the pistol away from him.

"Pussy," he says, smiling, aiming.

He sits in the ice plants for a long time, looking at his hands, feeling the breeze on his new skin, getting used to this.

The inside of the house throbs with the flickering lights of a TV screen. It's like watching someone weld inside a manhole.

From beneath the house a mama raccoon comes out and looks at him. She does so practically, as though trying to ascertain his threat level, realizes he's fine, goes back under the house, and slowly proceeds, one baby raccoon in her mouth at a time, to waddle through the hedge, dunk the whole litter of four in the pool water and then carry them back to the burrow.

When she's done and gone he stands up—hands on knees, testing his new, uneasy, collapsible legs—and stumbles into the house with a clear plan to do three things:

1. Drink a gallon of water
2. Get rid of the pistol
3. Live his new life

(. . . shards of m . . .)

I'm lying on my back and staring into the night sky, looking for the face of God. The sky is carved with projectiles. They leave cat scratches of white fire against the vast blackness. Things are exploding. The earth is quavering.

I'm murmuring ancient Arabic phrases that carry no meaning for me because I learned them phonetically when I was a kid.

I've shit myself. I've pissed myself. I'm cold.

I'm praying the only way I know how and hugging my empty rifle.

I'm halfway between the trenches.

Mustafa felt drained with uncertainty, frustrated by his confusion. He drifted in and out of sleep, dreams, memories. He slipped into the past, woke up in the present, dreamed about the future. Or he slipped into the future, woke up in the past, dreamed about the present. Or slipped into the present, woke up in the future, and dreamed about the past. The way his brain processed it, it was one of those things—his past was in the present tense, and his present was . . . well, the present was anything but explainable in terms of something as simplistic as past and present. The present was scrambled. The present was shattered, then scrambled. Shattered, then pulverized, then scrambled.

It was all fucked up.

In the darkness, Mustafa tried to express some of the pain but the pain there in his throat was terrible. It was in the cartilage. In the jaw. In the loose splinters of his Adam's apple, apparently wedged in his windpipe, causing him to wheeze.

"I'll fuck you into shaaaards!!!" a male voice shrieked in the distance, through walls, it seemed, down corridors. Something metallic and empty clanged against some wall somewhere and came to rest on an equally hard-sounding floor.

A pot? A tray?

"I'll break you like a vase! You'll crumble like Marshal Tito's bust!" shrieked the voice.

Mustafa became aware of other voices around him, four or five at least, weak, mumbling, grunting, swearing in the darkness.

Captured? Jail?

He tried to understand the here and now, but there was nothing on which to build a reality. Just darkness. He managed to rub his fingertips over the surface he was lying on and succeeded in suppressing his pain long enough to have an unmolested realization: *fabric.*

A bed?

Somewhere doors banged open, and beefy footsteps boomed louder as they got closer to the I'll-fuck-you-into-shards voice, which promptly became unintelligible shrieking, like tearing the living darkness in two. There were meaty thuds of bodies full of guts and breath, colliding with one another and the surfaces around them, whimpering and pleading to be left alone. But then, the voice slowly died down, and the beefy footsteps walked calmly away accompanied by the rhythmic squeaking of a wheel in dire need of grease.

A cart? A gurney?

Mustafa caught a whiff of human shit and peeled citrus over a more antiseptic underscent of industrial-strength bleach that tickled his throat and threatened to make him cough. He summoned some courage to try to move again, to test the weight that was pressing on his chest and throat, when something scraped against the floor right next to him.

A chair leg?

Someone whispered a name that was not his.

Who spoke? A woman? A man?

Someone's clothes rustled with movement and then a soft, cold hand tenderly cupped his clammy forehead and the mere thought of screaming in terror made Mustafa exchange the darkness around him for another.

Despite the shame and the embarrassment of the bee fiasco, he said yes.

Mustafa said yes because she was cute and petite and coquettish. Because she wore Doc Martins and ripped jeans and he kind of had a crush on her. Because he believed that they could end up being together for a long time.

Bullshit. He said yes because at that age you never, ever say no to anybody who one day, potentially, might pop your cherry.

When she winked at him and said, *Let's go,* he said yes. She said, *Yes, what?* and he said, *Yes, let's go.* They made out in the dewy grass in front of her building until ten minutes before the curfew when she had to physically push him off her. She gave him a handmade bracelet she always wore and asked him, *Do you know what this is?* He didn't really, but he said yes and she killed him with a kiss. Then he hauled ass home.

The very next night Mustafa made an almost fatal mistake by teasing her and calling her a little girl. She was fifteen then. They were in front of the Bosnian National Theater, the newest hot spot in their fun-filled besieged city. She slapped his face and stormed off just to come back a minute later and throw a bloody tampon at his head, right in front of everybody. He was more confused than a glob of human sperm in the third chamber of a frog's heart.

That same night, as he walked home alone, she jumped out of the bushes by the river's embankment and kicked him in the groin. The gun looked huge in her little hands. She squatted over his convulsing body and aimed at his right eye. She kept spitting into the grass over his head. She squatted there for a long time, spitting, looking.

There was no doubt in his mind that the brain behind those fierce eyes was going to send a motor stimulus to the muscles of her tiny hand, which were going to squeeze that trigger and send him to the land of wooden poles and toilet bowls for good. And he couldn't think of a single thing, to say or otherwise. His life didn't flash in front of his eyes. He didn't think of loved ones. He didn't think of hated ones either. He just cupped his nuts—a laughable instinct from the receiving end of a 9 mm Zastava.

He would later come to believe that she saw something in his eyes that made her decide not to kill him. Perhaps it was the total absence of him from himself. Whatever it was she calmly removed the bracelet from his wrist, walked away, and never looked at him again.

Things changed big-time for him after this incident. He stopped going out and spent most of his time with the basement dwellers, which is what everyone called those people who never accepted the war as normalcy and lived in fear underground.

A year later somebody found the body of a guy named Goran, who he heard was her second boyfriend, in the middle of Banja Park. He had been shot and stabbed numerous times. The story was that he pressured her into having sex with him and then, during a quarrel, threatened to tell her dad, a devout Muslim, about it. Apparently she convinced her little brother to help her take care of the problem and they killed him together. Since her mother was a judge, she ended up in Kreka Psychiatric Hospital.

And even though Mustafa was drafted and made to go and fight, and had seen people blown to bits, cadavers rotting in the trenches, children's heads atop wooden sticks, crosses carved into abdomens and foreheads; and even though he had a lot of close calls like that time the shrapnel went through the van and through the folds of his shirt around the midsection when he was bending to tie his boot, still the closest he had ever been to death was the moment before she reclaimed her bracelet. In all those other instances his life did flash before his eyes and he did think about loved ones and about those he didn't like.

"So . . . there was this kid they called Donut," said a raspy, Waitsian voice, and Mustafa came to and so did the pain. There was too much light on the other side of his eyelids now and he dared not open them yet.

"He was a little off, if you know what I mean. Drank barbecue sauce out of a glass, crapped in the elevator, threw firecrackers into people's mailboxes. He was some kind of a diabetic . . . something to do with blood sugar, too much or too little, I don't know. I once saw him out there in the parking lot setting a dead cat on fire and then pretending to take pictures of it with a piece of shrapnel instead of a camera. Craay-zee little bastard."

The man's voice was rushed but the words came to him with ease, like he had the story memorized, like he had told it a million times using the same words, the same pauses, the same inflections. Mustafa peeked out of his left eyelid, letting in streaks of white light, some of them stained with mint green, through the bars of his eyelashes. Still way too much light. He switched to the right eye then, trying to acclimate them both.

"They said he went nuts because of the war. Like the war is the only thing that makes shit happen. Kid gets Fs, it's because of the war. Husband cheats on his old lady with the lady downstairs, it's because of the war. Daughter turns gay, it's because of the war. Bunch of bullshit."

Mustafa opened his eyes and saw that he was in a hospital room, which explained the bleach and the citrus and the shit. It explained the weak voices and the grunts and the swearing. It explained the whiteness of light and pale, mint green walls. The cast he was in from the waist up to his chin explained his immobility and his pain, and the heavy bandage around his neck suggested that there might be a reason for the fire in his throat and the thunder in his jaw. The man directly across from him, a balding fellow with the head and neck of a buzzard, met his eye and smiled a deranged, yellow smile. Mustafa knew his face.

"Good morning, neighbor. Finally, an audience," he said. "All these other fuckers are as good as kindling."

The glee in his neighbor's eyes and his wiggling eyebrows like a hairy caterpillar cut in half on his Slavic forehead and the straps with which he was tied to the bed hinted to Mustafa what kind of hospital he'd just woken up in.

"What was I talking about? Oh yeah. So . . . every time a shelling dies down, out come these children to hunt for shrapnel. It's like a collecting deal . . . like children collecting marbles and things. So they are walking around with these . . . sacks of shrapnel, comparing and trading, whathaveya. But this Donut kid is fanatical. He thinks he can recreate a shell by putting together all the shards. Insane!"

Mustafa glanced around the room and counted seven other beds occupied with elderly men lying on their sides, their faces in agony and old and puffed with medication-induced slumber. Out the window the day was gray, and the tops of trees were in their flimsy underthings, shivering.

"So one day I'm sittin' there on the stairs and I overhear Donut and this other kid arguin' . . . about, you know, who has the biggest shrapnel, who has the weirdest-looking ones, and so on and so forth, and this grandma from the first floor there, what's her name? . . . Um . . . Shit . . . Mrs. Abdić! That's it! Anyway, she's on her balcony, hanging out, she hears them, and goes, 'That's nothing, my dears. I have one in my living room that's this big.'"

The man tried to show how big the shrapnel was supposed to have been but realized his hands were tied to the bed. He smiled sheepishly, as if embarrassed. For the first time Mustafa noticed a cluster of bruises on the side of the man's face.

"I'm thinking the grandma's a little senile, there's no way that there're shrapnel that big, I don't give a shit if it's a fuckin' Tomahawk. Little Donut cries that he wants to see it. Can he come and see it? Can he please come up and see it? Grandma says, 'Sure, come up.' I'm thinking, I better take a look at this shit myself. Knowing this kid, he might do something bad, and I don't want the poor woman having a seizure on account of that. So I wait a few seconds, then start up the stairs after him.

"When I go in, there's a sight to see. Right there, in the middle of the sofa, wedged in there, sticking half out, is a whole, goddamn shell! A whole, goddamn, unexploded, fucking mortar shell!"

Something in Mustafa's mind scraped and he . . .

We're here.

Everyone in the village is dead, piled up.

I'm choking and holding it in and choking and holding it in.

I can't hold it in anymore. I'm chok . . .

"What happened was that it hit the stove, mangled it but didn't explode, and ricocheted into the sofa. Grandma goes, 'It came through the window a couple of nights back, hit the stove, look what it did. I tried to get it out, I banged at it with a hammer. I can't move it one bit.'"

The man's eyes grew huge.

"I'm real shook up right now, you see. There's a damn explosive device in the house. I'm so shook up, I'm confused. And Donut, that crazy little bastard, goes right up on top of the damn thing tryin' to pull it out. If I didn't shit myself right then and there, I never will. You crazy little bastard! I pull him off the shell and he starts nippin' at my arm. Well I start hollerin', I smack him a good one across the mouth. I yell, 'Everybody out of the room! You'll blow us all sky-high!'"

Steamboat is crying, too. I can see that he can see me see him crying and he turns away and coughs. He kicks over the body of a dead Chetnik to see his face. The fucker looks like us but his face is splotched, a burgundy hole in his cheekbone, the eye above it swollen and closed.

"And as I'm getting them all out a 'Goddamn' slips from me, and the grandma goes crazy. Don't take the Lord's name in vain this! Don't swear that!

"God don't care, I tell her. It's just a word. But she has none of it."

Then the back of Steamboat's head is a red blur. And he drops. And I go as if to help him, instinctively, floppily, and someone yells:

"Ambush! Retreat!"

And by then I'm gone.

Then I had a dream that I was hanging out in the Albatros, only the place was bigger and it didn't have the stage but was more like a club I used to frequent. The floors were dirty granite and the walls were pure black. I stood watching the people come in and I could see both from the perspective of me in the dream as well as that of me as a camera on the ceiling. So there was me standing there looking out of my skull but there was also me looking down at myself looking out of my skull, and the feeling of psychic immensity overwhelmed me as I saw myself backing toward a corner and across the room of dancing people. To my right a curtain opened revealing a DJ behind a glass wall like in radio stations, and the DJ was a familiar face and he played vinyl records and I can't remember which ones and then there were Hare Krishna with their little percussion section chanting around. Then the music stopped and this muezzin appeared behind the glass and the DJ equipped him with headphones and a microphone, nodding his head. The

muezzin began to pray in Arabic and I didn't understand
what the words meant just that it was filling me up and
then everything stopped and I started to levitate up toward
the ceiling, into the lighting fixtures, and my chest bulged
with incomprehensible joy as I saw pure light pour out of
me and something in my chest kept saying *God is here God
is here God is here God is here God is here God is here God
is here* and it might have been my own voice saying *God is
here* and I could see all the oblivious people dancing in the
club as well as my own collapsing face agape, eyes open
with *God is here* and then

there was the dusk of the hospital room and the voice kept on saying
God is here, even though there was no transition from sleep to waking, no opening of eyes, no realization that one realm was different
from the other, just the continuous voice saying *God is here* until it
was Mustafa who was saying *God is here* out loud in his head and
the man across the room was tossing himself against his restraints,
tugging at himself, making terrifying monkey faces, exposing cords
in his neck and hissing in his throaty gravel:

"Fuck him! Shut up! Fuck him into shards!"

That night, way after visiting hours were over, a short woman
shuffled into the room. She had the posture of a reanimated corpse,
stiff and bemused, her right hand clutching a bulky, rectangular
purse. Her clothes looked worn out, brown pants stretched at the
knees. She paused at the door as if to adjust her eyes to the level
of light. There was a single, buzzing neon tube in the middle of
the ceiling, making the shadows of things throb and the things

themselves, the faces, the walls, the furniture, look as though made of smooth bone.

Mustafa shuddered when she, finally adjusted to the room's lighting, pinned down his eyes with her own. Her face spilled outward into an expression of concern and the welling tears gave definition to her eyes, making them obvious, unavoidable points of focus. She came forward, still not dropping her gaze, put her purse on the chair next to the bed, and laid her tremulous hand on his forehead.

"How are you doing, son?" was what she whispered, smiling excruciatingly.

He knew she was going to say that the moment he saw her. That was the cause of his horror. Because he recognized her as one would recognize one's personal angel of death. It was not the face, or the clothes, or the mannerisms. He recognized the archetype. She was a mother, all right. But his?

No, not his.

The geezer to the left of the buzzard man wheezed and gargled all night. He coughed and mumbled, yelped and howled, sobbed all night. He cried for the goddamned nurses, for his fucking doctor, for his mother. He cried for God. None of them showed. He kept on crying and swearing all night and then, at dawn, he stopped.

Buzzard man's eyes, though still crazy, signaled solidarity and relief, full of regret for the passing of human life but also saying *about fucking time*. He was gagged now, on top of being tied to the bed and on top of being nuts. He was restrained and silenced and in that respect in a similar position to Mustafa's.

They lay there all early morning, staring at each other with bulging, pain-filled eyes. They communicated commiseration to each other, told each other to hang in there, and eye-rolled when the geezers in the room farted, or rasped, or whimpered. The room slowly revealed all its details as the gray light seeped in through the windows. The trees knocked against the glass with the tips of their branches, urged by the wind.

Around eight o'clock a nurse finally came, wheeling in a cart. She looked like she had worked a night shift in the salt mines and this was her second job. Her feet dragged, her hair was nappy, her movements somnambulistic.

"I have to draw your blood," she said to the dead man.

The buzzard man first looked at Mustafa as if to say, *What the fuck?* then mumbled through his gag and engaged the nurse with globular eye contact that wouldn't be denied.

"Are we going to behave better today, Mirsad?" she asked him, pulling out a metal box from the bottom of the cart and picking out a syringe from it. Mirsad mumbled another garbled response. His eyes darted left and right frantically over his gag.

"See? There you go again. I can't take your gag off if you keep acting like that." She took the syringe out of its plastic wrapping. "If you want me to take it off you have to promise to be a good boy and stop yelling and cursing. Can you do that for me?"

Mirsad nodded.

"You promise?"

Mirsad nodded. She zombied over to him and started to untie his gag.

"If you show me you can be good and respectful I might even take off your restraints later."

The gag came off and Mirsad opened and closed his mouth, stuck his tongue out, tried to work some of the locked muscles loose. There was a mischievous twinkle in his eyes.

The nurse was bent over the dead man's arm trying to find a vein, not even looking at his dead face. She smacked the spongy flesh under his biceps with the tips of her gloved fingers, mechanically.

Mirsad looked at her with contempt, then at Mustafa to see if he shared his outrage. Her blindness seemed unfathomable to him. He watched her for a few moments longer, opened his mouth as if to say something, thought better of it, and just shook his head. She stuck the needle into the dead flesh.

"Better stick that needle into that wall there," Mirsad said. "You'll get more blood from it."

She gave him a tired look but he was now looking away, toward the window.

"What?"

But it was obvious he was not going to say anything else. The nurse finally looked at the dead man's eyes, waved her hand in front of them, held two fingers against his jugular and then backed away from the bed, her face flushed. She turned and left the room with a little more urgency, wiping her hands on her scrubs.

Mustafa burst into laughter, which lasted only a second before the terrible pain in his throat came back and silenced him.

It took a long time for the nurse to come back with a doctor and two buzz-haired beefcakes in stretched white coats, pushing a gurney whose duct-taped left hind wheel squeaked something awful. They worked fast. The doctor, a frumpy fellow with bloody eyes, ministered to the dead man. He held a pocket mirror to his nose, pulled down on his eyelids and stared into his eyes, picked up his arms and tried to lift them, yanking at the stiff resistance. He ordered the beefcakes to roll the dead man to his side, pulled the dead man's pajama top out of his pajama bottom and looked at the skin on his back, then chicken-scratched some things onto a sheet of paper clamped to a clipboard. Then he walked out. The beefcakes heaved the cadaver like a grotesque mannequin off the bed and onto the gurney and were gone, too, the wheel going *squeakety-squeak* down the corridor. The nurse, stuck with the cleanup, peeled off all the bedding into a plastic bag, flipped the thin, stained mattress and dressed it anew. When she left with her cart there was no trace of the dead man.

Nurses spoon-fed the geezers bread and briny, brownish broth. They talked to them like they were children, and the old men were nasty, spitting and cursing, showing them that they were still there. Mirsad kept turning his magnificent, buzzardly profile away from them, refusing his food completely. Eventually, the nurses gave up on all of them and left. As for Mustafa, he couldn't open his mouth at all and the IV dripped his tasteless breakfast directly into his vein.

"Grandpa," called a tinny voice from down the corridor and Mustafa and Mirsad both turned to the door. Mirsad chortled as if he already knew everything that was going to happen.

A blonde girl, about five or six years old, in a red hat and a matching Windbreaker, rushed into the room and scrambled to a stop halfway between the doorway and the empty bed. Her noisy sleeves stopped making noise, and although her mouth continued to smile, her eyes dashed open with surprise as she peeled her gaze from the unoccupied bed and then glanced from bed to bed, trying to recognize a face.

"Grandpa," she repeated with a little less vigor now, her smile already plateauing.

"Grandpa is not around anymore, little girl," Mirsad told her.

The girl's face turned red with confusion. Her little teeth bit her lower lip.

"Your grandpa died this morning."

She just stood facing the empty bed. Mustafa thought that if he had known what Mirsad was going to say ahead of time he would have chucked his IV stand like a spear right into his lunatic, scavenger face, his own pain be damned.

Something popped within the girl and she screamed a normal scream. Mustafa was glad that she had that in her.

She took a timid step backward but never made it all the way to the door. Instead, her mother, a pasty woman shaped like a pear, plunged into the room and picked her up into her arms, holding the back of her head gently as though she were an infant. She broke into soft, soothing ocean noises, saying *shhhhhhhh, shhhhhhhh, shhhhhhh,* and rushed out of the room.

A man poked his head in with a dumb expression on his face. He was gray but there was a ridiculous earring in his ear.

"Where did he go?" His question seemed to be rhetorical, considering the volume and the degree of inflection. Then he met Mirsad's gaudy eyes and directed his next question at him.

"Where did they take him?"

"Into the sky," said Mirsad.

The man's face turned even dumber and he disappeared from the door frame. Mustafa heard him say something to his wife and then yell for a nurse.

"People," Mirsad said to Mustafa, "they deserve everything that's coming to them."

There was a commotion in the corridor and the gray man with the earring barged into the room again, his arms slicing the air.

"He was right here yesterday," he cried. "We talked about his precious plum tree and I fed him some corn bread. Right here." He gestured at the creaseless pillowcase.

The nurse who tried to draw blood from his dead father appeared livelier and professionally reserved when she came in this time.

"My condolences, sir," she offered, looking down at her shoes. "There was nothing we could have done. It was his time."

Mirsad scoffed.

The man looked at him, then at the nurse. She ran her hand through her nappy hair.

"Are you sure he wasn't just transferred somewhere?" asked the man.

"I'm sure."

He went over and sat on the empty bed.

"If it's any consolation, he passed peacefully in his sleep," said the nurse with perfect intonation, putting her hand on the man's shoulder.

"Peacefully, my dick!" Mirsad shouted. "The man was in pain all night! He was screaming and shouting—"

The nurse was already next to him in panic, fumbling with the gag.

"Don't listen to this man, sir. We had to transfer him from the ward upstairs because there wasn't any room up there." She tapped her temple with her left index finger and rolled her eyes pointedly. The man stood up, gawking at both of them, unsure of whom to believe.

"—calling for personnel, crying like a baby because he knew he was dying, and none of you fuckers as much as walked down that corridor, let alone came in to check on him! On any of us!"

She attempted to slip the gag into his mouth but Mirsad snapped his jaws at her, growling like Archibald.

"Don't touch me! I'll fuck you into shards!"

She retreated to the grieving son.

"Come with me, sir," she said, taking him by the arm. "It's not safe here." She used his confusion to whisk him away, leaving the buzzard man to scream about breaking people like shot glasses against the fireplace. He tried to wiggle out of his restraints. It wasn't long before the beefcakes made their return, smiled creamily as they drew curtains between all the beds and, out of sight, silenced the raving man. They silenced him so well that he didn't wake up until noon the next day, at which point they silenced him again despite the fact that he made no sound at all.

Later, in the silence of that afternoon, a petite young woman with her hair in her face glided into the room as though on an excruciatingly slow conveyor belt, barely stirring anyone. She was in a pair of pink pajamas, the top of which was stretched open, exposing one of her small, pointy breasts. The cuticles around her fingernails were chewed raw. She was walking toward the window in a trance when some nurse finally tracked her down and took her by her shoulders.

"We're not supposed to be in here," said the nurse gently, turning her body back toward the door, pulling a flap of pink fabric to cover her puffy nipple.

"Hi, Momma," the girl said, tonguing the corner of her lips. For a moment Mustafa saw her face: her dead eyes, the deep crimson of her open mouth, and her small delicate nostrils. It wasn't until she spat on the floor that he realized who she was.

"Down! Down!" the Claw yells and we drop Steamboat's body into the mud and get down. Three or four shells hit in rapid succession, the closest one some twenty meters away. Up the hill, Ninja's smoke grenade, thrown earlier to cover our retreat, is dying, spurting its last white breath.

"The tree!" the Claw yells through the rain, motioning to an oak halfway between the trenches.

We grab Steamboat's shoulder straps and start our crawl and drag, crawl and drag. The progress is slow. Chetniks are blanket shelling everything, cavalier with their ammo. Two or three machine guns are blurting their repetitive syllables. Slugs fly over. Our noses in the mud, we blindly crawl backward.

I just keep going and going and the next time I find the courage to look around, the tree is right there, between us and them. I stop, my abdomen in a knot. The Claw stops, too. I can't take large enough breaths to accommodate the sudden need for them with my face in the muddy grass. I flip and face the ferocious skies. Raindrops grow bigger and bigger and hit my lips, forehead, cheekbone. I pant like Archibald for a while and then push myself under the foliage, sick of being rained on and shot at.

Something forced itself into Mustafa's mind's eye with the ferocity of a flashback. He was transported to another place, a small round park completely surrounded by a street (it's called a *roundabout*, he remembered,) in the middle of a city he somehow knew was Edinburgh. Everything was vivid. He knew what he was doing there, too; he was in the middle of a play, he knew his next line. Sure enough, there were his fellow actors, too. And even though he jumped right into his role, dropped down and did twenty push-ups, counting out loud in English and forcing his own face into the mud, a part of him was flabbergasted. Flash-forwards couldn't feel like flashbacks, could they? It simply wasn't possible to remember a place one had never visited, recall a play one had never read.

He dropped down to his knees with his back to a mighty Scottish oak and said his next line:

"Please, God, give us technical pencils and salvation," he crooned, his eyes closed, his face turned upward. "Bring back our mothers and let them splash in shallow cognac, O Mighty One. Give us spas for diving and walnut forests for pointy frolicking. Put fear in us so we don't lose our moral balance. Fuck us into shards."

All at once the other actors were leaving the park through a hole in a metal fence. Mustafa saw his director (Asmir's his name) talking to a portly female cop and emphatically trying to explain something. Her small white police car was up on the curb, flashing its lights, the driver's side door ajar. Passersby were converging on the scene in waves, gawking and sneaking snapshots.

He was alone in the park now, at the center of everything, and the cop came to the fence and pointed at him.

"You have not obtained the proper documentation to perform here, sir!" she said.

"Make our cunts wide so that we feel no pain of birth!" Mustafa screamed his next line.

"You have to discontinue!" the cop went. "This performance is over!"

Another police car pulled up and two male cops came out running. Mustafa turned away from them and approached the tree. He put his head to the ground and got up into the kneeling position again. He did it over and over again, unable to stop himself from performing. Every time he opened his eyes he saw that the crowd was growing in size. His fellow actors motioned for him to stop but he just kept on going down and up, down and up, again and again.

Somebody was taping him with a camcorder. There was a red dot in the crowd. Mustafa raised his head and screamed.

Then: magic. Out of the foliage above, a thick, dry branch broke off with a rich crack, shushed through the leaves, and thudded onto the ground in front of him.

I'm choking. It's crushing my throat. I'm trying to push it off but can't. My arms are boneless, fleshy. They bend when I push. I dig my nails into the bark, fighting for purchase. Twigs and bark fragments hit my face, eyes, fall into my mouth. Bullets are ripping up and down the tree. I cannot inhale. I cannot inhale.

Then I inhale and the air fills my throat, lungs, and mind with pain. I see stars. I exhale.

"Mustafa," the Claw calls, breathing his rotten breath in my face as I inhale another gulp. But the pain . . . The pain is . . .

Mustafa spun around and around, wielding the fallen branch and laughing. He remembered how he had remembered who he was in the first place. It came down on him like a hammer when the Claw came to visit him in that loony bin, in that hospital room with that birdly man, his neighbor. He had instantly remembered how the Claw had left him in between the trenches all night but had come back before dawn, tied a rope around him, and dragged him down the hill to safety. And spinning around like that he also remembered the Claw's strange demise later on. But what he still could not for the life of him remember was what it all meant.

The cops finally got the gate open and Mustafa, his face covered in mud, blood and spittle, calmly walked toward them and toward the red-eyed cameras.

*   *   *

Mirsad, the buzzard man, he was taken away. Not just him but his whole bed. The mint green gap that Mustafa was now forced to face all day was a smile with a missing tooth. The bed to the left of it, the dead man's deathbed, had another candidate in it, another slab of fed-up forehead, another pair of dry twig arms, another wheezing whine. The sky was invisible through the window from all the clouds. The rain was falling outside. And shells were falling. And the world was falling apart.

The nurses changed Mustafa's piss bags (often) and shit bags (seldom), commenting on the amounts, colors, frequencies. They squirted salty mush through his barely open mouth and massaged the sides of his throat to ease the swallowing. They dragged lukewarm sponges over the surface of his rapidly diminishing body, giving extra care to all the hairy nooks and crannies.

The doctor changed his jaw and throat bandages, looked at the stitches from all angles, smiled sad smiles, and always touched his shoulder. The family members of Mustafa's hospital roommates mostly ignored him, just as they mostly ignored their hapless old relatives. They moved around, working hard not to look into their eyes, and fussed about the blankets, curtains, and juice boxes. They gave quick pecks on the foreheads and short, crushing squeezes on the arms, mumbled feeble words of encouragement, and took their swift leaves.

His own family never came or came when he was out of it, but he never saw them while he was in there. He was having trouble even picturing them in his mind. All his memories of them seemed muddled and grainy. Only the woman who thought she was his mother came in every night after visiting hours were over, most likely sneaking away from the ward upstairs. She held his hand and patted his forehead. She sighed and cried, asked why he was so distant to her, asked him if he remembered this or that, gave him news about his supposed relatives: that his uncle Fajko was mobilized into the army, that a shell had hit his father's garage and totaled his car, that his brother was having a hard time acclimating to his new school, that he just wanted to sleep all the time. She even brought him a letter that he supposedly received from the army and started to read it aloud to him.

"We regret . . . to inform you," she read, sniveling, "that your unit . . . was . . . decimated in the enemy counterattack—"

Her emotions had their way with her and she abruptly started to sob, folded the letter, stuffed it into a blue envelope, and left it on his bedside table.

"I can't," she whispered. "I can't."

What conviction, he thought.

"They list most of your unit . . . they are all dead . . ."

As soon as the Claw walked in Mustafa remembered everything. He remembered the bulldozer, the ambush, and the rain. He remembered the tree and the chunk of the tree that fell on him. He remembered the stench of shit and the cold ring of his prayers in the night. He remembered his real mother, his real father, and his real brother. His family. He remembered everything.

He also remembered what the Claw did for him, how he called him by his name, how he came back for him because no man was ever to be left behind. He remembered that the Claw would die a week after the war was over, or rather he *knew. How strange*, he thought. He knew that his war buddy would be on the way to the command to receive the Golden Lily and that the asphalt would cave right under his feet and that he would fall into a deep hole caused by the town's saltwater exploitation and break his neck.

"What's up Mustafa, you pussy's worst foe?" boomed the Claw now. "Is that you or did someone take a shit?"

Mustafa wanted to tell his fellow Apache both what he remembered and what he knew but the pain in his throat was bursting. All he could do was look, and when he did, for a while all his eyes could do was cry.

"You're crying, you pussy," the Claw said, only this time he looked away and choked something down before it was too big. He walked around and sat on the chair. He ran out of words. He swallowed audibly.

"Sooty says hi. He's better now. They got him good, in the stomach and in the ass but he's better. The bulldozer rolled over his foot and they cut off his heel. He's gonna go to some place called Thousand Oaks in California to get a new one. They are letting him go."

Mustafa strained to look into his eyes but the Claw was leaning forward in the chair, his elbows on his knees, his hands exploring each other, going through all the poses. His eyes darted sideways and every once in a while his facial tic took over them. He noticed the blue envelope on the bedside table and picked it up.

"Motherfuckers," he said, scanning the contents. "I got one too: Your country thanks you for your valiant service in these times of war. We sent you on a fucked-up mission in a fucking bulldozer and you all got killed. Chetniks retook the village the next day so it was all for nothing. Thank you for your lives. In return we will list your names on this piece of paper and not even bother to find out your Apache nicknames, the fucking sacks of shit."

He took a pen out of his pocket and started to scratch out the soldiers' real names and write down their nicknames instead.

Almir Mutevelić became Steamboat.

Dragan Krstić became Ninja.

Vedran Delić became the Lump.

Damir Verlašević became Hammer.

But in the letter's salutation, the Claw had, for some reason, blacked out the name to which the letter was addressed and written Mustafa above it in a surprisingly bubbly longhand. When Mustafa later read over it he realized that he was right, that that woman was crazy and the letter had been addressed to someone else, not him. Looking at the paper all he could discern under that uneven rectangle of black ink was the first letter of the first name in the salutation, which looked like an *L* or perhaps an *I*. It was like reading a government-censored document; it was impossible to be 100 percent certain.

NOTEBOOK THREE:
BOOM-BOOM*

---

*The San Diego Police Department found the third notebook, titled
"BOOM-BOOM," in Izzy's car, which was parked on La Jolla Shores
near the university, some three hundred pages of it. In the notebook was
the following note: *"I, Ismet Prcić, the author and the characters of these
chicken scratches, residing in a silver 1981 VW Scirocco with licence plate
_____, generally located around San Diego County, being of (finally) sound
mind, do hereby declare this instrument to be the last will and testament of my
life. However, I do not hereby revoke any previous chicken scratches and codicils.
I direct that the disposition of my remains be as follows: Burn me until none of
me is left. I give all the rest and residue of my estate to Eric Carlson of ____
Los Feliz Drive, Thousand Oaks, CA 91362, to do with as he pleases, should
he survive me for sixty days. The only condition is that he read all of this and
try to piece me together."* Bound as I am by this last will and testament, I'm
including a portion of this notebook here.

(. . . the absurdity of reality, the mind-boggling, fucking unlikeliness of it all . . .)

. . . It came to me, Eric. It came to me in a dream. I finally understand EVERYTHING! Listen:

In the beginning there was Light. In the beginning there was the Word. In the beginning there was the Voice. In the beginning there was the Voice using Words to bring the Light into existence by uttering the word Light into the void. Thus, out of the void came the light and from it everything else. But if something can be created out of nothing then something and nothing are made out of the same material, so to speak. If something can be created out of nothing by the sheer utterance of sound that gives meaning to it, then the only difference between something and nothing is in the naming. By calling nothing something, nothing becomes something, but the truth remains that nothing really changes in the great scheme of things. The physical constitution of nothing/something, if it can even be called that, remains the same.

That means that heaven = hell = purgatory = void = return to God. Eternal life = death forever. Mahatma Gandhi = Adolf

Hitler. Al-Qaeda = UNICEF. Good and bad are indistinguishable. $0=1=2=3=\ldots=$forever.

Nothing is everything because there isn't anything.

Now, the sad thing is that some pieces of this nothing thought themselves up, imagined themselves up, then thought up and imagined and created this thing called *reality*. These little nothings got very caught up in all this *reality* they invented, and made it very complex and cyclical, so much so that it made them forget that they were really, in essence, still nothing. It made them stupid. It made them real.

We are the descendents of these stupid, real people who forgot that they were nothing. So we go on epic journeys, from nothing to nothing, we start in nothing and end up in nothing, we never leave nothing, but we perpetuate our delusions. On some level we know we're nothing but we're too scared to think about that. The whole time we're making this journey from nothing to nothing, we sense, we hope, that there is someone, something out there, a *third presence* that follows us, watches over us, narrates us, dreams us into being, and we hope that this being means something, is something.

What is this something we hope is out there?

1. Fill in the blank:

The third presence is _____?

a. God

b. The narrator

c. Ismet

d. Mustafa

e. What?

f. Me

g. You

h. Who gives a shit?

i. Something

j. Nothing
k. All of the above
l. None of the above
m. All/none of the above

If you answered "m. All/none of the above," you are on your way to become nothing.

(. . . monologue . . .)*

. . . back at the house out of habit, to sneak in a shower when you know your ex-roommates aren't home, even though you don't live there anymore, even though your old room is now an office and your old closet is full of Ben's outrigger paddles and moldy wet suits, and even though Jen said she would call the police if you used the washer and dryer, on the patio again you find the spare key under the terra-cotta Santa Claus underneath the fig tree and go in, strip out of your clothes, and use their soap and shampoo and a towel . . .

. . . although the love is gone, although she left sometime ago and moved away and took the computer and the bed and the jar of change and left you red hair in the lining of your sweatshirts and on your pillowcase and that scent in your nostrils and in your brain, since you can smell it even out at the beach where the cold winds blow . . .

. . . and although your mother longs to die back in Bosnia, where your father got up one morning and found her naked in the bathtub with her wrists slit the longitudinal way this time, with her stomach full of Valium and Ativan and aspirin and slivovitz, with her head

---

* In the margins of these fragments the following note appeared: "PRESTO! STACCATO! Perform almost breathlessly!"

full of thick blissful nothing, *but still alive,* and instead of calling for an ambulance, hauled her out of the tub, dried her body with the floor mat and some towels, put a pair of panties and a slip-on nighty on her, dragged her across the parquet and into the bedroom, where he hadn't noticed her not being all night, lifted her onto her side of the bed, started a load of pink-stained laundry, and slipped out of the house so as not to wake your brother, knowing this depressed young man would not get up before two in the afternoon, because he never does, and went to work as usual, hoping she would finish dying, finish killing herself for once, but was really disappointed when your brother called him in a panic, and after she came out of a three-day coma, bought her an apartment on the seventeenth floor of a skyscraper, the same one you saw a woman jump from when you were a toddler, and told her he couldn't handle the stress of being near her anymore and that they should separate, still denying his involvement with those other women, which brought your mother within an inch of her life in the first place, still denying he left her on her side of the bed to die . . .

. . . despite the fact that because of all of this your chest most of the time feels inflated with . . . full of what? wrongness? full of whatever the fuck is left in the wake of a lot of love, full of whatever the fuck love turns into when you figure out its insignificance, when you figure out you can't hold on to the loved ones, you can't help the loved ones, you don't know the loved ones, and you want to claw at your chest, stab your fingers through your own breastplate, and pull apart your rib cage like an accordion, the way Superman pulls apart Clark Kent's suit to get all that love out, all that wrongness out, all that pain, and although this is how bad things are all the time, this day of all days you feel fine . . .

. . . you feel better because your ex-roommates are gone until tomorrow (you checked on their crew's Web site at the library:

Kae Elua: two-day race in Catalina) and this means you will sleep in their bed, use their computer, and play video games, so you put on some clean clothes and run to the kitchen and make yourself a huge Travesty with their vodka first, then shake some dry food into Johnny Cat's bowl, and you hear him thump down onto the carpet somewhere in the back of the house and then in a flash he's there crunching away at the food, loveless and yellow-eyed, and driven crazy by some kind of skin disease that makes him chew his own ass, and you make your way into the office, turn on a video game, a first-person shooter, and choose to become a SWAT commander and lead a band of artificially intelligent police officers into a bank under siege and save three blonde bank employees from masked terrorists who are holding them hostage . . .

. . . your mission is to save and you have to find your way through the maze of offices and corridors adorned with potted palm trees, water coolers, vent systems, and you find and save two of the three employees but the third one is nowhere to be found, and you kill all the enemies and run around the repetitive gamescapes trying to find her but can't, you can't advance to the next level if you don't save all three, so you kill all the enemies and, out of boredom, kill your fellow squad mates, too, but they keep respawning and you keep on killing them, running out of ammo, picking up their weapons and using them on them . . .

. . . and then you find her and when you do you realize there's a glitch in the game's design, because she's stuck in a wall and you can't get her to come with you, because you can't click on her because she's in the wall . . .

. . . and you realize there is stuff on your real face, your face is wet and you cannot breathe through your nose from all the stuff in there and what is the point of saving anything anyway and you get up and go for more alcohol, blowing your nose into your sleeve, but instead pick up the phone and dial your mother's seventeenth-floor apartment and listen to it ring and ring in Bosnia, expecting her weak hello to crush you, break you, but it just rings and rings and the hum of the silences becomes louder than the electronic *toooots* and then a taped voice says, *Sorry, no one is home, please try your call later,* and you panic and dial again and suffer through this whole thing again and again, each time a little more because a part of your mind is screaming *WAKE UP,* part of it is praying, part of it is coolly observing *She's dead,* part of it is negating it, *She's not dead,* and you hang up and call your father's number for the first time in months, that fucker's number, and your brother answers, sounding sleepy:

— What do you want?

— Where is Mother?

— How the hell should I know? At her place?

— Shouldn't you?

— Whatever.

— Where's *he*?

— Sleeping.

— I wanna talk to him.

— He's in there with some slut. I'm not going in there.

— You need to go over to Mother's apartment right now and check on her.

— Do you know what time it is?

— She's not answering her phone, you fucker.

— Maybe she took a sleeping pill. Maybe she's visiting a friend. Maybe—

— You fucker! You fucker!

— She's taking a walk. Maybe she pulled the phone out of the wall.

— Maybe she's fuckin' dead, fucker? Maybe you two finally pushed her over the edge.

—Why don't *you* fly out here and *you* check on her? It all started with *you* leaving, fucker. Remember that? All of this. *You* should be over here, fucker. *You* should be here feeling this. Fucker . . .

. . . and the line goes dead and you throw the cordless phone into the butcher block, where it breaks into pieces, and you grab the bottle of vodka out of the pantry and chug until you can't think anymore, don't understand why you're in tears anymore . . .

. . . morning takes care of itself, chases away the other life, the Apache battle cries and visions of moving sneakers, and even though your jaw dully throbs and it's hard for you to swallow you go out to your car and grab all the clothes you can and start a load of laundry, then ransack the house for food and money. You try your mother but no one answers. You call your father. Mehmed hangs up on you before you can say hello. You drink the rest of the vodka and watch Judge Judy yell at people until the washer is done washing and the dryer is done drying.

You realize you forgot to turn off the video game and when you go into the office the bank teller is still running in the wall and your fellow SWAT people have respawned and are going through the motions of looking, covering one another, running to and from the truck, swarming around the woman in the wall whom they can never help, never reach, and you finally understand how absurd, impossible, stupid, shitty, everything is.

(. . . boom-boom . . .)*

Once upon a time there was a . . . Once upon a time there is a . . . prison. A human convict has transgressed against the human society and was put here. Here he has transgressed against the ego of a ʙᴏᴏᴍ! particular guard and for this transgression he is being led down a cavernous black corridor toward the *holes*. His punishment: forty days of solitary confinement. He has heard stories about the *holes*, how they dematerialize reality and materialize nothingness. How the particular kind of darkness in the *holes* can short-circuit the mind. The convict knows all of this, and so, as soon as the key is turned in the lock behind him and he gets the first glimpse of that annihilating darkness and its power, he reaches for a **BOOM!** button. He first touches his throat knowing that's where the collar of his prison uniform will be. He investigates in the general area there until he finds the collar and finds the button there, that one button he never uses anyway, because his uniform is too small and buttoning it, even if possible, would seriously hinder his breathing. He finds it, gets a good grip on it, and pulls it off. Th **BOOM!** e string holding the button in place snaps and suddenly it is in

---

*This is the final entry and it appears here exactly as it does in the original without any of my meddling. Bear with it.

385

between his fingers, away from the collar, the button. It is round shaped, he feels, because of the way its edges bite into the flesh of his fingertips. It's metal. It's flat when he holds it the other way but his skin detects an unevenness and his mind tells him that it's probably leftover string, so he pulls at it with his nails and sure enough little pieces of string that held the button in its place on the collar are loose between his fingers. He rolls them into a ball and lets it silently fall to the concrete beneath him. It's of no importance to him because it's too small. But the button. The button is just the right size. Not too big, not too small. He then extends both of his arms out away from himself in all four major directions and finds out that, standing where he's standing, he can touch the cell wall to his right and in front of him. His mind does a quick calculation and he makes **BOOM!** a small diagonal step to the left and back and repeats the arms-extending-in-four-major-directions routine to find that he cannot touch any of the walls now. This is when he starts to spin in his place in the middle of the *hole*, one, two, three, four, five, six, seven, eight, nine, ten times, and on the tenth time he tosses the button over his left shoulder and listens to it *plink, plink, plinkety-plink,* plink, plink on the concrete until all is silent. Then he goes down on all fours and begins his search for the button. He crawls around for as long as it takes until he stumbles upon it in the dark, picks it up, feels its edges bite into the flesh of his fingertips in that round familiar way, stands up, extends his arms in all four major directions, finds that he can touch the wall behind him now, does a quick calculation and takes a step forward, repeats the arm-extended-in-all-four-major-directions routine until he finds himself in the middle of the *hole*, spins around one, two, three, four, five, six, seven, eight, nine, ten times and then tosses the button over his right shoulder and listens to it *plink, plink, plinkety-plink,* plink, plink on the concrete until there's a silence, **BOOM!** goes down on his hands and knees and begins the search anew, and repeats this over and over for forty days. He does this because he knows that if he is to stay himself he needs to keep his mind busy and on-task. He knows he needs to do this because otherwise he is running the risk of losing it, short-circuiting it, the mind. He knows that in the midst of nothing in the middle of the hole, he needs to pretend that there's something, this task of finding the button over and over, or telling himself a story over and over, to keep the mind busy so it doesn't short-circuit itself but BOOM! I can't do it. I can't keep telling myself this story because the BOOM! shells are hitting closer and closer and the mint green hospital room is vibrating, the beams are creaking, the ceiling is flaking and falling down on me like plum blossoms, and at the same time, somehow, I'm up here staring down, down, and the firmament is melting into a California rain and my heart is climbing up my esophagus and into my throat, into my eye sockets, into my thoughts, pounding there, BOOM! as I wish I were in prison right now, in a *hole*, in the middle of it, on my hands and knees searching for a bBOOM!utton instead of suffering this pounding, the pounding of shells on this fucking hospital, this pounding rain, this pounding in my head, the pounding of memory, of bullets and tree limbs, the pounding of Mother, the pounding of red hair, the pounding of volatile muscles turning rigid in the fleeting world far below, down there, where into my (pounding) ephemeral ear the sidewalk

shall whisper the truth BOOM!.

In the Name of God, the most Gracious, the most Merciful.

Dear son,

Where are you? Are you alive?

I'm writing this even though I don't know these things. I'm writing this because I have to, because I have to tell you something that I cannot, that I never could, not even to myself. But it's killing me.

Everybody says you're dead. People I haven't heard from in years call and offer condolences, send food, money, say, *If you need anything.*

I donate what they send. I don't believe them. I know you're alive. I just know.

Americans sent me pictures of a body to identify. Porridge of meat and guts, shards of bone. They said you jumped off a building, killed yourself. They said they had partial fingerprints. But it wasn't you, was it? They couldn't find your appendectomy scar. Weren't sure. They couldn't find the birthmark below your knee. *Inconclusive,* they said. The body's head had good hair like yours but it was too gray for you. One can't go gray overnight, can one? They say it's possible but I don't believe it. How can I?

Your . . . father is the one who signed the affidavit of identification or whatever and got everybody believing in this nonsense. *Face the facts,* he said when I called to beg him not to do it. He's quick to wash his hands of people that way. He tried to wash his hands of me, too, but I'm still alive, right? That's the last and only time I spoke to him.

*   *   *

Right now I tried to write the impossible (truth) to you, what I can't tell myself, and couldn't. What a surprise. But I tried really hard, son. People are not saints. Some things can only be admitted to in person. There'll be time for that, God willing.

But at least I can tell you the news. Your brother moved to Sarajevo to go to the university down there and to get away from your father. They were fighting something awful, I heard. He's studying pharmacology and dating a girl he won't let me meet. He's either ashamed that I'm religious or that I'm crazy, or both. He calls once a month or so.

Asmir made a documentary film in Scotland about your guys' troupe and it played twice on national TV. Mehmed taped it for me. I watch it every day, so much that the parts you're in are getting worn and the images dance up and down. Asmir came to visit in August and brought me tulips and bonbons and cried for you a little. Gave me a disc of the film but I still don't have that player thingy. He said that Bokal married a woman twenty years his senior to stay legal in England. Also, he said that your friend Omar was in rehab for an overdose but that he's better now. He didn't know where Ramona was because they had a falling out.

Your friend Eric from America sent me a letter and a book by Faulkner, but I can't read either, as you know. We learned Russian in school. There was a picture, too. He has the cutest little blond boy and his wife looks strong and sturdy, which is good for women in that crazy America. They are all smiling—you know how Americans are in front of a camera.

Oh, I almost forgot. Do you know someone named Mustafa Nalić?

He writes that he knows you but I don't remember him. I've yet to meet him in person. He's more like an angel to me, invisible but good. He takes care of me. Every month he sends this kid to my door with all my medications and some money, too. He sent me a *kurban* for Bajram, nearly half a lamb. (I made some of it with okra, the way you like it. I froze most of it so you can try it when you come home.) He seems to think that he owes me. He sent me this note and thanked me for visiting him in the hospital. It says that I was the only one who ministered to him during the war when he was wounded when a tree fell on his neck, although I don't recall doing any of it. But, with my head, who knows.

Where are you, my son?
I feel you. I know you're out there somewhere.
Why don't you call me?
Call me when you get this.
Or just come back to me. I have lamb and okra waiting for you.
And sauerkraut. Who's gonna eat all this food? *I can't do it alone.*

I miss you like I would miss a limb.

I need to tell you what I cannot write here.

I'm alone. In the walls.

In God.

Waiting.

Acknowledgments

I'd like to thank the following humans for helping me to write this book:

My mother, for being an artist despite her life; my wife, for her unwavering love and for keeping my ego in check; Samir Mehanović, who opened the doors; Eric Carlson, for friendship, for Tom Waits and for editing my "*those boots that you use to go hiking-s*" to "*hiking boots*"; Aleksandar Hemon, for writing back; Michelle Latiolais, for teaching me how to read what's on the page and encouraging me to write *my* book; Ron Carlson, for teaching me how not to leave the room; Geoffrey Wolff and Gil Dennis, for taking me in; Christine Schutt, for knowing what—unbeknownst to me—my writing is all about; Brad Watson for all the stories and encouragement; Eileen Myles, Rae Armantrout and Allan Havis, for starting it all. Thank you so much.

For looking at a mess of five hundred pages and believing that it's a book I'd like to thank my agent P. J. Mark and my editor Lauren Wein. Much love to you both.

Thanks should go to these exquisite lunatics as well: Who-is-it-that-is-your-daddy Deborah, J. M. Geever, Stephen Cope, Frankozoid, Ramona-fauna-land, Merris, Byrnage, Lordy, Papa Max,

Momma Erin, Sizzlechest Summel, Lady-what's-the-fuck Marissa, Kevin I'll-filet-you-like-a-fish Lee, Michael hmm-deep Andreasen, Jacoby, Quinlan, Grostephan, Leila, Kim O'Neil, Nelson and Agent Sanchez for enduring me in various workshops. "*You motherfuckers are gonna believe it now!*"

I am also greatly indebted to the UCI School of the Humanities and International Center for Writing and Translation, Glenn Schaeffer and the National Endowment for the Arts for their generous financial support.

Last but not least I thank the Hansen-Johnston, Prcic, McNeil, Gutić, and Hukić clans for all the love and support. Extra thanks for my sister-in-law for being a great reader; chances are if you're holding this book it's because Jessica made you buy it.

Shards

Ismet
Prcic

ABOUT THIS GUIDE

We hope that these discussion questions
will enhance your reading group's exploration of
Ismet Prcic's *Shards*. They are meant
to stimulate discussion, offer new viewpoints and
enrich your enjoyment of the book.

More reading group guides and additional information,
including summaries, author tours and author sites for
other fine Black Cat titles may be found on
our Web site, www.groveatlantic.com.

QUESTIONS FOR DISCUSSION

1. The author begins the book with two epigraphs: an excerpt from *Hamlet,* in which the hero gives advice to the players, and lines from a poem by Iraqi writer Saadi Youssef. How do both epigraphs speak to the themes of the book? Might they be taken together as the author's statement of purpose? Are there similarities between Ismet's and Hamlet's preoccupations? And perhaps also Asmir's, who quotes from Hamlet's advice to the players (p. 106)? Where else in the book does the image of shards recur?

2. *Shards* plays with the conventions of both the novel and memoir, with Ismet acting as the novel's hero as well as the author of the memoir within it. How is this layering of fiction and nonfiction elements essential to the larger story? Ismet writes in his diary that as he was working on his memoir "things — little fictions — started to sneak in. I agonized over them, tried to eradicate them from the manuscript, but it made the narrative somehow *less* true" (p. 22). How might these inventions make his story more true?

3. Why is Ismet more affected by seeing what he thinks is Mustafa Nalic's grave than by seeing his own cousin's (p. 168)? How much of Mustafa's existence has Ismet imagined and what purpose do his imaginings serve? Does Mustafa help give shape to the pain of war that Ismet experiences? How do their life stories intertwine and then fuse together at the end?

4. The novel alternates between Ismet's stories (told in the first person point of view) and Mustafa's stories (told in third person) and jumps forward and backward in time. How would the meaning of the story change if it were told chronologically using only one point of view? Why has the author chosen to tell some parts of the story in the second person point of view (see sections beginning on pp. 78, 313, and 378)?

5. How does the author establish the setting as uniquely Bosnian? What do you learn about the culture? About family life and gender roles? About village life and values (see pp. 85–93)? About the role of religion in daily life? About the politics of the region and the war? How much of the story depends on this particular setting and how could it be seen as a coming-of-age story that might be set anywhere?

6. Notebooks, diaries, and letters are the forms the author employs to tell Ismet's story. How might a writer's tone, choice of content, and level of honesty be different in each form? How do Ismet's word choices and tone of voice help establish his character? Ismet is very self-aware, but are there things he doesn't see about himself?

7. How does Ismet develop a sense of identity as he grows up—what distinguishes him in his own mind from others? How does his sense of identity change when he leaves Bosnia and becomes "Izzy" in America? How does Ismet situate himself in relation to his fellow

refugees arriving at the airport? Ismet contemplates his friend Eric's existence and then thinks about his own on p. 43. Do you think his dreams of belonging and being anonymous can ever be reconciled?

8. How has Ismet's awareness of his mother's unhappiness and fragility helped shape him? What are his mother's strengths? Does Ismet's relationship with his mother change as he matures? Consider the symbolic implications of Ismet's cat/person dream (p. 342). What do you think his mother wants to tell him that she cannot bring herself to write in her letter?

9. Ismet's first two girlfriends, Asya and Allison, pursue him and he leaves them both. Does his relationship with Melissa represent a change? What attracts him to each of these women? What does he learn through his relationships with them?

10. As war is brewing, fifteen-year-old Ismet tells his mother, "I thought we were all Yugoslavs," then wonders why he's broached a question he already knows the answer to: "Maybe the Communist message of Brotherhood and Unity had been so thoroughly drummed into my head that it surfaced robotically and overrode my actual experience" (p. 6). Does this awareness of doublespeak and propaganda contribute to Ismet's comedic sense and ironic detachment? Return to Ismet's description of Tuzla's architecture and the naming of its municipal offices (pp. 97–98) — what picture do you get of Bosnia's

Communist legacy and its effects on its citizens' approaches to life?

11. Can Ismet's childhood experiences of faking appendicitis (pp. 34–36) and directing the ninja high jinks in the forest (pp. 51–56) be seen as his first experiments in theater? What does he learn from them and how does his relationship to acting deepen with his membership in the theater troupe? When Ismet and the others stage an impromptu tableau vivant in the park and the shelling starts (pp. 110–111), how does their act take on larger meaning?

12. Ismet relates Asmir's theory that "democracy is not the way of the theater and if theater is to be worthy there is lots to be learned from dictatorships" (p. 101). What sort of tactics does Asmir use to achieve successful performances? Do they echo the humiliation and submission tactics Mustafa endures in military life? How is the power struggle between Brada and Asmir described (pp. 105–108)?

13. Can Asmir be seen as an alternative father figure? What does Ismet admire about him? How is Asmir, though charismatic, also flawed, like Ismet's father? Do you have any sympathy for his father?

14. How are Bosnian Serbs depicted in the book? What sort of neighbors are the Stojkovics? What sort of person is

Nebojsha, the Chetnik who surrenders himself in Mustafa's trench (pp. 206–210)? When Mustafa (existing in some fusion with Ismet in this chapter) realizes he's at a party with a bunch of Chetnik-supporting Serbs in California, why doesn't he leave immediately (pp. 317–330)? What is his attitude toward Jovan?

15. Ismet explains that the war "had begun with politicians fighting on television, talking about their nationalities, their constitutional rights, each claiming that his people were in danger" (p. 6). The television is on throughout the book, including at important moments, as when Ismet's family talks with him about immigrating to America (pp. 183–185). How does TV affect Ismet's experience not only of the war but of his daily life?

16. Why do you think Mustafa's special forces unit chose to call itself the Apaches? What distinguishes the Apaches from the regular army? How does Mustafa come to identify himself with his given name, "Meat"?

17. How does the book investigate the boundary between what is real and what is unreal? Does war make this boundary less stable? Ismet asks in his diary, "How is it that I can exist in both the past and the present simultaneously, be both body and soul simultaneously, live both reality and fantasy simultaneously?" (p. 40). Does Ismet ever make peace with this sense of doubleness?

18. In what ways does the book's form mirror its content? What are some examples of the splintering, and examples of reassembling as they appear within the novel? How are these processes embodied by the novel's structure itself?

19. Eric plays Tom Waits for Ismet on his birthday, and he writes in his diary, "It was then, *mati,* that love was born in Izzy for America, for its sadness and madness, for its naiveté and wisdom, for its vastness, its innumerable nooks where a person can disappear" (p. 43). Are your own feelings of affection for particular countries influenced by those countries' artistic contributions? For what reason does Ismet say he wishes Lendo had allowed his theater troupe to travel to Scotland (p. 175)?

20. How do you interpret the epigraph from Samuel Beckett that precedes Notebook Two (p. 311)? How might wanting a story for oneself be a mistake? Ismet writes in his diary, "One thing about forcing a life into a story is that you become a character and when the story ends you do, too" (p. 339). What role does storytelling play in your understanding of your own life? Is there a way in which you feel as though you become a character when you narrate your experiences to others?

21. Ismet flirts with suicide by closing his eyes on the highway but he always opens them, which he interprets as

"a conditioned response, this choosing life; I do it out of habit" (p. 342). Why does he feel betrayed by his survival instinct in America when he has shown so much bravery and ingenuity in getting himself there? How does this square with his preoccupation with the meaninglessness and absurdity of life (existentialist themes shared by artists who interest him, like Beckett, Dostoyevsky, Tarkovsky)?

22. How do you interpret the novel's ending? Do you believe that Ismet actually killed himself, or is that left ambiguous? Consider the ending in relation to the scene where Ismet goes to visit Mustafa Nalic's alleged grave back in Bosnia. How might these two scenes resonate, reinforce, or even undermine one another?

23. When Asya and Ismet encounter the Great Dane, Ismet reconstructs the dog's life story (pp. 154–156). Has he had a sort of mystical vision, like the ones his mother has, or is this just his wild imagination? Given that the name "Archibald" comes to him and saves them from danger, is an argument being made here for vision/imagination as life-saving?

24. Throughout the book, Ismet experiences a split between his body and mind, wherein he is able to look at himself with detachment, as though he were looking at another person. What triggers these experiences? (p. 17, pp. 190–191, pp. 258–259.) Have you ever experienced something like them?

Suggestions for further reading:

Sarajevo Blues by Semezdin Mehmedinovic; *Nowhere Man* by Aleksandar Hemon; *Sarajevo Marlboro* by Miljenko Jergovic; *The Bridge on the Drina* by Ivo Andric; *The Ministry of Pain* by Dubravka Ugresic; *Scar on the Stone: Contemporary Poetry from Bosnia,* edited by Chris Agee; *How the Soldier Repairs the Gramophone* by Saša Stanišić; *Persepolis* by Marjane Satrapi; *What Is the What* by Dave Eggers; *Dancing Arabs* by Sayed Kashua, *Safe Area Gorazde: The War in Eastern Bosnia 1992-1995* by Joe Sacco; *Then They Started Shooting: Growing Up in Wartime Bosnia* by Lynne Jones; *Slaughterhouse: Bosnia and the Failure of the West* by David Rieff; *Love Thy Neighbor: A Story of War* by Peter Maass; *Café Europa: Life After Communism* by Slavenka Drakulic